BARBARA EWING is a New Zealand-born actress and author who lives in London. She is the author of eight novels, one of which, *A Dangerous Vine*, was longlisted for the Orange Prize. Visit her website at www.barbaraewing.com.

BARBARA EWING

First published in the UK in 2014 by Head of Zeus Ltd.
This paperback edition first published in 2015 by Head of Zeus Ltd.

9 7 5 3 1 2 4 6 8

A catalogue record for this book is available from the British Library.

Paperback ISBN: 9781781859834
eBook ISBN: 9781781859841

Typeset by e-type, Aintree, Liverpool.

Printed and bound in the UK by
Clays Ltd, St Ive's PLC

Head of Zeus Ltd
Clerkenwell House
45-47 Clerkenwell Green
London EC1R 0HT

WWW.HEADOFZEUS.COM

To Richard

1

MY NAME IS Mattie Stacey and my mother runs a lodging house in Wakefield-street near Kings Cross and I was that *angry* at everything that happened about Freddie and Ernest, that's why I stayed awake in my room after the others had gone to bed, sitting at my long work-table next to Hortense, and just writing everything down. Hortense is a plaster head. Ma got it from a theatre long ago and I painted red lips and big dark eyes on her and we chat. But really she's for trying hats on when I'm making them.

If your house got rude words writ on it and people yelled WHORE at you in the street and if your address was published in the newspapers and called a bordello and 'the seedy headquarters of criminal activity' and other lies wouldn't you pick up a pen and dip it in the ink and write what *you* know happened? course all the other people we found was involved, they didn't get their houses writ on, no one wrote on the grand houses did they?

And it's true my heart was caught up, and I know that part is stupid and you'll think I'm stupid, well – well that just cant be helped, you cant always tell your heart what to do.

1870

2

The sharp, brisk sound of a door-knocker echoed through the house in Wakefield-street, near Kings Cross.

A young woman opened the door.

An elegant, top-hatted gentleman stood there; behind him she could see a carriage shadowed in the crisp darkness of the chill February evening, and the lights of the rattling, passing carts, and cabriolets. Yelling street voices blasted in and she heard the bells on several of the nearby churches tolling the hour of ten, not necessarily in unison.

The young woman smiled at the visitor, and when he had haughtily stated his business, she called loudly up the stairs. 'Ernest! Freddie! A carriage is here! And a gentleman!'

'We shan't be long!' A man's voice shouted down.

'Shall I send the gentleman up?'

'No, no, Mattie! Certainly not!' Loud laughter. 'Advise him we shall be down in just a moment.'

The top-hatted gentleman at the front door, thus dismissed, felt in his waistcoat pocket for a cigar.

The young woman politely offered him the small parlour where a fire was lit; she saw him glance amusedly, dismissively, at the hallway and the narrow staircase, although everything was impeccably clean and tidy and there were flowers on a polished table by the door.

'I would prefer to wait outside,' he said.

She left the front door part open, deciding not to be rude by closing it in his patronising face; cigar smoke drifted in from the front steps with the cold air. Above the never-ceasing noise of passing traffic (even though the street was back from the main Euston Road) the young woman heard the waiting horse shift its feet on the cobbles, the bridle shook and jingled, and as usual there was the sound of angry, screaming voices further down Wakefield-street as if people were killing each other; occasionally they were. She also heard old Mr Flamp telling himself the story of his life as he often did, for company, in his room under the stairs of this house.

Then running footsteps and laughter exploded from above, and perfume and powder swirled downwards excitedly with Ernest Boulton and Frederick Park: the flattering light of the lamps caught them softly, petticoats rustled, silk-and-tulle and satin shimmered, corsets held, chignons towered upwards, bracelets tinkled. Ernest came first in a low-cut white gown decorated all over with pink roses; pink roses too in the fair chignon and wig. Freddie was in blue with a train, with a bright red shawl around his shoulders, and a red feather decorating his flaxen hairpieces.

The landlady, Mrs Isabella Stacey, appeared from the basement, carrying a large teapot. 'Oh my heavens, Ernest, look at you! You look fit for a royal ballroom – you could dance with the Prince of Wales himself! But – ah – there's two hooks broken! you can't go out like that – here, Mattie, we'll give old Mr Flamp some tea in a moment, to cheer him.'

Mattie took the big teapot from her mother, and Mrs Stacey took a needle and cotton from her apron and sewed Ernest together, and Mattie, even as she balanced the teapot, managed also to smooth Freddie's red shawl over the blue gown and she smiled and said, 'You look lovely, Freddie.' Freddie put his hand to her cheek in a brief thank-you and her face lit up with a bigger, warmer, beautiful smile even as he then put his hand to his own cheek in the manner of a coquette, and laughed.

'Where's Billy?' said Ernest, peering over his shoulder impatiently to see why the landlady was taking so long. Mrs Stacey caught a drift of gin. 'We would like a *masculine* opinion of our gowns!'

'He's not home from his work. He often has to work late.'

'Running the country,' said Ernest, preening and smiling, trying to catch a glimpse of himself in the mirror at the bottom of the stairs. 'Of course he is!'

'He wouldn't be half bad at it if he was,' said Mrs Stacey dryly, satisfied now with the propriety of the hooks on the pink and white gown, and retrieving the large teapot from her daughter. 'Are you performing tonight?'

Freddie shimmered and quivered, unable to keep still. 'Ernest has been prevailed upon to sing, Mrs Stacey – and it is indeed a ball, although not a royal one! – at Mr Porterbury's Hotel by the Strand, and the Prince of Wales *has* been known to occasionally attend such soirées. Although I expect, this month at least, now that his unmatrimonial royal activities are being discussed all over London, he is being somewhat more discreet than usual!' and everyone laughed.

'But I do assure you, my dears,' said Ernest as he pulled up his elegant gloves, and his eyes glittered in the lamplight and fumes of gin mingled with strong perfume, 'that, unlike that wearisome little martyr Cinderella, *our* fairy tale shall not end by midnight, nor in a pumpkin!' and he looked coyly at the landlady and her daughter from under his eyelashes. All the petticoats rustled with further impatience; both men were laughing and the perfume and the powder swirled again – and then they were gone, disappearing into the night in a fever of anticipation and excitement and – some other thing also: a *frisson* – daring? hazard? danger? . . . something . . .

As the sound of the horse's hooves echoed away in the darkness, the scent of the powder and the perfume and the gin lingered for a moment in the hallway of the house in Wakefield-street (they preferred brandy, but sometimes gin was a cheaper way to prepare themselves). And something unreadable lingered for a moment also in the face of the young woman, Mattie, as she listened to the last sounds of the carriage dancing away into all the other traffic, towards the Strand.

And then the house sighed and settled and became itself again, a tall, narrow terraced house near Kings Cross Station among a hundred such houses, and the mother and the daughter took the large teapot into the lonely room of Mr Flamp, another – less glamorous – lodger, so that he could, for a little while at least, have someone to tell his stories to, other than himself.

❦

Mr Amos Westropp Gibbings, a very wealthy young gentleman of independent means, had hired for this particular, private soirée the whole first floor – that is, a large central room with much smaller rooms leading off it – of Porterbury's Hotel in Wellington Street, just off the Strand.

'A few particular friends,' he had said to Mr Porterbury some weeks earlier, 'perhaps thirty? Let us cheer up these chilly days with beauty and pleasure! Music, entertainment, supper, etcetera, etcetera – the etcetera to include the best champagne. I shall also expect to pay for all extra *accoutrements* of course.'

And now, tonight, a clock in the distance striking ten, they waited at the top of the first-floor staircase: Mr Gibbings, and Mr Porterbury the proprietor, almost as if they were a couple, for although Mr Porterbury was attired in his best gentlemen's evening wear, Mr Amos Gibbings was dressed in a mauve gown and pearls.

There were fires burning for warmth. Everything looked beautiful. Large baskets of flowers scented the already heady room; straight-backed, gilt chairs lined the wall as was the custom at soirées; bowls of fruit and little plates of breath-enhancing pastilles stood on small tables, and the chandeliers threw soft shadows across the floor, embracing the visitors with that warm, flattering glow. The musicians were already playing a cheeky polka and many guests in their colourful evening gowns and sober dress suits had already arrived; excitement mounted as the room filled. And Mr Porterbury the proprietor smiled and smiled and rubbed his hands together slightly (for Mr Gibbings was a valued customer, and money had already changed hands, and it was clear that more than thirty guests had already entered the large room, therefore more money would be changing hands at a later date). Despite the extra guests it appeared to be a most respectably patronised occasion: a Member of Parliament and a member of the judiciary arrived together, followed by two members of the clergy; all were immediately served champagne by the handsome young waiters who looked so fine in their smart jackets and very well-fitting trousers.

Excitement and laughter rose as the orchestra played 'Camptown Races' with much panache, and champagne glasses were generously refilled. Already ladies and gentlemen leaned nearer and nearer to one another, waving dance programmes: *ladies? gentlemen?* – sometimes it was hard to tell.

'An interesting guest list,' murmured Mr Porterbury urbanely, observing them all.

'Indeed,' said Mr Gibbings as he smiled and waved, 'several

young gentlemen from St James's of course. And as you know the Prince of Wales himself has occasionally honoured us with his presence.'

Mr Porterbury's jowls quivered. 'Will he come this evening?'

'I expect he is being very careful of his whereabouts just at the moment, considering the newspaper coverage of the Mordaunt divorce case!' And they both laughed.

Mr Porterbury, taller, suddenly nudged Mr Gibbings. 'However, several attractive ladies from St John's Wood are ascending the stairs, Mr Gibbings, if I am not mistaken,' and he smiled urbanely, (St John's Wood being an area where high-class but not necessarily entirely respectable ladies were known to dwell.)

Mr Gibbings stepped forward. 'Alice! How utterly delightful to see you, my dear. So glad you have honoured us with your presence!'

'Ah, Amos, I was whisked here by some gentlemen friends, and I have whisked also my little niece, Nancibelle, who has not graced such a soirée as this before. I thought it would be good for her education,' and Alice twinkled at Mr Gibbings, 'so I do hope you will make her welcome!'

'My dear, of course! Welcome, Miss Nancibelle, indeed! How exquisite you both look.' (And Nancibelle wriggled her shoulders slightly smugly, knowing that she was indeed exquisite, and looked about the room with great interest.) 'And Mr Porterbury here is the proprietor,' and Mr Porterbury bowed to both ladies and Nancibelle nodded her head haughtily as if to say, *Really? The proprietor?* as taught by her mother. Who was not of course present. Mr Gibbings then snapped his fingers. 'Now here is a very handsome young man to take you to the powder room,' and a waiter who had stepped forward escorted Alice and Nancibelle away.

'Methinks Alice is showing her age slightly these days after all her life's adventures,' murmured Mr Gibbings to Mr Porterbury, 'but she is now so desperate for a monied husband that she accepts invitations to my soirées unconditionally, thinking perhaps that certain gentlemen present may need' – he paused, smiling slightly – 'may need a particularly understanding wife!' The orchestra suddenly burst into a gavotte. 'And this of course is half the fun of it all,' Mr Gibbings murmured further, nearer to Mr Porterbury's ear above the music, 'to mix everybody up! For of course as you know, Mr Porterbury, to forestall insinuations I always invite a certain number of "real" ladies – if we may call them ladies.'

And then Mr Gibbings's face lit up as Ernest and Freddie swept up the winding staircase.

'Stella!' he called to Ernest. 'Fanny!' he called to Freddie. 'I thought you would *never* arrive!' And he turned once more to Mr Porterbury. 'This dream of perfection in white with pink roses is my dear friend, Stella. As spring blossoms she will no doubt be the star attraction at the Oxford and Cambridge Boat Race and another twenty balls; this cosy evening she is ours, she will sing for us, and will, I promise, bewitch,' and Mr Porterbury bowed again, bewitched already, unable to quite take his eyes from the lovely figure in front of him.

'My dear, you look ravishing,' murmured Ernest to Mr Gibbings, although he was actually surveying the room from under his eyelashes.

'My dear,' Mr Gibbings answered, 'I have spoken to the orchestra. They have the music for "Fade Away" and "Eileen Aroon", and assure me they are familiar with both songs.' He turned back to the proprietor. 'And Mr Porterbury, this is Fanny, another dear, dear friend; Mr Porterbury is the proprietor here, Fanny, and the facilitator of our evening,' and Freddie in his blue gown gave a small, graceful curtsey.

'Fanny dear, blue is your colour, as I have often told you,' said Mr Gibbings in mauve, 'and that *beautiful* shawl is certainly the most ravishing scarlet colour I have ever beheld! Come now, a glass of champagne!' and Stella and Fanny were at once surrounded, not only by trays of champagne carried by the handsome young waiters, but by many friends and admirers. Hands reached out for the fizzing glasses.

A swathe of ladies and gentlemen, all wearing the latest fashions, now filled the ballroom and waved their dance programmes at one another and called to friends across the large room. The orchestra was playing 'Camptown Races' again, by request, and voices rang out: *doo-dah! doo-dah!* in time to the music. Couples stamped and twirled, there was laughter and music and excitement. And, again, under the flattering lamplight, with the rising smell of perspiring men, layered with the aroma of pomade and strong perfume and pastilles and alcohol – again some other thing shimmered there also, in the air . . . the scent of something – something that seemed almost a dangerous perfume itself, heightening the animation and the exhilaration. (Philosophers have for many centuries debated this last point, of course: the proposal that human beings sense certain particular matters exactly as do animals – and indeed, it is believed, butterflies.)

Such exquisite, sparkling, shining gowns; such handsome men; such pretty ladies – an evening like many others in London except that perhaps the laughter became by degrees somewhat more feverish than might have been considered respectable by young ladies' chaperones in other ballrooms. (Actually, the somewhat uninhibited laughter may in some circles have been deemed extremely vulgar.)

But of course there were no chaperones here.

Minutes passed, or hours: it is hard to keep count when the

champagne is flowing so freely and the noise so loud. Many of the gentlemen in their elegant evening attire, including both bishops, wanted to dance, in particular, with the lovely figure in pink and white, with the pink roses in her hair. (Mr Amos Gibbings was heard to comment favourably on a bishop's cassock and its suitability for the swirl of the waltz.)

Before the actual supper was served the handsome young waiters carried in plates of tiny savoury delicacies and, with little delighted screams, people swooped on both the waiters and the food like hungry, noisy, predatory birds, appetites aroused. In some corners ladies – perhaps they were ladies – sat in the little straight-backed gilt chairs, and gentlemen bent over them with champagne and chicken wings, and whispered; the laughter became even more ebullient perhaps (raucous, frankly) and the orchestra played another waltz and couples danced closer together and champagne continued to flow unabated. Occasionally now discreet doors opened and closed into the smaller rooms beyond the ballroom.

At midnight a large and luxurious supper was served in another room.

Mr Amos Gibbings looked around imperiously. 'Julius, where is Julius? It must be Julius!'

'Julius!' went up the cry. 'Julius!'

One of the bishops emerged from one of the side rooms with red rosy cheeks, fumbling at the very many cassock buttons and innocently smoothing his dishevelled hair. (Followed at a discreet distance by one of the waiters.) This bishop blessed the French soup and halibut and duck and roast beef and treacle pudding and caramel and cream and orangewater ices and profiteroles. All these victuals were immediately attacked by guests (including the blessing bishop) with much enjoyment, and in one corner of the dining room a party of inebriated gentlemen used the ever-growing piles of empty champagne bottles as skittles, with goose eggs as balls.

Champagne Charlie is my name, sang the skittlers,
Champagne Charlie is my name,
Good for any game at night, my boys,
Good for any game at night, my boys,
Champagne Charlie is my name!

Then when most people had drifted back into the ballroom an announcement was made by Mr Gibbings.

'Ladies and gentlemen!' He could now hardly be heard above the noise and the laughter. He looked to the orchestra and twirled his pearls impatiently at which there was immediately a very loud drum roll. 'Ladies and gentlemen! Ladies and gentlemen, please!' and Mr Gibbings raised his braceleted arms for silence. 'A special guest has kindly agreed to provide a little more entertainment! If you have not heard her voice, you have not yet lived for she has what I can only describe as a seraphic gift for song! Ladies and gentlemen, I present' – and Mr Gibbings lowered his voice dramatically as if imparting a secret, and people called *sssshhhh* as there was still much laughter in corners – 'ladies and gentlemen, I present: STELLA, STAR OF THE STRAND!'

The figure in pink and white was so very lovely, there beside the orchestra with pink roses in her hair. As she began to sing, the echoing, excited room became oddly quiet; a few last stragglers emerged from supper for the voice was lilting and pretty, and rather sad in an enjoyable kind of way, and people sighed a little as they listened. Violin strings chorused (with perhaps just a touch too much sentiment) around the pretty voice.

Rose of the garden
Blushing and gay
E'en as we pluck thee
Fading away!
Beams of the morning
Promise of day
While we are gazing
Fading away!

A tear or two fell, tumultuous applause ensued and Stella, Star of the Strand, gave a genteel wave with her white-gloved hand to her appreciative audience. Regrettably in the crowded ballroom just at this moment, a woman – perhaps it was a woman – fainted (or, to put it more prosaically, passed out); she was quickly handed through the crowd to one of the side rooms while voices called to the stage.

'More!' came the cry. 'More! Encore!' and finally Stella was persuaded to embark upon another number and again there was relative quiet on the first floor of Mr Porterbury's Hotel and the lovely old Irish song began.

When, like the early rose
Eileen Aroon
Beauty in childhood blows
Eileen Aroon
When like a diadem
Buds blush around the stem
Which is the fairest gem?
Eileen Aroon.

Stella, Star of the Strand, would then have sung another verse, but in chorus with the very last lovely line (slightly spoiling the ending), there was an exceedingly loud scream from one of the discreet side rooms: not so much a scream of terror, more a screech of outrage. (Unfortunately, however, whatever its origins, it was so very loud it was certainly heard right down to the Strand.) There was also the very clear sound of a slap, several slaps; they echoed slightly and at once voices rose. Doors banged, champagne spilled, enquiring footsteps hurried upwards from below. Mr Porterbury looked deeply alarmed; there were respectable guests staying at his hotel; he searched at once for Mr Gibbings in his mauve gown. A man with his braces showing for all to see emerged into the ballroom, hair ruffled; he was so angry he punched a wall, somehow ripping the elegant wallpaper, deeply offending Mr Porterbury who deplored violence, especially violence done to his hotel. Somewhere (it could be clearly heard) a woman was being shushed and placated.

'I have never been so insulted in my life! He – he—' But the voice obviously simply could not bring itself to elaborate further.

'Sssshhh, Nancibelle dear, sssshhh! The *whole* of London will hear you! It was a misunderstanding.'

'I want to go home! I did *not* misunderstand! It is disgusting! I want to go home!' The voice rose to a crescendo.

Another voice interrupted: a man? a woman? it was not clear.

'Well, dear, frankly I think you *should* go home to the nasty little abode from whence you emerged! It was *me* he beckoned to follow him into this private boudoir, not you, you cheap and ignorant little St John's Wood trollop!' and there was then further violent verbal altercation, screeches, further slapping, and the sound of sobbing: all these sounds emerged from one of the discreet side rooms very indiscreetly; whether it was male or female sobbing was difficult, at this juncture in the evening, to judge.

Stella, Star of the Strand, descended from the platform.

The orchestra tried to play on valiantly.

Several couples stepped on to the dance floor rather hesitantly.

But more or less, with champagne and eggshells everywhere, and the torn wallpaper, and rather shocked enquiries from below – and the realisation that it was almost four in the morning – the ball, at this point, disintegrated.

❧

Because of subsequent events, this ball at Mr Porterbury's Hotel, and several others like it, became somewhat notorious. They were gossiped about in gentlemen's clubs and particular back-street venues and certain private publications in what can only be described as a pornographic manner – with much mention of stiff pulsating members and open orifices spied in the side rooms off the ballroom. Nevertheless it is indisputable that those who had actually been present at this most amusing evening, those who had had the pleasure of hearing the dulcet tones and lady-like presentations of Stella, Star of the Strand, would of course have reacted with *complete outrage* – in a witness box in a court case, say – to such pernicious lies.

3

'Give me champagne, Susan!' cried the Prince of Wales, and he actually threw his hat across the drawing room of the house in Chapel-street of his most intimate and long-standing mistress. 'You and I have fifty minutes before I must dine with the Prime Minister and I, my dear, require much champagne and ministration from you!'

The Prince of Wales was *extremely* relieved.

It was perfectly well known (but of course never publicly mentioned), by the aforementioned mistress, and by the upper echelons of society, and by servants in fine and not so fine houses – and by hansom-cab drivers – that the Prince of Wales seemed to be able to manage several liaisons at any one time in little pre-arranged afternoon visits all over London.

However, today the Prince had finally emerged – only *just* untainted – from the scandalous Mordaunt divorce case in which His Royal Highness, among others, had been named by Sir Charles Mordaunt, the wronged husband. This accusation, which nothing could induce Sir Charles Mordaunt to withdraw, had been mentioned at some length in the newspapers.

The Prince – and his long-suffering but loyal and loving Danish wife, the Princess Alexandra – had been outraged that his unfortunate public naming (out of spite, obviously) had resulted in newspaper coverage that was less than supportive. Eventually the Prince had been forced to stand – oh, unheard-of impertinence! – *in the witness box* during the case. It had taken much political and judicial behind-the-scenes manoeuvring to prevent His Royal Highness facing any sort of cross-examination; it was inconceivable that the dignity of the heir to the Royal Throne of England should be besmirched in such a manner. Instead the Prince was questioned politely (the word 'deferentially' is a word that might perhaps be used) by lawyers for the defence.

'I would like to ask Your Royal Highness if you are socially acquainted with Lady Harriet Mordaunt?'

'I am.'

'I wonder if I might ask if it is true that on some afternoons Your Royal Highness paid visits to Lady Harriet Mordaunt when her husband was not present?'

'Very occasionally; only if I happened to be passing.'

'Did anything of any nature likely to offend her absent husband, occur between you on these visits?'

His voice was loud and clear and royal. 'Certainly not.'

'Thank you, Your Royal Highness.

'No questions,' murmured the prosecution.

But public opinion and journalistic coverage was not deferential in some cases, and apart from the unforgivable fact that *The Times* had actually reported the case and mentioned the Prince, an also unforgivable – nay, *disgusting* – article was splashed insolently over the pages of one of the less conservative newspapers.

The great social scandal to which we have frequently alluded has now become blazoned to the world through the instrumentality of the Divorce Court. Every effort was made to silence Sir Charles Mordaunt; a peerage, we believe, was offered to him. All the honours and dignities that the Crown and Government have it in their power to bestow would readily have been prostituted to ensure his silence.

We have no hesitation in declaring that if the Prince of Wales is an accomplice in bringing dishonour to the homestead of an English gentleman; if he has deliberately debauched the wife of an Englishman; – then such a man, placed in the position he is, should not only be expelled from decent society, but is utterly unfit and unworthy to rule over this country or even sit in its legislature.

However, today, the verdict had been given that had led straight to the Prince's champagne-imbibing and other delightful activities with his mistress in Chapel-street. Lady Harriet Mordaunt, aged twenty, the offending wife – who had certainly received letters from various gentlemen not her husband and who had recently given birth – was pronounced insane by the court, to the relief of many people (except her husband who therefore could not obtain a divorce). Because if she was insane, she was not, therefore, responsible for her wild accusations against other gentlemen, including His Royal Highness the Prince of Wales – who had given her two high-stepping ponies, certainly.

Which her husband had shot dead.

Mr Gladstone had already spoken gravely to Queen Victoria.

The Queen could not bear Mr Gladstone: his booming voice, his ridiculous high collar, his business antecedents, his pompous manner in addressing her.

'But I feel sure, Your Majesty,' the Prime Minister insisted in his – it is true – somewhat booming tones, 'that giving the Prince some real work to do, letting him see some official papers, perhaps sending him to Ireland, might be of great benefit to the renown of Your Majesty's family.'

But Her Majesty had answered disdainfully that she would not hear of giving her son and heir any work of importance, as he was not fit to have any hand at all in affairs of state. Her Majesty was now in the ninth year of mourning following her husband's death. She wore black at all times, and refused almost all requests to be seen in public or to carry out royal duties, but continued to ask for money – from the public purse – to maintain her family's position. She knew perfectly well that the unbecoming (not to say rakish) activities of her married, eldest son, the Prince of Wales, did not help her case but she did not quite understand perhaps the feeling about the monarchy that was growing in parts of the country. The Queen advised Mr Gladstone, with much certainty, that her subjects loved her.

It was Mr Gladstone who understood that royalty was becoming more and more unpopular in certain quarters with the almost-disappearance of the reigning monarch; he felt it might be difficult to weather another such 'revelation' as the present one. (He did not quite put it into those words.) But when he delicately raised with the Queen the subject of the *purpose* of the Royal Family, she remarked to her intimates that he addressed her as if she were a public meeting.

The Prince himself, ensconced with his family and his coterie in Marlborough House, did not want to go to Ireland in the least. But he had had a terrible fright.

His mother might not have admired Mr Gladstone but the Prince of Wales was extremely grateful to him, and (after his relaxing fifty minutes in Chapel-street) he and the Princess Alexandra dined with the Gladstones in their large house in Carlton House Terrace where more champagne was consumed (especially by His Royal Highness who was particularly affable and jolly). Late that night Mr Gladstone, who often wrote of discreet matters in his diary with no comment, was discreet once more, recording that the Prince and Princess of Wales had come to dine with a large party. But later he stared out at the dark, shadowed trees across the Mall and said to his wife Catherine, 'This is a dangerous time for the Royal Family and I do not know if they are entirely aware that it is so.'

The Prince had certainly been shocked at the public reaction to his private business. What is more, for some weeks afterwards, apart from his being written about so disrespectfully in many of the newspapers, the Prince of Wales was booed at race meetings and his carriage hissed upon in the streets. He and his wife grimly continued planting trees and cutting ribbons, regally.

As for the unfortunate young Lady Harriet Mordaunt, she might or might not have been insane at the time of the court case – perhaps she was merely pretending as the prosecution intimated (under her father's guidance, possibly in confidential collusion with the advisors to the Prince of Wales) – but she certainly became insane afterwards. She spent much of the rest of her life in a lunatic asylum, and never caused the slightest trouble to the Royal Family ever again.

That another scandal was about to emerge that could embroil both the Prince *and* Mr Gladstone was unthinkable.

4

EVERY SUNDAY MY brother Billy buys a great pile of newspapers, he reads every blooming newspaper in England it seems to me, the *Reynolds Newspaper* even though it shouts (especially about the Royal Family), and the *News of the World* and the *Weekly Times* (which calls the House of Lords "The House of Obstructives") and all those gentlemen's papers as well, like *The Times* and the *Telegraph* and the *Pall Mall Gazette*. He's newspaper mad! The one that entertains me and Ma the best is that shouting one, the mad old *Reynolds News*, the loud headlines make us laugh. And the *Illustrated Police News* always has big gory drawings on the front page.

Well. Well – well I have to start somewhere.

One Sunday, it was the first Sunday in May and a sort of chilly spring morning, well that Sunday we grabbed those newspapers as soon as Billy got them in the door, a bit like maniacs we were because we already knew that Freddie and Ernest, two of our lodgers, were in some sort of trouble.

Because on Friday a really unruly policeman had left his police cab right outside our house – neighbours heads looking out of all their windows like rows of cabbages – and he came rudely up to me scrubbing our front steps and insisted on pushing his way into our hall, asked for Freddie and Ernest's room.

'What do you want their room for?' I said, scrambling up from the steps still holding the scrubbing brush.

'Either a freak or a lark, young lady!' he said to me back, and he went straight in, looked about, took up gowns and corsets and powder, even old discarded stuff they kept in a portmanteau in a corner which was full of clothes they meant to clean one day, and photographs and papers, and then he had the cheek to put a lock on the door of the room and took the key with him.

'Bloody stop that!' I yelled but he didn't and I should've thrown the blooming scrubbing brush at him in his stupid policeman's uniform. But as soon as he disappeared with all the things Mr Amos Gibbings, another of our casual lodgers, came rushing in. And he smashed the police lock open, and took up a case of dresses and some jewellery in a hidden box and also some gentlemen's clothes and shoes and two top hats. And me, I went running after him as well: 'Whatever's *happening*, Mr Gibbings? Why did the policeman take Ernest and Freddie's gowns and things? Why are you smashing our door?'

'Sorry, Mattie, tell your ma I'll pay for it fixing,' and off he went moments later with the case and trousers and top hats, he had a cabriolet waiting. As Mr Gibbings when he lodges with us always pays his bills I wasn't thinking of the money at all, just the shock of everything – the rude policeman driving off with the gowns, and next minute a cabriolet driving off with Mr Gibbings and clothes and boxes and nobody explaining *anything* to me, as if I was just a demented rag doll requiring to be ignored in the hallway of our house.

Old Mr Flamp had come out of his room by now. 'The world's full of madmen, Mr Flamp!' I yelled at him and he nodded and said in his quaky old voice, 'I've always known that, Mattie,' and shuffled off again. Then later still that same policeman came back again, found the broken lock, and ranted that things had been *stolen*.

'They aint been stolen!' I shouted at him. 'They belonged to the gentlemen who lodge here sometimes and if you ask me it was you who's the thief!' He was in too much of a hurry to say more but over his shoulder he said 'I'll be back, young lady,' as he rushed off again.

After all that palaver I had sat on the front steps of our house in the spring evening, with a shawl still for the weather, waiting for Ma and Billy to come home, peering down Wakefield-street looking for any sign of them. Billy has all different hours at his work but he was home first that day so I took him inside so the nosy neighbours who'd already seen plenty wouldn't hear anything more and I told him what had happened and then we waited, a bit nervous, to tell Ma.

Ma is a bit deaf and can be sort of hot-tempered very occasionally, so we was glad she was out when the policeman came, we didn't fancy her and the policeman shouting our business – she'd gone to the market and then she was visiting one of the old lady neighbours she takes soup to – we call them her "soup-ladies". Maybe Ma would have shouted at Mr Gibbings as well as at the horrible policeman, nah, that's wrong, Ma doesn't really shout, not much. She looks. And sometimes she sort of ruffles up and that means she's angry, so be careful. And just occasionally she bashes bad people and she might nearly have bashed the policeman that day if she'd been here, he was so rude.

Most Sundays Billy keeps his own serious papers till later, and reads to us – not that we cant read ourselves but he reads out loud to us like our Pa used to, out of the *News of the World* or *Reynolds News*, or the *Illustrated Police News*: all sorts of weird and wonderful stories, and we dont clean the rooms on Sundays, most of the lodgers have vacated by Sundays anyway. Sometimes we'd have competitions to see how different the very same story – a murder, a scandal, a wild attack – can be told in each paper, our favourite papers and Billy's other papers, we would laugh till we cried almost, at the same story going through different tellings.

'Let it be a lesson!' Ma would say. 'Never believe what you read in the newspapers!' but the different stories was our entertainment. Or we'd read out some of the Advertisements:

MYRTLE: *contact at once, without fail. I'm warning you.*

ITALIAN LESSONS: *in your own home. Signora Spotuni, Lady Professor from Paris.*

PODOPHYLLIN: *a certain cure for liver, piles, wind spasms.*

Or we'd play cards for farthings. We sit in our little back parlour all cosy, often we light the fire, we did this cool spring day, Ma and me with our feet up and us all having a sip of red port, our favourite, and our Pa's old strange tropical plant still growing in one corner in a big pot even though Wakefield-street was hardly tropical. We'd had it as a little one when Pa was alive, we'd had it for years and years and it was still growing, we'd heard it was called a Joshua tree, we weren't sure, but we looked after it most carefully and polished its leaves and thought of our Pa. I usually love Sundays.

But there was no advertisement-reading this Sunday.

Billy read clearly, facing Ma so she could hear easily, and my heart was beating so fast and so loud after I heard the headline that I was thinking Ma might hear that as well even if she is a bit deaf.

APPREHENSION OF 'GENTLEMEN IN FEMALE ATTIRE'

At Bow-street Police-court on Thursday, Ernest Boulton aged 22 of 48 Shirland-road, Paddington, gentleman (son of Mr Boulton the stockbroker); Frederick William Park aged 23 of Bruton-street, Berkeley Square, law student (son of Mr Park the Master of the Court of Common Pleas, and grandson of the late Judge Park); and Hugh Alexander Mundell aged 23 of 158 Buckingham Palace-road, gentleman, were charged before Mr Flowers with frequenting a public resort, to wit, the Strand Theatre, with intent to commit felony, the first two-named in female attire.

'Felony?' said Ma. 'I thought felony was murder. Those boys aint going to *murder* anybody for God's sake!'

'Felony means other very wicked crimes,' said Billy. 'In their book. So it means life imprisonment.'

'*What?*'

'Hard labour, life imprisonment, ten years' penal servitude. That's what felons get.'

'For wearing women's clothes?' said Ma. 'Well in that case, they may as well lock up the whole of the acting profession!'

'They used to get hanged,' said Billy.

I didn't say anything. I was sure they could hear my heart going bang bang bang. One of the Gentlemen in Female Attire they were writing about was Freddie – Frederick William Park as they called him there – who was the least wicked person I had met in my life, he was the most kind loving generous person that I knew.

On being placed in the dock much amusement was created by their artistic make-up. Boulton was dressed in fashionable crimson silk, trimmed with white lace. He wore a flaxen wig, with plaited chignon. His arms and neck were bare. He had bracelets, and a white lace shawl round his shoulders.

'That's Ernest for sure,' said Ma, nodding and sipping port. 'I know that crimson dress.'

Park wore a green satin dress, with a pannier, flaxen wig curled, white kid gloves, bracelets and black lace shawl.

'Ah poor Freddie, never makes quite the picture as Ernest does.' And Ma sipped and nodded again.

'You know he makes a handsome woman, Ma,' I said, indignant, 'even if he's not pretty like Ernest.'

Mr James Thomson, superintendent of the E Division, said: 'At ten o'clock last night I went to the Strand Theatre where I saw the three prisoners in a private box, Boulton and Park being in female attire. I have been watching them for many months, in all sorts of places, especially the Alhambra and Burlington Arcade and balls and other such places and the Boat Race too. They do call themselves ladies' names, usually Stella and Fanny. I observed them nodding and smiling and winking to gentlemen in the stalls and making sounds. They were removed on leaving the theatre, to Bow-street Station. Mundell said that he was the son of a barrister and that a few evenings previously he had met the two other prisoners in male attire but he believed they were girls, in men's clothes. He made their acquaintance and agreed to escort them to the theatre last night.'

William Chamberlaine, detective, E Division, said: 'Last night I saw two persons in female attire come out of a house, 13 Wakefield-street, Regent-Square, with a gentleman.'

'Oh God Almighty!' said Ma. 'They've writ our address!'

'Never mind, Ma, it dont matter,' said Billy sensibly. 'They were only exiting from here, after all. It doesn't give our name.'

'They each had a satin dress on. They had chignons on (LAUGHTER IN COURT) and their arms naked and their necks bare. The gentleman called a cab and both ladies got into it. They drove to the Strand Theatre. I got into another cab and followed them. They got to the theatre where they met Mundell and another gentleman in the lobby. I still followed them. I saw them take their seats in the box.'

'But who's these people laughing in court?' I asked, puzzled, 'how did they straightway know about it, before it got in the newspapers even?'

'Ha! London gossip is faster than the newspapers,' said Ma in that dry voice she uses sometimes.

'The "ladies" came out of the box alone and had some refreshment. One of them went into the ladies' cloakroom and asked to have her dress pinned up. They were shortly afterwards removed to the station.'

'Was it for going into the ladies' cloakroom?' I said to Billy.

'I bet five shillings we soon see editorials written about that cloakroom: The Women of England In Danger,' said Billy.

'From Freddie and Ernest?' said Ma. 'Dont be ridiculous.'

Defence (Mr Abrams): 'On behalf of the prisoners, sir, I contend that the case of felony is not made out. Unless it is shown they were out for unlawful purpose, I submit that no such offence has been committed by them. They are young men, and no doubt did this intending it as a lark.'

'What?' said Ma.

'Lark,' said Billy.

'What?' said Ma again, not understanding, or maybe not hearing, or maybe just still shocked.

'*Lark!*' shouted Billy.

'Course it was,' said Ma.

Magistrate Mr Flowers (with severity): 'It is a lark then that they have been carrying on evidently for a very long time. I have, however, a doubt with respect to Mr Hugh Mundell. He may have been deceived by the appearances of the others, and the evidence does not show that he has previously been connected with them. I should have been deceived myself! But that, in my mind, makes the case all the worse for those dressed up.'

Mr Abrams: 'It was only a stupid act of folly.'

Mr Flowers said he was not sure of that yet.

After some further evidence Mr Flowers remanded the prisoners but allowed Mundell to be liberated on his own recognisances of £100. Mr Flowers refused, however, to accept bail for Boulton and Park.

'Oh bloody hell!' said Ma. 'Ernest and Freddie in prison!'

Mr Abrams later in the day asked Mr Flowers if the prisoners might be allowed to change their dresses before being removed in the van. They had already sent for their attire.

'So that's why Mr Gibbings came and smashed the lock,' I said, 'to take them their proper clothes.'

'And maybe take away his own things promptly,' said Billy, quite quiet.

Mr Flowers said, certainly.

Mr Barnaby (chief clerk), after the lapse of an hour or so, said that the crowd in the street had greatly increased and Mr Superintendent Thomson thought it would be better to remove the prisoners as quickly as possible although the required male clothing had not yet arrived.

'That's because of having to smash down the lock that rude policeman had put on the door,' I said to Billy, angry, thinking of people laughing and ogling and shouting at Ernest, and especially thinking of Freddie. I could imagine Ernest waving back and enjoying the attention and looking from under his eyelashes the way he did, but I thought Freddie would be shamed.

Mr Flowers consented to this, and the filthy fellows were then and there removed in the van to the House of Detention.

There was this sudden appalled silence in our parlour.

'And that's the end of *Reynolds News*,' said Billy, folding it up.

Without a word Ma poured more port into our glasses and shook her head, looking at the red colour in her glass. I suppose she was thinking about agreeing to let them have a room for a few days every now and then to dress for acting parts if they had an engagement – Ma used to be a theatre wardrobe mistress, everybody knew that. She had her glory days when our Pa was alive and they both worked in the theatre, this was before he got sick, and me and Billy were round theatres all the time, we even actually lived for a while in rooms right at the top of the Drury Lane Theatre and dropped plums on people going past way down below. (Billy was eight and I was three and I remember *clearly* that Billy told me that when the plums hit the hats they were going as fast as a train. Billy knew everything, even then.) Those were good days. Then the days weren't so good, but finally Ma got 13 Wakefield-street from Mr Rowbottom who was sort of like our stepfather when our Pa died. And now we run this lodging-house, mostly salesmen from the North stay here.

'But what are they actually charged *for*?' I asked Billy. 'It cant be just dressing up!'

'The felonious charge of conspiring to incite others to carry out an abominable offence,' said Billy, reading it out. He looked at me.

'All right, I know what that means, William Stacey, so there's no need staring at me like I was a baby.'

'Which, as I already said, since the death penalty was removed now carries a charge of ten years penal servitude or life imprisonment with hard labour. Which means the treadmill.'

Ma and I looked at each other, really horrified. Freddie and Ernest on a *treadmill*? Everyone knew what the treadmill was. A great big moving wheel going round and round for no reason and men were strapped to it and had to keep climbing its stairs to turn it and often in the end their backs broke.

'But Freddie and Ernest couldn't get *life imprisonment with hard labour*!' I said. 'Dont be silly,' but I heard my voice sounding all peculiar.

'Oh God above!' said Ma suddenly. 'What's this going to do for business, our address published and poor Mr Flamp paying no rent, this could send us to the workhouse!'

Billy rolled his eyes at me and I rolled mine right back. 'We're all right, Ma,' he said.

'What?'

'We're all right!' he repeated, firm, raising his voice a bit. 'We're nowhere near the blooming workhouse any more, you know that, Ma! Those days are over. We can perfectly well afford to look after Mr Flamp. It's Ernest and Freddie who's in trouble, not us.'

For a moment she looked slightly doubtful. She was fond of

them because they were – well it was fun when they were in the house, and it was so enjoyable to hear laughter and music floating down the stairs, and they used to sit and talk to Ma of fashion and costumes and quite seriously ask her advice about their gowns.

Now Billy threw *Reynolds News* into a corner. 'Ernest and Freddie aint done nothing, not really, Ma,' he said, 'not as far as we know. It's not a crime to dress up as a woman that I've ever heard of and that's all we've ever known them do, and they've stayed in our house for ages, off and on. Not one of the tenants ever complained, they applaud their gowns!' He looked quite ferocious finally. Billy can be quite ferocious. Clergymen make him ferocious, and liars.

'You're right,' said Ma, and she downed the red port. 'I'm foolish,' (and I saw she took a little look at me, she might be a bit deaf but she knows everything). 'I was just upset because of our address writ in the paper, and fancy them calling Freddie and Ernest "filthy fellows" when I never knew such pleasant tenants. Well they'll probably let them out tomorrow, dont fret, Mattie, have another port.'

And she held out the bottle to me and still she looked at me kind of old-fashioned, as if I wasn't a grown woman. I was still thinking, outraged, of Freddie being called a *filthy fellow.*

And Billy, thinking to calm us I suppose, went on to read us all the details of a woman who died after swallowing three sovereigns and a half while running round a kitchen table and when she died a doctor opened her up and said he couldn't find the money, but everyone said the doctor had pocketed it himself. But I was only half listening. And by the way, dont think I dont know what they're really talking about when they talk about felony and Freddie and Ernest, I'm not a child and I'm not a fool but I – oh – never mind.

When they first came to us Ernest and Freddie explained carefully to Ma that they already had rooms where they actually *lived.*

They would rent a room sometimes for getting ready for work, they might stay overnight just occasionally. They straightway explained that they played women's parts, so they would be bringing gowns to our house – there was no hiding what they were doing.

Ma, liking theatre people, and seeing they were real gentlemen, even if they were only lads Billy's age, agreed. (They were a bit – sort of unmanly – specially Ernest who was almost pretty, but we were used to people like that, we'd lived in a theatre for years.) They paid a deposit for one week. And next day we was most impressed when we saw them carrying in their costumes from a hansom cab: gowns, satin and silk, bustles and wigs and boots and bracelets and lockets and ribbons and bows and ladies' hats.

And they *were* sort-of actors – we have actually seen them acting, both playing women, as they had told – they asked us one night to a theatre show, me and Ma and Billy, we went all the way in a cab that a friend of theirs paid for who travelled with us, and he smoked about seven cigars and I was sick (I got out and spewed past Waterloo). It was in a little hall off Clapham High Street, not a real theatre, not really, but they played sisters, and Ernest – 'Stella' he was called – was the Star.

He – she – had several songs he used to sing that the audiences called for again and again – he had a sweet voice and it was like a woman's voice: 'Fade Away' was one song, it was sad, 'and it's a bit *mawkish*,' I said to Ma and she laughed when I came up likè that with some new interesting word I'd been reading. But I had a favourite of all Ernest's songs: that lovely old Irish song, 'Eileen Aroon'. Ma and me had heard it sometimes, by St Pancras, sad little evening fires with poor Irish beggars around them, thin and starving, gone from their own country, *who is the fairest gem? Eileen Aroon*, their voices longing and sad, breaking with the words in that way the Irish have with their songs. Ernest sang it just – simple. It was beautiful and I used to listen to that song and think about how it must be, to be the fairest gem, and be always remembered, like Eileen Aroon.

And Freddie, he was called 'Fanny' on stage, and well he did look like a woman too, but sort of not the main one, not with pretty Stella there singing away. Freddie's face was funny and kind and I often thought he looked like a man *or* a woman, he just looked like Freddie, whatever he was wearing. They weren't *real* actors, like at Drury Lane or the Haymarket, but their gowns swished and shimmered and Ma's a good judge and she thought they did well and looked lovely, and me and Billy did too, what I mean is we didn't think there was anything cheap, it was amateur but it wasn't laughable on the little stage at Clapham, it was better than that.

And that night at Clapham was the first time we clapped our eyes on a particular man who turned out to be Lord Arthur Clinton. He was there with a very elegant, pretty lady and they clapped and laughed together and they both talked and laughed with Ernest afterwards, and later Ernest told us who the man was.

'*Lord* Arthur Clinton,' he had said, 'and that was his sister with him, *Lady* Susan – and he introduced me!' And Ernest looked under his eyelashes in that coy way he had, and smoothed his hair fussily, pleased as anything and sort of quivering with excitement as he leaned towards us confidentially.

'She's a widow, her husband was insane and now she is a mistress of the Prince of Wales actually.' Smoothing his hair again and looking at us again from under his eyelashes, so pleased to think of himself as so nearly connected to Royalty.

But even though we'd seen them sort of on stage we'd always known, like I said, that they weren't real actors in real theatres like Ma and Pa worked in back in the olden golden days. And yes, we knew that they did parade about a bit sometimes, as women. But I thought it was just for the fun of it and not doing any harm.

From the very beginning of meeting them you could see: Freddie loved Ernest, really loved him. I dont mean like couples kissing – I mean real loving – they could kiss all day for all I care, but it wasn't like that. Freddie always – well – well what he did was always look to see that Ernest was all right. Over time we all saw that Ernest – who was the 'star' of their act, no doubt about it – was really spoiled. Once, when Ernest was flouncing off down the stairs and sulking and looking from under his eyelashes at us and calling up the stairs to Freddie, '*I need some money NOW!*' and slamming the front door – that was the time Ma said, 'I'd like to meet that boy's mother! I warrant she has a lot to answer for, he's a blooming little minx, Ernest is.'

But later he came back and we heard them laughing and then his sweet voice drifting down to us:

Be it ever so humble
There's no place like home

and even Ma could hear it, so clear and sweet it was as it came down the stairs, and she shook her head and smiled.

I suppose . . . well what do I suppose? I suppose – that Ernest must have been an exciting person to love: he was the star, he had the beautiful voice, he was – I suppose people would say – 'enticing' – you just couldn't help but see he's really pretty when he's all dressed up, no wonder people fell for him. In fact when he was dressed as a man, people often thought he was a woman trying to look like a man! Now there's a true conundrum! Ernest's too pretty for a man. When they booked a room he would arrive from the barber and the hairdresser – always very polite – 'Evening, Mrs Stacey, evening, Mattie, evening, Billy,' and even occasionally: 'How are you, Mattie?' but not very often for Ernest was more interested in how's himself than how we are! When I think about Ernest he reminds me of – I'm thinking now, trying to get exactly the right description. What I am trying to say is that Ernest is very pretty, but he reminds me sometimes of a beautiful cat, one of those ones stretched out in the sunshine – but it might suddenly scratch your eyes.

I noticed something about Ernest. He didn't like to be touched, he always drew away if anybody put an arm on him, or an arm about him, in a friendly way. As if other people were – distasteful. I felt sorry for Freddie because it was often Freddie who put out an arm, and then drew it away again, or had it shrugged off. But I saw Ernest move away quickly from others too, not just Freddie. Ernest liked himself best.

And Freddie. Well – well he's a young man who's the same age as my brother, and who's got a funny warm face whether he's dressed as a man or a woman – well, to me he's always Freddie whatever clothes he's wearing, he's a kind lovely man.

I dont think they were – well – look, I've already said, I'm not stupid and I know there's all kinds of love and people who pretend not have got their eyes closed and how do I know if they loved each other like that, I dont know how it all works. It doesn't matter. You meet all sorts in the theatre, my Ma and Pa knew some very strange people and we've had some very strange tenants in Wakefield-street, one man had a pet bumblebee, it was bright-striped, yellow and black, and he bought chocolate for it and talked to it and cried when it died in the bottle he kept it in, poor lonely man. But maybe, in the end, Freddie and Ernest were the strangest. And maybe once they had been – beloveds

– for all I know or care or understand but all I know is Freddie loved Ernest.

I know Ernest actually lived, for some time anyway, with that Lord, that Lord Arthur Clinton. After that performance in Clapham where we'd seen him with his pretty sister, Lord Arthur used to visit our house occasionally (he was the first Lord I ever met, and a bit scrawny I thought). And Ernest couldn't help it I suppose, he always said, 'This is *Lord* Arthur Clinton,' very proud and coy, he just couldn't help stressing the title, '*Lord* Arthur Clinton,' and do you know our Ma said to him one day, 'Where's your mother living now, Lord Arthur?' and Lord Arthur gave her a really, really funny look and said very grandly and imperiously – as if she hadn't the right to address him at all, even if he was inside our house – 'My mother lives in Paris.'

And Ma said: 'I met your mother many years ago, Lord Arthur. I worked at the Drury Lane Theatre. She came backstage one evening to meet one of the actresses. Your mother was a lovely and charming woman.'

Lord Arthur looked so surprised. But, for just a moment, pleased in a funny lonely way, or it seemed like that.

When Billy met him, another time he was at our house, Billy said: 'Lord Arthur, weren't you the Member of Parliament for Newark?' straight up, the way Billy always is. 'Before the last election I mean? I know you're not there any more but I work in the Parliament and I used to see you sometimes.'

Billy's a clerk at the Palace of Westminster, he got promoted from a messenger because he's so clever, he's been there since he was thirteen, he's twenty-three now, knows all the Members, he reads absolutely everything to do with Parliament, he's like a Parliament fiend, Ma and I tease him. Now Billy actually works sometimes in the Prime Minister's office, calm as anything about it he is. When suddenly more clerks are briefly needed for some reason Mr Gladstone's office – not Mr Gladstone himself of course, but his office – often calls for Billy.

'I used to see you in the Parliament,' said Billy again to Lord Arthur.

Lord Arthur looked again a bit thrown, not to say a bit annoyed, all this impertinent questioning from our family every time he crossed the threshold! – I suppose they're more respectful in the upper echelons (I read *echelons* in a book lately and asked Billy what it meant) – and again Lord Arthur nodded rather regally (except like I said he wasn't really a very regal-looking person, a bit small and bald me and Ma thought) but really, all he could do, Lord Arthur I mean, was moon and spoon over Ernest. He loved Ernest too, but in a quite different way, he was *smitten*, anyone could see. He was *berserk with love!* was what me and Ma used to say. That naughty Ernest could wind Lord Arthur Pelham Clinton (that was his whole name) around his little finger, Ernest held all the cards, it was clear.

Except money.

Then after Lord Arthur was made bankrupt we never saw him in our house again. Ages ago. (And if anyone had told that me and Billy would see him again, would be shut up with him, just us, in a tiny secret room, we would have told them to go back to Bedlam with such an unlikely story.)

Ernest and Freddie and their visitors never made a really spectacular noise or anything disturbing, they laughed loud, and sang a lot but – well, well not raucous and rowdy. There's a little piano in that upstairs room they usually took if it was free, that piano was there when we came and I learned to play it and dont ask me how it was got up to the first floor! I like to think of the previous owners huffing and puffing up and trying to carry it round corners on the narrow stairs, we couldn't imagine we'd ever get it down again. Me and Ma and Billy really enjoyed all the singing and laughing wafting down the stairs, even if one of the tenants in the room below, Mr Crosby, a salesman from Manchester, got cross. But he died (Mr Crosby I mean) so that's why he was cross I expect.

And then they'd go out, Ernest and Freddie, appearing in their gowns just like actresses going on stage, with maybe a gentleman escort waiting with a hansom or a cabriolet and they'd float out on a cloud of scents and powders (and gin, they had bottles in their room – sometimes brandy, sometimes gin), pulling on their gloves and patting their hair and adjusting their bracelets and necklaces – and always laughing and excited. I used to think the row of gowns hanging in their room made it like a theatre dressing room – a bit perspiration-smelling and a few grubby bits close up, and unwanted or dirty clothes just thrown careless into a portmanteau and just left there! but when they appeared all dressed up and perfumed they always looked lovely in the soft lamplight.

Ernest and Lord Arthur used to live together in various different places before Lord Arthur got bankrupt. I think Freddie still lives by himself in Bruton-street.

By himself.

I think.

All families have their own stories, but that's their business. Even, so it turned out, the Prime Minister Mr Gladstone has got his own stories just like we have, that are his own business, that he'd prefer to keep to himself. The Stacey family of 13 Wakefield-street – us I mean, me and Ma and Billy – we would have gone along, our own lives our own business – if Freddie and Ernest hadn't come to our house and made their story partly in our house, 'the seedy headquarters of criminal activity: 13 Wakefield-street'. 'Run by that prostitute,' people said (meaning me). And can you believe people came and hung around our house and *stared*? we would see them outside as the story went on, and sometimes things got writ on our walls, how would you like that on your house that you loved? SODOMITE LOVERS they wrote, no one wrote on the walls of 10 Downing Street did they?

Not that it was his fault I suppose, Mr Gladstone, he was just caught up too, like we were (but all *his* caught-up-ness kept secret of course) and actually he was kind – well I thought he was kind in the way he thought kind, I know this sounds a bit peculiar but I felt – I dunno, I just felt a bit sorry for him when I met him, he seemed – it just felt for a moment when he stood there in the dark that there were deep things that he literally *couldn't possibly* allow himself to think. So he didn't.

Still, no one wrote SODOMITE LOVERS on the walls of 10 Downing Street did they?

Our Ma, with her wardrobe connections, had got me trained as a milliner when I was thirteen (in case no one married me, I used to think), which perhaps gives you an idea that I was not the prettiest young lady in London. All right I'll just get it over with, I'm not ugly or anything but I've got something wrong with one of my feet. It doesn't make me either backward or ugly, so dont think it does, in fact because I'm always looking in the glass to try my hats I know perfectly well I'm pretty – not like Ma used to be, well – well, she's still beautiful even though she's old, everyone says so, Freddie told me he thought she was beautiful, so I dont mean I'm like Ma, but I'm a bit pretty, the only thing is I cant run like the wind like heroines do, like Cathy in *Wuthering Heights*, like heroines do in almost all the novels I've ever read and I've read more novels than most people I've ever met once my Pa got me going. But my foot is all that's wrong with me, got it? And it makes no difference to me, I walk everywhere, I walk and walk, just as well as everybody else, all the time. It dont even hurt most of the time, just maybe gets a little bit swollen and red if I dont stop walking for a bit. But that's all, got it? and that's all we're hearing about my stupid leg. But that's why I wasn't just called a whore, but a crippled whore as well and that's why I'm writing down who we *really* are.

Ernest and Freddie wore my hats sometimes (even paid me sometimes! well, Freddie usually paid for them both of course, and one time another man did, who was visiting). And I've got several good customers, they tell each other about me, and I work hard in the right light (Ma always saying to watch my eyes, and she knows because of being a wardrobe mistress). They both, Freddie and Ernest, used to come often and watch me in my room, stare at how I was sewing brims and feathers and flowers, and Hortense having my hats hung on her when they was part-finished.

Freddie and Ernest always said, 'Greetings, Hortense dear!' when they came in to try more hats.

'Why should Mattie have all the fun?' they said to Ma. 'Why should *ladies* have all the fun? – all the beautiful, elegant gowns and bustles and bosoms and boots and hats that ladies have, and look at us in our tedious gentlemen's attire! We were born too late to be dandies!' and they would laugh and take my half-finished hats and parade in front of the glass – they did it even when they were dressed in their men's clothes. Ernest in particular was so fascinated by himself – how he could change himself, how much he could look like a woman – he stood in front of the mirror wearing my different hats I was working on and preened himself, turning and posing and staring, fascinated. At himself.

Once, one night late I was still up sewing with Hortense when Ernest came in alone. I heard him fall in the door almost, and I went hurrying down into the hall. His gown was covered in mud and his chignon a bit battered and he did smell a lot of brandy.

'What's wrong, Ernest?'

'I've been to the Holborn Casino,' he said, staggering against the wall. 'I lost.'

He looked at himself in the glass in the hall and for a moment he made those chirruping noises at himself, like street ladies make when they're trying to catch attention, and then he fell on the floor. I helped him up the stairs.

'Where's Freddie?'

'Dancing,' said Ernest giggling. 'I have no doubt my sister Fanny is dancing her head off!' He was asleep, well, he passed out, before I got him properly on the bed.

By working really hard when I wasn't cleaning the house and that, I earned £18/18/4d from my hats in the last year and although Ma panics sometimes because of the past, money *isn't* one of our worries now, because Billy works at the Houses of Parliament on – listen to this – £90 a year now that he's a clerk – and when he was promoted to be a clerk from a messenger I made him a silk top hat because clerks have to wear top hats and we laughed, Ma and me, at this new Billy. But he looked so splendid we also nearly cried with pride. And Mr Gladstone's private secretary with an eye on him.

And we had our tenants – we were almost always full. So poor sad old Mr Flamp not being able to pay his rent was never going to put us in the workhouse! And though we were just one of hundreds of boarding houses round Kings Cross there was a group of cotton salesmen from the North came back to us over and over, said we were pleasant and clean and reliable. Course the salesmen were always telling us how to run our boarding house better, make more money – some of them had their eye on Ma and the business, that's what me and Billy used to reckon. Even me, some of them tried.

One of the cotton salesmen, Mr Plunger he was called, used to pinch my bottom in the hallway if I couldn't get out of his way quick, and one week he presented me with a pretty cotton shawl that I would quite like to have kept (as long as I didn't have to have him as well). 'Shall I wear it?' I asked Ma.

'What, that Mr Plunger's shawl? Well' – she felt it with her fingers – 'it's very nice cotton – as long as he doesn't plunge anywhere near my daughter without her permission!' and I saw she was glad when I laughed too, I hadn't been laughing much for a while.

So I wore the shawl once but Mr Plunger thought that immediately meant he could come and sit with us, a bit too close to me, in our little back parlour and look about and comment rudely about our Pa's Joshua tree and the chairs and why didn't we have a maid?

'You need a man to take over here,' he said. Billy was blooming well right there in the room! and at once I saw Ma starting to ruffle, and then Mr Plunger sort of put his arm round me, you could smell beer and pies, really strong. Ma was wild, for Billy's sake, and seeing me moving away carefully, trying not to be too rude, from Mr Plunger's sort of embrace.

But Mr Plunger didn't know Ma and he went on: 'I dont mind marrying a cripple.'

I'm used to it, I dont care, who cares, but Ma cannot stand that word: *cripple.* She sat up very straight and made a kind of strangling sound like she does when she's *really* angry (sometimes she reminds me of that turkey that lives on the other side of Regent-Square) and I looked at Billy and he winked at me very quickly.

'If you think, Mr Plunger . . .' and Ma sort of fluffed herself up, even more like that turkey. 'If you think you would be lucky enough to marry my beloved daughter and somehow receive 13 Wakefield-street as some sort of *dowry*, you have made an unfortunate mistake. We have a man in charge thank you and there is no way 13 Wakefield-street will ever have the word Plunger attached! Off you go!'

And off he went and me and Billy was laughing and in the end Ma recovered herself and she joined in too and that was the end of Mr Plunger. And you needn't think just because there's something wrong with my foot that I'm all virginal and innocent either, course I'm not, and I've been – well never mind about all that, I've had an interesting life and I know lots.

And we dont need a maid! We've always worked hard, we dont provide meals, just breakfast sometimes if they ask (and always something for Mr Flamp of course) and although we had acquired "Mrs Beeton" like everybody else in London we didn't use it much, except if we got stomach-ache or something.

And anyway it was Ma herself who decided *not* to let Mr Flamp go. He had lodged with us for ages, permanent, he was a merchant's clerk until he got too old and then one day after all those years living with us, he came to Ma and me and said, 'Mrs Stacey, I have looked into my situation and I have planned for the future. I have come to say goodbye.'

And he had packed up all his things in only a little bag and he was wearing his best jacket that he kept neat in the cupboard for special occasions. All his belongings in the world in one small bag.

'Where are you going, Mr Flamp?' said Ma, surprised, and he said, very dignified, 'I'm going to the Christian Mission sit-up, that will be my next home, it is a penny, and I thank you all for your kindness,' and Ma straightway said, 'Mr Flamp. You are not going to sit up all night for a penny in the Christian Mission or anywhere else. You've been here for years and you know everything about 13 Wakefield-street – we need you here, you are our watchman when we all happen to be away from the house. In fact the truth is, Mr Flamp – we cant manage without you. So you would do us a great favour by agreeing to stay, and your monthly payment, from us to you, is the room – plus five shillings, and I'll hear no more about it!'

Mr Flamp had a strange look on his old face. We realised it was him trying not to cry. We made him big thick potato soup and put two sausages in it and I helped him hang up his best jacket again.

Ma is the kindest person I know, no matter that she ruffles up sometimes. She's always kept a little bag of pennies in her cloak, for as long as I can remember, and every time she passes an old lady begging she gives a penny. Always. No one else, well if you gave one penny to all the beggars in London you'd be a beggar yourself but Ma always says to me when she sees an old lady: 'What was her life, I wonder, Mattie?' She talks to them quite often and she's always giving her shawl to someone.

We both clean our house, Ma and me, and do the washing, and I do the front steps and Ma does our cooking and I sew my hats by the window or under a good lamp, and when Billy comes home we all sit in our basement kitchen and tell of our day. Billy so likes his work at the Parliament, specially now that he does the clerical things, he often tells us such funny stories about the goings-on there, how Mr Gladstone speaks very loud, and gets secret letters inside other ordinary envelopes for instance!

'Who from?' we said.

'Spies? Mistresses? I dont know!' and we all laughed to think of the Prime Minister of England having one or the other.

'Very nice handwriting, William!' said Mr William Gladstone to my brother Billy years ago.

'We'll get maids when I'm old,' Ma said firmly when we asked her if she might like to do less, and Billy and me looked at each other and rolled our eyes, she's fifty now! She made Billy's shirts too, and pretty gowns for me, and finally we purchased her greatest treasure: a Singer Sewing Machine! We like the clicking hum it makes when the treadle goes up and down – she sews in our little back parlour in the evening sometimes, and on Sundays, and the Singer Sewing Machine hums and clicks, and Billy reads us books or the newspapers, just like our Pa used to.

That's enough. That's all you need to know about our life.

Well – that was our life I mean up till that first Sunday in May when we first heard of the arrest of Freddie and Ernest, with Billy reading to us from the *Reynolds News* in our little back parlour.

'You want to hear a bit about the case from *The Times*?' said Billy now to us.

'We know it'll sound different, course we do,' said Ma, sipping her port, only today she wasn't laughing, she sounded sarcastic.

Decent people may not willingly hear of these things, but a case presenting novel and extraordinary features is sure to be a subject of curiosity to hundreds of thousands, and acquires an importance which may demand some notice.

'Hundreds of thousands of people?' I repeated stupidly, not believing this. 'Reading about Freddie and Ernest do they mean?'

'Bloody hell,' said Ma, and she looked quite angry.

In the present day it is impossible to prevent such a case from being discussed by the public at large, and particularly by people who unite a strong appetite for the morbid and sensational with a credulity beyond bounds concerning the malpractices of the classes above them.

'Now that's enough!' said Ma and suddenly the turkey-ruffling started full-tilt. '*Credulity beyond bounds concerning the malpractices of the classes above them* indeed! They're jumping up and down at *The Times*, I know one or two of them hypocrite journalists who work there, they're getting excited about Lord Arthur Clinton and who knows who else being involved, "Cant have that," they'll say at *The Times*, I see they dont say his name, but *someone* knows and they're getting exercised about it! Freddie and Ernest may be "gentlemen" in ladies' gowns. But Lord Arthur is the Nobility – that's what's causing all the excitement, they wont care what happens to Freddie and Ernest, you'll see,' and she tightened her lips and she seemed suddenly really furious and do you know what she did then? she took *The Times* from Billy and stalked down to our kitchen, us following her, and she wrapped bones and rubbish in it, got it all greasy.

'I suppose Queen Victoria is reading this version, and shaking her royal tiara in horror, as if her children are little darlings – like the Prince of Wales!' she said, wrapping angrily. 'Ha! And dont think we're going to be sitting here next Sunday drinking port and reading gossiping newspapers. Next Sunday we're going to go and sit with Mrs Portmanteau.'

Billy and I rolled our eyes again but not too much because Ma was still ruffling. Ma loved Sundays in our parlour with our port and our newspapers just as much as we did, and always a lovely stew afterwards and we hadn't even had it today yet. Mrs P was an old character actress Ma had known at Drury Lane and she was about a hundred years old and *three* omnibus rides away in a sad room in Stockwell.

Me and Billy ate our stew politely. And finally Billy made Ma laugh about something at the Parliament and finally she shook her head and looked at us in a sort of rueful way which was her way of apologising for ruffling up.

And then we played cards, like we always did on Sundays.

5

On that first Sunday, the *Reynolds Newspaper* had given salacious details. But it was the paragraphs in *The Times* that had struck fear into the hearts of certain gentlemen of the Establishment. *The Times* opined that the two men now held in the case were part of an association of 'at least thirty' similar-minded young men who roamed freely, loose-moraled, about London. (Some of those members of the Establishment reading *The Times* in alarm were not young either.) In gentlemen's clubs all over London, gentlemen huddled on leather chairs under royal portraits and spoke together in low voices.

Some persons thought it expedient to take an early holiday on the Continent. Mr Amos Gibbings was one who made this decision urgently, quietly farewelled that Sunday by Mr Porterbury of Porterbury's Hotel by the Strand.

'I was going anyway. I had already arranged to meet friends in Calais. Just for a few weeks.' Mr Gibbings entered a carriage quickly. 'Keep me informed of course.'

An evening meeting of another group of gentlemen was hastily convened that Sunday. The venue was perhaps an unlikely one for the subject under discussion: a church vestry across the River

Thames from the Houses of Parliament. From that church, lamplight could be seen in the Victoria Tower, which rose at one end of the Palace of Westminster; odd lights flickered also in other parts of the seat of government. All of the gentlemen present at the church meeting wore clerical collars; some of them had been conducting evensong; many were members of the House of Lords. The organist was rehearsing Handel; chords wafted in and out of the locked vestry, notes echoing on the air.

That air inside the vestry was full of smoke and many of the gentlemen held glasses of amber liquid; the meeting had been proceeding for some time, the same ground covered more than once: there was an air of odd unease in the room.

'The arrests have already caused outrageous attention in the cheap newspapers, and have not been ignored by *The Times*, as they should have been.'

'We can hardly order that the matter be banned from being reported, and close the Magistrates' Court!'

'Very well, but too much is at stake for Lord Arthur to appear.'

This statement (which perhaps contained various layers of meaning) was not contested.

'His name has not been mentioned as yet.'

'Where is he?'

'We have not been able to ascertain.'

'We may be being overcautious. The whole matter may be over in the next few days.'

'Very well but I reiterate: there is too much at stake – for the country, I mean – for Lord Arthur Clinton's name to be mentioned or for him to appear. He was briefly a Member of Parliament: the honour of the House etc . . .'

A more pragmatic member of the group put it more bluntly: 'Lord Arthur is notoriously unreliable and impecunious. He cannot be relied upon to behave with the discretion that is expected from members of the nobility. Frankly, other names may come out if he is not prevented from appearing.'

Throats were cleared in the nervous, embarrassed silence that followed. Finally a very senior bishop spoke.

'Gentlemen. Lord Arthur may be unreliable but he is the son of the late lamented fifth Duke of Newcastle who was once Colonial Secretary, and Secretary of War for our country under Sir Robert Peel, and later Secretary of State for the Colonies under Lord Palmerston!'

Handel rang out as if to underline the credentials.

'Do not forget his notorious mother.' But that comment was muttered rather than uttered.

'It is of course possible that the young gentlemen already arrested – these – these "Petticoat Men"' – the voice now speaking was filled with disgust – 'may themselves mention – other names – if they fear the courts.'

The bishop who had blessed the large supper at the ball at Porterbury's Hotel banged his whisky glass violently on a pile of hymn books. 'Then they must *immediately* be stopped from doing anything so improper and immoral.'

'But they are already held in custody at the Clerkenwell House of Detention, Julius! Who knows what pernicious untruths they may already be disseminating!'

'Surely they are *gentlemen* and would not speak.'

(The slight titters that followed the unfortunate use of the word *gentlemen* in this context were quickly quashed.) Voices rose.

'But it is *exactly this* that looks so bad, so unlikely: that they are not Post Office delivery boys or waiters or labourers – *that* is what arouses such disgusting and popular excitement and lascivity. This is an anathema to Church teaching. These two prisoners must somehow be spoken to.'

'No, no! I tell you it will be the mention of Lord Arthur's name and the – the avenues to which that event may lead, that will destroy us – ah – when I say us, I of course mean this country and its respectable upper classes!'

'I think you are being overdramatic!'

When another cleric answered dryly, 'We are part of an over-dramatic profession,' the convenor of the meeting, one of the senior bishops who sat in the House of Lords, said: 'Gentlemen, we must now bring this meeting to a close. All contacts must be used to find out more—'

'Tomorrow someone must speak to that magistrate, that Mr Flowers.'

'Tomorrow someone must speak to – it would likely be more effective – the Prime Minister.'

'—but we must now, as I said, bring this meeting to a close,' reiterated the senior bishop firmly.

Slowly glasses were emptied, cigars extinguished.

'I think we all agree on two important things. The Church's view on this immoral and terrible subject must be preached, as always. And for the sake of the British Empire itself, Lord Arthur Clinton, a member of the English nobility, must not appear and we must hope that he has the sense to make himself disappear. We must fervently hope that the case will be dismissed this week as a silly prank. This is the defence case, I have been advised, and this outcome is devoutly to be wished for. Let us pray.'

... lead us not into temptation, and deliver us from evil, prayed the churchmen.

❧

Across the river, in the Houses of Parliament, so dangerous was the subject, such mental turmoil were some of the Honourable Members undergoing, that they did not even dare – some of them – to hold a meeting that Sunday in a committee room, as they might, in other circumstances, have done. There are many back stairs and dark corridors in the inner labyrinths of the honourable building. It was there that unthinkable words were whispered along dark passages: *life imprisonment* and *ten years' hard labour* and *penal servitude*.

They were at a loss to know whom to approach among the more powerful political figures (who were indeed holding their own private meetings elsewhere). Everybody knew that any connection, of any kind, to the *Gentlemen in Female Attire* would be political ruin and social suicide.

An air of apprehension and unease – indeed, of fear – stalked the green-patterned carpets – and the red.

❧

Meanwhile the Prince of Wales, still wounded by the recent ignominy that had attached to him with regard to the Mordaunt divorce case, was taking no chances this time. That same Sunday, having already been apprised of certain matters appearing in the newspapers, he went quickly, in a hansom cab, to the Chapel-street house of his most long-standing mistress (although Sunday was not usually his day for visiting in hansom cabs).

Instead of getting down to business immediately, as they sometimes did when time was short, the Prince lit one of his large cigars. Lady Susan Vane-Tempest smiled and reached for tobacco also; she lit a long thin Turkish cigarette. They had known each other since they were children, and smoked together often too; she was two years older than he and had given him his first cigarette. When his elder sister, the Princess Victoria, aged seventeen, became a royal bride (her father had arranged a most suitable marriage with the heir to the Prussian throne), the eighteen-year-old Lady Susan had been a bridesmaid. Bertie (as the Prince was called by his family) and Susan had danced together that day, regally as they had been taught, and smiled demurely. And then later, together with Bertie's younger sister, Alice, they had smoked cigarettes and drunk purloined champagne and giggled, in a hidden place.

'My dear Susan,' he said now.

She, surprised (but delighted) by this unexpected Sunday visit, was alerted at once by his tone of voice, became very still: she knew him so well.

'My dear, to come, at once, to the point: you may not have read the newspapers today. You know it is absolutely impossible for me to be involved in another scandal. I regret to inform you that you and I cannot be alone together again under any circumstances, until and unless this Gentlemen in Female Attire business is quickly dismissed. My contacts tell me it is certain that your brother Arthur is involved.'

Her face paled. She had indeed read the newspapers and had at once understood better than he knew; she had hoped he would not hear so immediately of Arthur's connection. Quickly she put the cigarette to her lips so that she would not speak without consideration. She could not lose him – she had always been part of his life; after his marriage other ladies always came and went or turned insane, but Lady Susan had not only known him since childhood, she had also been his mistress now for over three years; they loved each other, of course.

Who is to say which of them knew about love?

Who is to say which of them had had the most unhappy, privileged childhood? Small Bertie, the Prince of Wales, or little Susan, Lady Susan Clinton, only daughter of the fifth Duke of Newcastle? These unmothered children.

Bertie's mother had admitted she could not love her eldest son and even as a young child he had been aware of this fact.

Susan's mother had run away for the last fatal time from her husband – and from her five children – when Susan was nine years old; the girl wept night after night at this abandonment. Mrs Catherine Gladstone, who lived next door to their London town house, sat beside the bed trying to comfort the weeping, trembling little girl, whose mother never returned.

For years, Prince Albert, impatient at what he saw as his son's stupidity, at how easily he was swayed by other people, insisted that Bertie be educated alone, with no companions. For years also, in another stately home, the cold and cuckolded Duke of Newcastle watched his growing, only daughter sternly, over-anxiously; all the time wondering if she had inherited not just the name, but the proclivities, of her dangerous, degenerate mother.

Lady Susan, aged twenty, rebelled first. Perhaps tired of lovingly and respectably mothering her motherless brothers, just as she sometimes mothered the unmothered Prince, she insisted to her father that she wanted to marry a wealthy and exciting (but extremely unstable) nobleman, Lord Adolphus Vane-Tempest, who had declaimed to her, passionately and with much extremely expensive jewellery, that he was unable to live without her.

'I absolutely forbid this marriage, Susan. You will do nothing so ridiculous. The man is an inebriate. And he is mad, apart from any other consideration.' The unbending Duke of Newcastle brooked no further discussion with his daughter as they argued in the town house next door to the Gladstones, in Carlton House Terrace. 'I unequivocally forbid it!' said the Duke, and he left the room.

In a few moments his children heard the front door slam.

Susan addressed her eldest brother imperiously. 'I shall walk to St Mary's tomorrow morning, Linky. If Papa will not give his blessing – not even make a settlement upon me, I shall simply place my life in dear Dolly's hands. *You* must give me away, Linky, instead of Papa!' She put her hand to her forehead in a dramatic manner, as she remembered her mother doing, so long ago. 'Take a message to Dolly, with my heart. Tell him my plan and my wishes.'

There was nobody to even suggest caution: certainly not her brother Linky. He may have been heir to the Newcastle dukedom but he owed an extremely large amount of money in gambling debts, both in London and in Paris; he knew that the very wealthy Adolphus Vane-Tempest, who was so wild about his sister, would "lend" him money when he became part of the family.

'Tell Dolly: eleven o'clock tomorrow morning!' And her eldest brother sped to do her bidding.

The next morning Lady Susan Clinton arrived at the church on foot, with her governess, and married Lord Adolphus Vane-Tempest (who was somewhat the worse for wear by eleven o'clock, and singing).

The whole of noble London buzzed with the scandal: the mad Adolphus Vane-Tempest and one of the Princess Royal's bridesmaids, after all! At society dining-tables bets were placed, amid much laughter, as to whether the bride or the groom would be confined – by a surgeon of lunacy or a surgeon of maternity – first.

Queen Victoria who had always thought Susan such an agreeable and attractive girl was shocked also. She consoled Lady Susan's father, the Duke of Newcastle, for his continuing misfortunes by sending him to accompany the eighteen-year-old Prince of Wales on a visit to Canada and America.

Lady Susan's marriage was indeed dramatic, as so many had foretold. Lord Adolphus drank riotously and threw expensive ornaments and sharp knives at his beloved bride. Her father having disowned her, she several times had to hide for safety with her quite horrible mother-in-law, who resented having to support her daughter-in-law in the manner to which she was accustomed and complained loudly to anyone who would listen of her extravagance. (In the meantime the Prince's royal tour, with Lady Susan's father as escort, was a great success.)

So it seemed for a moment that Lady Susan may have been damaged by her unloved childhood, but that the unloved Prince of Wales was made of sterner stuff.

Alas, no.

The young Prince had been briefly permitted to be attached to a military camp. Bertie's first sexual activities – with a lady who had followed the brigade – had been discovered, causing great trouble between father and son, and very soon thereafter Prince Albert had died – it was said to be typhoid but Her Bereft Majesty insisted that her beloved Albert had passed away from distress over his eldest son's behaviour.

The Queen could not bear to have the Prince of Wales near her. The suitable marriage that was already being arranged with a Danish princess soon provided annual children. And Lady Susan became a young widow, perhaps providentially: her late husband had, before his death, thrown at her many more heavy items, including himself; had broken a bed in half in Paris, and had finally been escorted to a hospital for the insane where he died.

And here they were, this Sunday afternoon, these two lucky, unlucky people, together in her house in Westminster, smoking together still, conjoined by their background, and their childhood, and – perhaps – their mothers.

Lady Susan Vane-Tempest, widow, sister of Lord Arthur Pelham Clinton, had a certain kind of confidence with His Royal Highness the Prince of Wales that others did not. She knew perfectly well of his passing actresses and courtesans and foolish young married women; she was his confidante as well as his mistress.

She even knew of the Prince's personal and private physician, Dr Oscar Clayton, who was called upon should any of these alliances become medically troublesome, and not many people except the Prince's private secretaries knew about this man. The Prince did not know that Lady Susan had even met him. Quite by chance she had arrived early at a soirée at Marlborough House just as the doctor was being discreetly and hurriedly shown out; she heard him being quietly addressed, so she addressed him herself with some curiosity.

'Dr Oscar Clayton, I think,' she had said.

The man had bowed over her hand – and from his dark oily hair she was almost overpowered by the emanation of strong-smelling pomade of roses, something the lower classes were apt to wear. (The idea of such a man bending over ladies filled her with distaste: she ever after felt sorry for any of the Prince's women medically attended by Dr Clayton.)

Lady Susan Vane-Tempest knew many of the secrets of the Prince of Wales.

Now, this Sunday, she suddenly stubbed out her long thin cigarette and laughed. 'My dear Sir! You know my brother perfectly well!' She leaned towards him and put her hand to his cheek. 'Arty will surely have flown away if there is the likelihood of danger to himself of any kind!'

He looked at her, so beautiful there before him, her familiar, knowing face; he took her hand in his for a moment. 'Arthur never has the funds to fly away, dear Susan, and he is bankrupt still! Have you had contact with him lately?'

'Your Royal Highness knows very well I hardly ever have contact with him. I have not seen him for months. Perhaps he is in Paris with our mother.' (She never told the Prince she did sometimes meet Arthur; she gave him money: whatever her brother's predilections, she had brought him up, and she loved him.)

'Have you ever seen these particular female-dressing gentlemen?'

'Of *course* not!' she answered immediately (remembering the pretty, pretty boy, who sang).

'I have seen them,' he said. For a moment he leaned back in her comfortable armchair and smiled slightly. 'Across a crowded theatre only, I need hardly say! One of them was most attractive, hardly seemed a man at all!' But then he shook his head and sat upright again. 'Arthur is of course, as we know, unreliable and unpredictable, as he has been since he was a child, and his choice of friends is not always what one would wish. You know I do not want to lose you – I absolutely do not – but I would have no option but to do so if scandal threatened. You must obey me in this matter while all is uncertain. You will attend the court soirées as usual for I will not be deprived of the sight of you. But that will be our only contact.'

Immediate tears formed in her eyes. *I cannot not lose him now.* The Prince of Wales might have had no real power while his mother lived on, but in his own Marlborough House circle his authority was absolute.

'I must insist on this,' he said. 'For a short time at least. But I will speak to Mr Gladstone. He will, of course, be disturbed by this news.'

She pulled herself together with an effort. 'Arty was always

Mrs Gladstone's favourite when he was a small boy. And she was so good to me also.'

'I will talk to the Prime Minister, my dear Susan. Something must be done.'

And she smiled at him. 'Your Royal Highness is always so very, very kind.' Her voice was demure but her eyes offered something entirely different. 'Kind, although often *very naughty* . . .'

She looked so lovely, and so – willing, and just a little wild, as she had always been. He took his watch from his waistcoat. 'However, since I am here . . .'

Lady Susan smiled at the Prince of Wales in a certain way that promised much.

And knelt before him.

To – among certain other things that pleased him – undo his boots.

6

I LAY WIDE awake after I first started writing all that stuff, about Ma and me and Billy – our life. That was all I cared to write. Some things are just our business.

But – oh . . . well . . .—

Well, I missed out some things. But I knew I would have to write at least one more bit down. Because of Freddie. I dont really want to write this next bit, it's my private story.

But also it's about Frederick William Park. One of the Gentlemen in Female Attire. So I put my shawl around my night-dress and lit the lamp again and went back to sit by Hortense with her big painted eyes.

When I spewed that time when the man smoked all those cigars in the carriage when we went to see them acting in Clapham, I was pregnant. I was seventeen by then, but should've known better, me, course I should've, because I'd tried and tried to get a baby when I was younger and I didn't, so I thought I couldn't. I have to keep explaining in case you're getting the wrong picture, I'm not *stupid*, I've just got something wrong with my foot that's all, that hasn't stopped me having all sorts of adventures in my life. Neither however am I a crippled whore, and nor was our house at 13 Wakefield-street a bordello. And I hadn't fallen pregnant when I'd so wanted to, so I thought I wasn't going to fall pregnant at all in my life. Well then.

Ronald Duggan had a room at 13 Wakefield-street. Ronald Duggan. He worked at the railways and kept odd hours because of bringing a train back from Liverpool or wherever. He actually *drove* a train, that was his work, and one day he took me all the way to Birmingham and back again, it was wonderful, you should've seen that engine with all the steam puffing out like big white clouds, and the coal to heap on to the fire to make the engine go blazing, and the chuffing huffing sound as we raced along – Ronald said *sixty miles an hour, easy*, well that was the fastest speed my body had ever, ever been – oh it was a lovely exciting adventure, rushing past the country. I wished I could have stayed on the train for ever, the bell ringing, people crowding on at all the different stations, other people waving from the roads and the fields. Ronald had put me in a first-class compartment (with the guard knowing), I wore gloves and one of my nicest hats, and waved to people all day, even Ma and Billy were impressed when I told them all about it, for when you live in the centre of London you dont have much call to go on a train, people come *to* London, but we're already here, in our funny lovely old city.

London's where me and Billy was born and our Ma and Pa too, he was a stage carpenter and painter (and magician we called him), he built rooms and mountains and rooftops on stage and he painted big white clouds that he could make blow across from one side to the other. And he always had this one particular idea: always he wanted to make *real* doors and windows on stage, doors that opened and shut, not pretend painted ones. But the theatre managers always said the doors would only get stuck, something about the way the scenery was hung, so our beloved Pa was dead before proper doors got used on stage.

But we *have* seen real doors now, Ma and me and Billy went to the Prince of Wales Royal Theatre to see this new play with 'real doors' – Ma knew the manager of the theatre and he specially gave us tickets to a performance because of knowing our Pa and we sat there in the audience and saw doors opening and shutting, and a blind going up and down at the window, and everyone clapped and clapped at it all being so lifelike. But then sure enough, after the interval, one of the doors *did* get stuck, with an actress trying to get out, she'd said goodbye to the others and she was rattling the doorknob over and over and the other actors who were on stage tried to pull it open or push it open and all the time making up lines, '*Oh aren't you leaving, Polly dear? Thought you were going! Here, Polly dear, let me help you!*' and they banged and pulled the door and finally a man had to come on stage with a big hammer to move it and everyone in the audience was laughing by now, big huge laughs and Ma and me and Billy was laughing loudly too, and thought of our dear Pa who thought of this first.

It was Pa that got me and Billy educated, Ma's not such a reader. And yet it's funny, Billy and I often ponder on this: Ma knows more knowledge, and more people, than anyone else we've ever met. That's being a Londoner for fifty years and working in Drury Lane Theatre I suppose, and later the Haymarket Theatre, everyone came there. But her knowledge isn't out of books, and he just loved books our Pa, he had gone to the Mechanics Institute when he was a young man and eaten up education like a starving person. He read *Oliver Twist* to us when we were little, the first book I ever knew, and we all cried at the sad bits, and I love that book to this day.

And he got us into a new elementary school by Covent Garden, me as well as Billy, '*your leg dont hinder your handwriting, Mattie.*' And by the time I was about eight I was already coming home with Billy to Drury Lane from Mudies Lending Library in New Oxford Street with high piles of books borrowed, clutched in our arms like treasure – by the time I was twelve I had read *Jane Eyre* and *Frankenstein* and *Agnes Grey.* So we're good at reading and writing, well here I am, writing this and Billy always has his nose stuck in a book or a serious newspaper and like I say he now writes down lots of Parliament business.

Oh damnation, that's about London and our Pa and everything, all that's a long time ago, I'm supposed to be telling about Ronald Duggan. So. Mr Ronald Duggan the train driver. He was nice, and he was good to me, good to Ma, paid the rent – away a lot mind, well that's a railway man, we knew that. He liked me, we started walking out, and Ma was pleased to see me cheerful again, and then this happened. Me having a baby. Ronald knew, he didn't seem to mind, and me, I was glad, even though I was so surprised, *a baby*. After all that trying before! And even Ma, after she'd checked to see if I really was happy, and after she got used to the idea of being a grandmother after all, was pleased, and called Ronald 'Ronnie' and if he was here on a Sunday he came and drank stout in the parlour while we drank our port and we played cards sometimes, and Freddie and Ernest had just started coming and going to our house ("those *girls*" Ronald used to call them, but only laughing) and sometimes we heard the singing drifting down the stairs and our house was so cosy. I was only a bit sorry that Ronald never read any books, only the penny papers.

'Have you ever tried a book?' I asked him one day. He laughed.

'Mr Isambard Kingdom Brunel once said – and he was the cleverest man that ever lived, ask any railway man – well except for his father who built the Thames Tunnel. But Mr Isambard Kingdom Brunel, he said, "It is impossible that a man who indulges in reading should make a good engine driver." Your

Billy would be a disaster with a steam engine,' and Ronald laughed more, and pulled me on his knee.

But one summer evening I went into Ronald's room with some yellow daisies in a little pretty vase, I always kept it nice for him, never knew when he'd be back. The key was in the door, he must have come home already and I – well I just gave my knock and went in, the way I always did.

And there was nothing there.

Not his railway clothes and boots, not his timetables he loved, not his timepiece, not his couple of bottles of stout he always kept on his table. And he paid his rent in advance so he didn't owe us money. I suppose he didn't owe us anything. I looked for a letter, or a note. No letter.

It started to get dark but I didn't light the lamp, I sat at his table for a while, just me and the yellow daisies in the little vase and the usual evening sounds and shouting from Wakefield-street as it got darker. I hadn't really expected to get married of course, it didn't matter, Ma didn't marry Mr Rowbottom, after our Pa died, course not. Ronald was over thirty, and we all supposed he must've likely had a family at some time but he didn't speak of them and so we didn't ask and he never got letters or messages all the time he'd been here, months and months. And I had expected him to keep being here unless he told me different because he seemed very fond of me and I was fond of him and I think I dreamed we'd take our child on railway journeys with the steam and the clanking and the engine bell ringing, whatever else might happen, and I forgot my rotten leg altogether.

Anyway, he was gone for good with no message.

Ma and Billy said, 'Never mind, Mattie, we're a family, and we'll be a family with an extra one, and never mind Rotten Ronald Duggan, we'll be cosy like we always are,' and although it wasn't Sunday we all had a glass of port by the light of the moon, looking out towards Regent-Square where that turkey lived, there were couples there arm in arm I remember, and from upstairs we heard Ernest singing that song I loved:

When like a diadem
Buds blush around the stem
Which is the fairest gem?
Eileen Aroon.

and the moon shone so bright and cold and that was the end of Ronald Duggan.

Even though I was getting bigger I still cleaned the rooms easy, and made my hats, a very pretty one for this lady who always employs me in Mortimer-street, and I wasn't heartbroken like you read in the novels, I was – a bit sad, course I was, but I wasn't heartbroken, no I wasn't, I'd got over all that sort of thing, we'd be a family for this baby, course we would. We wouldn't be shorter of money either, I could still make hats, and the Houses of Parliament must know how lucky they were to have Billy, so he'd always be employed, and the rooms were all let, we always had the cotton fabric salesmen who came down each week from the North with their samples.

Freddie and Ernest had this other actor-ish friend, Mr Amos Gibbings, and he sometimes took the railway man's room now that it was empty and kept *his* gowns there at certain times and that was that. I was fine, and I was happy in a funny way and if it was a boy I certainly wasn't calling it Ronald, and I had this nice thought that I might call it Freddie, for Freddie upstairs, who was always so kind and sometimes gave me and Billy books to read, once he gave me *The Woman in White*, and once I saw him helping Ma with the coal-hole which was stuck, even though he is a gentleman and had a nice suit on! We always liked him, Freddie.

And then one night I woke because everything was hurting and hurting. I was suddenly bent almost double with pain and bleeding and I tried to run out my bedroom door for Ma and almost bumped into Freddie, all by himself coming up the stairs in a yellow satin gown and a bright blue shawl, his chignon was a bit loose and he was trying to take it off and I remember his bracelets and bangles jangling like I was jangling and he saw me.

'What is it? *Mattie?*'

'I think I'm—' and I couldn't talk because of trying not to scream with the pain but he could see of course and you know what? Freddie didn't care about his gown, he just ripped off his chignon and his hat and then he half carried me to the water closet, we had one inside the house and we were very proud of this for our tenants, and I was trying not to scream but I had to scream by then, and he held me and helped me and the blood was on me and on him and on the floor and still he held me and helped me and then Billy appeared and he saw, and he ran for Ma to wake her, and while they weren't there but Freddie was there – it was over.

We saw it. It was a little tiny real person, dead.

When Ma came Freddie had already picked up the little white shape and wrapped it in his blue shawl and he and Ma went outside in the dark, you couldn't leave it in the water closet, not for the other tenants to see, and Billy took me to my bed and Ma came and bathed me and sat with me and I fell asleep.

For more than two weeks afterwards I kept the lamp lit on the big table in my room where I made my hats so I could see Hortense, and I kept the one on the chest of drawers lit, and the small one on the table by my bed lit, because I didn't like the dark just then, because if it was dark – well if it was dark I saw it. I left the lights on and Hortense in the corner, well she was with me like a friend. Ma said to come down and sleep with her but I said 'I'm fine' and slept in my own room. Billy would always come in before he went to bed and talk to me for a bit and try and make me laugh, and I would try to laugh, and then he would go to bed. But I kept the lamps on all night.

On one of those lamp-on nights Freddie and Ernest knocked on my door, past midnight, they'd been playing the piano earlier, but not loudly, and I suppose they saw my lights.

'Greetings, dear Hortense!' they called gaily, like they always did.

They were dressed as gentlemen but – well – they still looked – like they looked. They had powder on, and no cravats, and cutaway jackets that showed their figures more I suppose. I hadn't seen Freddie, or Ernest, since – well since what had happened to me when Freddie helped me – they didn't say anything about it but they were very bright and gay and they had obviously decided to come and visit me and to be cheerful (even though it was so late and I was in bed but with all my lights on) and they sat on the edge of the big work-table very elegant in the lamplight with brandy breathing round my room and they told me about going down to the fashionable Burlington Arcade the previous day and all the shops that were there, selling elegance and jewellery, and after a while Ernest was yawning (but very prettily with his hand over his mouth, all graceful, like a girl).

'I better go home to you know who! But what use is he to me now, he was made a bankrupt months ago! *And* he's losing *more* of his hair.' Ernest shuddered slightly. 'Goodnight, Mattie!' and we heard him running so lightly down the stairs and gone into the night and I felt (though it might not have been true at all) that Freddie was a bit sad, listening to the footsteps fading away, and then the front door closing.

'Did Lord Arthur Clinton go bankrupt?'

'He did, poor man,' (and I didn't say, but I thought, *I bet it was Ernest that made him bankrupt*). 'And he is no longer a Member of Parliament. But – he is – in the meantime at least – someone for Ernest to – go home to.'

And again that odd sadness, it was in his voice, I heard it.

'Well I better go home too,' he said. 'Are you all right, Mattie?' and then I saw he looked at me carefully. 'You're shivering.'

'No I'm not.'

'You *are* shivering, Mattie.'

And he came and sat on the bed and took my hands and rubbed them to make them warm and then after a few moments, not embarrassed at all, he moved the covers and took my feet including my mad foot and did the same. 'They're like ice,' he said, and seemed not to notice my rotten foot as he warmed it.

'I'm perfectly all right,' I said, and I burst into tears like a blooming child, and Freddie held me and held me and I could smell brandy and "Bloom of Roses" and him but the arms were holding me, Freddie holding me. After a long time I stopped shivering and then I stopped crying and finally I said, 'It was nearly a little person,' and I felt rather than saw Freddie nod as he held me, because of course he had seen it too.

And slowly he began talking to me about this and that while he was holding me, about his life. He'd had a grandfather who was a Judge – Freddie hadn't known him but he was a 'Sir' Park. And Freddie's father worked in something called the Court of Common Pleas whatever that was.

'And I'm a disappointment to my father, the Senior Master of the Court of Common Pleas to give him his full title, for all sorts of things, and because I haven't finished my law studies and I should have. And I miss my favourite brother Harry, who has gone away.' And I felt his body, it was a sigh I thought.

'What's the Senior Master of the Court of Common Pleas?' I asked at last.

'Well, they usually call him the Master, but he likes his long correct title even though it's only a very senior clerk,' and he laughed and I did too, I supposed he was teasing me, because Freddie certainly wasn't someone whose father was a clerk.

So then I told him about my Pa when he was alive, and how he painted wonderful scenery and clouds drifting across the stage, and about the doors sticking even now in modern times and the actors making up words more and more desperate, *Goodbye, Polly! Aren't you leaving, Polly?* and we laughed again, and I said, 'I'm sorry your brother has gone away, I'm glad I've got my brother right here in our house,' and then I was sleepy at last, and at last he turned down the lamp on the table.

'Is it elegant and beautiful?' I asked.

'Is what elegant and beautiful?'

I was almost asleep but I thought of them telling me of all the little shops and the women's gowns bustling by.

'Burlington Arcade.'

'When you are recovered I will accompany you and you shall see for yourself. Should you like that?'

I opened my eyes and there was his kind, odd, funny-looking, lovely face.

'Yes.'

He turned down the lamp on the chest of drawers but he left the one by the bed and he said, 'Goodnight, dear Mattie,' and I heard his steps going down to the front door too, and then he was gone.

He did take me too, he just arranged it one day. They hadn't taken a room with us for a while (I'd missed him but I'd never have said so in three million years), he said Ernest had been ill and was better now and had gone to Scotland. We went to Burlington Arcade in a brougham! We clip-clopped through London where usually I'm walking, past the squares, along Tottenham Court Road, into Oxford-street. When we got to Piccadilly he helped me down outside the Arcade and we walked in through these stone columns into the passageway and we strolled slowly through this money-elegance, like any couple might, my arm resting on his. I was smiling all the time, I thought it was just like the theatre! Crowds of people, fashionable ladies in stylish gowns and hats, and these little tiny shops with their windows filled with shining treasures, lots and lots of jewels, probably diamonds even! and I thought it was so beautiful and exciting and there were these lovely, lovely smells: soap and perfume and chocolate and cognac and leather.

A big tall man in a gold and black uniform with a gold and black hat to match suddenly stood right in front of us.

'Now then,' he said looming over us as if he was a policeman. 'I dont want any trouble from you,' he said to Freddie. What a rude fellow.

'Excuse me,' I said. 'It's a free country,' and from the corner of my eye I saw Freddie smile slightly but he put his hand on top of mine where it rested on his arm, as if to walk me away, but I stood my ground. 'Could we pass, officer?' I said in my best elegant-haughty voice.

The Beadle (as I found they were called) looked at Freddie and looked at me and next thing he's *staring down my bosom*!

'She's real, is she? No stuffing dropping out of her like it did out of you last time I seen you here?'

He was still staring down at me, and I felt my cheeks go all red and my mouth go open in sort of amazement, Freddie was guiding me past but now I was feeling for my sharp stone in the pocket of my cloak, I would've scratched his rude fat face hard, only just at that moment one of the stylish ladies cried *Thief!* in a very loud voice next to us and the Beadle ran fatly after a thin man who was slipping like a snake through the crowd and me and Freddie looked at each other and I grinned to show it was all right, so he did too, and so we continued walking, past gloves and perfumes and hats and there was a nice smell now of cigars as we passed a tiny tobacco shop with fine pipes in the window, and there was a whip and umbrella shop, and even a magic tricks shop! And it was all *lovely*, that Arcade! (except for the Beadle), people sweeping along laughing and talking and stopping and buying and I looked at everything and I looked upwards. And I saw a thin red shawl or maybe it was a big handkerchief in one of the windows, lit by a lamp just behind it. And across the lamp a lady leaned from the window, looking down at everybody and making those little chirruping sounds like birds. Well course I know what that all means, we've got plenty of those red lights and chirruping ladies down by Kings Cross but I was a bit surprised to see them in such a place as Burlington Arcade! I looked at Freddie.

'Are they – street ladies?'

'Yes,' he said.

'Thought so,' I said and I grinned as I stared upwards again, same the world over then, dont matter if it's Burlington Arcade or Kings Cross. Then one of the ladies leaned right down, chirruping, not at Freddie but at a group of noble gentlemen in their fine-cut suits and their hats just ahead of us. And the gentlemen looked up and laughed and one of them made a discreet sign to the lady and left the group, winking at his companions. He wasn't very handsome either, spotty skin, poor her.

'Come and look in here, Mattie,' said Freddie and he took me inside one of the little shops, it sold gloves, gloves laid out everywhere. Some customers were just being served and I could see Freddie was waiting for them to go before he approached the serving-person. Then I saw that there was a small spindly red-carpeted staircase in the shop that wound upwards – maybe to a lady sitting with a red scarf and a lamp! Is this how the customers got upwards I wondered – through the shops? The shop assistant winked at Freddie, as if to say *be with you in a minute* and then the customers were gone, the bell tinkled as the door was opened for them to leave and then tinkled shut again.

'Well, Freddie dear!' said the shop assistant and he was looking at me with some curiosity. 'Who's this then?'

Freddie took me to the counter and I saw that the shop-man noticed me limping but I didn't care of course.

'This is my friend Mattie Stacey, Claude,' said Freddie. 'She lives where we dress up in our paraphernalia.'

'Stacey?' said Claude. He looked at me carefully for a moment. 'Did your mother work in the theatre?' I nodded. 'Are you her little girl with the funny leg?'

Guess what, turned out he knew Ma, she'd given him a job in the Drury Lane wardrobe when he was young, when Billy and I were staggering home with piles of books from Mudies Lending Library.

'The books were bigger than you!' said Claude. He was so pleased with this connection he gave me a pair of gloves from behind the counter, 'Take these for yourself Mattie, and tell your Ma Claude says hello!' and he smiled, so pleased, and then leaned on the counter. 'So where's Ern, Freddie, haven't seen him round here lately. What's new?'

'Thank you, Claude,' I said, fingering the soft gloves.

'Put them on,' he ordered and he drew off my own and helped me put the new gloves on, they smelled of lavender and they were soft and beautiful. He wrapped my own ones in some special blue paper and I put them inside my cloak and wore my new ones.

'Ernest's gone to live in Scotland for a while,' said Freddie. 'Fresh rich fields.' And they both laughed.

'Thank you, Claude,' I said again and we were both smiling. Good old Ma, she pops up everywhere even when she aint there!

'Can I take Mattie down, Claude?' said Freddie. 'She's never been to the Arcade before,' and Claude giggled and waved his hand in permission towards a very small downwards-winding staircase I hadn't noticed, no red carpet on this one, and then the doorbell tinkled and more customers came in and Claude turned to them at once and Freddie and me disappeared downwards (me holding very tight to the wall as I went even with my new gloves and not letting the wall go till we got to the bottom, wondering whatever in the world we were doing).

There were two tiny rooms down there, one was filled with boxes and one was like a little kitchen, it had a fire. Two boys had been sitting smoking; they got up quick and put out their cigarettes as they saw feet that didn't belong to Claude emerging from above.

'What's your name?' said Freddie to one of the boys.

I think the boy thought he was somehow going to get into trouble and he answered very sulkily.

'George, sir.'

'I'll give you a penny, George, to take this young lady and myself out to Piccadilly along the passage.'

'Thruppence,' said George immediately. 'We aint allowed if we aint messaging, sir. So it's got to be worth my while.' Freddie took a threepenny bit out of his waistcoat but didn't give it yet but I saw George look at it as if it was a sovereign.

'You hold guard now, Alf,' George said to the other boy and next thing I know he bent down and dashed out in front of us through a very small side door I hadn't even noticed, straight into a long, long, narrow, underground tunnel. It was a bit scary and dark, though there was some lamps dotted along the way, I saw their flames flickering in the draught and some huge rats shadowed and running. I couldn't run of course, though George was running, also the roof sloped downwards as we got nearer to Piccadilly, making it harder. But there we were, me and Freddie, hurrying along underneath the Burlington Arcade. True!

'Hold on there, lad!' called Freddie.

My gown and my cloak touched both sides, the passageway was that narrow, but another boy came running past us with a large wrapped parcel, *'scuse me, 'scuse me, customer waiting*, and we had to stop and press tight against the damp walls as he squeezed past with his big parcel, panting and red-faced in the flickering light. It was the queerest place I'd ever seen, I couldn't think I was underneath all that bustling money above us! but we followed George and at the end we had to climb up a few rungs ('It's all right, Mattie, I'm right behind you,' said Freddie), and George knocked and a boy above opened a small door. It was a bit hard to climb the rungs and my bonnet was all crooked but I was so amazed that I just somehow pushed up through that door – and there was Piccadilly again and the stone pillars at the entrance to the Arcade!

Freddie straightened my bonnet and gave George his threepence and George disappeared downwards again and it had all been such a strange and unlikely adventure that I couldn't stop laughing even though my new gloves had dirty marks on them.

'Do they all know?' I asked in amazement, still laughing, as the ladies and gentlemen sauntered through the entrance portals.

'It is considered extremely vulgar to carry your own parcels in the Arcade, Mattie,' Freddie explained.

'Why?'

'As I say, *vulgar*, my dear. Commerce is *vulgar*!' but he was laughing with me. 'The boys bring the parcels through the tunnel and meet the customers at the entrance. But I do not expect the customers consider how the parcels get here. This is a high-class establishment, Mattie! Of course as you know Ernest and I only ever appear at high-class establishments!' and he grinned.

I blinked and stared at the London gentry and at my friend Freddie, and then I grinned back, entranced with this unlikely adventure. When he took me home I was so hoping he would come and be with us for a while – he brought me to the door and to Ma – but even in his gentlemen's clothes he was already rushing off to somewhere else with that odd, excited look in his eyes. That I recognised.

'I have to meet someone at the Euston Railway Station,' he said.

Well. It's told now.

I lost the baby. Freddie was there. Months ago.

All that's how I came to – to feel about Freddie the way I do.

Listen, I know about men who like men better than women, course I do. Sodomite it's called. And buggery. I know they like men better than women and I know people call them filthy and dirty and dogs and people's faces get all twisted up when they're saying it, as if Freddie wasn't a real person, so kind and good and – no, I'm just trying to explain. About Freddie, Frederick William Park, law student, aged twenty-three, same age as my brother Billy.

I cant forget him helping me, and holding me – that feeling of him holding me – and talking to me and being so kind and good, those stupid newspapers dont know *anything*.

I dont know exactly what it is that I feel about Freddie. But this feeling feels like loving someone and that someone is arrested for being a sodomite and called a filthy fellow and sitting in a prison.

7

Big Ben boomed.

The slightly ominous sound of the chimes echoed, muffled, through the Houses of Parliament; they rippled along the busy, crowded River Thames near by; finally dispersed upwards into the sky where, perhaps, a stern but benevolent God looked down on this great city, this London.

Inside the Parliament buildings, in the busy rooms of the Prime Minister of Great Britain, private secretaries sorted and wrote and copied missives of great import. In one corner of the outer office one of the parliamentary clerks was sitting and writing. This particular clerk was Billy Stacey, called in today to help deal with the usual Monday pile of unimportant but nevertheless persistent letters from the world outside, most of which were from people that the Prime Minister did not know. Invitations to dinners the Prime Minister would never attend; requests for appearances he would never make; begging letters, proposals of marriage or other suggested gifts: all had to be acknowledged. Mr Gladstone's private secretaries had a formula for each kind of letter. Billy Stacey had been instructed to use the appropriate formula each time, and a pile of beautifully penned, ready-to-be-signed letters already lay there beside him, neat and tidy.

Even though the letters were mostly uninteresting Billy enjoyed this part of his work more than any other; he liked the idea of being an extra cog in this special office: his beautiful handwriting, learned and perfected in the elementary school in Covent Garden his passport to the fringes of the centre. It was not to Billy's occasional corner that the real words of power ever came and went, but nevertheless he liked the feeling of sometimes being part of the bustling activity and the heightened tension of Mr Gladstone's outer office.

Billy Stacey had worked in the Houses of Parliament for ten years. He was, soon, the fastest messenger employed there, speeding about long corridors with outside post, or letters between Members: hard-working, reliable, known. At some point he had fallen in love with the huge buildings that he traversed so often; he breathed them in to himself; he loved the high ceilings and the Gothic arches and the sudden, hidden staircases; he loved the wide corridors and the historic paintings on the walls and the heraldry and the gilt and the statues. He loved the red carpet and the green. The Head Doorkeeper, who had taken Billy under his wing, explained that the different coloured carpet was to differentiate between the nobles' part of the Parliament, and the others.

Eventually, Billy's reliability and handwriting admired, he was promoted to the position of parliamentary clerk. He still had messages and letters to deliver but much of his time was spent sitting in the clerks' corridor, bent over the long desks with the other clerks, writing what had to be written to maintain parliamentary business and records. Mountains of paper, hundreds of pens and nibs and bottles of ink: Billy understood himself to be only the latest in a long line of unremembered government clerks, stretching back far into history. Once he saw a small, ancient wall painting in the Egyptian Gallery in

Regent-street: a scribe sitting cross-legged before his master, holding a marker and a piece of papyrus. Billy stared at the picture for a long time, smiling to himself in wry recognition.

Some years ago he had been delivering one day more and more urgent letters between the Prime Minister of the time, Lord Palmerston, and his Chancellor of the Exchequer, Mr Gladstone. Towards mid afternoon, as the House of Commons was about to sit, the urgent letters were still rushing to and fro, Billy running from one office to the other. Mr Gladstone was deeply immersed in a conversation in his office with another Member of Parliament about the upcoming Budget when a further communication arrived in Billy Stacey's hand and was placed into Mr Gladstone's.

Mr Gladstone read it through quickly, still speaking to his companion; without looking around he said: 'Very well, agree, give time of meeting etc etc.'

The Chancellor's office was at this moment otherwise empty. 'Me, sir?' said Billy quickly. 'Shall I write this?'

Now Mr Gladstone saw there was nobody else; he looked at Billy properly for the first time. '*You* write it?'

'Yes, sir. It is said I have a fine hand.'

'Let me see.'

He dictated quickly; quickly Billy sat at the nearest desk and wrote.

Mr Gladstone looked for a moment at the letter, then showed it to his colleague. 'What is your name?'

Billy stood again at once. 'William Stacey, sir.'

'William like me.'

'Yes, sir. I know, sir.'

'Where did you learn?'

'At the elementary school at Covent Garden, sir. My father sent me there.'

'You were lucky.'

'Yes, sir. Like you, sir.'

Mr Gladstone looked at the boy sharply. Billy observed up close the odd, high collar that Mr Gladstone wore, that everybody noticed, and this day he was wearing a small flower in his buttonhole, as he did quite often.

'How old are you?'

'Seventeen, sir.'

'How long have you been working in the Parliament?'

'Four years, sir.'

The door opened and Mr Gladstone's son, who was also his chief private secretary, came in.

'William,' said the Chancellor to his son, 'we have a third William in a crisis!' and then he signed the letter and they all turned back to Budgetary matters except Billy Stacey, of course, who sped off to Lord Palmerston's office with the letter.

But sometimes, after that, Billy Stacey was called for by Mr William Gladstone Junior to assist when the office was particularly busy; and this practice continued – more often – when Mr William Ewart Gladstone became Prime Minister. Billy Stacey would sit in a corner in the outer office and write out those unimportant but necessary letters in his excellent handwriting. Very occasionally the Prime Minister, working on an Education Bill, would ask Billy about *his* education as if he were a specimen from another world (which indeed he was); Mr Gladstone was interested in the boy's replies about his learning; deeply disappointed, however, that Billy had not been interested in the school's religious teachings.

'Without our honouring God we are nothing, William.'

And Billy Stacey bowed his head politely and wrote on, neatly.

Mr Gladstone might possibly have rejected Billy's assistance after that conversation. But he understood this odd and clever clerk to be a kind person; twice he had seen him helping a very pretty crippled girl across the busy, dangerous street beside the Parliament with great courtesy and patience. And more importantly, his son, Mr William Gladstone Junior, knew a good and reliable jobbing clerk when he saw one.

'I knew you'd do well, lad,' said the Head Doorkeeper proudly.

Which is how Billy Stacey, now aged twenty-three, was sitting in a corner in the Prime Minister's outer office writing letters while Big Ben boomed on that Monday morning, just after *The Times* and the *Reynolds Newspaper* and many other newspapers had first reported in such detail the felonious case brought against Ernest Boulton and Frederick Park.

All the official private secretaries were working with the Prime Minister today as well as Mr William Gladstone Junior: all gentlemen of excellent education whose families were of course known to the Gladstone family; there was much coming and going; doors opened and closed all day long.

Billy wrote neatly in a far corner.

The door opened now. Nobody in particular looked up.

'William!' The voice called out: loud, confident. Now everybody looked. Billy saw a gentleman of religious persuasion; his white collar and cassock announced his calling.

'Julius!' The Prime Minister's busy, furrowed brow part-cleared, he nodded in hurried recognition. 'Julius, a pleasure. But you must excuse me. We must meet another time, not now.'

'Now, William,' said the visitor. Something in his voice.

'It is impossible, I am due in the House to speak on the Irish land question now.'

'You need to speak to *me* now, William. And in private. I come on behalf of the other bishops in the House of Lords.'

The something in his voice was louder. Mr Gladstone looked impatient. Outside the door someone was calling urgently for him; the House was waiting.

'I shall return, Julius, in an hour or maybe two. It is a long speech and a complicated matter. You of course know my son, William; he will look after you if you need to wait.' He was already reaching for his coat.

'Did you read about the court case concerning the apprehension of the Gentlemen in Female Attire?'

Mr Gladstone's coat was half on, his son helping him. They both stopped, stared at the bishop, amazed at the bizarre turn the conversation had taken. Billy waited, disbelieving, to hear what would be said next, bent over his letters. His pen scratching was the only sound; the office was otherwise silent for a moment, despite all the noise and calling from outside.

'Of what possible interest is that dirty, squalid little case to me?' said Mr Gladstone and he impatiently nodded to his son to help further with his jacket. He then picked up some papers from the big desk in the centre of the room.

'Arthur is involved.'

'Arthur?'

'Arthur Clinton,' said the churchman.

This time Billy Stacey did look up from his desk. Again Mr Gladstone's movements were arrested, only this time he automatically put out his hand to a chair, as if for support. And Billy saw something; saw it happening – the colour drained from the Prime Minister's face. The silence in the room was absolute; they could hear a man whistling in the courtyard below. Nobody in the room moved.

'Arthur Clinton.' Mr Gladstone stared at the visitor. The gentleman of the Church said nothing more, just looked back at him. 'He has not been arrested also?'

'Not yet. But I have been advised by a contact that damaging and compromising letters have been found.'

'Where is he?'

'No one can find him. But it is likely there will eventually be a warrant put out for his arrest also. It may seem nothing but a squalid dirty little case to you at the moment, William. You are always an innocent about public opinion – and, incidentally, it is our opinion in the House of Lords, as you know, that the death penalty should never have been repealed by previous, ignorant governments for such a terrible offence against God! Ten years and hard labour is nothing! However the Great Unwashed have already shown an enormous interest in this case – there were apparently huge and very unruly crowds outside the courtroom – and that interest will increase an hundredfold if Lord Arthur's name appears in any way, and my contact tells me it is very unlikely that we can prevent this. If I have this information about Arthur, it is likely that many others will already have it too and whatever happens we – the bishops – feel that it is imperative that nothing at all, however innocent, is published – ah – that is with regard to yourself, or this Parliament. You know very well how foolhardy Arthur is. What is to stop him standing in the witness box and—'

Mr William Gladstone Junior suddenly turned and said hurriedly to the occupant of the desk in the corner, 'Thank you, William, that will be all for the moment.'

Billy stood quickly, leaving the room and the pile of letters that were not completed. As he left, he saw Mr Gladstone and his clerical visitor going into the private office, speech on Ireland or not.

He walked slowly back to the clerks' office downstairs: the pens and the inkwells and the never-ending parliamentary papers.

He wrote neatly and quickly, as usual. But his mind went over and over the conversation he had heard, the officious words of the bishop and the pale face of the Prime Minister. Billy did not know that his own face was slightly pale also. If Mr Gladstone had been so affected by the mention of Lord Arthur's name, would that affect the fortunes of 13 Wakefield-street – the address already recorded in the newspaper? Could it affect Billy's own work here?

I cannot – I must not – lose this position, thought Billy Stacey.

Billy had been intrigued, since that very first meeting, by Mr William Ewart Gladstone. He knew now quite a lot about him. He knew that his father had owned sugar plantations and slaves in the West Indies. Billy studied articles and pamphlets and even looked at a book called *The State in Relation to the Church* written by Mr Gladstone many years ago, but was unable to agree with it, or finish it. But most of all Billy studied the great man himself. He knew that Mr Gladstone was a most courteous man, to everybody. But he had a temper, which he restrained by sheer will; from his quiet corner Billy had several times seen the Prime Minister when he was displeased, breathing deeply, his face redder, but controlling himself. Mr Gladstone often addressed people, even in his own office, in a manner that was pompous, loud, and sometimes long-winded. Billy understood that Mr Gladstone was very clever. He understood that he was deeply, and strictly, religious with high moral principles.

Therefore Billy had stopped stock-still in the street in utter amazement the first night he had seen Mr Gladstone, now Prime Minister, walking with one of the street-girls along the Strand. The girl was talking and Mr Gladstone leaned down, listening, as they walked. The second time this had occurred,

Billy had discussed it with his friend, the Head Doorkeeper, Elijah Fortune.

Elijah Fortune had laughed.

'He's mad of course. Terrible risks he takes, most people consider. He is often lately seen in the company of a most notorious lady who has social aspirations – notorious, but she has recently found religion – and that to Mr Gladstone must be a combination that makes her irresistible.' Elijah shook his head. 'But he is basically a good, very sincere man, I believe. Tormented, I would say, but – good essentially.'

'Tormented by what?'

Elijah had looked at Billy speculatively for a moment, knowing that perhaps he, Elijah, was the nearest thing to a father Billy Stacey now had. Perhaps Billy was also the nearest thing to a son that Elijah Fortune had. Billy was a very serious lad, and sometimes Elijah worried about him.

'Since you ask me specifically, not that it is our business—' He stopped, trying to find the most suitable words and then spoke very quietly. 'In my own very personal opinion, he is tormented by too much upright morality which is – which is at war, perhaps, with his – personal temperament. A common difficulty maybe.' And then Elijah moved to deal with an enquiry from a member of the public, whistling 'I Dreamt that I Dwelt in Marble Halls' as he bustled about, arranging something. Elijah always whistled.

But later when he and Billy were almost alone in the Central Lobby Elijah thoughtfully contemplated the carvings of saints and monarchs that stood everywhere above them, and resumed the conversation.

'I've known Mr Gladstone longer than many people here, and I believe he's a good and very moral man as well as a significant Prime Minister.' Elijah stared at the marble saints. 'Everyone has demons, Billy. That is part of life. But the God I believe in is a little more merciful and less judgemental than Mr Gladstone's perhaps. In my opinion he does, as I say, take stupid risks – so do many people, but they're not all Prime Minister of England and Empire are they! But – he doesn't care about gossip. He seriously thinks to rescue those street-girls from their wicked ways, that's what you saw him doing. Been doing it for years. It's part of his nightly activities.'

'Does he rescue them?'

'Well, that, lad, is hard to quantify. He talks to them about God, I believe. Seems to me Mrs Gladstone has some success – he takes some of them home and she tries to get them proper work.' Elijah looked at Billy dryly and again spoke very quietly. 'What he is *actually* thinking when he walks with them in the night you and I are unlikely to ever know, and it is not our business – although as you may gather I do sometimes make conjecture, having observed him for so many years.'

And Elijah whistled as he tidied papers on his counter.

Billy noticed that Mr Gladstone and Elijah always greeted each other, both long-time members of this institution. Billy also observed Members of Parliament emerging from Elijah's cubbyhole behind his desk in the marbled Central Lobby with tears in their eyes: Elijah Fortune appeared to be a combination of head doorkeeper and father confessor. At first Billy had supposed that he must be giving his visitors strong spirits for strength and succour. But when he was invited into the inner sanctum himself, he saw that only tea was provided, made by Elijah in a pot hung over his small fire.

And Billy was surprised to find that Elijah and his wife actually *lived* on the premises, actually lived in this wonderful, historic building. Not quite the splendid apartments where the Lord Chancellor lived, Elijah explained, nor the gracious establishment for the Speaker of the House, but in small living quarters just above the basement and the drains, and the sewerage pipes.

It hadn't taken Billy long to understand that Elijah knew everybody and kept many secrets. Indeed, Elijah Fortune, hearing the name of the new keen young messenger at the Parliament, had befriended Billy Stacey when he first started work, without mentioning that he had known Billy's father and Billy's mother. Isabella might not have wanted him to talk of the past, Elijah thought; he knew what had happened to her, what she had had to do, how hard it was for her, and Elijah Fortune was a man of infinite discretion.

'Elijah Fortune!' said his mother when Billy had described him soon after he had started work, aged thirteen. 'Well.' And for a moment she said nothing more. 'He didn't mention we were known to each other?' Billy shook his head. She nodded. 'How like Elijah,' was all she said then. And then she did not mention Elijah Fortune for years.

But very much later, long after they had moved to 13 Wakefield-street, Mrs Stacey said: 'Well. We're friends from the past – Elijah used to be at the stage door at Drury Lane in the olden, golden days – Elijah and your Pa and me and his wife Dodo who was a dancer and a singer in the music halls, and loved everything that was coloured red! Elijah was very fond of your Pa, your Pa missed him when he went to the Parliament, it's a long time since I've seen him. A good man down to his shoes. He knows everything about everybody in London, and he's a discreet man, thoughtful as to how he uses his information.'

Billy and Mattie rolled their eyes. (Not so their mother could see, of course.) Elijah Fortune might know everything about everybody in London. It had been their opinion from a very young age that the same could be said about their mother.

After Billy had seen the Prime Minister with street-girls, he said to his mother: 'Elijah says Mr Gladstone's been rescuing street-girls for years.'

Mrs Stacey laughed. 'Peg Turnball runs one of the houses off the Strand and Peg said to me a few years ago: "Listen, Isabella, that man, Mr Gladstone, he's a bloody great nuisance and I wish he'd keep out of my street – my girls complain – Edie Barnes moans that he reads her blooming Shakespeare! Well, I don't care about that in their own time, Isabella, but he puts people off approaching the girls, the way he hangs about them so, he's blooming bad for business!"'

And then his mother asked Billy, in that droll manner her children were used to: 'Did Elijah mention Peg's other observation: that Mr Gladstone helps only pretty girls, and young, not ugly old ones?' and Billy had laughed too, because that indeed had been his observation also.

'Where does he walk?' asked Mattie curiously. 'The Prime Minister of England walking in the Haymarket? He *wouldn't*!'

'Not the Haymarket, Mattie, he's not stupid!' said Billy. 'After the Parliament business is over at night he goes up Whitehall – right past Downing Street as if he didn't have any connection to it, and then from Whitehall he often doesn't turn towards Carlton House Terrace where he lives still, but down the Strand instead.'

'Ten Downing Street is quite small for a family,' said their mother knowledgeably, which made her children roll their eyes at each other briefly, for it meant that, sometime, through one of her multitudinous acquaintances, Mrs Stacey had probably been inside.

'And how do you know he goes down the Strand?' said Mattie, laughing at her brother. 'You walking the streets too?'

'Mind your own business,' said Billy mildly.

He didn't say he had once or twice followed Mr Gladstone, so fascinated was he by this strange and powerful man who had helped Billy get promoted, probably without realising it. And finally Mattie had seen the famous man herself. She had met Billy outside the Parliament, and Mr Gladstone had passed them in the street, and courteously raised his hat.

'Say hello to Elijah from me,' his mother said at last. 'And to give my love to Dodo. Tell him—' She stopped, bit her lip. 'Tell him it all worked out in the end.'

And Billy had looked at his mother carefully, and nodded.

Now Billy sat at the clerks' desks, having been banished from the Prime Minister's office, writing neatly. But his thoughts went round and round. *What is the connection between Mr Gladstone and Lord Arthur Clinton?* The scene he had observed tumbled about in his curious mind. Billy had seen Lord Arthur, the Member for Newark, in the Houses of Parliament occasionally (but not often), and at the little theatre in Clapham with his pretty sister, and a few times in Wakefield-street with Ernest. Billy's father had taught him long ago not to judge what he did not know, and Billy lived by this precept, but he had quietly thought Lord Arthur a dispiriting fellow.

'He's had a dispiriting life,' Elijah had said.

But this dispiriting person was no longer a Member of Parliament. He had lost, or resigned, his seat at the last election. He'd been made a bankrupt, Freddie had told them, and they had never seen him at Wakefield-street again. But whatever his proclivities, of what real consequence could he be to the government now, that Mr Gladstone had turned so pale? Something knocked at Billy's brain, some piece of information.

Lord Arthur Clinton.

Newark.

Billy, such an avid reader on the Parliament, knew something. Newark had been known as one of the 'pocket boroughs' – in the pocket of the local lord, to give to whomever he pleased.

Billy suddenly jumped up from the long clerks' desk, knocking over some ink and receiving complaints and swear-words from other clerks as they worked. He put papers under his arm, to look official; he knew where records were kept, and scrolls of past election results. Mr Gladstone was now the Member for Greenwich. And before that, Billy now read, for South Lancashire. And before that for Oxford University. (*Bit odd*, thought Billy, *a university having a vote.*)

He kept going back and back patiently, following Mr Gladstone's successes (and sometimes his failures; sometimes he had stood for two seats at once, to be sure of getting one somewhere). Back and back the records went; the light was going from outside; Billy did not notice, he had a task, he simply bent nearer to the old pages.

Billy Stacey had been old enough to understand what had happened to his family when his beloved father died. He knew what had happened to his mother. He knew what she had had to do, to make them safe. And today he had understood what his mother and his sister did not: that their safety could now be affected by what had happened to Ernest and Freddie.

And then he saw it, in the shadowing evening light.

He must have known it, read it somewhere, or his mind would not have niggled in that way. Billy Stacey found that from 1832, when he was first elected to Parliament, till 1845, Mr Gladstone had been the Member of Parliament for the pocket borough of Newark.

The same seat that Lord Arthur Clinton had briefly held.

Billy felt slightly dizzy. Was that the connection? *Who gave Mr Gladstone his very first parliamentary seat? Whose pocket was it in? The same seat that Arthur Clinton had held. Who gave it to Arthur Clinton?* But Arthur Clinton had lost the seat, or stood down.

Billy sneezed in the dust. Did this dry old stuff have anything to do with Ernest and Freddie dressing in their ladies' gowns? It didn't seem very likely.

But Billy had seen Mr Gladstone's face go white, and Billy Stacey never let things go.

8

The bishop who had visited the Prime Minister in his office had also made it his business to then call at the Gladstone family house in Carlton House Terrace, to speak to the Prime Minister's wife.

Which is why, as Billy Stacey bent over old documents in the falling light, the aristocratic and confident Mrs Catherine Gladstone (above her husband in birth, with the advantages that brings which can sometimes be useful in a crisis) was seen to enter a carriage which quickly deposited her, after a very short journey, at the doors of Marlborough House at the end of Pall Mall, where the rotund Prince of Wales and the beautiful Princess Alexandra were waiting out their long years, for their destiny. And where this evening a soirée was being held to which Mr and Mrs Gladstone had been invited. She never minded going to such things on her own for everybody knew Mrs Gladstone, and her husband would join her later if he was able. And she was interested this evening in who else might, or might not, be present also.

The soirées held regularly at Marlborough House by the Prince and Princess of Wales were not, of course, similar to the memorable soirée held at Porterbury's Hotel by the Strand, although there were straight-backed gilt chairs for the ladies, and plates of fruit, and laughter and chandeliers. But in Marlborough House there were beautiful old paintings on the walls and two magnificent staircases leading down to the main reception room. There were also over a hundred rooms and very many servants and two grand pianos in one corner from whence Haydn's 'Variations' wafted. Royal portraits stared down regally. A fruit cup was served by respectably uniformed staff.

There were other members of royalty present (Queen Victoria, never); there were ladies of society and best lineage; and most of all there were the racy, rich members of the 'Marlborough House set' as it was known. (It helped to be rich, to enter this magic circle: the Prince of Wales required a great deal of entertaining, which often turned out to be surprisingly expensive.) The Prince was a genial and genuinely welcoming host; the beautiful Princess of Wales, hurt by one matter or another (for they came with growing frequency), nevertheless stood graciously with her lovely head held high. Also present was the person whom Mrs Gladstone had hoped to see: Lady Susan Vane-Tempest, daughter of their old, now-deceased friend: Henry, the fifth Duke of Newcastle.

'Susan, my dear!'

Mrs Gladstone drew the attractive woman aside and as she did so she saw that Susan's eyes were anxious as she watched their host over the heads of the guests. But nothing after all was more natural than that they should know each other well; Susan and the Prince of Wales had been friends since childhood. (Mrs Gladstone had of course heard the rumours of a slightly different relationship.)

Susan did give now her whole attention to the older woman and smiled at her with genuine affection.

'My dear Mrs Gladstone, how lovely to see you!' and she kissed her warmly. 'I think of you often. How is the Prime Minister?'

'Sitting in the House, alas, unable to attend. He too would have been glad to see you, dear Susan, as am I.'

There was a burst of male laughter from across the large room and people smiled at the sound and drank fruit cup.

'You look lovely, as you always do, my dear. And how are you? It is some time since we have seen you.'

'I am – very well,' said the lovely Lady Susan, but again her eyes seemed anxious as she involuntarily looked once more for the Prince of Wales.

'I am glad. And your brothers? We were just wondering, Mr Gladstone and I, if you knew the whereabouts of Arthur?'

'Arthur?'

And Lady Susan pulled herself together at once. To Mrs Gladstone, Susan's voice seemed nonchalant; she shrugged her noble shoulders. Perhaps had not yet heard; perhaps had more important things on her mind. Then Susan laughed. 'My brother Arthur is never to be found – unless he requires financial assistance of course. You know that perfectly well, Mrs Gladstone!' she ended gaily.

'I believe he may be in some sort of – difficulty.'

Lady Susan looked at the older woman. Of all the people in the world to whom she might have confided, Mrs Gladstone was the one of whom she was most fond. Mrs Gladstone had been so good and loving when her own beautiful mother had run away. Susan had a sudden, desolate longing for Catherine Gladstone to put her arms around her and stroke her hair and comfort her, tell her all would be well in the end, as she had done so often long ago. But Mrs Gladstone would not understand that, although Susan loved her brother, it was also the way Arthur's actions were affecting her *own* life that troubled her at the moment.

She disguised a tiny sigh with a cough, and shrugged again.

'Is not Arty always in difficulty!' she said ruefully. 'Is that not a way of life with Arty?'

The conversation might have proceeded further but they were suddenly surrounded by gentlemen; the Prince of Wales himself approached. First he smiled at Lady Susan, who curtseyed at once. Then he turned his whole attention to the older woman.

'My dear Mrs Gladstone. I suppose the Great Man is unavailable – we hope he will arrive later as he sometimes manages so to do. But in our opinion no soirée of ours is complete without your presence. My wife wishes to speak with you, and I myself wish you to partake of some special wine from Madeira that I have acquired.'

Mrs Gladstone was drawn away by His Royal Highness but not before she observed an exchange of, frankly, intimate looks between himself and Lady Susan, who was then swept off by some of the Marlborough House set, laughter echoing.

Mozart had succeeded Haydn. 'Eine Kleine Nachtmusik' emanated now from the two grand pianos.

When Mrs Gladstone tried again later to find the younger woman, she was advised that Lady Susan Vane-Tempest had had to leave early.

9

THAT SAME RUDE policeman who took their gowns away and put a lock on the door came back again. He had a summons to the Treasury, and then to the Bow-street Magistrates' Court, and, good, I was the only one home, Ma was at the market with her shopping list and her big basket and visiting who knows what lonely people and soup-ladies, and Billy was at work.

'Where's the man who owns the house?' was the first thing the rude policeman said to me this time.

I fixed him with a very rude look back. 'I'm one of the owners,' I said. He looked at me, I was sweeping as it happens and I was blooming hot, the weather was suddenly boiling, and only May.

'How could someone like you own a house?' he said. 'I dont own a house. How come you own a house?'

I just held on to my broom and stared at him.

'You know it's an offence to lie to the police,' he said.

'I am not lying. I am one of the owners of this house. I own it with my mother and my brother.'

'Well where's your brother?'

'He's at work. Wont be home till after midnight,' (well that might be true, he might go observing his hero Mr Gladstone!)

'Where's the landlady?'

I made a Plan, very quick. 'I'm the landlady,' I said, very firm and sharp. 'As you can see.' I was still holding the broom.

'You look a bit young to be the landlady,' he said, sarcastic. 'I expect you're the maid.'

'I may look young but I'm not,' I said. 'Besides my brother and my mother may own the house with me, but he works elsewhere and has nothing to do with the running of it, and she is very old and she may be the landlady in name, but she's – well well Ma's nearly seventy-five, she couldn't possibly come to Bow-street,' but I did have a quick look round to make sure Ma wasn't anywhere near, she might've got very ruffled if she heard me say that, well – well she's *quite* old, she's turned fifty.

Lucky for me at that very instant one of our regulars Mr Connolly came up to the door with his battered old portmanteau full of different patterns of material for ladies' gowns and with black smuts from the railway on his face. Mr Connolly always walked from the railway station, he said too many people got their belongings thieved if they parted from them, even for a moment, in an omnibus or a cab.

'Morning, Mattie, just arrived at Euston. It's a bit hot!'

'Good morning, Mr Connolly.'

He took no notice at all of the policeman. 'Got my room three nights, Mattie?' he asked me.

'Yes, I was expecting you, Mr Connolly,' I said grandly. 'Come in. The back room first floor, this week,' and in Mr Connolly went and up to the first floor and I grinned at the policeman, cheeky I suppose.

'You better watch your step, miss. We'll close you down if it turns out this is a whorehouse!'

I was so surprised, so shocked, I held on to the broom for support, what if people like Mr Connolly heard them words, and before I could answer him he said: 'Right, young lady, you'll appear at the Bow-street Magistrates' Court on Friday,' and he handed me a paper. 'And you'll come with me right now and make a deposition at the Treasury.'

'What's that mean?'

'Tell what you know so it can be writ down. It's the law.'

'What do you mean, *what I know*?'

'About this matter of the men and their fancy frocks. Come along now.'

I pulled myself together. I knew I'd better go and see what I could find out so I took Mr Connolly's money and locked it away, and gave him a room key, and I yelled to Mr Flamp, 'Mind our house, Mr Flamp! Tell Ma I'll be back soon!' and I grabbed my hat and off I went with the surly policeman.

Mind you, Mr Flamp couldn't save our house from a rat let alone an intruder but funny though it seems, our house was safe usually, too much coming and going for thieves and murderers.

When I got back, having answered all their stupid questions and told them Ernest and Freddie were gentlemen, and ordered to be in the Magistrates' Court to tell the same, Ma wasn't back yet and Billy wasn't home yet.

I sat on our front steps in the warm evening, waiting for them again, like last week when the policeman rushed in and took their things and Mr Amos Gibbings smashed the lock (which was still smashed). I thought about dear, kind Freddie. I thought about what the policeman had said about 'closing us down' – this is our house, they cant do anything, well I'm nearly bleeding sure they cant close us down. I thought about what he had asked me and what I had answered. I thought about what I could say to help them. Ma laughs sometimes when she guesses I'm thinking over one of my Plans. I hope she'll laugh this time, I might not tell her the 'closing down our house' bit.

When she came home looking hot I got up from the step and

helped her inside with the big basket and gave her a big cup of cold water. 'Sit down, Ma,' I said, and then I told her what I'd done, my Plan, that I'd said I was the landlady. I thought she might stop me but she just looked at me, very careful, and then she just said, 'Are you sure, Mattie?' and I said, 'Course I am! I've already given my statement to the Treasury, that's what you have to do apparently, before you go to court. Actually Ma – I, well – well I told them you were a bit old and we had a relative who was like a maid.'

Ma looked very surprised. 'Whatever did you do all that for? What's the matter with you, Mattie? It's foolish to lie to the police if they're writing it all down.'

'I wanted them to think I was the landlady and that we were exceedingly respectable, with maids and that.'

Ma laughed instead of ruffling. 'I am indeed old, you are the landlady partly, and we *are* exceedingly respectable!'

'The thing is – *I* wanted to give the evidence, Ma,' I said. 'I might be able to help Freddie,' and she just looked at me funny again but she nodded.

'You'll hear the questions in court better than me,' she said, 'but I'll be coming with you.'

'No, I can do it by myself!'

'I'll be coming with you,' said Ma.

I swallowed. 'Well – well I actually said you were seventy-five so they'd believe I was the landlady.' I could feel my face, looking ashamed, would she get mad now?

But Ma only shook her head and looked at me, still half laughing. 'Sometimes I feel seventy-five having you as a daughter!'

Then Billy came home and we told him and he went very quiet. He's often quiet, too busy thinking about his books we say but this was a funny quietness, and then later he said: 'I'll give the evidence of course, Mattie. If you'd like me to. It might be a better idea.'

'I *want* to do it,' I said. 'I want it to be me, I've already told them Freddie and Ernest are gentlemen and excellent tenants. I might be able to help them!' and they thought I didn't see but Ma and Billy exchanged a little look, I saw it.

'All right, Mattie,' said Billy.

10

The evening was so hot, for May.

Mr Gladstone was unable to sleep.

He had already written earlier in the evening to his old school friend the Solicitor-General.

He wrote now, in the middle of the night, to Mr Frederick Ouvry, the lawyer for the Newcastle Estate.

Among his many official duties and long hours in the House of Commons that day, he had seen the Prince of Wales, who reiterated that he did not care to go to Ireland, although that was not the only subject they discussed. Mr Gladstone lay thinking in the warm night; sleep would not come.

Next day, during his long hours in the House of Commons where he made several speeches, and had the usual many gatherings with Members and bishops and businessmen, Mr Gladstone saw His Royal Highness again. There were several official meetings with his cabinet; he also found time to see, privately and unofficially, certain members of his cabinet with whom, like the Solicitor-General, he had been at school and university. There were dinners to be attended and letters to be written and important papers to be read and his diary to keep.

Again, that night, he could not sleep.

11

ON FRIDAY MA and me – it was hot and sticky, peculiar weather for May and I could feel my heart beating a bit fast – went off to the Bow-street Magistrates' Court, dirty old place it is too, and the first horrible shock was seeing such an enormous, pushing, noisy crowd outside, all laughing and gossiping and eating and obviously they'd got a view of the 'filthy fellows' being brought back to court again from the House of Detention, and other witnesses already gone in. A policeman saw I had a witness paper and took my arm and helped me through and some of the crowd stared at me, limping in: *who's that cripple?* and Ma just turned back and punched the man in the crowd who said that, much to his surprise, and I felt like punching ten people, I was that mad at all the gawping and gossiping. The policeman finally got me inside and Ma slipped in too by pretending she was a witness with me and I thought to go in with her and at least see Freddie and Ernest, but I was told I had to sit on a bench outside the courtroom until it was my turn, all hot and dark and gloomy.

And next to me on the bench, guess who? That big bullying fellow who had looked down my bosom, sweating in the same black and yellow uniform and funny black hat with a gold buckle – that blooming Beadle from Burlington Arcade, and he was so pleased with himself and full of himself (and taking up most of the bench of course) and he couldn't stop talking and he didn't remember me at all thank goodness. I sat half on the end of the bench and half on nothing, to get away from his spreading fat bottom.

'I presume we get paid for coming,' was the first thing he said to me and then he went on and on about Freddie and Ernest. 'Course I know them, them two, course I do, I seen about them in the paper, so I went straight down to the police station, I know all them coppers, they're all friends of mine, and I told them I had evidence to give. Those poncy boys come to the Arcade all done up in their ladies' clothes trying to catch the passing gentlemen's attention, vying they are, making trouble with the street *ladies*,' and he put great emphasis on the word *ladies* to make sure I understood and he kept laughing at his own stories, *ha ha ha!*

'And several of the *real* ladies stroll about my Arcade with my permission, and I make a bit on the side, but not from them two, mind, they was mean as crows, them. Once they ran into a ladies' stocking shop, they knew I wouldn't follow there, but me I just waited outside and ejected them from the Arcade as soon as they came out. And another time one of them had the cheek to address me as "*O you sweet little dear*". So I ejected them again, the dirty buggers. And I writ it down, them words, here they are,' and he waved a little notebook, read them out slowly: "O You Sweet Little Dear," which made me want to laugh even in this horrible heart-beating place, 'and I shall give them in evidence! Not that I'm at the Arcade now, I got fired but I volunteered to come and give evidence in me old uniform, ha ha ha!'

He had two chins and the bottom one wobbled over the collar of his beadle's jacket.

'Why were you fired?' I asked.

'They say I took drink! Well that's wrong, I took money, not drink! I bought the drink with the money, ha ha ha!' and at that moment he was called in: GEORGE SMITH, GEORGE SMITH and I was left by myself on the bench outside. And I couldn't really hear anything much from inside the court except a bit of laughter, and I did blooming hope it was about Ernest (I bet it *was* Ernest) calling that fat George Smith a sweet little dear.

And then it was me: MARTHA STACEY, MARTHA STACEY and I marched in (well limped in), and there they were at last. My heart really did turn over then – Freddie and Ernest in the dock as if they were criminals, and the most unshaven I'd ever seen them. (In their gentlemen's clothes so Mr Gibbings must have got them to them eventually, though we hadn't seen Mr Gibbings since.)

At once I saw that Ernest was enjoying it, he had that look, that special look of his, all coy, but knowing too, and he gave me a little wave and a smile. But Freddie looked grave, and he was pale and he held a pencil and a little notebook for taking notes and every now and then he'd pass one to his lawyer. He nodded very slightly at me and I smiled at him and I only half looked about the crowded hot court and thought, *they know nothing, all these people, specially about Freddie*, and I gave my name and I suddenly wasn't nervous at all. A gentleman asked me questions quite politely and I tried to answer quite politely back.

'My name is Martha Stacey, I live at 13 Wakefield-street, Regent-Square. I live there with my mother and my brother. I am the landlady.'

'Do you have any children, Mrs Stacey?'

That punched me. I couldn't help it, I looked at Freddie. And even in his own troubles I saw his kind face straightway look back at me, as if he was saying, *I know, Mattie*, helping me to answer.

'No children,' I said.

'How long have Mr Boulton and Mr Park rented a room from you?'

'The gentlemen first took lodgings with us – oh – more than a year ago. Sometimes they kept the rooms for a good few days, and sometimes just a night.'

'How were they dressed when they took the room?'

'Of course they came dressed as gentlemen. They are gentlemen.'

'Did you see them also dressed as females?'

'Course, they explained they were actors, we knew they dressed up as women for the purpose of performance and I have seen them acting.'

'You have seen them perform upon the stage?'

'I have and they were very good!'

There was some clapping in the court much to my surprise and Mr Flowers banged on the bench but Ernest was smiling at the applause and bowing and even Freddie was smiling, looking down at his hands.

'Did you understand they had lodgings elsewhere?'

'Yes, they lived elsewhere.'

'Did they receive visitors at Wakefield-street?'

'Sometimes other gentlemen came. But always very respectable and quiet. Some friends of theirs also took rooms with us sometimes. Mr Amos Gibbings who broke down the door after your rude policeman put a padlock on it, he sometimes took a room too. Sometimes they all dressed as ladies before they left.'

'Did Boulton and Park sometimes sleep the night at the house?'

'Occasionally, if they came in late.'

'But it was not their main place of abode?'

'I *told* you that already.'

'Were they ever troublesome?'

'Course not. They were good tenants, pleasant. And' – I wanted to look at Freddie again but I did not – 'very kind. And they always behaved in our house with propriety.' I took a breath. 'The only troublesomeness in our house was when the policeman came and took their clothes and put a lock on the door of the room that I am supposed to keep clean!'

'Thank you, Mrs Stacey,' said the man politely. 'That is all.'

It was only then as I turned to get down from the witness box that I properly realised the boiling hot dirty old Magistrates' Court was crowded with very well-dressed people, society people, people from the theatre, all leaning forward and then talking among themselves, and then I nearly laughed because I saw – guess who? – that actress from the play where the door stuck! It was a bit hard to get down with my rotten leg and I was looking for Ma but I was quickly offered a seat, I squashed in on the end of a row near by, next to a rather beautiful fashionable lady who smiled at me and made room.

'Good girl,' she said, as if I was a child.

The magistrate was called Mr Flowers and he looked to be a kind man.

The man who had been with them when they were arrested who was given bail, Mr Hugh Mundell, told his story. He said he'd only met Ernest and Freddie recently. The first time he met them they were dressed as men, but he believed they were really women dressing up.

'In fact,' he said, 'I gave them some hints about being more like men if they were going to dress up, using their arms more when they walked, like men do.'

There was very much laughter in court and Mr Flowers said dryly: 'Thank you, Mr Mundell.' And then Mr Flowers said, 'Somebody earlier used the expression *going about in drag*. Can someone please explain that expression to me?'

One of the barristers said very gravely (because there was a mighty lot of twittering and tittering in court it seemed to me), 'The term *drag* is a slang term employed in certain circles to mean men wearing women's clothes.'

'Why is that? I understood a drag to be a four-wheeled vehicle.'

'I believe it is something to do with the brakes of such a vehicle, Mr Flowers, that is, the brakes slowing the vehicle, dragging things along, say like the train of a lady's gown slowing a person's movement, as it were.'

His language was very inelegant and he got very muddled-sounding and the court laughed at him, but Mr Flowers nodded and said, 'Thank you, sir, for your elucidation,' and the naughty crowd clapped and it seemed from all the whispering in the audience that Mr Flowers was about to give Ernest and Freddie bail at least, for they'd already been in custody for more than a week. I was suddenly so nervous for them I could hardly breathe even though I hadn't been nervous when I was answering the questions. But a short man stood up urgently. This was Mr Poland, he was the main prosecutor.

'Mr Flowers, I am afraid there is much, *much* worse to come. I would urge you still not, at this stage, to allow the prisoners bail.'

But there was immediately a sort of hiss in the court, as if all the fashionable people and the actors didn't agree. I looked at Freddie then and I swear he went paler. Even Ernest looked thrown at last and I realised they had completely expected to be released today.

Mr Poland said: 'It was not just female attire that was removed from the room in 13 Wakefield-street, and other rooms around London, Mr Flowers. There were also photographs. And, most importantly' – and he sounded really blooming triumphant – 'there were letters that are going to be extremely important evidence in this case.'

'What do you mean, letters? What sort of letters?'

'I mean letters to and from the prisoners that will make your hair stand upended.'

As Mr Flowers was bald there was some more laughter in the

court but it was nervous laughter now. Then Mr Poland went and whispered to Mr Flowers. The court was very quiet. Whispering and whispering between those two and at one moment I thought they was looking at me.

'Very well, Mr Poland. Very well.'

Mr Flowers thought for a while and took his watch from his waistcoat and his eyebrows were frowning and then he addressed the audience (well it seemed like an audience in a play).

'I have been given information that makes me think that although this matter has been taking some time it would be best if I ruled that the prisoners be remanded further in custody, at least overnight, and I will call the court again tomorrow. I hereby recall Martha Stacey to return again then for further questioning. Return the prisoners.'

Just like that. And Mr Flowers went out a side door, and those policemen went and escorted Ernest and Freddie out, Ernest was waving and smiling at the fashionable people but Freddie passed me on the end of my row, and stopped and gave me a little smile, and shook my hand briefly and I put my hand over his, didn't care who saw.

'See you tomorrow then, Mattie,' he said. 'Thank you. I expect we'll surely be released tomorrow,' but I saw a queer little twitching under his right eye and he gave a sad little shrug of his shoulders, oh, I so wanted to give him a big hug.

When we all piled out of that hot dirty old room it seemed that there were blooming hundreds and hundreds more people outside and we saw Ernest and Freddie being put into a van and the driver got up and cracked his whip and they were driven away and people banged on the van and yelled and some of them yelled out, 'Filthy fellows!' And some of them cheered.

And Ma took my arm and said, 'Well done, dearie, you did well, shame you have to go back tomorrow.'

'I don't care,' I said. 'I know how to do it now! I cant tell them anything else anyway. And surely they'll get out tomorrow.' *And I'll see Freddie again,* I thought.

Ma said, 'Shall we take an omnibus?' but I wanted to walk, and I knew so did she, after this peculiar day, and Freddie and Ernest taken off in a van like criminals.

'Where are they being taken?' I asked my Ma.

'I expect they are going back to the House of Detention in Clerkenwell,' she said and I thought how queer and cold that sounded. Ma keeping to my pace we walked in silence, arm in arm as the strange, warm evening fell and gaslights shone into the smoky dusk that is London.

'Ma,' I said at last, 'that policeman said he could "close us down".'

'What d'you mean?'

'If we were a whorehouse, that's what he said.'

And my Ma stopped sharp in the street and ruffled as big as any turkey ever seen in Regent-Square.

'It is our house, Mattie. It *belongs* to us!'

'Lucky we knew Mr Rowbottom, Ma.'

'We've got the papers. It belongs to me and you and Billy. And it is not a whorehouse, and over my dead body will anyone say what we can or cannot do inside our own house, bleeding cheek!'

And then, just as quick, she ruffled down again and took my arm again and we walked on. Back to Billy who'd come home as early as he could and was boiling us some sausages and waiting to hear what had happened, and to 13 Wakefield-street our home, which suddenly was in all the newspapers.

12

While the business of the Gentlemen in Female Attire was proceeding, and reported in the newspapers, Mr Gladstone was confined to his bed in Carlton House Terrace with one of his rare bouts of complete nervous exhaustion. Normally a robust and healthy man, he had to be away from Parliament for several days on doctor's orders.

He turned in his hot bed. He listened to the eternal passing of carriage wheels. And the voices of caring women, instead of the voices of ruling men.

These nervous turns came at moments of great stress in his life, and of course there were indeed many things to stress him. The Education Bill that meant so much to him and the planning of the best ways to instruct religion in the rate-provided schools. The immense and complicated difficulties of the Irish Land Bill. Presiding over the whole of the British Empire in the way he knew best; the colonies were, as he said so often, one of the best means of advancing and diffusing civilisation by creating so many happy Englands, where the Anglican Church at its highest, and the Anglo-Saxon race, could plant a society of Englishmen. Dealing with Her Majesty the Queen, the most difficult woman he had ever known in his life. Long hours of attendance in the House of Commons. Letters, meetings, dinners. And the diary he kept, briefly noting most – but not all – of his actions, his letter-writing, his state of health, his meetings: recorded for posterity.

But there were other matters on his mind also, when he briefly noted in the diary that he was confined to his bed by his doctor as the horses and carriages clattered by in the uncomfortably warm May darkness.

13

SO BACK TO the court I went next morning, Saturday, it was a lovely May day, spring that felt like summer and you could see the sunshine clean and clear for once, not all foggy and cloudy. There were flowers in strange places – bright yellow dandelions in the cracks of the pavements that looked as if they were smiling, like good omens, and I wondered if Freddie and Ernest could see a flower, well surely there was a little window in the House of Detention and they could see the sunshine at least. And today it would probably be over and they could see all the flowers and sunshine they wanted. Ma and me again pushed past all the waiting loud crowds with our piece of paper, Ma squeezing my arm before she melted into the audience (yes, yes, I know it isn't an audience, but that's what it *feels* like, up there in the box thing).

And there I was standing up there in the dark old stuffy court again, and there was Mr Flowers, and there were Freddie and Ernest in their place, and I could clearly see they both had not shaved again. Freddie was passing a note to his solicitor; he was a law clerk after all, and he probably knew very much about the law with all those legal people in his family that he'd told me of. I so hoped that today would be the end of all this and our life could go on as usual and Freddie and Ernest and their gowns and their music often in our house. I wanted it like it used to be.

The fashionable crowds were crammed in again – big hats and lovely gowns – and I thought the man who was asking me questions this time was rude, this horrible short person, Mr Poland, the main prosecuting man. All I thought of was them getting out today, even on bail so I tried not to get mad and to answer politely, me and Ma and Billy had talked last night about how to say things and then I'd decided a few other things to say when I lay in my bed. Mr Flowers the magistrate did look quite serious this morning, but not unkind, he had a face you could trust I thought. I wondered if someone had told him that Freddie's grandfather was a Judge? and that his father was important in the courts? but understood it was not for me to speak out about any such thing. I just smiled at Freddie before Mr Poland began.

'Mrs Stacey, you are perhaps rather young to be a landlady.'

'No I'm not.'

Silence.

'We run a particularly well-regarded establishment. And my mother may be rather old but she would certainly not stand for any disrespect.' I hoped Ma wouldn't stand up and ruffle. I thought I saw Freddie smiling to himself.

'And who is the actual owner of 13 Wakefield-street?'

'As I already explained to the policeman who put a lock on one of our doors, the house belongs to myself, my mother and my brother.' I felt much more confident today.

'The boarding-house trade must therefore be very lucrative, in Kings Cross.' Everybody would have heard the sarcasm.

'The house was left to our family by a – relative, in his will, when I was nine years old.' I couldn't punch him but I could punch him with words. I remembered Ma's words: *It BELONGS to us, Mattie!* I looked at the magistrate and smiled at him. I hadn't read lots of books for nothing, I knew how words could go.

'Perhaps, Mr Flowers, you would like me to go home and get the legal papers for you to peruse since it seems to be implied that they are relevant to this case, though I dont know how, I'm sure.' Mr Flowers coughed and harrumphed and looked at Mr Poland and Mr Poland left that line of questions.

'Mrs Stacey, how many beds were there in the room they first rented from you?'

I was on the alert at once. This Mr Poland was looking for things to go in *Reynolds News.*

'There was one bed. A large one.'

'So if they stayed the night the defendants slept in the same bed?'

There was that sort of hiss again, from the actors and the fashionable people.

'Well, I s'pose they did, Mr Poland! Like I sleep with Ma if we're short. But I didn't go up to their room in the middle of the night and investigate their sleeping arrangements. And anyway like I said they didn't stay very often, they had their own homes to go to.'

Another noise in court, not a hiss but agreement.

'However, Mr Poland, when they first came to our address they asked most specifically for two rooms but we did not have two available.'

Take that, Mr Poland, I thought to myself.

'Did gentlemen visit them?'

'D'you mean did they have any friends?'

'Were they visited by gentlemen at 13 Wakefield-street, Mrs Stacey?'

'I told yesterday that other friends rented a room sometimes. Mr Amos Gibbings had a room. Sometimes they had a visitor or two, or Mr Amos Gibbings had a friend, and sometimes they sang which was really enjoyable.'

I got a bit carried away here, remembering Ernest's sweet voice, *which is the fairest gem? Eileen Aroon*, drifting down the stairs.

'Do you mean music and dancing?'

'Just humming and singing, Mr Poland, perhaps you do the same in your house? We like music in our house, actually.'

Another murmur of agreement from the crowd.

'And lately we hadn't seen them for ages before they started coming again about a month ago, I believe, Mr Boulton went to Scotland for some months because he had been ill, to get better.'

'Did he indeed?' and Mr Poland gave a little nasty smile. 'And tell me, Mrs Stacey, have you met Lord Arthur Pelham Clinton?'

What a queer little ripple there was in the audience after that question, it was like a gasp. Somehow my answer was listened for in a funny silence as if it was very important but I did not dare look at Freddie because everyone was looking at me and waiting to hear what I would say. I remembered what Ma said: *Everyone waiting for the nobility to be involved.* I felt sweat trickling under my arm. I had no way of knowing if anyone else had talked about Lord Arthur.

'What was the name?'

Sarcastic: 'Lord Arthur Pelham Clinton.'

'I may have. Maybe many months ago. I have a busy life.'

'Surely somebody of your – class, Mrs Stacey, would notice if a member of the nobility arrived at 13 Wakefield-street?'

I looked at him. He looked as if he kept nasturtiums, a flower I had an aversion to. 'Mr Poland, perhaps your "class" would notice other people's class, but my mother and I run a very busy lodging establishment—'

'Some people may use other terms than merely a "lodging establishment", Mrs Stacey.'

Blooming pig. I turned to Mr Flowers on the bench. 'Mr

Flowers, could you ask him not to cast further aspersions on our very respectable home?'

Mr Flowers looked at Mr Poland over his spectacles. Mr Poland bowed in apology and Mr Flowers indicated courteously to me to continue.

'—because my mother and I run a very busy lodging establishment and very many people visit us from time to time, including many cotton salesmen from the North of England who are also regular patrons which perhaps you would like to verify. Possibly the person you mentioned came to the house but I cannot be absolutely certain and if he did it was a long time ago.'

And I folded my arms, making it clear that was the end of that. *Take that, Mr Poland.*

'You say the defendants always came to your house dressed as men. Did they leave always as women?'

'Course not. In fact' – I suddenly had this idea – 'Mr Frederick Park had a moustache a while ago as a matter of fact, for months actually, so he wasn't always dressing as a woman, though they did quite a lot.'

Mr Poland looked at me very suspiciously. 'Thank you, Mrs Stacey, that is all.'

Again I found it hard to get down but there was the noble lady from yesterday near by, beckoning me, again she squashed up and made room for me on the end even though we were all hot, while the policeman read out a list of the things that had been found in our house. The more the list was read out in the policeman's flat voice the more the people in the court laughed and sort of applauded and Ernest seemed quite cheered at this and looked at the audience pleasedly, and sort of fluttered.

'Sixteen dresses, silk. Moiré antique, ditto, white Japanese silk trimmed with white lace and swansdown, pink stripes, green cord silk. Thirteen petticoats in tulle, tarlatan, white frilled cambric, white book muslin. And a crinoline. Nine coats, ermine jacket and muff, crimson velvet shawl.'

The lady I was sat next to found this all very funny and laughed – her laugh sounded like a bell, ding-dong-ding-dong – in an elegant sort of way, other people laughing too of course, and Ernest looking coy. And she laughed even more at the next things.

'Ten pairs of stays. Two pairs of drawers; garters, stockings, eight pairs of boots, shoes, etc. Curling tongs. A bottle containing a quantity of chloroform.'

'Did you see these?' the lady asked me, tears of laughter in her eyes now.

'I did,' I whispered back, 'and some of the gowns were beautiful though some were a bit battered. But I never saw any chloroform, whatever that looks like.'

'Now listen, if they ever ask you about chloroform, say it is for toothache,' she whispered.

'Is it?' I said, surprised.

'Never you mind,' she whispered back, laughing still.

'Seven chignons of different colours, chiefly of the prevalent golden hue. Two long curls. Ten plaits for hair and a grey beard.'

Here the court erupted and Mr Flowers made a banging noise with a hammer thing. Still the policeman hadn't finished his list.

'Artificial flowers and a great quantity of wadding, used apparently for bosom padding. Four boxes of powder and two of "Bloom of Roses".'

Mr Flowers leaned forward. 'Is it suggested by the prosecution, Mr Poland, that the aforementioned grey beard is an article of female attire somehow to be worn with "Bloom of Roses" which I presume is some sort of ladies' powder?'

'No, sir. Rather it is my opinion that the beard would have been used as an article of disguise. It is possible that the moustache mentioned by Mrs Stacey was a disguise also and she did not recognise it as such.'

I went to stand but the lady stopped me with her gloved hand. 'It's all right,' she whispered.

And again I thought, *they will be let out on bail today and then we can all laugh about it together, it will be all right.*

But it wasn't all right. It was terrible. Because we realised that it wasn't just ladies' clothes that that horrible lawyer was going to tell of. Or even photographs. Well they were just photographs of them dressed as women, I'd seen them plenty of times when I cleaned their room, both of them dressed as ladies in all sorts of different gowns, and often photographs with Lord Arthur Clinton – he was always playing the man and they were playing women – theatrical photographs, that's all, and never Lord Arthur dressed as a woman, I couldn't see how such photographs could matter in the least.

But it was the letters they'd talked about yesterday. They must have been in a drawer. (Well I didn't look in their drawers when I was cleaning, I'm not a blooming spy.) And Mr Poland had kept the letters for his grand finale.

'We have seized letters from several addresses, including 13 Wakefield-street,' he said triumphantly, 'that are very relevant to this case.'

'You implied yesterday there was something in the letters we should know about,' said Mr Flowers.

And the prosecutor held up a packet of them and then he said: 'I would like to read just one of these letters to the court.'

'Very well,' said Mr Flowers.

And he stood there, that prosecutor, and he was smiling in a nasty way and all the laughing and gossiping people in court suddenly went very quiet, taken by the look on horrible Mr Poland's face.

He started reading. It was from Scotland where Ernest had gone to stay.

My darling Ernie

And my heart did sink at once, because men dont write like that to other men.

My darling Ernie,
I had a letter last night from Louis. He tells me that you are living in drag. What a wonderful child it is! I have three minds to come to London and see your magnificence with my own eyes. Would you welcome me? Probably it is better I should stay at home and dream of you. But the thought of you – Lais and Antinous in one – is ravishing.

There was another funny gasp in the audience then, not a laugh. I looked at the lady who I sat next to, I wanted to ask her who Lais and Antinous are but she was looking serious now and muttered something to the lady next to her on the other side.

Let me ask your advice. A young lady, whose family are friends of mine, is coming here. She is a charmingly dressed beautiful fool with £30,000 a year. I have reason to believe that if I go for her, I can marry her. You know I should never care for her; but is the bait tempting enough for me to make this further sacrifice towards respectability? Of course, after we were married I should do pretty much as I pleased. People don't mind what one does on £30,000 a year, and the lady wouldn't much mind, as she hasn't brains enough to trouble herself about much beyond her dresses, her carriage etc.

What shall I do?

You see I keep writing to you and expect some day an answer to some of my letters. In any case, with all the love in my heart,
I am yours etc
John

There was a funny feeling in the courtroom in the silence and I thought it was mainly because the letter was so cruel, but maybe it was the *all the love in my heart* bit.

But Mr Poland hadn't finished. He turned to Mr Flowers and said: 'There are many more letters of this ilk and much, much worse, Mr Flowers. I have another which I think will persuade you, but I do feel, sir, that I cannot read it aloud as its contents are much too shocking, and mention is made of – a certain lord – who has not yet been called to give evidence. I do suggest that you retire to read it, before you make any further decision about the prisoners.'

'I think if the public can be saved the reading of them it will be beneficial,' said Mr Flowers in a dry tone and he slowly got down from his big bench and disappeared, clutching the letter he had been given.

The good feeling in the court wasn't so good now. I looked at Freddie and Ernest and I suddenly thought, very clearly: *all this is Ernest's fault.* Whatever Lais and Antinous might mean it was quite clear to me that most of this was about Ernest, and not Freddie. Even Ernest looked pale now and had stopped smiling and nodding, he was in men's clothes, yes, but it was true, he *did* look as if he was a woman trying to be a man. Whereas to me Freddie looked like – Freddie.

After a while Mr Flowers came back. He didn't say anything at first but he looked serious. Again I wondered if he knew that Freddie's family were important in the law. Surely that would count, *surely*?

'I have decided to keep the defendants in custody,' he said rather shortly. 'This court is adjourned for a week.'

A week? They'd already been incarcerated for blooming ages.

Now they both had their heads down and looked really distressed as they were escorted out to the van. There were such huge crowds waiting outside now, even bigger than before, it truly looked like thousands now, stretching way back down to the Strand, all yelling and peering and craning to have a look, it was like a Royal Procession or something. Ernest and Freddie couldn't get to the van, the police had to move people, some were cheering and some were shouting. Ernest and Freddie did manage to wave and took off their hats. Before he entered the van Freddie spoke briefly to a man in a suit, I looked carefully but it wasn't anyone I'd ever seen, maybe it was someone from his family; they shook hands. And I thought, *his family will be looking after him, of course they will, both of them, Freddie and Ernest are gentlemen and their families will know what to do* and then as he was stepping into the van Freddie saw me, and gave a small wave and I waved back.

When we got home I told Billy that they'd gone back to the House of Detention and a letter had said that Ernest was *Lais and Antinous in one* and that it made a funny feeling in the court and what did it mean?

'They're getting a bit literary down there at Bow-street,' said Billy in that droll voice, like Ma. 'Lais and Antinous were both famous lovers in history. Antinous was a man and Lais was a woman. Lais was loved by many men.' He looked at me. 'Antinous was loved by men also.'

And Ma said, surprising us the way she does so often: 'And if I remember rightly, both of them died in mysterious circumstances.'

14

In Paris, Susan Opdebeck (once the young and beautiful putative Duchess of Newcastle, now banned from English society and married to – English society found it hard to forgive this also – a Belgian courier) stared with incomprehension at the telegraph message from her daughter, also named Susan. It required her to keep Arthur with her at all cost, should he turn up, because he was in extreme trouble should he be found in London. She shrugged in exasperation.

Her son Arthur was not with her.

None of her five children was with her.

Her children were a disappointment to her. They were all somehow flighty; bereft of money, unable to support her in her old age (she was fifty-six, but still beautiful). She had thought that at least, when Linky became the sixth Duke of Newcastle on his father's death, proper allowance would be made for her at last. But he was too busy selfishly gambling: a disappointment indeed.

A disappointment, as was her first husband, Henry, Lord Lincoln, who became later – without her at his side – the noble, honourable fifth Duke of Newcastle. But only she knew what that paragon was *really* like: upright, religious, tedious, selfishly sexually demanding. Serious. Boring. No fun. Like all those religious hypocrites among his friends.

A disappointment, as was her lover Lord Walpole, who had deserted her after they had run away to Italy together over twenty years ago, and she had borne him a son. They had put it about that the baby, Horatio, had died but she knew perfectly well that he lived in Italy still, in rude health, having been educated by nuns in a convent there.

A disappointment, as were her loving, extremely indulgent parents who had both died, unbelievably leaving her as short of money as ever, and no one with the grace to at least bring to Paris her mother's furs.

And for her cruel fate she *still* blamed the long-ago actions of Mr William Gladstone, her husband's best friend, who had, in their youth – she was well aware – been a little in love with her himself (and had written her dreadful poetry).

She had run away several times before: that is, before the last, fatal adventure. Her tedious husband had always taken her back after her escapades, as long as she wept many tears and grovelled with sufficient repentance (she had known the routine by heart): '*Henry, dearest Henry, my darling, forgive me, forgive your penitent wife. How could I have been so stupid, I believe I must have been ill, I am losing my mind, I believe I shall die, Henry,*' tears pouring down her face as she clasped his knees. '*You are the only man for me, you, Henry darling, I will be good, I promise you I will be good, you know, my darling, how very good I can be, I kiss your feet and ask your forgiveness, feel my heart, Henry, feel it, feel how it beats so fast*' (and she would at this point take his hand and place it upon her heaving bosom). '*I know I will die if you do not forgive me,*' and she would cling to him and her gown would somehow fall and she would once again endure his gross and greedy (and unfulfilling to Lady Susan, who knew very well how fulfilling sexual encounters could be) sexual appetites. After which, there she would be again, on her husband's arm, part of British nobility and society, curtseying to the Queen. And, of course, soon pregnant once more: Linky, Eddy, Susy, Arty, Alby.

And to this day she knew still that if the sanctimonious William Gladstone had not come running after her that last time, bringing God and Duty, she could have left the illegitimate Horatio abroad, gone back to England and performed the usual grovelling apology, Henry would have forgiven her surely, and she would have become the Duchess of Newcastle. With nobody any the wiser.

Her family background was immaculate: daughter of the Duke of Hamilton, no less. Queen Victoria was fond of her children; why, her daughter, also called Susan, had been bridesmaid at the wedding of the Princess Victoria *after* the scandal! *Of course I could have returned.* Susan Opdebeck could never believe that it was actually her dreary husband, the fifth Duke of Newcastle, of whom Queen Victoria was so very fond and, therefore, the children. When Susan Opdebeck had heard that Queen Victoria had actually travelled from the Palace and visited him on his deathbed, she was amazed.

But the interfering, moralising, tedious, holy Mr William Gladstone had come charging across the Channel on a steamer as if it were a white stallion, to find her and spy on her; to take the news of her condition back to England; and later to have the effrontery and hypocrisy to say that God had led him to her, eight months with child to another man, on the banks of Lake Como.

As she thought of the past, *Lady* Susan (no one could take her own family title from her) Opdebeck sipped laudanum, which she had had to have in large doses for many years on account of her fragile nerves. For if things did not go her way she became – literally – ill: suffered from nervous prostration and spasms;

her life could hang by a thread. (Only that last, fatal time had these often useful symptoms made no difference to her fate.)

In Paris now, Lady Susan Opdebeck let the telegram from London about her son Arthur flutter to the floor. She observed that the hand that let the message fall, and the arm above it, were still firm, still elegant.

The only person not a disappointment to Lady Susan Opdebeck was herself.

15

'*. . . my ghost will haunt you . . .*'

The English weather that year had suddenly become even warmer – most unseasonably warm – but Mrs Catherine Gladstone shivered slightly as the words echoed round and round in her head: *my ghost will haunt you my ghost will haunt you . . .*

Mrs Catherine Gladstone was not a fanciful woman in the least, but she could not shut out these words this evening as she walked with her husband. She suddenly shook her head slightly: puzzled, anxious, as if the ghost from her past was too near. William Gladstone walked, with his stick, beside her slowly, as if he was older than his sixty-one years, but he was recovering from his nervous exhaustion.

There was no proper garden at Carlton House Terrace. Mr and Mrs Gladstone were walking together, as they occasionally did, in the garden at the back of 10 Downing Street. The official residence was used for offices, and the occasional official reception; the garden was tended carefully. Tonight the evening was lowering and humid, rosebuds already bloomed and the scent of lilac lay on the air. In the distance, the sound of passing carriages; here, small birds sang and conversed as they came like a dark chorus to settle in the trees. The couple walked now in silence but they had been discussing the scandalous newspaper coverage of the trial that was the talk of London.

And they were both thinking about the same woman.

They had been, long ago when they were young, such close friends, the four of them. Lady Susan Hamilton had married Mr Gladstone's dear friend, Henry, Lord Lincoln, who one day would become the fifth Duke of Newcastle. The aristocratic Miss Catherine Glynne married Mr William Gladstone, who would one day become Prime Minister of Great Britain. The men had been to Eton together, Oxford together, served under Peel and Palmerston together. The couples spent much time in one another's company, lived as neighbours in London, visited one another's country residences. Mr Gladstone had, indeed, written Lady Susan poetry – courtly poetry only of course – for he had found it hard to take his eyes from her on those long-ago memorable evenings in the noble Newcastle country mansion, when the beautiful and charming Lady Susan stood beside the piano in the lamplight, and sang so sweetly.

But all had turned to dust and ashes more than twenty years ago and the runaway wife had not only blamed Mr Gladstone for all her troubles to anyone who would listen, but had threatened, in a letter to a mutual friend, to *haunt* Mrs Gladstone if she ever spoke badly of her to her bereft children.

Mrs Gladstone had tried to care for the lost young people; never once had she spoken disloyally to the children about their mother – yet tonight the mother seemed hauntingly here anyway, drifting through the darkening leaves, blaming and accusing still.

The birds had settled now. It was almost dark.

Mrs Gladstone spoke at last. 'Dearest William. I have said this to you many times: we cannot rewrite the past, neither our own nor other people's. This is all twenty years ago! You did as you thought wisest, and I agreed you should go. Henry asked you to look for his wife and Sir Robert Peel himself concurred that you should and so you went to Italy. It was a most honourable quest: to bring her back and save her marriage and her reputation – you did that for them both because they were our friends. How can it be your fault what you found!' She sighed in the falling dark for what, indeed, had been found. 'But those motherless children were damaged by everything that happened between their parents. Perhaps Arthur most of all.'

He seemed not to hear her. Again they walked in silence.

The Prime Minister passed his hand wearily across his face, saw himself now as he was then: young still, full of ideals, a knight on a mission: to rescue a beautiful woman. From Naples to Milan to Como he had followed her: there he had been advised that an English lord and lady were living at a large villa on the banks of the lake. He delivered a sixteen-page letter to Lady Susan there, telling her of her duty to her family and to God.

The letter had been returned unopened.

So then, intoxicated by the nearness of the quarry, he decided to go himself to the villa in the night, to try to actually speak to the maiden in distress. He arrived there with – he swallowed even now at the embarrassing memory – a *guitar* as a disguise; should there be others present he thought to appear as a musician (as if Mr Gladstone could ever look like a musician). Then, approaching the villa with his guitar clasped in his arms, he saw his old friend's beautiful wife hurriedly departing, wrapped heavily in cloaks, but not enough to disguise her condition. Light from a lamp caught her face as she entered a carriage and fled across the lake from the friend who had wanted to save her from herself. All his dreams of heroic rescue, of scandal averted, dead from what he saw in the night. Which he then had to report to his heartbroken friend.

Then of course there was only one course of action left: a course of action almost too terrible to be thought of and, at that time, as was right and proper, available only to the very rich.

Divorce.

When this terrible event at last took place, through the House of Lords and the Ecclesiastical Church, a solicitor for the husband confided to Mr Gladstone that he thought Her Ladyship was possibly deranged. Mr and Mrs Gladstone knew that Her Ladyship was not necessarily deranged but she was certainly laudanum-addicted – and how well they understood, from their experience with Mr Gladstone's unhappy sister Helen, that laudanum addiction and madness were closely entwined. Towards the unhappiness that led to such addictions, however, they were not sympathetic, in either case, for Mr and Mrs Gladstone both strongly believed that, in the end, Duty mattered most.

And Henry, the fifth Duke of Newcastle, had never really recovered, right up to his death five years ago.

William Gladstone spoke aloud in the evening garden his own train of thought. 'Catherine, I miss Henry. He was my dear friend, one of my oldest friends, and we shared so much together. I owe him so much. He was a fine, honourable, deeply religious man with many burdens to bear, and he bore them with dignity.' Mr Gladstone sighed heavily. 'How could I not still mourn such a friend?'

Silence. Only the distant rumble of traffic. His wife knew when to interrupt and when to listen.

'And how could I not want to protect him still? I suppose I should rejoice that he is not alive to suffer this latest scandal spread across the newspapers in a vile and vicious manner!' He struck at the grass, vicious also, with his stick. She restrained him gently. 'A scandalous divorce from that beautiful charming woman we thought we knew so well, who is married now to *a courier from Belgium*! And now his son's name in the newspapers in the most disgusting and shameful way possible.'

They reached the bottom of the garden where a wooden seat was built into a stone wall. The Prime Minister stood silently but struck the wooden arm of the seat, angry still. 'And if his daughter is not infinitely discreet in her relations with the Prince of Wales, she will be next. Is it a curse? Is it a curse in the bloodline?' But he shook his head in answer to his own question. 'I cannot believe that.'

He at last sat wearily on the seat; his wife sat down quietly beside him. Somewhere an owl called: that haunting, night sound. But he did not hear. 'The Prince of Wales needs proper work! His mother refuses any such notion. His energy is therefore dissipated elsewhere, especially in scandalous dalliances and liaisons, and it will go on being so.'

Mrs Gladstone refrained of course from making any comment about work and energy and dalliances, although she might have done. For she knew, as Elijah Fortune knew, and indeed as many people knew, that her husband dallied also – apart from the actual act: she knew him so well: he could not have lived with himself if he had been physically unfaithful – with a lady of much repute. Mrs Gladstone loved her husband. She had decided – gallantly and perhaps wisely – to live with a situation that she could do nothing about, but it had pained her nevertheless that he shared even a part of himself with another woman. She was not sorry that family ties and duties often called her away from London.

They sat in silence as darkness fell and ghosts hovered.

'I am answerable only to God and to my conscience,' said Mr

Gladstone as if he could read her thoughts. But he was actually thinking of Arthur Clinton. 'Nevertheless I do not require my – our – past close relationship to Lord Arthur, although it is beyond reproach, to be spread all over the newspapers also. It is not a matter for the public. It is our own private affair. It would be inappropriate – and totally unnecessary – if it became anything else.'

'They would not dare,' said Mrs Gladstone comfortably. 'The newspapers would not dare. Even if they knew.'

'The *Reynolds Newspaper* dared to pontificate quite disgracefully on the appearance of the Prince of Wales in a divorce court not long ago. Journalists have no sense of what is appropriate!'

'The Prince of Wales had exasperated the benign allowances that are made for his behaviour, and which he thinks are his due because of his position,' said his wife, just a little tartly. 'The populace – and the newspaper men – expect some respect.' She sighed, and then she added loyally: 'You, my dear, respect the people of your country, and have never taken advantage of your position. The situation is entirely different.'

'I do *not* respect the *Reynolds Newspaper*, which I see seeks to raise its tone by mentioning paramours from classical history!' He laughed shortly: if Lais and Antinous could appear in the *Reynolds Newspaper* the world was probably doomed.

Of Lord Arthur Clinton's actual crime they did not speak, for there were no words for the unspeakable, even between themselves in the private garden. William Gladstone stared down at his hands, saw that they were no longer young.

And then the Prime Minister of Great Britain bowed his head in the night, and prayed for guidance.

The following week – still recovering from his nervous illness, while the only news in town, the scandalous trial of 'The Men in Petticoats' as they were now called in the cheaper newspapers, continued in the Bow-street Magistrates' Court – the Prime Minister wrote three times to his school friend the Solicitor-General, as he often did, and also met with him privately on several occasions. He also met the Prince of Wales a number of times.

The contacts were, perhaps, more frequent than usual.

16

I'm deaf, yes, but I'm not as deaf as Mattie and Billy think. It suits me to be deaf, it's no blooming joke running a good-class rooming establishment round near Kings Cross and Euston and St Pancras and if anything happens to me I want those two to be forever safe. Sometimes I find it sensible to slightly exaggerate my deafness, ha! and just keep my eyes open. And – well – all right, yes, I have also read Mattie's account of what has happened, it was lying on her work table when I went in to take thread I had purchased down Gray's Inn Road. I'm not proud of myself but I have been so worried about her these last years, and I cant have her hurt more. She's such a true girl, my Mattie. But in telling our story she's entirely left out the most important thing in her life. She has every right to do that – it is too hard, and nothing to do with all this. Except it has made her who she is.

My true girl.

Yet I know she must tell her story her own way and I'm not reading her private writing again, I felt like a bleeding snoop. But there is something I have to make clear also. About 13 Wakefield-street, for everything to make some sort of sense.

Even I know who Lais was, and Antinous. I hardly missed anything when I was attending the court with Mattie, except a couple of witnesses early on who mumbled, but I observed that Mr Flowers was slightly deaf as well, he was sitting nearer than me, but he asked them to speak up! Most of the people talk as if they are giving a speech, I'm glad to say.

And even I know who Lais and Antinous was - if you work in the theatre for years and years, especially in a theatre like Drury Lane, you'd be surprised how educated you get. And I was married to a very knowledgeable man, like Billy is knowledgeable. I've seen a picture of a statue of Antinous, a very beautiful young man who looked like a woman. I think it was that Hadrian, the one who built that Roman wall, who loved him. And some of the actresses used to talk about that courtesan, Lais, like a kind of heroine. They identified with her I suppose because of all the offers *they* got from gentlemen who hung about the theatre - we all knew some of the actresses got money that way. (And who am I to mention that.) In Drury Lane they used to laugh in the dressing room and tell the story that Lais was once offered a thousand - well not guineas but the Greek equivalent I suppose - anyway it was a huge amount of money, but Lais took one look at the person offering and said nah, it had to be ten thousand.

'Ten thousand!' they used to say to each other when they saw an ugly rich man hanging about them.

Yes.

Ah - the real truth about deafness is that instead of hearing other people's voices all the time you hear your own thoughts too much. I wonder if other people have things going round inside their heads that they find *literally unbearable* to think about? There are three unbearable things inside mine.

The first is that I cannot bear to think of Mr Rowbottom.

When we first moved to Wakefield-street they was just digging up the main road nearby to build the Metropolitan Underground Railway – dust and dirt and blooming loud digging all day long and rats, big rats from under the ground running down Wakefield-street. And carts and coaches going past our door at all hours of the day and night, trying to find their way out of the mess on the main road – it all made Drury Lane seem like a country avenue! But now of course that Metropolitan Underground Railway carries thousands of people. I wish my Joe was still alive to see such modernity – he'd find some theatrical equivalent to put on stage in Drury Lane, I bet! I know – he'd build a tunnel, with a light at the end of it, that was Joe, cheerful and optimistic and clever. But, actually, it's smoky and odd and windy down there in the tunnels, where the underground trains now run so easy, I dont like it. I'm so glad I can still use my feet and walk.

But every single day I thank our luck that this house, 13 Wakefield-street – every day I thank our luck that it was not the *other* side of the main road. Euston and Kings Cross Railway Stations were already here when we came of course, all the crowds and noise and dirt and stinks and of course good for our lodging-house business. But when they decided to build St Pancras Station much later, do you know what they did? they just pulled down hundreds of houses on the other side of the main road that were in the way, *smash!* and left so many people with nowhere to live. If you've ever seen people weeping in the streets with their children and their pans and their shoes, or fighting to crowd into an already overcrowded tenement – well then, you know how lucky we are.

Here in Wakefield-street we're safe. And Mattie and Billy have to be safe for ever: that's what matters to me most in the whole world. We know about being unsafe, and now we're safe and no bleeding policeman can do anything. When Billy reads to us, specially on Sundays when we dont clean and us all cosy by a fire and drinking our port in our back parlour at the end of the hall and me remembering the old days in Drury Lane when Joe used to read to us all so often – that's when I know the decisions I made were the right ones.

As Mattie says, if they call your house that you polish and care for 'a bordello' or 'the headquarters of criminal activity', well, although you know it's not true and you try to laugh it off it's not blooming pleasant. But then it wasn't blooming pleasant getting this house in the first place either. That policeman had the cheek to ask Mattie how we could afford to own a house – 'people like you', he said to her. And all that questioning about who owned the house in court – our private own stories getting batted about like shuttlecocks. What's that got to do with them? What's that to do with Freddie and Ernest?

It was cruel and sad what happened to us – and it happens to hundreds. There we were, us all safe and cosy and happy in our room at the top of Drury Lane Theatre, me and Joe working there, us able to put Billy and Mattie in the elementary school in Covent Garden, them learning reading and writing and adding, coming home with all the books from Mudies Lending Library, so keen and eager and happy. And then so suddenly – like almost in a week – Joe so ill that he couldn't work. So ill, and the pain so bad that I couldn't work either, I had to be with him.

There's a lot of talk about warm-hearted theatre folk. And it's true – the actors and the stage-hands collected some money for some of the medicines we needed and I loved them for that. But the managers: no sentiment, just businesslike, we were given a week to leave the room, needed for the next people who were to take our place. There was an opera coming on at the time, Joe getting ill just when the workload was the hardest. We weren't paupers, we had had work and we had some money but how fast does that go when it stops, and the doctors and the medicines costing so much? In the workhouse – why do they call it the 'workhouse' when you go there when you aint got any work? – anyway, you know what they do there? – they have female paupers in one part and male paupers in another part and children taken separate. And most of all Joe in such pain and needing me and quiet and us with nowhere to live and having to pack up everything very quickly and go – go where? where could we go? who could take four people and one of them dying and no money to pay, I used to spew everywhere from the agony of it all. I have never been so desperate in my life.

Mr Rowbottom. All right here comes the story of Mr Rowbottom who Mattie called 'sort of our stepfather'. Ha. He was one of the gentlemen who hung round the dressing rooms of the actresses, only Mr Rowbottom, from the very beginning, started hanging about me for God's sake. I was in and out of the dressing rooms all the time and there were plenty of young actresses and I was married to my Joe, but no, he used to hang around me and he was a pest. But there it is, I'm supposed to be beautiful, or, rather, was, I've turned fifty now and not beautiful at all. (Mr Rowbottom certainly wasn't beautiful, Lais the courtesan would have had something to say about him!)

In the end I think it was because although he had made money and strutted about like a gentleman and sat in the best seats in the theatre and hung about backstage with champagne, he wasn't a proper gentleman, not really, and I think he felt more at home with me, it was probably as simple as that.

'I own many houses,' he said to me several times.

'I'm glad for your sake, Mr Rowbottom, now please get out of my way.'

When he heard of our dire story he straightway came to me while I was trying to find someone we might stay with, and said he had two rooms empty in the Strand and we could have them now, they was furnished and ready.

'Mr Rowbottom, go *away*, I cant pay any rent.' I was frantic and I dismissed him like a fly.

'Yes you can, Isabella,' he said. And he grabbed at my arm and stared me straight in the face. 'You can pay me. Later.' And I stared back.

And that was that really.

Two rooms in the Strand.

Elijah Fortune who'd gone to the Parliament by now came to see Joe soon after that, knowing he was ill and we had been evicted. He knew the situation, Mr Rowbottom told everyone the situation, sort of rubbing his hands together, but never once did anyone we knew make me feel they judged me or blamed me when they came to visit Joe at the end.

Two rooms in the Strand.

Joe lived another miserable three months but at least we had a home. And we looked after him and used all our money for medicine and flowers and chicken to make soup he could still swallow and we loved him and talked to him about when he was better and loved him. When an – uninvited – churchman came and told us Joe was going to a better life and it was God's will, Billy shouted, 'We *had* a better life before, so God is rotten,' and punched the churchman who threatened to sue for assault.

And after Joe died I paid Mr Rowbottom for the rooms.

In the way he expected, most nights, in the rooms in the Strand that he gave me 'for free' before he went home to his family. Mattie was so young still, and hardly ever saw him, fast asleep with her arms around a book before he would even arrive.

But Billy knew.

Drury Lane Theatre wanted me to return to work, but I wouldn't go back there. I went to the Haymarket Theatre and I stayed for years. Finally Billy turned thirteen and his teacher found him the position as a messenger in the Parliament because Billy was so clever. I longed and longed to get away from Mr Rowbottom, I'd paid my debt over and over, and Billy and I found another room to rent, the three of us, in Bedford-street, and decided to keep Mattie longer at the school that she loved so much, till she was thirteen, and then I should be able to get her work sewing. I told Mr Rowbottom, thanked him for helping us when we needed it most but that we would be leaving now. Mr Rowbottom cried. He sat one night in one of the rooms in the Strand, the children asleep next door, with tears dripping down his face and off the end of his nose.

'Stay with me, Isabella, and I'll give you a house when I die.'

The words were almost ridiculous. No one in my family, or Joe's family, had ever owned a house.

I thought how wonderful it would be, to be free of Mr Rowbottom. God, he might live to be a hundred years old. I might die first, we would surely manage now that Billy was working too. We could afford a room, nothing else could go wrong now.

Then I thought about how nearly we had sunk into the poverty of the city. Because nothing, ever, stays as you think it will.

'Which house?' I said.

He took me to 13 Wakefield-street, I saw it could be a lodging house with a bit of paint and polish.

'Legally,' I said. 'To Billy and Mattie as well as me in case I die.'

He brought a lawyer to the Strand, and we both signed – but not until I'd had the contract checked over, clause by clause, with a very clever lawyer I knew from the Haymarket.

And I stayed with Mr Rowbottom. You might find me disgusting. That's fine. It's what many women do all the time. In their way. I think Lais the courtesan was killed mysteriously by jealous women but I'm not likely to die a mysterious death, I dont think anyone was jealous of me when Mr Rowbottom came beaming into the theatre at night to claim me and take me to the two rooms in the Strand.

Then God smiled. (I dont believe in God either, but still.) Mr Rowbottom died about a year after Billy started at the Parliament.

We got the house.

We own the house.

We are safe.

Or we were until Ernest and Freddie's story intertwined with ours.

Billy. He's a true, real scholar. He knows so much – of course he's worth more than running around with messages from Honourable Members and writing down their every word – not that it isn't a very good position mind, and so well paid, we know how lucky we are. But he could have done anything, Billy, if he'd just been born a bit upwards and known a few of the 'right' people that you have to know in this world.

Billy reads and reads – even poetry. Once he saw Mr Matthew Arnold at the Parliament, come to speak to Mr Gladstone, and next thing I know he's reading all Mr Matthew Arnold's poems too! There's something basically 'good' about Billy. That's the only way I can describe him really, Joe was like that too. Billy's a good person, and a very, very clever person. And: there's something – I dunno – immovable about Billy once he makes his mind up about something. Mattie said once over some small thing: 'It's like sitting at dinner with God, sitting eating stew with you, William Stacey!' but as Billy has immovable thoughts on matters of religion too we all laughed then, the three of us!

Billy knows perfectly well the price of our house. He knows how near we'd been to the workhouse and he knows why we stayed with Mr Rowbottom and he understood and has made me know he understood, always.

But once – him and me alone in our downstairs kitchen, we were discussing something or other and I said, 'You're as stubborn as a bleeding ox, William Stacey! An ox as huge as Big Ben! You dont have to carry the whole blooming world on your shoulders!'

And my son said to me quietly: 'I just want to carry us, Ma, that's all,' and I nearly wept then. I knew what he meant, dear loving responsible Billy. But I think – I think everything that happened has somehow made him a lone person. And that is a sad thing in my life.

And, Mattie. Always so bold and brave and making her famous 'Plans', but I know her heart inside. I'd like to kill that Ronald Duggan – nah but I was taken in by him too, he seemed a nice and reliable man who cared for her and I did make him welcome. I thought, *it will get her thoughts away from Jamey and the sad past.*

It's Jamey she hasn't mentioned.

She might not ever, it goes very deep with her, which is why I've encouraged her to walk out with others. And she had so, *so* wanted her and Jamey to have a baby, so when this happened with Ronald Duggan I was taken aback (and of course I thought he might be a fly-by-night who had taken advantage of her) but I could see that he did care for her (or so I thought) and I could see that it made her happy to think of being a mother at last, so I was happy too. You might think I should've kept her more carefully. But – she'd been a married woman. I could hardly treat her like an innocent young girl.

Jamey. Mattie and Jamey had known each other since they were about nine years old when me and Billy and Mattie came, at last, on our own, to live in our very own house, in Wakefield-street. It was paradise, after everything. Truly, *paradise.* My soul breathed.

There was a big, moving population in all those streets round Kings Cross but Jamey lived near and was not much older than Mattie and he and she, these two children, just took to each other and were inseparable. I think he never even noticed her leg, she was full of life, tough as a nut, and full of her reading, and Jamey loved books too, right there in Wakefield-street, these two young people and their beloved books, chatting away, scaring themselves half to death reading *Frankenstein*, writing in notebooks even, telling their own stories. One day I found them at the back of our house, digging with a huge shovel that was bigger than both of them. They had decided to plant some honeysuckle that they'd found in the old churchyard at the end of our street, so that it would grow over the old cesspit and 'smell lovely'.

Young Jamey was a grand lad and when he was thirteen he got work with Mr Bloom, who owned a printing press down Kings Cross – so many big and little businesses started up there, that station is the worst in London, like a big public meeting all day long, yelling and travelling and buying and selling and thieving. And all the mad, dangerous bloody, *bloody* traffic, round and round the station.

Soon as he turned sixteen Jamey asked me, very formally like in one of their novels, if he could have my permission to marry Mattie because he loved her. 'I'll do better than help in a printing press,' he said to me with his dear earnest face, 'I'm going to start writing stories like Mr Charles Dickens! I've already started, and Mattie and I will be rich and happy!' Mattie wasn't even turned sixteen but it seemed right and fine and they'd been cuddling by the fire for years.

'Course you'll do well, Jamey!' I said. 'And you can marry her if she wants it too,' and course I knew she did, like I say, we'd known him for so long and Mattie and he were so close and fond, and she looked so happy and she is so pretty when she is happy. If they wanted to be married that was fine by me. So we had a little wedding party, best china, Billy in his suit, Jamey's mum came and his sisters and brothers and we all went into the old nearby churchyard that smelled of honeysuckle, it was a lovely sunny day and we sat on the old graves in the sun and thought the world was a fine place indeed, and Jamey's mum and me, we even sang a few of the songs of our younger days after we'd had a few bottles of stout – there was this popular dance song, that kids sang later, and I do believe we danced in the old churchyard that day as we sang it!

Up and down the City Road
In and out the Eagle

That's the way the money goes
POP Goes the Weasel!

And Jamey came to live at 13 Wakefield-street, and he was a good boy to have around – though a bit dozy at times, forgot things, because he was writing stories in his head, but we only laughed and he really tried to help Billy fix things in the house, they put up some new wallpaper with little roses on, and chopped wood for the fire from old logs they found in the graveyard. (But you had to watch that Jamey with an axe, he was too dreamy for an axe, he might be thinking of a story and cut his leg off, we joked.)

Mattie teased me about being a grandmother, and I said, 'Dont be in so much of a hurry,' and she said, 'Why? I can still make hats as well as have a baby!'

And I expect she could have, only – although they so wanted to have this big family I used to hear them chatter about, she didn't get in the family way.

And then, after only about six months, Jamey got knocked down by a stupid, *stupid*, STUPID, drunk cart-driver delivering things to Kings Cross. There are always accidents with bloody carts and carriages all the bloody time everywhere round the bloody station but somehow you dont think it will happen to your own loved ones do you? Jamey died, carried here bleeding and unconscious by Mr Bloom and another man, with his legs all out of shape and Mattie falling as she tried to run fast down the little steps by our front door to get to him. We thought Mattie would die herself, she got ill, she couldn't stop crying, me and Billy were at our wits' end, finally we got a doctor but he couldn't do anything, he said we were spoiling her and he told Mattie she was a pretty young girl with her life ahead of her and it was God's will and she must 'pull herself together'. That advice cost four shillings and I was glad to see the back of him or Billy might have punched him too.

She sat at the table so pale with us that night after the doctor left, not eating anything, and pulled and pulled at her thin arms.

'Whatever are you doing, Mattie?'

'He said I have to pull myself together,' she said. 'And I am trying but what does it mean?'

Mattie pulling at her thin arms at the table that sad night is the second thing in my head I cannot bear to think about.

Luckily a lady in Mortimer-street who had had one hat from her sent a note just at this time, asking for another. I made Mattie go to see her, I mean I took her myself and the lady had very large-hat ideas, it was to meet Royalty no less because her husband had won a medal although it wasn't the dreary old Queen they was to meet of course, no one ever met *her*, but one of the younger Princes, at a ceremony in the Palace.

That was the start of Mattie getting better but it was long and sad and I was probably at fault when I encouraged her to walk out with others but I thought it would help the healing.

I still feel so angry with Ronald Duggan the railway man, to leave her without even a word or a note. Coward.

The third thing inside my head I cannot bear to remember is that I was sound asleep as well as deaf and didn't hear her pain until Billy came to wake me and there she was so pale and Freddie covered with blood in his yellow gown and his chignon lying on the hallway floor and it all over – without me being there to help her. Freddie and I went outside with the little bundle wrapped in his bright blue shawl. And buried it in the dark little yard next to where Jamie and Mattie had planted the honeysuckle. The honeysuckle had died long ago, there was no sun at the back.

Buried it in Freddie's shawl. Freddie still in his gown all covered in blood and me in my nightdress, like a couple of madwomen in a stage melodrama only it was real.

And all that story is why Mattie loves Freddie so much, because he was kind to her when she needed him, and Ronald wasn't, and she wants to be cherished and loved again. Me and Billy we cherish and love her so much, but I see that it isn't that that she wants, she wants to be loved and cherished by a *man*, more than by her family. Somehow as if that is the only loving and cherishing that really counts. And she thinks that Freddie, when he realises she will stand by him and love him, will be that man. And I dont expect he will.

Kind, sad Freddie.

Surely something will happen to prevent all this going further. Probably Lord Arthur Clinton's family will intervene – and hadn't Lord Arthur told Ernest his sister was a mistress of the Prince of Wales? Let Him intervene then! And Freddie's father works in the courts and his grandfather was a famous judge wasn't he? Something will happen; they cant let this go on and on. Although, of course, after the next court day something had happened

already. That could never be taken back, however it might end.

Once your bum has been in the newspapers how can things ever be the same again?

17

'I'M GOING BACK to the next hearing at the Magistrates' Court,' I announced.

Ma looked at me. That way she has. 'Well then, I'm coming too,' she said. 'We'll have to go early to get in.'

'I can *do* it you know, Ma.'

'You're not going by yourself,' she said.

So we all got up in the dark, Billy too, we were even too early for the omnibuses, and he walked with us all the way, before he started work at the Parliament, he and Ma took my pace, and I walked as fast as I could and Billy whistled sort of absent-mindedly in the early morning, he's been a bit distracted these last days, Ma and I both noticed.

'Do you think he's got a sweetheart?' I asked Ma but she didn't answer me.

It was hardly light but the streets as we walked were already crowded, hundreds of carts with vegetables piled up high, some orange pumpkins fell off and rolled over the dirty old cobbles and they were gone in such a flash, children appeared so quick, and an old lady with a sack.

'There'll be a lot of pumpkin soup today,' said Ma, and she laughed, 'the driver told them to be ready on the corner!'

And in the streets there were animals and milk-girls and

street-girls and a whole bunch of cows, what a stink, and huge wagons of Burton's beer from the vaults at St Pancras Station, and all the costermongers with their fish and their fruit and stuff in big baskets and all the dogs slinking about, and rats in gutters. But not many coaches and carriages at that hour. We could've had breakfast on the way at one of the little stalls but Ma made us have bread and tea before we left. And you know what? there were lots of people crowding about the Magistrates' Court before us, even then, even though we'd left home in the dark – that's how much interest this case had made – and guess what? some of them were servants for the noble people, keeping their places in the queue, what a cheek. Billy waved us goodbye seeing us safely at the court, and we were early enough and when the doors opened Ma and I knew exactly where to go now of course and hurried in and we got a good place.

And then of course I wished we hadn't.

At first it was almost fun; and we were sure that this time it would all be over like a bad dream. There was this very angry businessman, Mr Cox, he gave great booming evidence about kissing Ernest – thinking he was a young woman. He kept looking at Ernest, really enraged and his face all red as he told it.

'I met Ernest Boulton with Lord Arthur Clinton, oh, some time ago now. Over a year I should think. They were with a solicitor, Mr W. H. Roberts, I was introduced, they didn't say what W and H were. Mr W. H. Roberts left but I had lunch with the other two in the Guildhall Tavern. They were dressed as men, of course. Boulton said, "Oh you city birds have good fun in your office, and have champagne," and he said it in a womanly flirtatious way so I thought he *was* a woman and I said, "Well you had better come and see." And they did, both of them, Ernest Boulton and Lord Arthur Clinton, they came to my offices in

Basinghall Street, my partner came in, and we opened champagne, which we laid out in the office. I treated Boulton' – he cast a really furious glance at Ernest – 'as a fascinating woman and I think Lord Arthur Clinton was jealous for he left the room and while he was away Boulton went on in a flirting manner with me and I kissed him – or her. Or it.'

All the noble ladies and actresses and gentlemen in the audience laughed so much I thought the trial could not go on, and Ernest and Freddie couldn't help but laugh too! But Mr Cox took absolutely no notice and just went on talking angrily, so everyone was quiet to hear what he might say next, and the journalists in particular were looking very interested.

'Shortly after the kiss Boulton complained of being chilly and my partner whipped off the tablecloth and wrapped up Boulton's feet in it and placed him in an armchair.'

'I beg your pardon?' said Mr Flowers. 'Could you repeat that series of events, Mr Cox? You wrapped Mr Boulton in a tablecloth, you say?'

'He complained of being cold.'

'So you wrapped him in a tablecloth? Is this usual?'

Mr Cox got angrier and angrier. 'We are gentlemen.'

There was so much laughter now that Mr Flowers had to bang his hammer many times.

'Then what happened, Mr Cox?'

'Nothing. They left. And then I heard from others that Boulton was definitely a man.'

'And you had kissed him.'

'I thought he was a *woman*! They tricked me! But after I heard that, you can imagine how angry I was to have been tricked in such a manner! I was disgusted. I went to Evans' Restaurant in Covent Garden. There were Park, Boulton and Lord Arthur Clinton, all dressed as men. Well I pointed them out to the waiters, and spoke of their nefarious tricks but the waiters seemed not to wish to turn them out. Do you hear that? Waiters hindering a gentleman? So I spoke severely but calmly to the waiters again. "Let me pass," I said, "I will make no disturbance but let me pass." And they did and I went straight up to the table where they were sitting. I said, "You damned set of infernal scoundrels, you ought to be kicked out of this place." And I remained some little while near the table. And I used this language three or four times, I knew they heard it. But they did nothing. In fact they went on speaking to each other as if *I wasn't there,* the scoundrels. Soon after, I left.'

This witness, Mr Cox, had such a red face now that I thought he might expire.

'What I dont understand,' he said, very much aggrieved, especially by the laughter, 'is why I am having to say all this in public! I cannot bear to see these – creatures! I am a public-spirited gentleman and I saw reports of this case in the newspapers. So I took it upon myself to go with my evidence to Superintendent Thomson last night as any reputable citizen would do – and frankly it is a mystery to me why I am subpoenaed here today.'

There was much applause and laughter from the audience even though Mr Flowers told them they must be quiet or they would not be allowed to stay, but I thought even Mr Flowers was smiling a little bit now. And Ma and I sort of relaxed and smiled at each other. And soon we were smiling even more. The next person giving evidence at first struck me as quite mad and her hair started falling down as she was talking.

'My name is Ann Empson and I let rooms to respectable gentlemen only at 46 Davies-street and I let rooms to Lord Arthur Clinton, specifically advising him of the rules of my establishment, no women, no noise, etc, etc. He agreed with the rules. And because he was a Noble Lord I lent him money, he said he was temporarily unmonied and so I helped him out, expecting to be repaid almost immediately – he was a Lord after all, how did I know he was about to be declared a bankrupt, how was I supposed to know that, eh? Then he said he had a cousin called Mr Ernest Boulton and he would like him to stay occasionally. "Well where is he going to sleep?" I asked. "There's only one bed!" And with Lord Arthur's persuasion I obtained another bed. Next thing I know valises and portmanteaus are being dragged up my nicely polished staircases by various gentlemen, including that Mr Park I think, and a *lady* was seen late at night, but when I confronted Lord Arthur with this information and reminded him very firmly of the rules he assured me I had been mistaken, he only had gentlemen visitors.'

There was definitely something a bit – a bit peculiar about this landlady's way of talking, well like I said I thought she was mad and at this point Mr Flowers started to intervene but by now Miss Ann Empson was in full flow, with her hair flying about.

'And when I went to clean the room I examined the sleeping arrangements and it was clear to me – I will not go into detail of course' – and she paused dramatically, her voice full of horror – 'that Mr Ernest Boulton had been sleeping in the same bed as Lord Arthur Clinton!'

Having delivered this piece of information she swayed slightly. All the journalists were writing furiously and breaking their pencils, Lord Arthur had been mentioned before today of course but only in passing; this was what they had been waiting for, as Ma had foretold.

'She's *inebriated*,' whispered Ma, and she couldn't help laughing. One of Ernest's and Freddie's lawyers, called I think Mr Straight, got up.

'Can I ask you, Ann Empson, if it is just possible that you are drunk?'

'You mind your tongue, you cheeky beggar!'

'Are you married, Ann Empson?'

'Certainly not!'

'It might have been an advantage to you.'

'Not if I had been married to Park, or Boulton or any of that lot.'

This was the loudest laughter of all and Mr Flowers had to give a very severe speech while banging his hammer on his bench, saying the next person to cause a disturbance would ensure that every spectator in the court would be turned out. Nothing seemed to stop the housekeeper, however, who just went on talking.

'Now you listen to this! Lord Arthur owed me money, as I say I had lent him some because I thought he was an Honourable Lord and he wasn't at all, he was a bankrupt bugger! And to reimburse myself I took some of their things, I took photos and letters, hundreds of them, I kept some, listen, you just listen to this!' and she actually waved one from Ernest to Lord Arthur and read it before anyone stopped her.

My dearest Arthur,
I am just off to Chelmsford with Fanny, where I shall stay till Monday. We are going to a party tomorrow. Send me some money, Wretch!
Stella Clinton

The audience erupted and she was about to embark on another one, dropping papers, and pointing at Ernest and Freddie in a vague manner but Mr Flowers intervened and told her extremely severely to give the letters to the court where they should properly have been deposited. But she was unstoppable.

'I did deposit them,' she said, 'but I kept one or two as evidence!' She pointed dramatically at Freddie. 'That's him!' she cried. 'I'd know him anywhere even if he's not in a negligee! That's Ernest Boulton!'

'Excuse me,' said Mr Flowers leaning forward politely. 'For the clarification of this court would you identify Ernest Boulton again.'

She pointed again at Freddie. 'That's Ernest Boulton!' and as it was Freddie she kept pointing to, this made her sound even more mad and everybody in the court laughed and started shouting out almost and she was almost physically removed from the witness stand, still speaking, amid great applause.

I saw that the next witness prepared herself before she spoke, a bit like as if she was in front of a mirror, she patted her hair and lifted her head and looked about and smiled at the audience as if she was about to give a performance – and then she began – and did the faces of the journalists become even more excited as they wrote down the words for their newspapers!

'My name is Maria Duffin. I know all about this matter because I let rooms at 36 Southampton-street to Lord Arthur Clinton and I'm telling you that dirty Ernest Boulton masqueraded as Lord Arthur's wife and what's more, you listen to this, Ernest Boulton ordered – I know this – I seen them – he ordered visiting cards with LADY CLINTON writ on them.'

There was a huge explosion of noise in court at that but I could feel Ma ruffling, quite wild, next to me. 'That woman is *not* the landlady of 36 Southampton-street,' she said. (Ma knows everything as I've said so often before.) 'She's only a bleeding maid, leave it to me, I'll fix her,' and Ma just got up and left the courtroom!

Maria Duffin waited for the noise to subside and then, giving a small nod as if in pleased acceptance of all the excitement she was causing, went on. 'Now, listen to this, everybody, that dirty Ernest Boulton drooped about all day in a negligee, and they slept in the same bed – I know, I checked the sheets! – and Lord Arthur called Ernest *darling* and *my dear* and *Stella*.'

The activity among the pressmen was now frantic, and rushing for the door, all this stuff I suppose being what they were waiting for. This Maria Duffin observed this further and puffed up her hair under her hat and actually almost bowed to the court as if she was taking a curtain call as she was dismissed.

'Why is Lord Arthur Clinton not here to speak for himself?' asked Mr Flowers rather testily, and you should've heard how quick the noisy court went completely quiet. A policeman spoke at once.

'He has been asked for, sir, all about, but he is not to be found.'

'Well I hope further efforts are being made to find him.'

By the time the court came back from the lunch adjournment Ma had done her mission and brought the real landlady of that Southampton-street address who was wearing a very respectable bonnet and her white curls shook in indignation. She insisted on being heard, took the oath, her eyes sparkling with rage.

'My name is Mrs Louisa Peck. I am married to the Managing Clerk of the Sacred Harmonic Society.' (And I wished Billy was here so we could roll our eyes at how Ma knew everyone, as usual.) 'I have already given a deposition at the Treasury and you people had no right to call my maid instead of me! That woman, Maria Duffin, who purported to be the landlady at 36 Southampton-street instead of myself, is a wicked liar. How dare she make my very respectable establishment sound so unrespectable! This is not only a slur on me and my business but on the Sacred Harmonic Society. Maria Duffin was only a kitchen maid and she stayed with me no more than a month, and she mostly worked in the kitchen and she did not make the beds. If she heard Lord Arthur Clinton call Mr Boulton *darling* and *dear* and *Stella* then I must be deaf and if she saw Mr Boulton lounging about all day in a negligee handing out cards saying LADY CLINTON then I must be blind. And Maria Duffin did all this because she is *desperate* to get a husband!'

'By speaking in court?'

'By coming here and making herself all important with her lies, and hoping to catch the eye of some male person who may pass by out of interest!'

And then, in her respectable bonnet, she looked almost pityingly at Mr Flowers and the lawyers.

'I believe there have also been comments about – if I may be allowed to use the word – about the *gender* of Mr Ernest Boulton. I think there is a possibility that there are some things that gentlemen dont understand. Which women do of course. Mr Boulton's parents came to visit one day, and I *distinctly* heard his mother address him as Ernest. Now, excuse me, gentlemen! A mother would know if anybody does – so *of course* he must be a man, if his mother called him Ernest!'

The audience laughed and applauded and Mr Flowers banged his bench. Ma was now standing at the back but I turned round and gave her a wave and in the general moving about between witnesses being called Ma got back in to a space beside me.

'Good for you, Ma!' I said and we laughed in a whispering sort of way. 'They'll get bail now!' I said.

But.

It came next.

The next thing.

Well – well I'm just going to write about it as quickly as I can, I'd rather leave this bit out but I suppose I have to write all that happened, and this is when – when everything changed.

It was the police surgeon in the Metropolitan Police, called Dr

Paul. He had black greasy hair and he talked as if he was talking about nothing important.

'When the prisoners first appeared in this court the morning after they were arrested at the theatre I was asked to examine them afterwards for the purpose of ascertaining their sex. They were still dressed in their women's clothes that they were arrested in.'

'There was no authority from the court for you to do that,' said Mr Flowers very severely.

'I dont need authority, sir. I am a police surgeon. I have constantly to examine prisoners as directed by the police, Mr Superintendent Thomson gave me orders. "Take off your clothes," I said and I took a desk stool and said, "Bend over," and in turn they did, Mr Park first. Both had on as well as a dress and petticoats, etc, etc, tights or drawers, over white stockings. I examined them not only to assess if they were men but I had another idea – I did this on my own accord, it was my own idea – I wanted to ascertain something more, which came from a belief that men so attired might commit unnatural offences. First I looked at the anus of Mr Park. The muscles round the anus were easily opened and I could see right down into the rectum, and the appearance I saw could be accounted for by the insertion of a foreign body – that is the thrust of a foreign body many times.'

Ma looked at me then, my face felt as red as a tomato, I suppose I looked funny, I felt funny, how could such words be allowed to be said like that in front of everybody?

'Do you want to go?' whispered Ma, but I held my hands together very, very tightly and shook my head.

'I looked also at the anus of Mr Boulton. Both anuses were much dilated, and the muscles readily opened. I attributed this to the fact of them having frequent unnatural connections – one insertion would not cause them. I do not in my practice ever remember to have seen such an appearance of the anus as those of the two prisoners presented.'

And he said all this loudly and calmly as if it was nothing, talking of Freddie and Ernest in that way.

And then Mr Poland called another doctor from Charing Cross Hospital, who was a Fellow of the College of Surgeons and not greasy-haired like Dr Paul. But he pointed straight at Freddie.

'He came to Charing Cross Hospital, perhaps three months ago, and I treated him for a syphilitic sore on the anus with mercury and iodine of potash over several weeks.'

Not a single sound in the courtroom.

'Do you have a record of his visits?' asked Mr Flowers.

'We do keep records but there is no mention of the name Park. He probably used a false name.'

'Are you sure he is the man?'

'When I went to an identity parade I had some doubt, but then I was sure, and I see him here today. Park is the man I saw at Charing Cross Hospital.'

'Adjourned for another week,' said Mr Flowers grimly.

That was the evening we got home and found FILTHY PIGS and SODOMITE LOVERS writ on our house in paint. Ma and Billy and I all went out with buckets and soap and scrubbed and scrubbed, even as it got darker, and when we finished there might have been marks but you couldn't see what it was saying. That was the evening I finally understood that it wouldn't, ever again, be like it was.

Indoors I couldn't stop crying, not for the words on our house so much, though that was bad enough, but for thinking of the shame Freddie must feel, Ma and Billy tried to tell me that Ernest and Freddie had influential families – especially Freddie – and they would not let this happen, they *could* not, they would find a way to stop them going to trial.

'They are in a trial *now*!' I yelled at Billy. 'You didn't hear what was said about them, it's all changed and horrible now! And they only have the blooming hearings once a week and they're stuck in gaol in between, that's not fair!'

'Well I expect they have to hear other cases at that court all the time, burglars and murders, as well as this one,' said Ma.

'This is only the Magistrates' Court, Mattie,' said Billy, patient and kind like he is, 'to see if there is enough evidence for them to appear at the Old Bailey for a proper trial.'

'Well you can keep on saying that, William Stacey! but it already seems like a proper trial to me, all the disgusting things they are saying in public to go in the papers for the world to read! Their lives will never be the same, you know that, they'll go to prison for years and years and years, or for ever, you know they will!'

'I dont think that medical bit will go in the papers,' said Ma. 'How could they write the words?'

Billy said calmly again: 'Freddie comes from an important legal family, Mattie. They will find a way to stop it from happening.'

'I keep telling you, *it has happened already*!' I yelled at him, 'and I'm going to bed rather than listen to you!' but in my room I didn't make a proper Plan, like I often do, that I think about carefully, I was so upset I just sat at my table with Hortense and wrote a letter to Freddie.

I addressed it to him at the House of Detention, Clerkenwell, and I didn't care if my letter was read out in any court in the land. I tried not to think of the horrible medical things that we had heard, I tried not to imagine that they would be sent to another trial to have more terrible things in the newspapers for everybody to read, instead I asked Freddie if he would like to marry me and then nobody could say these things about him and I would look after him and care for him and we could have a baby and I sent my love, signed Martha Stacey, 13 Wakefield-street.

Then when the house had gone quiet I got out the front door, my sharp stone was in my cloak pocket with the letter and I walked to the House of Detention, I knew where it was. It wasn't all that far but not very easy streets, a bit of screaming and dark shadows on corners and a wind had got up and made that moaning noise round the houses but I didn't care, I'd have killed anyone with my stone if they tried to stop me, I think I must have gone a bit insane, like how did I think I was going to find Freddie at one o'clock in the morning? The House of Detention was a grim old place, all locked up, a few lamps but mostly darkness and iron railings with spikes, I went round and round, big metal gate, no place to sneak in, that wind whipping at me, I started crying with frustration that I must be so near to Freddie but no way of giving my letter. I could've hung it on the inside of a railing spike I suppose but it would likely blow away.

'Oh look! Look at that drunk tart stumbling everywhere! Let's give 'er one!'

Some drunk men weaved and rolled further down the street. That must've brought me to my senses, I cant run like the wind maybe but I can hurry and hide and take side streets and they were too drunk and falling over to get close to me and I got away, clutching my letter and my sharp stone. And I tore up my letter into tiny pieces as I came towards Wakefield-street, course I did, Freddie was a gentleman, he had a family and they were very important people, and they would find a way and of course someone like Freddie wouldn't be marrying someone like me in a boarding house and little bits of white paper blew about me and upwards and back to Gray's Inn Road and far away in the horrible windy night.

And then on Sunday every single word of that medical evidence by that horrible Dr Paul, and the doctor from Charing Cross

Hospital, was *actually published*, the things about anuses and syphilis, not in every newspaper but right there in the *Reynolds News*, under the heading HORRIBLE AND REVOLTING DISCLOSURES – so that not just the people in the court at the time heard that medical evidence but everybody in the whole world!

And then we saw the advertisements. There was a pamphlet pictured, with Ernest and Freddie drawn on the front in women's clothes. It was called 'THE LIVES OF BOULTON AND PARK: EXTRAORDINARY REVELATIONS'.

The price was one penny.

18

Next morning Billy was ordered to the Head Clerk's office.

He was, of course, expecting it.

The Houses of Parliament had always been the greatest hive of gossip in the country. Everyone (whether in the clerks' office or the cabinet office) had been following the 'Gentlemen in Female Attire' case since it began, talking about the details; there were huddles and whispers and laughter (some of it very nervous laughter) all over the venerable building: in clerks' offices and cabinet rooms and in the servants' quarters. People remembered the rather silly and ineffectual Lord Arthur Clinton and his brief career as Member of Parliament for Newark, the seat he had lost at the last election. Most of the present cabinet had known and admired his father, the fifth Duke of Newcastle.

A number of clerks had gone down to the Magistrates' Court before starting work to see Ernest Boulton and Frederick Park being brought in a police van from the House of Detention, very disappointed to perceive that they were not still wearing their gowns. When it was so quickly realised all over the building that they had kept their female attire in the house of the clerk Billy Stacey, there was further great excitement and enormous surprise. He had not seemed to be that sort of person, people murmured. His young colleagues wanted to discuss the case in great detail.

'Did they wear stays? Did they wear stockings? Did you go with them?'

There had already been a fight that was quickly concluded by the Head Doorkeeper, Elijah Fortune, when Billy had finally punched someone.

So the day after the medical evidence was published in the *Reynolds Newspaper* Billy was simply waiting to be called into the Head Clerk's office.

In a dark, poky little room Mr John Jenkins sat at his paper-crowded desk. Mr John Jenkins was a self-important man, and very particular. But he was an honest man and he and Billy were used to each other. Mr Jenkins was about twenty years older than Billy and used spiced pomade on his hair. They addressed each other formally: Mr Jenkins. Mr Stacey. There was a very strong smell of spiced pomade in the room now, as if Mr Jenkins had applied some extra portion, to prepare himself for this difficult meeting.

'Well, Mr Stacey.'

'Sir.'

The Head Clerk cleared his throat, felt for a handkerchief in his jacket. He was deeply embarrassed. 'I am afraid there has been a complaint about you.'

'And what sort of complaint would that be, Mr Jenkins?'

'Oh, not about your work of course, Mr Stacey.'

'I rather thought it would not be about my work.'

'Of course. Of course.' He cleared his throat. 'One of the bishops from the House of Lords has been to see me.'

Billy rolled his eyes. The Church, sticking its nose in. He remained silent.

Mr Jenkins said: 'It has of course been revealed in the

newspapers that – erm – the defendants in a certain criminal case had been living at your house.'

'Not *living* at our house, Mr Jenkins. It has been made quite clear in all the evidence that Mr Boulton and Mr Park rented rooms from us sometimes. To dress for their theatrical engagements.'

'Of course. I noted that distinction. Mr Boulton and Mr Park, yes, yes, that is the names. Your sister, I believe it was, giving actual evidence.' (Mr Jenkins, like everybody else, poring over the newspaper reports.) 'I have told him that you are one of my top clerks and that I cannot manage the business required of us without you. The bishop feels that it would be very bad for Parliament if it was revealed that someone involved in – in that rather scandalous case – of course I am not speaking, Mr Stacey, of any personal involvement of your own – worked in any capacity in this ancient and honourable establishment.'

Billy smiled grimly. Having pondered for some time as to the likelihood of Lord Arthur Clinton bringing the Parliament to its knees, it was rather odd to hear it was now considered that it might, in fact, be himself who would do so.

'And what do you feel, Mr Jenkins?'

Mr Jenkins cleared his throat again. 'I think, Mr Stacey, that that bishop, in particular, is a hypocritical person of the highest degree.'

Billy was so surprised he laughed.

But Mr Jenkins did not laugh. 'It is unfortunately no laughing matter. This clerical gentleman says he is the spokesman for the bishops in the House of Lords. He told me that he has already spoken to Mr Gladstone and that your personal involvement in the case is dangerous because the good name of the government needs to be protected.'

'From *me*?'

'From – any connection with this – scandal.' Mr Jenkins stood. 'I said I would speak to you myself but I am not sure how long I will be able to – safeguard you, Mr Stacey. I thought you should know.'

Billy stood also and looked across the table. 'You're a good man, Mr Jenkins, when all is said and done, and I thank you for the warning.'

'We will hope that the case will soon be over. To be replaced, I have no doubt, by other scandals.' Spiced pomade moved towards the door as Mr Jenkins went to open it. 'I would be very, very sorry to lose you, Mr Stacey. It would not be my choice.'

Billy put out his hand, and Mr Jenkins took it.

'Thanks, John,' said Billy.

That evening straight after work he went to Clerkenwell, to the House of Detention. He said he was the landlord of Boulton and Park, and needed to speak to them about their goods and chattels. He was let in. But a young policeman stood there at their meeting, which Billy hadn't allowed for.

Ernest and Freddie were brought in and Billy, who had not been at any of the court hearings, was shocked at their faces, these men his own age. They looked pale and unhealthy and depressed. Freddie had some whiskers, Ernest a very small moustache.

'Hello, Billy,' they said, very surprised.

'Well,' said Billy. 'How are you both?'

They shrugged.

A little bit of the old Ernest: 'It's not exactly the Prince of Saxe-Coburg Hotel of course. Which we would prefer. Wouldn't we, dear?' he said to the young policeman, looking from under his eyelashes in that way he did. The policeman blushed.

'How's Mattie and your mother?' said Freddie. 'We see them there.'

'Yes,' said Billy.

'Thank them for their support. Mattie was a good witness for us.'

'Yes,' said Billy.

Silence.

'Come and sit with us, dear,' murmured Ernest to the policeman. 'On your feet all day.'

The policeman blushed again. 'I'm going out for a pipe,' he said. 'But I can still see you. Five minutes you can have and no trouble,' and Ernest smiled at him again as he left.

'For God's sake, Ernest, *stop* it!' said Freddie in exasperation.

'Billy won't be shocked! The police are not immune to my charms – we all know only too well that policemen can be tempted – or indeed tempting!' Ernest tossed his head sulkily. 'I'm so bored with having just you to talk to! I can't stand it, I can't stand being locked in a pig-pen! I can't stand anything.' His voice rose higher. 'I want a drink, gin or brandy or sherry, anything! I wish I was dead!'

And although Billy was used to Ernest's emoting manner wafting down the stairs in Wakefield-street, this was something different. And then, to the consternation of both men, Ernest began to weep.

'What is going to happen to us, Billy?' he asked pathetically. 'What is everybody saying out there in the world? What are they saying about me? Even my own mother lies to me – mind you, she has lied to me all my life anyway, and she didn't bring me any liquid refreshment either.'

'Stop it, Ernest,' said Freddie, more gently now.

'I think most sensible people feel the police have gone too far,' said Billy.

'They'd been following us for weeks,' said Freddie disdainfully.

Ernest blew his nose daintily. 'I suppose everyone sees us as – dirty, do they?'

Billy heard Mr Gladstone's imperious distaste – *this dirty, squalid affair* – and felt pity. 'Hold fast, Ernest,' he said firmly. 'Mattie says so many of the people in court are on your side.'

Ernest brightened slightly. 'Yes,' he said. 'They are a lovely audience.' He wiped at the tears. Freddie said nothing and the silence lengthened, Ernest still gulping but mostly recovered.

'Where's Lord Arthur Clinton?' said Billy at last. They both looked at him in surprise.

'*We* don't know,' said Ernest. 'Or care much. Why should we? He's hiding, I suppose, he was always a coward. I threw him over, months and months ago. A bankrupt even if he is a Lord!' But his face looked strained and white, and it was clear to Billy now that all the performance with the policeman a few minutes earlier had been bravado.

'Why are you asking, Billy?' said Freddie.

'I'm having trouble keeping my position. At the Parliament. I need to find Lord Arthur Clinton urgently so that I can ask him something.'

'Why? I mean, why would you be fired?' asked Freddie. 'Mattie told me you were the best clerk in the whole place.'

Billy shrugged; they had enough problems. But then Freddie guessed.

'It's all in the papers, we know. Your name and address as well as ours. My father has been in, white with fury. Sorry, Billy.'

And Ernest understood also, said it like a little, sad echo: 'Sorry, Billy.'

Silence.

Ernest gave a little sigh. Billy looked at him and thought: *It is true. He looks like a pretty young woman, dressed in men's clothes. In spite of the moustache.*

'His sister will know,' said Ernest casually, looking not at them but at his fingernails. 'How are we supposed to keep *pure* in this place? Look at me!' He held out his hands; they were grubby and the nails were rimmed with dirt.

'His sister?'

'His sister, Lady Susan. She was the only one of his family I ever met, just the one time. He brought her to see us perform, remember, Freddie?'

'But we were there!' said Billy. 'At Clapham. We saw her too, with Lord Arthur.'

'Yes, yes, that time. And – you saw, didn't you – Arthur actually introduced me, think of that! And she was *very* complimentary to me, actually. Of course he never introduced me to any *others* of his illustrious family – I don't believe he even saw most of them. But he would see his sister sometimes. She married a rich man who went mad and threw knives at her and died – or that is Arthur's story. But how would *I* know! Still, she was fond of Arthur, she gave him money sometimes, I know she did.'

And for a moment he was himself again, throwing back his head and then looking at them from under his eyelashes. 'The money was for me, of course! Oh God, I long for a drink. I shall be ill!'

'Do you know where she lives?'

'No idea.' And then he suddenly smiled up at them both. 'But you could go to Marlborough House! Because Arthur once told me she was the mistress of the Prince of Wales! But he was probably boasting to impress me. Though of course, my dears, *think of it*! That would have made me – well, more or less – sister-in-law to the next King of England, wouldn't that be marvellous in the present circumstances!' And he laughed but it was hysterical laughter and his eyes were quite wild. Freddie and Billy looked at each other in alarm. 'Find his sister Susan!' Ernest ended, in dramatic tones. To Billy, Ernest seemed to be a little insane.

'Shut up, Ernest,' said Freddie.

'Thanks, Ernest,' said Billy politely.

But he felt his own shoulders fall. He thought it highly unlikely he would gain entrance to Marlborough House.

'And *He* knows *us*, doesn't he, Freddie? Remember that time in the Lyceum – we took a box across from that of the Prince of Wales, and he came in during the performance and he saw us! Remember, Freddie? He picked up opera glasses and stared at us – I gave him a tiny elegant smile and I *know* he smiled back!' Ernest fluttered a moment longer, and then was quiet.

'What do you think will happen to us, Billy?' said Freddie. 'As Ernest says, you're out in the real world.' And Freddie looked about him with enormous distaste: the grim building; the smell of not enough soap, and old onions; the policeman outside the window. Freddie's face was drawn and drained and his hands seemed to shake, almost as if he was a different person. Billy thought of them both at Wakefield-street: the singing and all the laughter in the house.

'My father says many new lawyers have been' – Freddie laughed wearily – 'retained. Well, what use is it to be the Senior Master of the Court of Common Pleas if you can't retain lawyers at least!'

Billy thought of Mr Gladstone's pale face. He said: 'I truly think you have enough well-wishers, and – connections – to – protect you.' He did not say more, stood up. 'I haven't – I should've thought of it, I'm sorry – I haven't brought you anything from the outside world. I came straight from the Parliament. Is there something you want? I could come again.'

'Gin,' said Ernest.

Billy felt in his pockets. There was a half-sovereign, some

shillings and pennies, and half a chocolate bar. He put them all down on a little table, embarrassed but determined.

'Thanks, Billy.'

And Freddie actually took the bar, broke it, and gave some to Ernest. Ernest looked at the chocolate almost with distaste, and then suddenly ate it all at once.

'We hope we'll get bail soon.' Freddie spoke in the same weary tone. And then: 'Have you seen Amos Gibbings?'

'He hasn't been near Wakefield-street since he came for your clothes the first day.'

'He can talk about amateur theatricals better than anyone I know. I thought he would be here, to give evidence for us. Gibbings of all people.' Silence. 'Why do you think Arthur could help you at the Parliament?'

Billy shrugged, pulling at his jacket. He hardly knew himself what he'd hoped for. If they could have helped him, and he had found Lord Arthur Clinton, what would he have asked him anyway except: 'Why does your name make Mr Gladstone go pale?' All he was certain about was that he had to keep his place at the Parliament.

'Lord Arthur used to be an MP,' said Billy, shrugging again, and the policeman, who had seen him stand, had come back now, and before the three men had time to say much more Freddie and Ernest were escorted away.

19

HEROINES IN NOVELS – people who love someone – dont abandon them because of HORRIBLE AND REVOLTING DISCLOSURES. That wasn't Freddie's fault. I decided that people who actually believed that Freddie and Ernest's private parts should be splashed about for everyone to read of were mad people, in fact I decided that so many of the people we'd seen because of this trial were mad people, like those landladies, either drunk or preening. And others – we *saw* them. Outside the court we'd see people with placards. One said SODOM AND GOMORRAH and one said ABOMINATION and the men who were carrying them were surely on the same side, but they were drunk and they were hitting each other with their placards and yelling.

And inside the court we'd see people like the man from the Society for the Suppression of Vice asking Mr Flowers if he could urgently intervene to prohibit the newspapers from publishing *dirty* details of this *dirty* case and so Protect Families. And then this man, having made his appeal, squashed in the front row to listen to the rest of it, leaning forward especially at the *dirty* details. And the manager of the Alhambra in Leicester Square, one of the most notorious places in London, protested that people like Ernest and Freddie gave his notorious establishment a bad name. Ha! as Ma would say.

Maybe I was mad as well, one of the mad people. I'd been a bit mad to go to the Clerkenwell House of Detention in the middle of the night. The weather was mad certainly, it was so hot now I couldn't sleep, or maybe it was thinking of Freddie and Ernest and how they had to listen to those – those medical details and Freddie's kindness to me and his pale face.

Finally one night I got up and crept into Freddie and Ernest's broken-locked room with my little lamp. I hadn't touched it since everything happened, though Ma told me to: 'We have to be able to rent it out, Mattie,' but I told myself they'd be back, singing up the stairs and coming down in gowns and perfume. But the room stayed silent. And, really, I knew now they wouldn't be back and singing.

When I went in, it was the saddest room you ever saw. I put the lamp on a table and it looked like a room that had belonged to someone who'd died. Things on the floor, spilled powder, hairpins everywhere, and a bottle half full of something called 'Crème du Peche', which I opened and breathed in. It smelled a bit peculiar. And a skirt left, and a waistcoat and a half-open portmanteau, some 'Bloom of Roses' on the bed, dust everywhere of course. The piano was dusty and silent, I played a few notes very quietly, *which is the fairest gem? Eileen Aroon*, but the notes sounded lonely. There was a white petticoat, half showing out of the big cupboard, as if there might be somebody there, I stared at it and in the lamplight it didn't move, just hung there like half a ghost.

I sat there for a while and thought, *cant I do something?* What I really needed to do was find where that Lord Arthur Clinton was, who had been so besotted with Ernest – he was the one who could say it wasn't Freddie, all this trouble, that it was really all about Ernest. But I didn't have any idea how to find Lord Arthur, maybe he was staying with his noble family and they were hiding him in an attic and taking him soup. So I had to do something else.

And then, sitting there with their left-over things, I thought of a Plan. I sat there in the shadowy dusty room working it out, thinking of fantastical falsehoods that I could embroider. Like hats. But in the end I decided to keep to the truth, but to tell it so it sounded different – I think I really must've seen myself like one of those heroic heroines in novels, those ones who run like the wind.

I picked up my lamp, I saw my own shadow move towards the door. But suddenly I turned back quick – *did something move?*

I felt my heart beating. At last I moved to the wardrobe and pushed at the petticoat half showing out of the cupboard, hanging like half a person. Just in case.

Nobody. No ghost flew away. Just a petticoat.

Then I went back to bed. With my Plan.

Next morning very, very early I went in again and I cleaned that room from top to bottom, I got really hot in that mad weather, but I didn't take any notice of being hot just went on cleaning and polishing, polished the poor silent piano, packed what was left of their things into the portmanteau, including the ghostly petticoat and some 'Bloom of Roses'. Even the hairpins. I just kept one, a darker one, that Freddie would have used, I put it in my own hair. I arranged for a man down the road to fix the door that Mr Gibbings smashed.

I waited till Ma called out she was going to the market. Billy was long gone but it was still early. I left a note: *Gone to see if I can help Freddie, back soon, dont worry.*

I had a wash and dressed in my best gown, and one of my best hats and my Burlington Arcade gloves, oh it was so *hot*, then I went back to Bow-street, but to the offices round the end of the court.

I hate it when people look at me limping.

He stared at me, the policeman at the desk, but I took no notice.

'I wish to speak to the Senior Master of the Court of Common Pleas. Mr Park.'

'Do you indeed, miss. Well you wont find him here,' and he directed me about and about to other buildings in other streets and I walked in, bold.

I said to the man on the desk, 'I wish to speak to the Senior Master of the Court of Common Pleas. Please. Mr Park.'

He looked surprised. 'I dont think he sees people, miss. Have you got some sort of appointment?'

'No.'

'Well I dont think it's possible, miss.'

I'd planned everything of course.

'I have a note for him that you should deliver. Please very specifically advise him it is about his son. I will wait.'

They knew of course, they all knew about Freddie, there was a certain rustling along the desk where other men were working but listening.

Poor Mr Park, I suddenly thought, everyone reading *Reynolds News* and terrible things about his son. Poor Mr Park.

I handed the man a sealed note and sat down in a leather chair in the hall that was obviously for judges and large gentlemen, my feet hardly touched the ground. I didn't look at anybody. Out of my basket I took *Oliver Twist* by Mr Dickens, the one my dear Pa had read to us when we were children and I opened it at the beginning and I began to read: *Chapter One: which treats of the place where Oliver Twist was born, and of the circumstances attending his birth.* There was no air in the big building but I didn't care, in fact if I fainted all the better.

I read and read and read and I was kept waiting for hours and hours and hours. After a long time I heard my stomach making funny rumbles even though I had eaten some bread before I came. But I just kept on sitting in the leather chair that was too big for me and reading about Oliver Twist asking for more, I decided if anybody tried to move me I would just scream and scream and call for Mr Park. There were high-up windows and beams of hot grey sunlight started coming through them as the sun moved round London, the sunbeams only showed up all the dust swirling around in the stuffy air.

I was hungry. Men kept passing, you could tell the clerks from the proper law men, their suits were different and I thought about Billy's suit, maybe it shows him to be a clerk too and I thought me and Ma should talk about this, Billy being so clever and sometimes seeing Mr Gladstone himself, maybe we should get him to have a very good suit made by a men's tailor.

Finally after about a hundred years a man came and said, 'Miss Martha Stacey,' and I thought, *he's read my letter, he knows my name*, and I said, 'Yes,' and I looked up. A young man about Freddie's age.

'Come this way.'

He walked off and I had to somehow wriggle off the big chair and hurry after him, ungainly, I know, I know. He took me to a small room near by with one small high window and when I went in he closed and locked the door behind him which I found a bit peculiar, locking himself in with a young lady but I always carry hatpins and a sharp stone. But I suppose it was to be private. It was even hotter, even he ran a finger round his neck as if to loose his cravat. But he wasn't Mr Park and I wasn't going to talk to him.

'Now look here,' he said. 'Is it money you want?'

He must've seen surprise on my face – I hadn't even thought they would think that – because he said: 'What are you writing to the Master for?'

'I have nothing to say to you, Mr Whatever-your-name-is, because you haven't even had the courtesy to introduce yourself.

What I have to say regarding Mr Frederick Park is only to be said to his father.'

The clerk cleared his throat. 'George Pearce at your service, miss. It would be quite impossible for you to speak to the Master.'

'Then it will be quite impossible for me to leave this building, Mr George Pearce. Did he read my note?'

'That I cannot say.'

'Then I cannot say anything either so I will leave you if you will kindly unlock the door which is by the way no action of a gentleman with a young lady like myself and I may faint from lack of food and air. If the Senior Master of the Court of Common Pleas does not want to hear something which I think would be advantageous regarding his son, he is a bad father and you may tell him so, and so I will bid you good-day and I will wait until the Master shows himself and no, I do not want, or need, money.'

He didn't unlock the door.

'If you keep me locked in here I will scream very loudly, at which I am extremely talented.'

He did unlock it then, rather hurriedly. 'Wait here and I will talk to the Master,' he said but I could see he was angry. 'Do not scream.'

And then the rotten man locked the door again, from the outside! All this seemed very illegal to me in what was supposed to be premises of legality. I considered my options including screaming the fact that I was locked in and starving. But at last I sat down under the small high window and began *Chapter XX: wherein Oliver is delivered over to Mr William Sykes.* I knew perfectly well what happens next but I love this book.

I got all the way to *Chapter XXXII: of the happy life Oliver begins to lead with his kind friends.* That's how long they made me wait that day. The sun had quite gone, it was a little bit cooler, not much, the dim light was hurting my eyes now and I knew Ma would be worried and probably Billy would be almost home by now, I must have been in the building all day. And I was *so hungry*.

Then I heard the door being unlocked. I was so mad I just sat there reading (well pretending to read). There was a pompous loud *Ahem!* if you can imagine that sound being done pompous. I looked up. Course it was Freddie's pa, I nearly dropped the book because I could see some of Freddie in him and he was in a very good gentleman's suit and collar. He closed the door but didn't lock it. I closed the book and didn't stand (I didn't want him to see me ungainly).

He looked at me and I looked at him. His face was like Freddie's only – different. At first I only saw he was angry at me and I thought I wouldn't like him to be in charge of my Common Plea (whatever that actually was).

'What's this?' He waved my note.

'What does it say?'

'Do not speak like that to me, girl, I know what it says! I want to know why you have come here with it, bothering me.'

Just as well I loved Freddie so much, in fact I loved him even more when I saw the angry face of his father and Freddie so gentle and kind, and sad sometimes. I sat with my hands clasped on *Oliver Twist*.

'The note says, Mr Park, that Freddie held me in my bed and it is signed *Yours sincerely, Martha Stacey.* I should think you would be pleased to receive a note of that nature, in the circumstances.'

'How dare you! How dare a – a—' (he was trying to find the right word to say to me) 'a chit of a girl from the lower orders speak to me like that! How dare you call my son Frederick *Freddie*!' His face was red as anything.

'Mr Park, Freddie calls himself Freddie and as he appears at my house quite often, so do I call him Freddie. It is more useful at this point, surely, than calling him Fanny.'

I thought he might actually hit me then; I saw him restraining himself and his face was even more red and I quickly went on while he was so speechless.

'I have sat, Mr Park, in these inhospitable premises for almost the whole of this day and I hope your clerk advised you that I do not come for money. I do not need money, Mr Park. I know Freddie intimately' – I let that word hang there a bit, ha – 'because my mother and I are the landladies of 13 Wakefield-street where if you have been following your son's trial you will know he and Ernest Boulton lodged sometimes, and two more pleasant lodgers we have never known. If you visit your imprisoned son, Mr Park – as long as you show him my note first – you may discuss me if you wish. I make no claims on him, upon you, or upon any of your family and I reiterate once more I do not want money. But I believe my intervention in this matter could help your son's – reputation – in a way, and at a time, that he may most need it.' (Oh, it was good I'd been reading Mr Dickens all day, I had the swirl of the words, just like him!)

'Good-day to you, Mr Park.' And then I did stand up, too bad if he saw.

'Wait.' His face was calculating things, I could see. 'I—' He cleared his throat in that pompous loud manner again. 'There has been a gross misunderstanding of my son's behaviour of course.'

'Of course.'

And it was then that I at last looked at him more carefully. And then I saw how strained he was, he had that same tic under his eye that I'd seen on Freddie's face. Of course I didn't know everything then, but I did feel suddenly sorry, because I understood his face.

'There are – many lawyers working on his case at this very moment.'

'I am glad, Mr Park.'

The next words burst out, I dont believe he meant to say them to me.

'This case will *never* be brought to a trial at the Criminal Court.'

'Really?' I sort of gasped in surprise. 'I'm so glad, Mr Park, to hear you say that.'

He tried to collect himself. But he suddenly looked so frail that I moved the chair I had been sitting on near to him and he did sit down. 'No, no, by that I mean – there are ways – it will not . . .' and then I could see that he recollected that he was talking to a chit of a girl from the lower classes. 'Thank you, Miss Stacey,' he forced himself to say, 'but your "intervention" will not be needed,' and he stood up again.

'Oh I am so glad, Mr Park, to know that you feel all will be well,' and he gave me a funny sharp look to see if I was being rude but of course he could see I wasn't, I was *glad*, so glad, if he thought there was to be no big trial, wait till I told Ma and Billy. He still stood there, poor old thing, and he looked a little bit more like Freddie. I limped to the door, him looking at me, I know.

He stopped me. 'In fact, Miss Stacey, I would prefer that you did not say any more to anybody about our conversation today. Or about my son, ever, unless you have to,' and it couldn't help sounding as if it was because I was a limping lower-class chit of a girl but I didn't care.

'I am so so *glad* you think there can – be a solution! And Freddie will tell you that I am a very trustworthy person, Mr Park,' and I smiled and smiled at him, I think he must've known I meant it. 'Perhaps I should go home now,' I said, 'as my mother and my brother will wonder if you have locked me up permanently seeing as I've been here nearly all of the day and I am awfully hungry!' but I think he saw I was teasing him just a little for he gave a very, very small smile.

He opened the door of the funny stuffy hot little room then, and I went out without looking back, *of course* he could see clearly how I walked and would wonder what a gentleman like Freddie was doing holding a cripple in her room but I didn't care. It was nearly dark and I was so hungry and so keen to tell Ma and Billy what had happened that I even caught an omnibus towards Wakefield-street even though it's so hard to get up and down from the steps, specially when they're crowded.

And all the way home I thought about Mr Park working in the courts and his son arrested for what they said was filthy and I thought how hard it must be for him but he had shared something with me, even if he hadn't quite meant to: he must have lots of influential friends of course. It sounded so important: the Senior Master of the Court of Common Pleas, if he was a clerk like Freddie said he must be a very very big clerk.

'I dont think there's going to be a big trial!' I had called on the stairs, before I even got to the downstairs kitchen. Billy was home, Ma was a bit frantic that I was so late as if I was a child and not a life-experienced person and she and Billy were looking deadly serious. 'Freddie's father told me! Well, sort of told me.'

'Freddie's *father*?'

'I went to see him. I told him Freddie was my boy. I thought it might be useful.'

Ma and Billy stared at me. I poured myself water from a jug, I needed that, Ma had made a beef stew and it smelled so lovely I thought I would swoon but they had that look as if they had been talking very serious and me not there.

'What did he say?' said Ma quietly.

I faced her so she could hear clearly. 'He said there are lots of lawyers working on the case, and he said he believed there wouldn't be a trial in the Old Bailey! Could we eat, *please*, Ma? I haven't eaten since this morning and I'm really hungry.'

We sat down then and Ma served out the stew and it was raptureful to me and I ate and ate but I could see Ma and Billy were uneasy and a bit quiet and I noticed I ate more than them. 'But aren't you pleased?' I said at last, still eating.

Ma looked at me. 'Is that *exactly* what he said? He wouldn't say something like that to you, Mattie.'

'He didn't mean to. But – I think it is what he believed.'

'Jesus!' said Ma. 'If that's true,' she said to Billy, 'surely your position will be safe.'

'*What?*' I put down my knife and fork then.

'It's all right,' said Billy, calmly. 'I will not let them take away my position. And Mattie, I meant to tell you, Freddie asked me to thank you for giving the evidence so well.'

'You've seen him to properly talk to?' Now I knocked my fork and it clattered on the floor. 'You went and saw them and talked to them?'

'I thought they might help me to find Lord Arthur but they had no idea where he was.'

'Oh. Oh. I would give anything in the world to see Freddie by himself and make him know that no matter what evidence is said – I – I care for him and I am his friend.'

'I think he knows that, Mattie,' said Ma in her dry voice.

I suddenly felt fear at the bottom of my legs. 'Is your position unsafe in the Parliament because of our name and address being in the newspapers about Freddie and Ernest? Oh Billy, is that what has happened? but Billy, listen, didn't you hear me? you wont have to worry any more, I've told you, I think – I think it's going to be all right, I think there isn't going to be a big trial, course you wont lose your position, Freddie's pa didn't even mean to say it to me, I could tell, *but he did*, so he must know something we dont. You mustn't worry, Billy.'

Billy looked at me as if I was a babbling nincompoop. And then he suddenly grinned and his face creased just like our Pa when he smiled or laughed. I love Billy.

'We're just getting a little bit too famous, Mattie!' he said.

20

NOTHING MORE HAPPENED about Billy's job, he still went to work every day and on the next Friday I said to Ma, quite cheerful: 'We have to go back to the court, even though we think it might be all right in the end – and if it's all right in the end then Billy wont lose his position. But we do have to go back to the court because otherwise Freddie and Ernest will think we are not their friends any more, that we've been shocked.'

'Have you been shocked?' asked Ma and I just looked at her.

'I'm not stupid, Ma.'

'I know you're not stupid, Mattie,' said Ma, gravely somehow. 'That wasn't what I was asking you. And we are not certain that it will "be all right" altogether.'

'Mr Park *told* me.'

'All right, Mattie.'

'As long as we dont have to hear any more about – about their – private parts,' I said, but still trying to be cheerful.

Soon as we got in I stared around for the Senior Master of the Court of Common Pleas now that I knew what he looked like. But he didn't seem to be there. I wondered if they gave him a secret place at the back.

When they brought Freddie and Ernest in I could see that Freddie's whiskers had grown more, even Ernest had a few.

But. They both looked – different in another way somehow, more despondent, and – I dont know what the right word is – puffed up in their pale faces, as if they were sick. As if they didn't know anything about anything good at all. And I felt a big jumping feeling somewhere in my heart, had I misunderstood? his father would certainly have told Freddie if he thought there would be no trial, and Freddie simply looked ill.

'Ma, they look *terrible*. Do you think – do you think I might have misunderstood Mr Park?'

'I think perhaps you might have,' she said back, she was looking at Freddie too.

Then, a gentleman was called from the Royal College of Surgeons and my heart jumped again. He was *so* much more respectable-looking than that police surgeon with the greasy hair who said those disgusting things. Mr Flowers treated this medical person with great respect and you could tell he was a gentleman. But – oh well – well the surgeon still had to say things it must have been hard for Freddie and Ernest to listen to, if someone spoke publicly on and on about my private parts I cannot imagine how I would bear it because private parts are called private, and here were theirs being discussed again all over London.

'I am a friend of the father of Ernest Boulton and I went to the House of Detention at his request,' he said, 'where I found the young men despondent and, I thought, almost unwell for the worry of this case. I examined Park's private parts and his anus. I did not discover anything to indicate the presence of disease or the probability of anything having existed within two or three months past.'

I looked at poor, poor Freddie. Of course this was evidence *for* him, unlike the police surgeon. Freddie stared at the floor, unmoving and I thought, *this man held me tight when I needed him, I would hold him now if I could in front of all these people I would hold him and protect him and let them say what they liked.*

'I also examined Mr Boulton. I could not discover anything to suggest a suspicion that he had been guilty of an unnatural act.'

Ernest looked at Mr Flowers from under his eyelashes, that look of his, but Mr Flowers remained impassive as always.

'I did not perceive that the anus was dilated. The muscle was intact and it had the natural function of retaining control of the bowel. Of course I speak theoretically rather than practically as my experience of such cases has been extremely limited. I only apply my general knowledge to this case.

'However, I wish to make a particular and important point: I do not believe, as the police surgeon in his overzealous – so it seems to me – examination of the two defendants obviously does, that sodomy can be identified by physical examination.'

And this time the audience's applause was respectful and loud. There was no shouting or laughing.

Ma whispered to me, 'That's their defence lawyers done this.'

I nodded. But what I was thinking was, *I hope I never have to hear anything about Freddie's bottom ever again*.

No sign still of Lord Arthur Clinton. No sign of Mr Gibbings. Ma said in her dry way: 'So much for noblemen.'

'Is Mr Gibbings a *nobleman*?'

'I've heard he has some vague connection.'

There were more witnesses called. I was still looking around for the Senior Master of the Court of Common Pleas while we heard about Ernest being in Scotland: tales told, all the men who seemed besotted by him, letters read out. Soppy letters to Ernest.

And then there were two more letters read out. They weren't to Ernest. Or from Ernest.

These letters were from *Freddie* to Lord Arthur Clinton.

At first I actually thought there must have been some sort of mistake, they weren't written by Freddie, they couldn't have been, well they didn't *sound* like Freddie, not the Freddie I knew and it made everything sound – different than I thought it was. And when Mr Poland read the letters out he had a snarky way with his voice, well his voice was already snarky and it got even worse when he was reading out letters. From Freddie.

My dearest Arthur,
How very kind of you to think of me on my birthday. I require no remembrance of my sister's husband, as the many kindnesses he has bestowed upon me will make me remember him for many a year and the birthday present he is so kind as to promise will only be one addition to the heap of little favours I already treasure up. So many thanks for it dear old man. I cannot echo your wish that I should live to be a hundred, though I should like to live to a green old age. Green, did I say? O! ciel, the amount of paint that will be required to hide that very unbecoming tint. My campish undertakings are not at present meeting with the success they deserve. Whatever I do seems to get me into hot water somewhere; but n'importe, what's the odds as long as your-rappy? Believe me, your affectionate sister-in-law, once more with many, many thanks,
Fanny Winifred Park

I could feel Ma looking at me but I didn't look at her, as well as not looking at Freddie. Somehow the letter wasn't the same as dressing up for a lark. And what came to me suddenly in that dusty old court was the glittering, excited – dangerous – look in Freddie's eyes when he – when he rushed off somewhere. But Mr Poland raised his hand – there was a lot of talking excitedly in the court – and began to read the second one, I dont know blooming well *why* they had to read out more like that, and everyone went quiet again.

My dearest Arthur,

You must really excuse me from interfering in matrimonial squabbles (for I am sure the present is no more than that); and although I am, as you say, Stella's confidante in most things, that which you wish to know she keeps locked up in her own breast. She may sometimes treat you brusquely; but, on the other hand, how she stands up for your dignity of position. As to all the things she said to you the other night, she may have been tight, and did not know all she was saying; so that by the time you get my answer you will both be laughing over the whole affair, as Stella and I did when we quarrelled and fought down here – don't you remember, when I slapped her face? Do not think me unkind, dear, as really I have told you all I know, and have not an opinion worth having to offer you . . .

Ever yours,

Fan

'I dont think Freddie could have written that,' I whispered into Ma's ear.

Ma looked at me with that exasperated look she has sometimes. But there must have been something in my face that stopped what she meant to say, and she said something else. 'It seemed like a kind letter,' said Ma to me. 'He was trying to cheer Lord Arthur.'

I was having trouble saying words.

'We – we only knew part of their lives, Ma.'

She looked at me so surprised. 'Of course, Mattie!' she said. 'Did you never understand that?'

I hadn't, not really, understood that. I thought 13 Wakefield-street was the important part.

When we came out of the court that day there was a poem fixed on to one of the walls near by:

There was an old person of Sark
Who buggered a pig in the dark
The swine in surprise
Murmured, 'God bless your eyes
Did you take me for Boulton or Park?'

We walked home. Not speaking hardly at all. But Ma, comforting, as she held my arm in hers. A carriage went rushing past us up by Gray's Inn Road and we had to jump out of the way and I was slow because of my leg and I looked up to shout at it. And I saw Lord Arthur Clinton, sitting right back inside it, he must've been pushed forward when the coach swerved past us, he was right by my eyes for a moment and then quickly sat back.

It was hot again in the night that night, hot and stuffy, as if a big thunderstorm might come. I lay awake again, all that awful old lying awake in the darkness as if I was mad, *my sister's husband. . .your loving sister-in-law* . . . and probably I had made a mistake about Mr Park and been even more stupid, *there was an old person of Sark who buggered a pig in the dark did you take me for Boulton and Park*, my thoughts going round and around, and stupid tears on the blanket as if I was a little girl like when Pa died.

And Jamey.

(There. I've writ down his name.)

I know I sound sometimes in this story like a stupid person, but I'm not a stupid person.

Finally, I understood.

I wasn't crying about the poem, although I couldn't get it out of my head, *buggered a pig in the dark did you take me for Boulton or Park.* Or even about what the newspapers said. What I was crying about was my dream that I'd kept going through the whole trial, whatever was said. I'd made up a whole dream. Me and

Freddie and our little family and my love even though I wasn't a real lady I'd be standing beside him and *changing* him and he would love me too because I was so strong, and he wasn't like Ernest, not really.

Go on go on write it down.

I was crying because the letters from Freddie to Lord Arthur Clinton had somehow hurt me – I know I know, they were nothing at all to do with me, but they were in a way – because then I knew that the Freddie in my dream wouldn't write that kind of letter and so the Freddie in my dream wasn't real but somebody I made up. I wasn't thinking about the *real* Freddie. I had really been thinking about myself. And despite all the evidence I'd kept hearing, it was hearing the letters read out that made me understand at last how far away I was from Freddie's real life, and not part of it hardly at all.

It was a stupid dream I'd made up because he had been kind.

Yes.

21

And then suddenly the trial at Bow-street Magistrates' Court was over.

The usual raucous, hooting, unruly crowds outside the court doors, eating pies, and carrying placards and babies, people stretching down towards the Strand and up into Long Acre, long after the court proceedings had recommenced. For weeks they had ogled and shouted as the prisoners were brought in yet again, and if they had the time available people simply waited about to see who would be called in to give evidence, and to catch a glimpse of the prisoners again at the end of the day. Some were clerks, some were street women plying for a bit of day trade, some were servants, some were children. Some were pickpockets, some were a higher class of citizen who nevertheless had not been able to get a place inside. These latter finally repaired to a nearby coffeehouse to discuss further the eternally interesting developments. Buggery had its own fascinations.

Mattie Stacey and her mother were there; they knew how to arrive early and secure a place. Today Mattie Stacey's face was very, very pale but composed also, as if some resolution had been reached; her mother, without seeming to, watched her daughter carefully.

Mr Flowers appeared on his bench at exactly 10 a.m. and the proceedings once more commenced.

That last morning the much missed Mr Amos Gibbings, host (or perhaps hostess) of the ball at Porterbury's Hotel, did appear after all. Mrs Stacey and Mattie exchanged glances as his name was called. For there he was: if he had run away, he had returned. He appeared very confident and gentlemanly in a ladylike sort of way, and he introduced himself clearly as 'Amos Westropp Gibbings at the willing service of this court, having arrived from Calais this morning'.

'You are familiar with the charges in this court, Mr Gibbings?' said Mr Flowers gravely.

'I am indeed, sir, and I am sure the whole business is simply a terrible misunderstanding, which I hope I can explain in relation to my own life if you will allow.'

'Continue, Mr Gibbings.'

'It is simpler to explain, Mr Flowers, than you may imagine. I began dressing in female attire myself six or seven years ago, for charades – I have several times during the last three years acted in female character for charities – something for which I have a talent, so I am told by my friends – who used to enquire of me how I could keep up my feminine roles with such delicacy, being a man myself. And so occasionally I would appear at their social gatherings dressed as a woman, to show them how it was done. But I work in the theatre! I have played Lady Teazle in *The School for Scandal*, Mrs Mildmay in *Still Waters Run Deep*, Mrs Chillingtone in *Morning Call*.'

People in the court laughed, entertained; Mr Gibbings himself held up his hand for silence so that he could continue in his confident and cultured voice.

'I have played Helen in *The Hunchback* – I could go on, Mr Flowers, there are many other trifling parts. I have played these parts mostly in small halls and schoolrooms but I have also had upwards of twelve hundred persons in the audience when I played Mrs Atwell. I have, as I explained, some talent in these renditions, and have indeed received praise.'

For a moment Mr Gibbings seemed to be expecting praise from this audience also, who were enjoying his evidence, as he was well aware. And then he continued, 'I have known Mr Frederick Park for some time – we became very good friends for I knew he played female characters, especially dowagers, like myself.'

This entertained the audience mightily.

'He introduced me to Mr Boulton, and I have never known any impropriety in their behaviour at any time. They are gentlemen. I had heard of Mr Boulton's talent as a singer and so I asked him to sing at my ball earlier in the year at Porterbury's Hotel, Where I have to say he was a great success.'

He would have simply gone on, taking over the court, until at last Mr Flowers intervened.

'Do you know Lord Arthur Pelham Clinton, Mr Gibbings?' he asked politely.

Mr Gibbings answered at once, 'Why, of course.' And he added with some nonchalance: 'There is some remote connection, I think you will find, between his family and mine. He was not present, however, at the ball that I have spoken of.'

Mr Flowers looked at some court officials and said, 'Neither will Lord Arthur Clinton be present here as a witness, I take it.'

A bald man suddenly stood.

'Sir,' he said to Mr Flowers, 'Mr W. H. Roberts, solicitor. I am here in court for two reasons. First, I wish to completely disassociate myself from any involvement in the story told to the court previously by the witness Mr Cox, which included champagne and tablecloths. I was not there. I was merely with

Lord Arthur Clinton one morning at the coffeehouse – at the request of his family – to discuss the matter of his bankruptcy. We were joined presently by Mr Ernest Boulton, and then by Mr Cox—'

'Nothing prejudicial to yourself was taken from your presence at that meeting, Mr Roberts,' said Mr Flowers briskly. 'You, Mr Roberts, are not the matter under discussion. Your second reason?'

'The second reason for my appearance is that I am here to represent Lord Arthur Clinton – against whom, at this moment, no charge has been laid – who is unavoidably detained from giving evidence at the moment, but is hoping to present himself at the earliest opportunity.'

'I see, Mr Roberts,' said Mr Flowers dryly. 'Well, we are grateful indeed for your presence at least.'

One of the defence lawyers stood immediately.

'I should have thought, Mr Flowers, that the Treasury would have done one thing or another – either put the unavailable Lord Arthur Clinton in the box as a witness, or in the dock as a prisoner.'

A lawyer for the prosecution jumped up.

'It is not so easy to just "put people in the dock", sir.'

'It is easy to avoid if you are the son of a duke,' murmured the defence lawyer, looking at the new man, Mr Roberts, but Mr Roberts said nothing, just sat down again, and Mr Flowers banged his gavel and turned back to the witness.

'Mr Gibbings. Do you know 13 Wakefield-street?'

'There is no need for him to make our home sound like a house of ill-repute,' said Mrs Stacey loudly, and Mr Amos Gibbings heard, and turned, and gave a small and graceful bow in Mattie's and Mrs Stacey's direction.

'I too sometimes kept my theatrical wardrobe at the very

respectable establishment at Wakefield-street,' said Mr Gibbings urbanely. 'It was not a place I stayed very often – not above one night ever, I think – but the landlady was very accommodating in allowing me to rent a room for our theatrical attire – everything there was suitable costume for modern comedies or parts. It is true, I did break open the door the police had locked at Wakefield-street, but only to take some clothes to the two gentlemen in the dock. Most importantly, I have swiftly returned from Calais, arriving here this morning, on purpose to give this evidence for my friends. I have always been ready and willing to give evidence at any time, and should have done so sooner, had I thought the case had taken so serious a turn.'

'Ha,' said Mrs Stacey, under her breath.

'Thank you, Mr Gibbings,' said Mr Flowers pleasantly. 'And I would like to compliment you on your clear evidence.'

He was a change from inebriated housekeepers, and tablecloths, and drunken beadles, certainly. And, of course, he was noble.

'Just one more thing,' said Mr Gibbings who seemed reluctant to leave the stage. 'That beard found among the gowns. There was lately a production of *Faust*, and it was for that production that it was used.'

Somehow the court erupted with laughter again and Mr Flowers banged his gavel. But there was much applause as Mr Gibbings sat down with some of the noble ladies, and Mrs Stacey and Mattie exchanged further glances, both wondering if he had run away to Calais after that first day and then decided to come back again. But they knew he had been a good witness and surely would have helped Freddie and Ernest.

The solicitors started arguing about the charges. Frederick Park's solicitor suddenly stood and addressed the bar.

'Mr Flowers, sir. Before you make your decision I must now point out to you that nothing has been proven against *my* client, Mr Frederick Park. I leave Mr Boulton in the capable hands of my colleague for whom I have nothing but esteem. But every one of these charges, apart from the dressing in women's clothing, which I think we all agree was a stupid prank – and indeed not worthy of my client – applies to Mr Boulton, not Mr Park. I wish to make application that the two men standing here today be tried separately.'

Mattie leaned forward quickly. Perhaps this was what Freddie's father had meant. She looked at Freddie. He did not look at Ernest, but stared straight ahead. Mattie thought Ernest looked frightened, but in a different way.

Mr Flowers simply addressed Mr Park's solicitor in a very dry manner. 'What would you therefore, sir, make of the letters from your client, Mr Frederick Park, to Lord Arthur Clinton – and which he also signs, "*your sister-in-law*"?'

'That was just stupidity, not felony, and if I may also point out—'

But the solicitor got no further.

Mr Flowers suddenly banged on his bench with his gavel very loudly and the court became immediately silent. Somehow everyone knew that, after so many weeks, this was the moment. It was assumed that Frederick Park, at least, would now be set free.

Mr Flowers said very slowly: 'I have had no doubt for some little time past that it is my duty to commit both the prisoners for trial, both on the graver charge of buggery in the indictment, and upon the charge of misdemeanour also – and without bail.'

Mattie and her mother looked at each other in disbelief. Now there was a different sound in the court. It was astonishment. It had all been so very entertaining. But this was not how the entertainment should end. Frederick Park and Ernest Boulton looked so suddenly shocked it seemed they might both faint. Unbelieving faces in the crowded room; the fashionable ladies and gentlemen, and actresses with big hats: all silent.

'There will presently be warrants for the arrest of several other people about whom we have heard in this case,' Mr Flowers continued ominously. 'The prisoners should now stand.'

They stood, stunned. Not a sound in the courtroom, not a cough. Just people holding their breath.

'Ernest Boulton and Frederick William Park, you are charged that you did, with each and one another, feloniously commit the crime of buggery. And, further, that you did conspire together with divers other persons to induce and incite other persons feloniously with them to commit the said crime. And, further, that you, being men, did unlawfully conspire together and with divers others to disguise yourselves as women and to frequent places of public resort so disguised and to thereby openly and unlawfully outrage public decency and corrupt public morals.

'The prisoners, and others whom I shall name in a separate hearing, will be committed for trial at the next sessions of the Central Criminal Court as a matter of course.' And Mr Flowers stood. 'This hearing is now adjourned.'

But Frederick Park, before anybody else could move, lunged towards the magistrate; he suddenly looked, not like the heretofore contained prisoner, but a wild, pale stranger.

'I am entirely innocent of any thought of that crime!' he cried and he pushed off a policeman who tried to restrain him.

Ernest Boulton had been standing holding on to the chair for support, which he now accidentally knocked over, bewildered. 'I say the same as Mr Park,' he said.

Mr Flowers said, 'You say that you are entirely innocent of the charge?'

And this new, wild, pale prisoner Mr Park said: 'Of any *thought* of committing such a gross crime!'

Ernest Boulton simply swayed.

Mr Flowers was still standing at his bench, ready to leave, papers in his hand.

'The prisoners are to be taken to Newgate Prison to await their trial,' he said blankly, as if for the last five or six weeks they had not been on trial at all.

There was an uproar of rage in the court. Frederick Park seemed to be crying. Ernest Boulton stood unbelieving: no fluttering eyes, no bows or waves or smiles. The court was cleared by policemen; the van was waiting outside. The news spread; crowds of people pushed and crowded round the van like a big sea. There were lots of calls of SHAME! but it was not clear if it was directed at the verdict, or at the two prisoners.

Mrs Stacey and her daughter were buffeted about in the crowd, as indeed were many people. They waited, silent, as first Frederick Park climbed up into the van. He suddenly turned, bent down to speak briefly and urgently to a gentleman, clasped his hand for a moment and was then gone. Ernest Boulton then climbed up into the van; at the doorway he too turned. He gave a small wave to the crowd and then disappeared inside. The driver whipped the horses, people banged on the van – in support, perhaps, or disgust – and they were being driven away to be locked up in Newgate Prison. Everyone knew stories of Newgate Prison; it was whispered that it was like going to hell.

Just as the van was moving away a group of men suddenly threw rocks, big rocks, as if they'd had them ready. They yelled 'FILTH! SODOMITES!' and their faces were twisted with something like hate; a rock hit one of the horses and it reared up and cried out; for a moment it looked as if the van might overturn and voices shouted in alarm, and then somehow the van righted itself and continued its journey, rattling in an ominous manner.

'FILTH!' yelled the same men still. 'SODOMITES! DIRTY BASTARDS!'

Then the van was too far away and the rocks fell short and on to the street and the shouting men laughed and Mattie Stacey thought of how it would be at Newgate where there would be lots of ugly-faced men like that. Suddenly she ran and punched one of the rock-throwers and screamed at them all, 'DIRTY BASTARDS YOURSELVES!' and she managed to scratch one face with a sharp stone that she took from her pocket before they knocked her over and shouted, 'CRIPPLED WHORE! CRIPPLED WHORE!' And then a policeman and her mother were running towards her and the ugly men quickly disappeared and the excitement was over.

'All right, miss?' asked the policeman quite politely, and Mrs Stacey wrapped her shawl quickly about her daughter's arm, which was covered in blood, and brushed at her skirt. One of the noble ladies said, 'Well done!' and shook Mattie's hand even though it was bleeding. Little groups of people stared at the two women quietly as they left.

The mother and the daughter walked, arm in arm, slowly.

'I must've misunderstood Mr Park,' was all Mattie said, in a flat voice.

The streets stank that late afternoon, the heat making them worse than usual; fish and piss and burnt onions. And still Mrs Stacey stopped at an old lady beggar, spoke to her for a moment and gave her a penny. The main streets near Wakefield-street were crowded and stinking also, full of evening people, and there was a lot of singing and drinking and laughing, and two shabby men were rolling with beer and singing *Champagne Charlie is my name*, and a slither of a summer moon came into the sky, even though it was not yet dark.

22

WHAT A HORRIBLE Sunday the next Sunday was.

We used to love Sundays.

It started with us all shouting at each other, we weren't usually like that.

'We dont have to read the bleeding newspapers every blooming Sunday like ghouls, we were *there* for God's sake!' yelled Ma when Billy came in with all the newspapers as usual and I tried to grab them. 'What can they tell us that we aint seen with our own eyes? And no doubt they'll embroider it with fancy rudeness! We're going to go and visit old Mrs Portmanteau again!' shouting at Billy as much as at me – for bringing the papers home I suppose, she *never* usually shouts at Billy, and hardly ever at me – and there she was, ruffling and shouting and bustling about and getting ready, banging things, looking for her cloak behind the door, and I just jumped up and screamed at her and Billy: 'I want to read the papers! I want to see what they are saying about our friends – you two go and visit old Mrs Portmanteau again for all I care, we only saw her the other week! I'm going to read *Reynolds News* and *The Times* and any other paper that has writ, I'll go and buy my own copies, you cant stop me, I might have made myself foolish about Freddie, well I'm finished with that, but they are still our friends and they're in prison!' and I actually snatched the

Reynolds News from Billy and if I hadn't had a big bandaged-up arm from the fight outside the court, and my rotten leg, I'd have locked myself in my room before they could catch me, I was so wild and angry and sad.

Billy stopped me of course, but gentle, as he always is.

Finally Ma said, 'All right, Mattie, all right.' She sighed and looked at Billy again, blaming him. 'But first we'll all settle down like we always do and we'll have a glass of port.'

'That wont make no difference to the words!'

'No, Mattie, but it might make a difference to how we hear them,' said Ma firmly as she filled our glasses – she sloshed some over on to the rug and she didn't even seem to notice which was so unlike her, you dont run a nice place like ours by not noticing port sloshing on the floor.

On some days rays of sunshine came into our little back parlour, and they did today, June rays of sunshine trying to cheer us, catching Pa's old Joshua tree, the leaves were shining because Ma and I looked after it so well. They shone and gleamed, green in the sun.

And so finally we settled as we always did.

'Read everything,' I instructed Billy, but you dont instruct my brother, he just looked at me without saying anything. Course he'd been funny too, Billy, lately, worried about his position of course because he loves working in Parliament so much, so I shut up. And he finally started to read to us as usual. *Reynolds News* seemed to have given the case much more coverage than a war or the Queen or a triple murder.

'THE HERMAPHRODITE CLIQUE,' he read.

'What's a hermaphrodite?' It was hard to say, it was a word I'd never heard before.

'It's just a word to get people's attention.'

'Yes but what does it *mean*?'

'A hermaphrodite is half a man and half a woman.'

I just looked at him.

'Mattie,' said Ma, quite quiet. 'Do you remember Aggie? He did the wigs at Drury Lane? Do you remember him from when you were little?'

Well, everyone knew Aggie. Aggie was – he was just as he was, well – well he had a man's arms and legs – and – and, well you know, the other stuff men have stuck on their bodies, but well – well he was a woman too – but in a different way from Ernest because Aggie – it was a bit strange – he had a real bosom, quite large, not a stuffed one like Freddie and Ernest, and long lady's hair that he done up in a chignon. He dressed in sort of men's clothes for his bottom half and ladies' clothes at the top, he was fussy and fidgety and wore ribbons – he used to give me ribbons to play with and talked a bit funny and fluting and ladylike. Aggie wore floating coloured scarves and curled his own long hair at the same time as he was doing the wigs, just pinned it up like women did. So that was a hermaphrodite then. Ernest and Freddie weren't anything like Aggie. I took a deep, deep breath.

'Keep reading,' I said.

THE HERMAPHRODITE CLIQUE

The moral sense of the nation has of late been receiving severe shocks.

Nearly a century ago, the poet Cowper gave a graphic description of the evils engendered in 'proud, gay, and gain-devoted cities':

> *Rank abundance breeds*
> *In gross and pampered cities, sloth and lust,*
> *And wantonness and glutinous excess.*

What would the poet say if he lived in the present day?

‘Well he’d be able to catch a train to pampered cities these days,’ said Ma calmly, drinking port. ‘And if he had an operation in the hospital he could be chloroformed.’

‘I dont think Cowper would approve of the railway system,’ said Billy dryly.

‘Keep reading,’ I said.

How would he be affected by the glaring infamies and the grave ‘freaks’ perpetuated by the aristocratic orders and by people ‘highly connected’? So deep would be his sentiment of disgust, that no language could adequately express it.

Boulton and Park obviously had influence and interest at their back. It is interesting that there was no lack of friends to engage counsel for their defence even when before a magistrate. The public will await with interest the forthcoming trial of the prisoners. But should the evidence against the prisoners be such that the jury will bring a verdict of ‘Guilty’, what then? Why, the impression will be conveyed thereby that this London of ours is as foul a sink of iniquity as were certain Jewish cities of old which, for their flagrant wickedness, met with retributive destruction by fire from heaven.

‘Oh for heaven’s sake!’ said Ma, ‘do we have to endure all this rubbish! That’s enough, Billy! Mattie, what is the point in listening to this?’

Billy stopped. Even I didn’t have the heart to hear any more. Ma poured the most port I’d ever seen her pour, spilling it on the rug again and I understood that she was upset too. I wondered if people read *Reynolds News* in Newgate Prison, and I thought of all the ugly men throwing rocks and I wondered what was happening inside Newgate to poor Ernest and Freddie, maybe they were having rocks thrown at them there too and I closed my eyes, trying not to think about it.

All of a sudden Billy, who was now reading a different part of the paper, started to laugh. It was so unlikely, and so unlike him, I dont mean Billy doesn't laugh, but he was now looking at the very same newspaper with tears of laughter in his eyes, almost right after reading all those stupid paragraphs.

'Listen,' he said.

However there is another matter relating to this case which we cannot let pass without notice. The Times *in a leading article of its Tuesday impression says 'the existence of such a scandal is a social misfortune. The charges made by the prosecution are such as are seldom made in this country, except against the lowest, the most ignorant and the most degraded.' Of course the writer here implies that the most abominable offence attributed to the prisoners, is confined to the humbler orders of society. We have no hesitation in saying this assertion is a foul calumny. We do not hesitate to say that if called upon to give an opinion as to the particular grade of society most given to the perpetration of unnatural offences, we should at once point to the episcopacy. Only a few years back the Right Reverend Bishop of Clayher was caught in the act of committing an abominable crime with a private soldier. Within the last twelvemonth two more right reverend fathers in God, Dr Twells, a Colonial bishop, and the other a Scots prelate, have been detected in abominations of a similar kind. These facts alone give lie to the assertion that the humbler classes are more addicted to the commission of these execrable offences, which at all events, seem prevalent amongst the prelacy.*

And Billy laughed even as he read. Billy has always hated religious men since that one told him God knew better than us and was taking Pa to a finer place, when we'd been so happy in the place we were already in.

A few days later the same rude, horrible policeman came again to Wakefield-street early in the morning and told me the proper trial was going to begin soon, at the Old Bailey, and that I must 'hold myself ready' to give evidence. Hold myself ready. Like pull myself together. Funny things we're supposed to do to ourselves.

'So it's going ahead after all,' was all I said to Ma.

Billy got hold of a copy of the new indictments against other people in the case. He brought it home, late, we'd eaten without him and left his dinner warming on the stove. I was washing some dishes and pots. Ma gave Billy his dinner, he gave her the paper with the indictment writ on.

'You read it,' he said.

Ma had magnifying spectacles. She read it out, sitting at the table with Billy.

Ernest Boulton and Frederick William Park are charged with buggery; also with committing buggery with Arthur Pelham Clinton, commonly called Lord Arthur Pelham Clinton; with conspiring to solicit other persons to commit to the crime and with conspiring with Clinton, Marin Luther Cumming, John Salford Fiske, Louis Clark Hirst and C. H. Thomas to attend places of resort in the disguise of women, thereby outraging public decency and offending against public morals.

'How did you get this?' she asked Billy.

Billy looked at her. 'Inside help,' he said, sarcastic. 'Elijah gave it to me in his little private cubby in the Central Lobby to copy. He said "because you are an interested party". You'd be surprised what's delivered to Honourable Members in the evenings.'

'So they've decided to arrest Lord Arthur Clinton at last,' Ma said. 'That'll cause bleeding bedlam, mark my words. And in your workplace too, Billy.'

'Why's there suddenly all these new people?' I asked Billy.

He shrugged. 'They're people who wrote letters to Ernest mostly. And it all starts again tomorrow.'

'Right.' Ma's voice was suddenly very cold and businesslike. 'This is the real trial with a judge and jury and all that palaver. You cant go in before you're called to give evidence, Mattie. Billy, you're obviously in real danger now of losing your work now that it's a proper trial, and no doubt our name and address plastered all over the newspapers again. Our home is already called a brothel and we've lost some of our regulars. We might find ourselves with hardly any income at all. So I'll go to the Old Bailey tomorrow to find out the worst.' She sounded scary, not like our Ma at all.

Billy said, 'Everyone's now looking at me out of the corner of their eye, that's true. But dont worry, Ma. If I do lose my position I'm going to get it back.'

'How?'

He was silent for a moment. 'I've said over and over: Mr Gladstone wasn't just shocked in an ordinary way when he heard about Lord Arthur Clinton.' His face was set like it gets sometimes. 'There's something odd, something else. I dont mind what his secrets are, that's his business, but I'm going to find out about him and Lord Arthur Clinton if I get dismissed and he doesn't, and I'm going to ask him to help me.'

That was the end of that conversation. Billy ate his dinner, silent, but I saw he ate hardly any. I washed pots. I wondered if I could make more hats by working later at night, earlier in the morning. We heard the clang of the letter flap on the front door and Ma went upstairs.

Billy ate.

I washed pots.

Ma came back with a letter she'd already opened. She put it on the table for us to read without saying anything. It was from Mr Connolly, one of our cotton salesmen, saying he felt it necessary from now on to find other 'more suitable' lodgings in London. He was the third of our regulars to decide not to use our rooms any more.

Outside some cats were screaming. When we first came to Wakefield-street I couldn't tell the difference between cats screaming and people screaming, but I can now.

23

Billy escorted me at dawn to the Central Criminal Court in his suit and his top hat, hoping I might somehow get inside. Both of us not saying much, well we didn't need to. This was a dark hour for us, and all for letting a room to Freddie and Ernest.

'I hope you'll keep your position, son,' I said to Billy by the corner of the Old Bailey. Billy is a most undemonstrative person but he gave me a little kiss on the cheek. 'See you tonight, Ma,' he said, 'we'll be all right somehow, I promise,' and then my Billy was gone on towards Westminster, to his own troubles at the Parliament.

It was a blooming circus outside the Old Bailey even at that hour, crowds and crowds of people even though it was only just getting properly light, all pushing and waiting for this big proper trial with Judges and Juries and more excitement. There was a man with a placard:

> THOU SHALT NOT LIE WITH MANKIND
> AS WITH WOMANKIND
> IT IS AN ABOMINATION.
>
> LEVITICUS 18:26

and all the usual clerks, and street-girls offering "just a quick one, before the trial" and men in top hats and women carrying babies, pie-sellers of course, footmen holding places for their Masters.

But the ones in charge were having none of it, not this time – nobody allowed into the Old Bailey without permission – they actually shoved people away with their police sticks! Those noisy press reporters were pushing and waving passes, but there were strict rules, only the people with the right to be there were let in. I understood I would not likely be one of them and I just stood there for a few moments, in the middle of all the people, just thinking of many things and the twists and turns of our lives till now, and then a tap on the shoulder, bloody hell, one of the policemen – was I going to be blooming shoved about too? – but it was Algie Thornton of all people, his pa done building work at Drury Lane so course Algie knew me.

'Auntie Ma!' he said, there outside the court, as if he was a small boy still, and we both laughed. 'Heard you and Mattie was involved,' he said. He gave me a wink, escorted me away from the crowds and took me to a side door to wait, and when the court doors finally slowly opened Algie actually escorted me in, one of the first! He was always a good boy, I looked after him sometimes, years ago, when his mother was having another, and he heard Billy and Mattie call me Ma, so he called me Auntie Ma.

I sat as near to the front as I could and hoped I'd hear it mostly. Although I was scared in a way, I *made* myself think positive. We still had some of our other regular salesmen from the North, cotton people, they still came to us all this last month, they knew Freddie and Ernest in a casual way, knew about the case, didn't seem to care tuppence. Just so long as they all didn't stop coming like Mr Connolly and some of the others . . . I told myself we'd manage somehow. But if Billy lost his job . . . I couldn't help it, there was a strange, tight, pressing feeling round my heart, God, I'm not having a bleeding heart attack in here! I said to myself. Then I got a tap on the arm: Emma Goodrich, she was an actress I knew from the Haymarket, sitting nearby and wearing a fine gown and cloak, very elegant. She moved to sit beside me, whispered to me very loudly several times, told me she had a "barrister gentleman friend" who'd got her in, she was a pretty Celia in *As You Like It* but years ago now. So here we sat, me and Emma and noble ladies in big hats and gentlemen with their hats removed and ministers in their church collars. There seemed to be a large amount of lawyers with their wigs on, from nearby courts I s'pose – all wanting a look at Ernest and Freddie no doubt.

Then they swore in the jury, seemed very quick to me, all swearing by Almighty God with righteous enthusiasm, ha! one was Beetle Turner, his nose as red as ever, publican at the Lord Russell down by the river. He was a bit of a rogue, dealt in stolen watches and jewellery, bet he was a bit blooming uncomfortable finding himself called to the Old Bailey! And then at last there was someone crying, *Silence in court,* and they said we all had to rise for the Judge in his long black gown and his long white wig, escorted in a slow procession of Sheriffs or Aldermen or whatever they were, and the bigwig legal men following – the Attorney-General, the Solicitor-General, the big barristers – all the Stars eh! and a great hump of lawyers behind them, that nasty little prosecutor Mr Poland, Freddie's lawyers, Ernest's lawyers, all taking their places on the Stage. Well it *was* like the Stage it seemed to me, I half-expected a blooming theatrical fanfare any minute, like in a Royal scene from Shakespeare!

And then just before Ernest and Freddie was brought in, me and Emma - at exactly the same time - observed a gentleman come in and sit at the back of the barristers benches - we turned to each other, sort of surprised at who we'd seen and Emma started giggling - we *knew* him, it was Sir Alexander Cockburn, the Lord Chief Justice, he was in charge of *everything* to do with the Law, everyone knew that. But he must be off duty, he wasn't even wearing his wig, just sitting quietly at the back, I never saw him quiet before! He was at the theatre often, that Sir Alexander Cockburn, knew lots of the actors - he was always coming backstage - I remembered he was sweet on young Ellen Terry at the Haymarket, before she became so famous. He was a very elegant, sociable fellow, always bringing bottles of champagne!

Then Freddie and Ernest were brought in.

Ah God, those poor boys.

It had felt we was at the theatre, but of course now suddenly it didn't, it was alarming and serious and the court was suddenly still and silent and hot. Just the prisoners' footsteps and the guards' footsteps as they were escorted to the dock, even I could hear them. I was glad Mattie wasn't there, they looked blooming terrible. It was Freddie I was most worried for, they was both deathly pale but Freddie looked to me as if he might faint right here in court. His face was so white and puffy, he kept holding the bar of the dock and then trying to make his collar loose. While Ernest was still. As if, in the end, Ernest was the strong one after all. Who looked like a girl in a man's suit, standing there. Blank face. They stood as far apart from each other as they could, as if they didn't know each other and I saw them in my mind, laughing in their gowns down the stairs at Wakefield-street with perfume and powder and excitement and gin and their shadows dancing on the walls.

The charges Billy had showed us the night before was read out loud, in public, with the new names of people to be arrested and as soon as Lord Arthur Clinton's name was said about four of the pressmen jumped up and made for the door. A Nobleman arrested for buggery.

Then there was a strange silence.

And then a barrister suddenly stood and said to the Judge: 'My lord, I would request, with the new charges and new indictments to be studied – which have only just come to us, and new evidence including new medical evidence, to be presented – I would therefore request a postponement of this case.'

And – *at once* – I thought of Freddie's father. And what Mattie had said. Maybe it was *this* he knew was going to happen? But even if it was, it hadn't gone as the poor man had hoped, the trial wasn't cancelled, only postponed maybe, with a warrant out to arrest Lord Arthur, which would mean more publicity than ever before. Freddie was staring and staring at his lawyer. The Judge made Freddie and Ernest answer the charges before he gave any decision. All them things read out again, felony, buggery, misdemeanour, blah blah; after every one Freddie said, 'Not guilty,' in a shaky voice. Ernest said,

'Not guilty,' like a girl, they were both even paler now than when they came in.

The Judge then sat cogitating for a minute and then he turned to the Attorney-General and politely asked his opinion. The Attorney-General said something like if all parties agreed the prosecution would not demur about a postponement, for he too had more preparation to make. I looked at them all, all the Sirs and Lords, all the ones with the real power. And I suddenly thought, clear as can be: *they've planned this.* Because me, I've worked in theatres all my life and I know a rehearsed piece when I see one.

And watching it all, in the background, the Lord Chief Justice, Sir Alexander Cockburn and I know this was fanciful but to me he looked like a theatre director, watching the actors from the back of the stalls.

And then the Judge leaned forward and said: 'If all parties agree, of course there can therefore be no objection to a postponement till the next sessions' (as if they hadn't all breakfasted together earlier in some gentlemen's club, ha! well that's only my opinion but that's what I thought).

I looked at Freddie. There was colour back in his cheeks, he was staring at his lawyer still. The jury was dismissed and that Beetle Turner looked as if he was making straight for his public house on the Strand, as if he couldn't get there fast enough. The pressmen were furious – Lord Arthur Clinton mentioned and the whole thing postponed at once! one threw his hat on the floor in disgust, probably from *Reynolds News*! Freddie and Ernest were led away once again and us all pushing to get out, talking and muttering. Emma disappeared – then I saw her having a word with her "gentleman barrister friend". Outside Ernest gave a few little waves to people but Freddie saw no one I think, just stared ahead. But they both looked as if going back to Newgate Prison in the police van was preferable to going on with the case.

Emma came rushing back up to me. 'Just fancy, Isabella! That old party fellow, Sir Alexander, skulking in the wings! You know the Queen refuses him a peerage because he's too naughty – all those children by a lady not his wife! And Isabella, listen, I just saw my friend, and he told me there's been another case about Lord Arthur Clinton in another court! A cab driver was suing for a big fare not paid – he said he'd driven Lord Arthur all round London for hours, and then Lord Arthur told the driver to wait outside the Opera Hotel. And he didn't come out again, and when the driver finally went into the hotel he found Lord Arthur had skipped out the back way! They called for Lord Arthur Clinton to appear in court – but nobody came! Isn't it all exciting!' and Emma rushed off again. And I remembered then how sure Mattie was that Lord Arthur had passed us in a cab. So he must be hiding in London, somewhere.

I also saw Algie again outside, proud in his policeman's uniform, thanked him for getting me in, asked after his pa. Algie said his pa had lost his mind.

I stood there, wondering if I was going to lose mine. Postponed till next month, us no idea about our future or our fate. It wasn't even lunchtime.

I didn't know if I should go on with my heart attack, or laugh.

24

On Monday, when Billy went back to the clerks' desk at the end of the day, having delivered piles of copied documents to the Colonial Secretary's office, he found the same old verse by his place.

There was an old person of Sark
Who buggered a pig in the dark
The swine in surprise
Murmured 'God bless your eyes,
Did you take me for Boulton or Park?'

A message was also waiting: he was to go at once to the office of the Head Clerk Mr Jenkins.

The Head Clerk's room smelled strongly of spiced pomade. This time they didn't even sit at the desk. 'I'm sorry, Mr Stacey,' said Mr Jenkins at once. 'That same bishop, a hypocritical gentleman if I may reiterate, has got his way now. As Lord Arthur Clinton is now accused, and no doubt the trial becoming more sensational, and likely more publicity for your home, I'm afraid your position is be terminated immediately.'

'Just like that?'

'You have been here for ten years, Mr Stacey, I know that. I tried very hard to make them change their minds but I am afraid it was impossible. The House of Lords is bursting with bishops, as you know, and this one is their spokesman (self-apppointed, I wouldn't mind wagering). He said no references, but I've written you one anyhow, to hell with Bishop Julius.' He handed a paper to Billy.

'Bishop Julius?' said Billy. He remembered him, coming in to the Prime Minister's office when Mr Gladstone had turned so pale.

'He's a hypocrite as I say,' said the Head Clerk. 'I am sorry, Mr Stacey.'

'Thanks, John,' said Billy, and he was gone to Elijah Fortune.

'I've got to find Lord Arthur Clinton in a hurry,' said Billy to Elijah.

'You and everybody else apparently,' said Elijah. 'Why?'

'My position is terminated.'

Elijah whistled a few bars of 'Home Sweet Home' while looking at Billy carefully.

'I suspected it might be. What makes you think Lord Arthur is the clue?'

'I need this work, for our family. I have to get it back. And I want to keep working here. I refuse to let them get rid of me when I'm good at my work – and I believe Lord Arthur and Mr Gladstone are – connected in some way.' And there was something about the way Billy spoke: some anger but some certainty also. Elijah beckoned to one of the other doorkeepers.

'Stay here for ten minutes, Cyril,' he said. 'Come with me, Billy.'

The Central Lobby, the Members' Lobby, and the debating chambers were on the 'principal floor' of the Parliament. Daylight could be seen through leaded windows and a few steps led down from various doorways into the London streets. Billy thought he knew most nooks and crannies in the Parliament where Elijah, whistling still, led him, but Billy did not know the tiny staircase far along the corridor from the Central Lobby. He just knew he was going downwards, past the clerks' offices under the Central Lobby, and then down again towards the basement where the sewerage pumps spewed their waste into the Thames. But between the clerks' offices and the basement there was another floor: other rooms down some back steps past anonymous oak doors, dark corridors lit by gaslight, then a darker, tiny passage.

Elijah took a key from his waistcoat and they seemed to enter an almost invisible door.

Inside everything was red. Red velvet curtains, red-covered cushions, red lampshades, red wallpaper. And under one of the red lamps, reading, a great pile of books beside her, sat an old bent woman with claws for hands it seemed, and wearing a red hat.

Billy couldn't help it: he laughed, and she, looking up, said at once: 'Good heavens! You must be Joe Stacey's boy, how lovely. Have a cake, dear. Your dear pa always liked my cakes.'

'This is my wife, Dodo,' said Elijah. 'Used to be a singer and a dancer in the music hall, comedy songs mostly, but the arthritis has got her. I'll have a quick cake too, my dear. Sit down, Billy.'

And as Dodo got up laboriously from her chair, Billy stood again, to help her, but Elijah motioned to him quickly. And when she had gone from the room he said, 'She so wants to move and she can't always, so let her try.'

Billy looked about the red room. 'This is handy and nice!' he said. The cosy red hideaway underneath the workings of the state somehow made him want to laugh again, just with the oddness and the pleasure of it.

'We're very lucky and comfortable down here,' said Elijah. 'Dodo and me.' He pulled aside one of the red curtains. If they looked upwards they could see dusk and feet passing in a concrete alley. Elijah closed the curtains again.

'After she left the stage, and before the arthritis really got her so bad as now, Dodo used to work here as well as me, so we got this place. Dodo was one of the housekeepers. Kept the Members in cakes – some of them nearly cried when she had to retire! Now listen, lad. I don't know all the ins and outs because the nobility try to keep everything quiet from people like us, but I do know Mr Gladstone was very friendly with the late Duke of Newcastle, Lord Arthur's father, and had something to do with helping him get his divorce from Lord Arthur's mother in the old days when divorce was almost impossible.'

'Have a cake,' said Dodo, appearing with two plates, each holding an iced cake, and the two men smiled and ate and she smiled back. 'Just like your pa,' she said to Billy. 'And how's your ma?'

'She's well, Mrs Fortune. She told me of you, that you were a singer and a dancer, and she and Pa used to go to the music hall to see you.'

And Dodo smiled and smiled, and Elijah smiled at her too, for she had been so lovely. And he loved her still.

'Thank you, my dear,' he said to her, for the cake. And then he turned back to Billy. 'The present pathetic Duke,' said Elijah, 'Lord Arthur's eldest brother, Linky they call him, is a nitwit and a gambler and usually lives in Brighton or Paris, and is obviously not giving any assistance. If he had any sense at all he'd get his brother away to France where these things are not a matter for the law. Just keep that information in your head. And I know where Lord Arthur is.'

Billy was so surprised he stood at once, spilling crumbs.

'He's staying at a hostelry in Christchurch, the King's Arms, he's trying to leave the country. I got a message, asking if I can help him.'

Billy looked at the Head Doorkeeper in surprise. 'How could *you* help Lord Arthur?'

'He needs money,' said Elijah. 'He never has any money. He thinks someone in the Parliament might help him, and the Central Lobby is where everyone passes. I'm to send it to the name of Hamilton. If you see him, don't tell him how no one wants to know, and I'll keep trying anyway.'

'Thanks Elijah.' And the men finished up their cake.

And Dodo said, 'Isn't it sad that Mr Dickens has passed away.'

When Billy got home that evening, down in the kitchen that smelled of herrings, where Mattie was folding clean towels and his mother was just about to put an apple pie in the blazing oven, he stood at the bottom of the stairs for a moment, quite still.

'I've been dismissed,' he said.

'*What?* Even though the trial's postponed?'

'Especially as the trial's postponed apparently. They expect there'll be much more publicity with Lord Arthur called for.'

Mrs Stacey did not ruffle or speak of the workhouse, just stood there with the apple pie, as if she had forgotten where to put it. Both women were silent-shocked, even though he had warned them.

'Don't worry,' he said to them both. 'I told you, I'll get my position back. I am going to Christchurch, tonight, because I believe that is where Lord Arthur is. And if I can find him, I just might find out why Mr Gladstone went so white in the face.

Surely it can't just be because he knew Lord Arthur's father, for goodness sake! So can we eat dinner now, Ma, please, before I leave.'

'He'll hardly want to be found by you,' said Ma quietly after a moment, 'if the police can't find him.'

'I'm not going to arrest him,' said Billy dryly.

'I saw him here in London,' said Mattie. 'I *told* you I saw him, Billy.'

'He certainly was here in London,' said his mother. 'He apparently tricked a cabman in London not long ago, it was in one of the courts. How do you know he's now in Christchurch? Some rumour? It'll be like chasing a pin.'

She opened the oven and the heat came rushing out but still she clutched the apple pie to her, looking at her son.

'Elijah told me.'

'What?'

He raised his voice. 'Elijah! And I met his wife Dodo. She's got terrible arthritis, Ma, all curled up. She asked after you.'

Mrs Stacey then quite slowly bent down again and put the apple pie in the hot oven; when she closed the door it was a relief that the extra heat was cut off.

'Dodo was such a clever dancer in the music halls long ago, till that blooming arthritis started. And she had a lovely, laughing voice and she sung them comic songs. And she made delicious cakes.'

'She gave me one. It was delicious too.'

'The audiences really did love her, me and Pa used to go, I told you. Well, if anyone will know what's to be known, I expect it will be Elijah.'

'He got a message about Lord Arthur needing money. Why would Elijah get such a message?'

Mrs Stacey looked at her son. 'Elijah's that sort of person.

Everyone has always relied on Elijah somehow, it was always like that at Drury Lane too when he worked there.'

'I'm coming with you,' said Mattie to Billy.

'Don't be ridiculous,' said her mother.

'Don't be ridiculous,' said Billy.

'Let me *come*, Billy. I'll help you. I'll help you find him, I'll be useful, no one will hide from a lame girl, you know that – I could approach him first and he wouldn't be frightened that I was from the police or anything, he might remember me, limping.'

The top of the stove now banged and clanged.

'Sit down and eat, both of you,' said Mrs Stacey. She took a pot off the top, 'Do you really think you can do it, Billy? Get your position back?'

'Yes,' he said.

'I'm coming to help you,' said his sister.

Their mother served out food. 'Here, there's herrings and mash, while the apple pie cooks, and if both of you are minded to hare off like insane policemen you'll need some money.'

Her children looked at her in astonishment. She *never* gave them money; they earned their own, and gave part of it to her. She used to hide it all away, for the day they were all carted off to the workhouse – which was now more likely than it had ever been in their new lives.

'And there'll be a railway train, part of the way anyway, in the morning. Which there won't be at this hour.'

And while her children ate obediently, Isabella Stacey disappeared. She returned some time later with an old tin from some secret hiding place of her own. She gave them three gold sovereigns each.

Billy and Mattie, deeply shocked, spoke in unison: 'We've got some money, Ma!'

'Take it,' she said to them both. 'It's worth all this if it gets your position back, Billy.' She bent down to the oven. 'Now eat this apple pie!'

And as she laid the hot pie on the table, she said, smiling slightly: 'Does Dodo still love red?'

25

IT WAS NEARLY evening when we finally got to Christchurch next day, even though we had left Wakefield-street so early, me and Billy, not even sure how to get to where we were going, keeping our wits about us for everyone knew the stories of thieves at railway stations and we had our new riches. It was all like a huge adventure, only the second time I'd been on trains, and as we puffed and chuffed along leaving our London behind I thought of Mr Ronald Duggan the perfidious train driver, but not much; and I thought of Mr Dickens dying and how he had taught me to stand up and speak with words, and mostly I thought of Freddie and Ernest in Newgate Prison and if we could find out something to help them while we were helping Billy. It's all right, it's all right, I didn't have any stupid dreams left in my head. That was gone. I wanted to help Billy and I still cared for Freddie, but no dreams. In my head I often saw his terrible face when they sent them to Newgate.

We passed villages and big towns, we got off a big train and on to a coach with beautiful white horses, there were no beautiful white horses in London, they were grey in a week. Then we saw the sea. And then we got a last, smaller train that took us to Christchurch Railway Station and then we had to walk into the High Street and dear Billy, patient as ever, gave me his arm when he saw I was a bit tired, like he always did. And I knew I was lucky Billy was patient with me when I slowed him down a bit, because I knew how much of a hurry he was in. He had a bag on his back too, just the things we needed. And all that money, clinking in our pockets, I never had that much money in a pocket in my life! Ask yourself how you'd feel if your mother gave you nearly about a *sixth* of your year's earnings and told you to just put it in your pocket!

Christchurch was full of friendly people, they directed us to the High Street, and then to the King's Arms, just along Castle-street. We looked at the front of it, it was quite big, and a bit too grand for us, we knew not to spend our money on a room there; friendly people told us of the Old George Inn just on the near corner, 'You'll get a cheap room there,' they told us.

But first we did a good investigation of the rest of the King's Arms in the dusk, down some little alleys that wound round Castle-street, I tripped a bit on the uneven cobbles but we kept winding round and we came to the back of the hotel, just so we could have a good idea of the whole place.

'Why dont I just go right in and ask for Mr Hamilton?' I whispered to Billy. 'Or should one of us wait here at the back, and one of us at the front and just hope he comes out? but I s'pose he might be hiding in an attic or a basement or something.' Lucky we'd both actually seen him before, a bit balding and a bit thin and a bit snooty. Sort of small somehow.

Billy doesn't believe in God – *very firmly* he doesn't believe – but something had got us there, some lucky chance, in the half-light, at the back of the King's Arms Hotel in Christchurch just at that moment, looking across carriages and horses to where lights were shining inside the building. One of the doors opened. Three men came out and I heard Billy's sharp breath. We were quite far away but Billy quickly moved near and I followed him, there were enough carriages there and horses rattling their bridles for us not to be clearly seen but *we* could clearly see that one of the men was Lord Arthur and we could hear voices though they weren't talking very loud. Lord Arthur stood beside a small cabriolet where a driver was waiting.

'Mudeford,' said one of the men. 'Johnny Hewlettson. He lives above the quay. And I hope I'm getting my money back,' and that man laughed but it was only a half-laugh, as if he expected he wouldn't.

'I'm expecting something big to arrive here for me tomorrow, name of Hamilton. Bring it to Mudeford immediately.' And Lord Arthur climbed into the cabriolet.

And the two men standing in the courtyard waved him away as another carriage arrived and the small cabriolet came right past where we were stood concealed and we both instinctively turned away as the driver used his whip gently and the horse trotted out into the alley and away from us.

Almost not believing our luck we walked back towards the inn. We asked a man we passed about Mudeford, was it a person? was it a place? It turned out it was a place just a few miles away. Billy wanted to go now, asked the same man how to get there.

'You a smuggler, lad?'

Billy laughed. 'Do I look like a smuggler?' he said. He indicated me. 'With my sister along with me?'

'I cant rightly see you in the night,' said the man peering at us. 'But they come past Mudeford escaping the patrols, and then run into Christchurch, up the narrow channel.'

I said to Billy if Lord Arthur was waiting for money tomorrow, he couldn't leave till then, so we could stay here tonight and go to Mudeford very early in the morning. 'Not because I'm tired!' I said quickly.

Billy grinned at me, but in a very nice brotherly way. We got a room at the Old George Inn and sat to eat a steak pie at a little table in a big room with dark brown rafters where others were munching and drinking and talking and smoking and we weren't left alone for long.

'Where you from?'

'Where you going?'

'What's your name?'

They talked in a slightly funny way, slower, they sounded a bit different than us, but it was still English.

I thought to myself how odd and interesting it was to be having this adventure with my brother and sitting with everybody all talking to us and asking our business.

'What for are you going to Mudeford?'

'Who do you know in Mudeford?'

'We dont know anybody,' said Billy. 'See my sister? She's hurt her leg.'

I nearly punched him. Of course they can see that I limp but there's no need to draw attention.

'Sea air,' said Billy. 'We hear there's good air, in Mudeford.'

Friendly people looked at my leg and my boot and even poked me, as if I was public property. But a lady serving ale brought me a cold cloth. 'You could walk to Mudeford,' she said to Billy, 'but look at the girlie's leg. And it'll be hot again tomorrow, I can tell by the sky.'

'I can walk,' I said, loud, 'I walk everywhere in London.'

She brought a bucket. 'Here then,' she said. 'There's clean water in here, before I sluice the floors. You put that leg in here, and the swelling will go down and you can walk again tomorrow morning,' and she took off my boot like Ma did sometimes. I never knew the world had such kind people in it, my leg was a bit swollen too. 'Wont take you more than an hour or so to get there at an easy pace, the postman does it twice a day and back again.'

'We'll leave early,' said Billy, 'even before the postman. Who is Johnny Hewlettson?'

There was a funny little silence in the room.

After a while a man said, 'You sure you're not a smuggler, lad?'

'I'm not a smuggler, I'm a clerk! And my sister is a milliner.'

'I made this hat,' I said, and I took it off and showed my sewing to the lady who took off my boot. She studied my sewing on the hat with great interest.

One of the men said, 'Johnny Hewlettson, he's a big man in Mudeford,' and then everyone laughed. 'Mind you, there's not very many people live in Mudeford! But he owns fishing boats, Johnny Hewlettson.'

'Fishing boats?' Billy was careful not to sound surprised or look at me but I guessed we were both thinking of fishing boats maybe carrying people as well as fish. Elijah had said Lord Arthur was trying to run further.

'We'll leave very early,' said Billy.

And we said goodnight to our new friends but I knew they watched us as Billy waited for me to go ahead and I limped up the narrow stairs to the little top room and this was the first night I ever slept in a real inn but after all it was only a bigger version of our boarding house really, I said to Billy.

Even though it was still dark next morning already people were working in the Old George Inn, and the woman behind the bar who had helped my leg last night gave us a big duck egg each and a pickled onion and bread and wouldn't take any extra money.

When we'd been walking along the Mudeford Road about half an hour a man came past on a horse.

'They said at the Old George to look out for you two,' he said, the same slower way of talking, different from us. 'Hop up, girlie, and I'll drop you at the Nelson Inn to wait for your brother, not so far now.'

'Are you the postman?' asked Billy quickly.

He laughed. 'Do I look like a postman?'

He was old, about forty maybe but he had a very fine face and a beard, a bit wild, in fact he slightly reminded me of those old paintings of Jesus. Only because he was a bit old maybe he looked more like Joseph the carpenter than Jesus who was the son of God – or possibly who was the son of Joseph depending on how you felt about things – anyway I hoped Billy wouldn't be rude.

'The postman does walk to Mudeford, twice a day in fact. He's famous for it.'

He had a deep rumbling voice. I'd never actually been on a horse but Billy helped me up and I took our bag on my back and sat behind the man.

'My name's Mackie,' he said. 'I'm a fisherman. Hold tight, girlie,' so I waved to Billy and I held tight and the horse trotted away and I was jumped up and down for a bit but then I got the feel, holding tight to Mackie, and I thought I hadn't felt anybody to hold to since Freddie had rubbed my foot and held me, all those months and months ago. If you dont know what I mean, you haven't been used to holding, and then suddenly that holding is gone. So you wont know what I mean but it's like a pain.

'Do you live in Mudeford, Mackie?' I asked, into his shoulder. When he answered me I could feel his voice, you know that? you can feel someone's voice vibrating if you're leaning into their back?

'Often I do,' he said. 'I like to hear the sea always.' And I heard it too, as we came near.

And when Billy arrived I was waiting with a room booked at the Nelson Inn, well I ran a boarding house didn't I? it wasn't so different and I paid in advance with some of Ma's money like any old experienced traveller. And although he had called me 'girlie' as if I wasn't a grown-up person, that Mackie the horseman was very kind, and had asked me my name and about me and told me he couldn't live without the sea and gave me an apple.

When Billy had washed his face and drunk a cold drink we walked down to the Mudeford quay. It was a wonderful place to us visitors from London, boats and nets and people and the smell of fish and rope and the open sea further out there, I could feel the warm sea wind on my face as we walked to the end. It was mid-morning, some of the fishing boats had come in now, fishermen were cleaning fish, women helping them, some little girls too, and the very youngest ones looking for crabs and laughing, I looked for Mackie but he wasn't there. Someone offered us some whelks to eat so we sat on wooden posts and ate them: looking, listening. Then I held on to a rail and walked to where the quay sloped down, near where the little children were crab-fishing. I suppose it was where they dragged up nets. I bent down and rinsed my hands and felt the lovely cold sea, and the bottom of my gown was suddenly all wet and I laughed with the children and ran backwards in my clumsy way.

We looked very obviously strangers of course.

'You here on a visit?' said a man finally, who was pulling ropes together, winding them into a bundle.

'We're looking for Johnny Hewlettson,' I said to him before Billy had time to answer. There was silence for a while.

'I'm Johnny Hewlettson,' he said finally.

'Mr Hewlettson, we're looking for – for a man who is hiding, just now, he came last night.'

'Never heard of him,' still pulling the ropes, winding them, coiling them.

'Mr Hewlettson,' I said, 'we dont know what name he is using, but it might be Hamilton, and he will be hiding but if you do just happen to see him could you just tell him that Mattie and Billy Stacey from Wakefield-street are staying at the Nelson Inn tonight and that we have a message from – from Stella.'

The rope winding stopped just for a moment and then started again. 'Is that so?' he said.

'Yes,' I said.

He looked at Billy. 'And what do you say, or do you let her do all the talking?'

I saw the two of them, sort of taking the measure of one another, like – well have you ever seen a fight where people dont just go at it straightaway but look at each other carefully first? I almost expected them to put up fists.

But Billy was smarter than that. 'If you do happen to come across this person, Johnny Hewlettson, will you tell him you saw us?' he said. 'Tell him who we are, and that we're at the Nelson Inn if he wants to see us, and if he doesn't we'll be going back to London tomorrow morning and will leave him alone. Nobody knows we came.'

'And what made you come to Mudeford of all places?'

Billy looked at Johnny Hewlettson. 'Elijah. Tell him Elijah Fortune.'

Johnny Hewlettson shrugged. Went back to winding ropes.

'Goodbye, Mr Hewlettson,' I said politely.

We walked slowly back to the inn, breathing the sea, wondering if we had lost our chance.

'Something will happen,' said Billy calmly. 'You'll see. It was good you said "Stella", and Lord Arthur knows Elijah is a trustworthy friend.'

'He might think we're bringing money from Elijah,' I said

suddenly. 'Can we give him at least something, Billy, do you think?'

'Maybe we can,' said Billy, nodding.

The weather had got hotter and lowering even though we were by the sea. The day was darkening, I was getting uneasy by then, we'd waited a long time. Seagulls were wheeling and calling in their sharp voices.

'Perhaps he's already gone,' I said finally but Billy said, 'Just wait.' We'd eaten a pie, we were sitting on a seat in the dusk at the back of the Nelson Inn.

Then a little girl appeared.

I'd seen her on the quay earlier – she must have been about ten years old and she had a dirty face but bright, inquisitive eyes and she looked us over, and then carefully looked at my feet, before she spoke. 'Aren't youse the visitors? For Mr Hamilton?'

'Yes,' said Billy at once. 'We are the visitors for Mr Hamilton.'

'Come then.'

And she led the way, back along the road towards the quay, ahead of us, not with us, but every now and then looking back.

'You were right,' said Billy dryly. 'If it was just me I might not have been so lucky. Somehow a limping girl is a guarantee!' but he's my brother so he knows how to tease me without really annoying me, though I flicked him with my shawl.

'Why do you walk funny?' The little girl threw the words over her shoulder.

'I've got something wrong with my leg.' I saw her look back again, and then shrug.

'No one will marry you,' she said, 'you'll be like the egg lady.'

'Who's the egg lady?'

'She keeps hens and lives by herself because she's a hump-back.'

She stopped outside an old cottage, dark and unkempt and damp-looking, perhaps it was more cheerful in the daytime, I wondered if it was the egg lady's cottage.

'In here,' said the girl.

She opened the door of the cottage and lit a little lamp from a shelf. She led us upwards – the stairs were so narrow and so steep that I had to pick up my petticoat and my skirt and hold them in front of me with one hand while I held on to the wall with the other so that I wouldn't fall.

'I'm here,' said Billy. 'Just behind you.'

The girl knocked on the door of the room at the top and then stood back so that we could squeeze in. She gave the lamp to me and disappeared downstairs.

The heat of the tiny attic room hit us because the window was closed and the curtain drawn. Lord Arthur Clinton was lying on a small bed in his clothes but without his jacket. There was an old blanket beside him. No one else was there, well that was lucky because no one else could have fitted into the room anyway with me and Billy there, and the ceiling so low and it being so *hot*.

'What is the message?' he said, sitting up as we entered. 'Have you brought money?'

He was pale and perspiring. I put the lamp on a tiny table beside the bed.

'I believe Elijah is trying to arrange to send you money, Lord Arthur,' said Billy. 'But in the meantime I have – two sovereigns for you.'

Lord Arthur's face fell. 'That's nothing!' he said but he put out his hand quick for Ma's sovereigns nevertheless. 'I sent Elijah a message asking him to send some. I thought he had sent it with you. That's why I agreed to see you. Where's the money? When's the money coming?'

'I know he's trying to raise a sum,' said Billy. 'He told me himself yesterday. And Elijah is one of the most reliable men I know.'

'Well he should have sent it by now! I cant wait longer!' Lord Arthur picked at the old blanket with the hand that wasn't holding the sovereigns, and sweated, and our three shadows mixed together on the sloping walls as the lamp flickered.

Billy waited for a moment. And then he said, very politely: 'Lord Arthur. What is the Prime Minister to you?'

Lord Arthur wasn't expecting such a question it was clear; he stopped picking at the blanket. 'Where are all my friends?' he said plaintively. 'Why are you people here at all if you haven't brought money?' He was clutching our mother's sovereigns while he spoke. 'Why am I by myself?'

Silence in the small, stuffy, shadowy room. Breathing. My breathing. Billy's breathing. Lord Arthur's strange nervous breathing. Scuffling sounds in corners.

Finally: 'What did Stella say?'

'I have seen them both,' said Billy. 'I went to Clerkenwell, to the House of Detention. Before they were sent for trial at the Old Bailey. They were sent to Newgate Prison at the end.'

Lord Arthur seemed to literally flinch, as if he heard clanging gates. 'I am not going to prison! I would rather die. I have the means!'

'We do not want any of you to be in prison,' said Billy patiently. 'Not you, not Freddie and not Ernest.'

'What did Stella say?'

The trouble with Billy is he's hopeless at lying, even when it is useful. Billy really tried, bless him. 'He – we were wondering where you were, how you were. But – he and Freddie are – in a very distressful position.'

Tears came in Lord Arthur's eyes and then they fell down his cheeks, poor thing, and I remembered Ma and me saying about him how he was 'berserk with love'. I felt in my cloak for a handkerchief, I wanted to throw off my cloak in the stuffy sweating room, open a window, anything.

'Stella broke my heart,' he said.

I leaned towards him, gave him the handkerchief, my strange shadow leaned with me across the sloping ceiling. *I have to open the window.* I moved towards it.

'Why didn't Mr Gladstone stop the trial?' Lord Arthur cried out very loudly, stopping me, now he was clutching the handkerchief that our Ma had embroidered, as well as her sovereigns. 'He is the Prime Minister of England, why didn't he stop it for my sake!' He sounded insane.

I watched Billy's face. He didn't show anything. 'I do not think even the Prime Minister of England has that sort of power, Lord Arthur,' he said, very still.

'Well he *never* helped me anyway, and my father and my grandfather helped *him* and he wasn't even the nobility. His family were just business people, owners of slave plantations in the West Indies, not nobility, like us. Yet my family gave him his first seat in Parliament because he was my father's best friend, my grandfather owned the seat. Thanks to *us* he became Prime Minister of England but when I wrote to him and asked him to help me get a position at Court – that would have solved all my problems and none of this would have happened – he didn't assist me in any way whatsoever!'

By now Lord Arthur's voice was harsh and crying but Billy's was so quiet, calm and gentle, like a little brook going quietly along under trees.

'Was it because he was grateful to your family that he should have helped you?'

Lord Arthur's voice went higher. 'What's a guardian for if he doesn't guard you?'

'*What?*' Yet even in such surprise Billy somehow kept his voice low.

Lord Arthur was silent but only for a moment. 'Well why shouldn't everybody know! He was made one of our guardians, years ago. One of the times our mother ran off. He was legally made one of our guardians, me and my sister and my brothers, my father insisted, in case my mother's family tried to – claim us.'

Silence. Perspiration pouring down Lord Arthur's pale face, Billy's face, my face, and of course I couldn't open the window for his wild shouting words. Moths already in the room were banging against the lamp on the little table now, wanting the light, hurling themselves at death. He picked again at the old blanket.

'Mrs Gladstone was kind. She used to take us to the zoo.'

Silence.

'*And* he's a trustee for the Newcastle Estate, my family's estate. He's not even the nobility – and all he does is withhold our birthright. He never lets any money out, not for anything, and *I need money*! Look at me here! Me: Lord Arthur Clinton, my brother Duke of Newcastle, my old guardian the Prime Minister of England in charge of our noble estate – and yet me in this room in this place with no money, not a penny, and charged with buggery!' The word shocked out.

'There was a legal person spoke for you,' I said, trying to be calm like Billy now, 'at the end of the first trial. I was at the trial, I think his name was Mr Roberts. Maybe Mr Gladstone arranged that.'

Again Lord Arthur was silent for a few moments before he spoke.

'Not Mr Gladstone. There's a lawyer for the Newcastle Estate, Mr Ouvry. Linky – my ridiculous, useless, selfish brother who's now the Duke – is always trying to get him fired because he was our father's lawyer and holds on to the money too and wont give us extra, he says it is to run the estate, and Linky's a gambler and always in debt and says, "Bugger the estate", but – he's – Ouvry's all right. Ouvry would have arranged for Roberts to speak for me. Roberts helped me before, when I was made – when I had some little difficulty. He used to be one of my father's private secretaries in the Parliament years ago – so he knows all the family secrets.' He wiped his face with his spare hand. 'Anyway I'm sure if my actual family were involved at all – which I doubt – they only arranged a solicitor to speak for *them*. To protect *them*, not to help me. I know that. He was there to protect *them*, not me!'

'What do you mean, *them*?' said Billy.

'The Family. The Duke my brother. The Newcastle Estate.' He shrugged in his little bed. 'The Family. Everybody.'

I thought of our little everybody: me and Ma and Billy.

Silence in the hot room again.

'Why did you come to Mudeford?' asked Billy finally.

'Royalty used to come to Mudeford,' said Lord Arthur. 'And the nobility, like us. There's a castle along the shore and beautiful houses. That's where I *should* be.'

Our breathing in the small, unbearable, un-noble room. The mad moths, banging.

'I thought I might get to France. My mother lives in France. There is no such crime as buggery in France.'

'Shall you go?' I asked him.

'How can I go?' he burst out. 'No one will help me! You haven't brought enough money and I haven't got the money to pay someone to take me! The King's Arms wouldn't give me more credit so I end up in this rat-hole! I cant go back to London! I wish I was dead!'

Tears fell down his face again and this time I couldn't help it, I took the handkerchief, the mad way he was clutching at it, and wiped his face, I wished there was some water to make it cooler for him.

'Lord Arthur,' I said, as I wiped at his tears and his perspiration, 'I dont of course have any personal interest in the case – except that Freddie and Ernest kept their clothes at our house and stayed there sometimes, as you know. But I was thinking – and one of the lawyers said this also. The case is about Ernest – about Stella really, isn't it? Not Freddie.'

'What does that mean?'

'Freddie is – different.'

'*Different?*' Lord Arthur started to laugh but it was a very hysterical kind of laugh. 'Fanny is less beautiful, that is all! Fanny is on the town looking for chances every night of every week, Stella or not! Everyone in London knows his arse is as big as the Thames Tunnel, and most of them have been through it!'

I stepped back from the bed as if he had punched me in the stomach. Moths banged at last to their death against the lamp and fell downwards.

'I am going to see Mr Gladstone, Lord Arthur,' said Billy. 'What would you like me to say to him?'

'Tell him he has to help me! Tell him to send money absolutely immediately so that I can go to my mother in France. He loved my mother, she told me so. We laughed about it. His best friend's wife, he used to write her love poetry and then talk to her about God, for God's sake! "He is a hypocrite," she told me, "like all the rest. It's his fault I had to leave your father," she told me.'

'Have you been attended by a doctor, Lord Arthur?' Billy asked him.

'Whatever for? Because I am telling the truth about the man of the people, Mr Gladstone? You needn't think I am delirious! I know of what I speak! You would be ill if you were me! Shut up in this shit-heap with no air! Scared of every footstep! Wondering if

I'm going to be thrown into prison as a debtor or a bugger! That would make anybody ill. If you hadn't mentioned Stella and Elijah you would never have found me because I am in hiding – and you have brought me nothing!'

(But he was holding very tightly to Ma's sovereigns as he struggled up in the bed again.)

'Listen! I will kill myself rather than go to prison – and I have the means to do it – tell them that! Tell them all! Tell Stella! Tell Elijah! And make sure you tell the Prime Minister I will blame him as my mother blames him, and my ghost will haunt him, tell him that!'

His face was now so red and terrible I felt quite frightened for him, I couldn't think what to do, all I really wanted to do was get out of that room, but I tried to calm him, to smooth his arm but he pushed me away violently and clutched the sovereigns to him.

'How dare you touch me!' he said. 'Just because Fanny and Stella kept their gowns in your cheap and nasty little establishment it does not make them your friends – and it certainly does not make *us* intimates!' but his poor face looked really terrible and he sounded delirious.

'We will send a doctor,' said Billy. 'Just in case.'

'Get out! Get out of here!'

'Only a doctor that Johnny Hewlettson suggests. No one else. I promise.'

It seemed most terrible to leave him but in truth I went quick as I could manage down the narrow stairs, I couldn't wait to get out of that awful, unforgettable *boiling* room and the awful, unforgettable words, I left the handkerchief that Ma had once embroidered so beautifully. But Billy went back up the stairs for a moment with a cup of water he got from the little girl, who was still waiting downstairs with another small lamp. I wondered if she'd understood all that mad shouting upstairs. But I couldn't speak. I wanted to get out of the cottage but that seemed even ruder.

Lord Arthur's words about Freddie went round my head: *Fanny is on the town looking for chances every night of every week. Everyone in London knows his arse is as big as the Thames Tunnel, and most of them have been through it.*

Now I know what speech-less means.

Billy came back down the stairs. 'Is Johnny Hewlettson your pa?' he asked the little girl.

'Might be. Might not be.'

'We need to speak to him.'

She shrugged. 'He's out.'

'Is this your house?'

She gave a funny sharp laugh. 'No.'

He squatted down to her level. 'Where's your pa, little girl?' he said gently. 'We really do need to speak to him to help the poor man upstairs.'

She stared at him.

'My name's Billy,' said Billy. 'What's your name, little girl?'

'Marigold.'

'That's a pretty name.' She stared at him a moment longer. 'Follow behind me.'

Oh the relief of air! In the darkness we followed her and her lamp towards the quay and then down to the water and along the stony shore, I stumbled and Billy took my arm. Around us, odd houses were outlined in the night, there were lamps at windows and the strange smell and sound, of the sea.

'Wait,' said Marigold and she walked away; finally her lamp went inside one of the houses.

I couldn't stop shaking as I stood near Billy in the warm night. He must have felt me, he put his arm round me. We looked at the dark water, a little breeze came while we stood there, my hair blew across my eyes, we could hear waves. Lights flickered back along the quay, moving and then disappearing.

'Perhaps that's the smugglers,' said Billy. 'Maybe that old fisherman Mackie is there, smuggling away.'

'Do you think it's true? What Lord Arthur said about Freddie?'

Billy didn't answer for a few moments. Then he said, 'Lord Arthur is frightened and he seems – hysterical.' That didn't help the words in my head. 'It's a different world from ours, Mattie.'

Just then we heard a door, then the light of a pipe came towards us, we could smell the tobacco on the air.

'Give me a sovereign, Mattie.'

I gave it to him, quickly feeling for the money in my cloak pocket.

The outline of Johnny Hewlettson moved towards us in the dark.

'Well,' he said.

'He's very frightened,' said Billy. 'We dont – know him very well but he seems in such a state he could do anything. Maybe it would be a good idea to have a doctor, just in case.'

'He's a nuisance,' said Johnny Hewlettson. 'He owes money all over the county as well as all over London. He hasn't got money for a doctor – and what can a doctor do for someone who's scared?'

Billy handed the sovereign to Johnny Hewlettson with another half-sovereign.

'For a doctor you trust maybe? And some food maybe?'

The sea shushed on the gravelly sand and my thoughts mixed with the sound: *most of Ma's precious sovereigns left in Mudeford, to help Lord Arthur Clinton.* I wondered what she'd think of that. How odd it all was.

Johnny Hewlettson looked down at the money in the darkness. 'We're not exactly savages down here, boy. My wife made him food last night and twice today. He wouldn't eat it.' He turned towards the houses, holding Ma's money in his hand, and then he stopped and turned back to us. 'I see you mean well, lad, and the only people who've come anywhere near him.' Tobacco drifted across to us. 'We dont have any doctors in Mudeford. I'll get a good doctor in Bournemouth that's known to us, not any of those elegant-refined Christchurch ones. I'll get Robbie Thompson with your money. We dont want him cutting his own throat or dying of fright on us just because nobody else will take him in. But tell his family he needs proper help,' and then he left us, there on the shore. He threw the last words back over his shoulder, 'Not to leave him with strangers like a rat in a corner.'

We walked back to the road, along to the inn. Billy took my arm in his again and, unusual for him, put his hand over mine just for a moment.

'You got the information you needed, Billy, didn't you?' I said.

'I think I did.'

'But – Lord Arthur's too old to have a guardian.'

'He is now,' said Billy. 'But he wasn't once. I dont expect people like us are supposed to know that story. I think it would be – bad for Mr Gladstone if they said in the trial of the Men in Petticoats that he was Lord Arthur's guardian and a trustee of his family's estate. It makes him like a – much too close a connection to the trial.'

'Are you going to – blackmail him, Billy?'

Billy laughed. 'That's in novels, Mattie! I dont think Mr Gladstone could be blackmailed by anyone, he's the sort who would call a constable if he had to because he thinks he is in the right and to hell with what the world thinks. That's different from just keeping his connection very quiet. But – I just feel he's an honourable man and – that I could explain to him.' And he sighed in the night. 'We need my job, Mattie. And I love working there.

I'm glad I know the truth now. I hope I can just see him and say to him that I was caught up just like he was, only I lost my position and he didn't.'

He still held my arm and I sort of squeezed it, so he'd know I understood. We walked in silence for a while, you could hear our footsteps and the sea further away, that's all, it was all so quiet and not like London.

'Do you think Lord Arthur is sick, Billy? Or just frightened?'

'I dont know,' said Billy. 'Frightened I think. Hysterical and wild and frightened.'

'Will that man get a doctor?'

'I believe he will. They wont want the risk of him ill in Mudeford and police snooping about.' And I saw that Billy shook his head in the dark. 'Looks like a smuggler has to take charge if nobody else will.'

'But – Lord Arthur wouldn't *really* kill himself, would he?'

'I dont know,' said Billy.

Again we walked in silence.

'I know I've been very foolish,' I said at last. 'It was because Freddie was so kind. Other people must make up dreams besides me.'

And now Billy gave a small nudge to my arm hooked in his, just like I had, as if to say, *I understand.*

After that we didn't speak again. And we didn't pass a single person, just me and my brother, walking along the dark Mudeford Road. We could see lights, warm and welcoming as we approached the inn. I didn't want to talk to anybody, not even Billy who wanted an ale. I said goodnight to him and went to our room. Someone had left a lamp on, turned low, as if someone was waiting for me to give me a hug. But not really of course.

26

Before dawn next morning two figures walked along the Mudeford Road towards Christchurch. The young woman walked with a limp, the man kept her pace and carried their bag.

This day was a Thursday.

At first only the sound of their footsteps on the hard dirt road. Then the first notes of morning birds, singing as they sensed the first light before the walkers did. The grey light in the sky grew brighter. They heard horse's hooves far behind them, pounding nearer and then slowing. It was Mackie the fisherman, travelling towards Christchurch in the growing light with a large number of mysterious bundles attached to his horse. They could smell fish.

'Room for you, Miss Mattie,' he said. 'I'll drop you at the Old George and you can wait for your brother there.'

The girl got up behind the rider with the help of her brother, and took the bag. The brother waved to them as they trotted off into the light. The girl looked back several times and saw the stoic figure getting smaller and smaller.

'Did you find who you were looking for?' asked Mackie. She felt his voice rumbling in his back as she held on to him once more.

'Yes,' she said shortly.

She supposed the whole of Mudeford knew their business by now. But he did not ask her anything else, and she did not ask him about the bundles tied to the horse. He talked occasionally, about the sea. Almost she fell asleep against his warm, rumbling back.

Billy, walking, was almost at Christchurch when a small horse and trap passed him, going in the opposite direction: the doctor got from Bournemouth. Paid for by Mrs Stacey's sovereigns.

But Billy did not know this that morning, as he raised his hand in greeting, the way people always did on empty roads, still so early.

27

Nor did Billy Stacey know that, later that same Thursday, even before he and Mattie got back to London, a telegram regarding Lord Arthur Clinton arrived to Mr Frederick Ouvry, solicitor for the Newcastle Estate. It was marked EXTREMELY PRIVATE, was signed J. HEWLETTSON, ESQ. and it, also, was paid for by Mrs Isabella Stacey's sovereigns.

The telegram advised Mr Ouvry that Lord Arthur Clinton was ill, under an assumed name at a certain address in a small fishing village called Mudeford, near Christchurch, where money should be sent to J. Hewlettson, Esq. at once. After a most urgent conversation with Lord Edward Clinton, the only sensible Clinton brother (this was Mr Ouvry's opinion, and indeed most people's), Mr Ouvry made some hasty arrangements.

He instructed the solicitor Mr W. H. Roberts, who had already appeared in the Magistrates' Court on behalf of the absent Lord Arthur Clinton, to immediately depart for this place mentioned: Mudeford. He instructed him further to find J. Hewlettson, Esq., and therefore, presumably, Lord Arthur Clinton, urgently. He must travel overnight.

Mr W. H. Roberts departed London at once. Mr Frederick Ouvry provided funds out of his own pocket for this to be done, otherwise the matter would have had to be discussed at great length with the Trustees of the Newcastle Estate.

Very little is secret in certain circles. Several gentlemen, hearing rumours, met quickly with others in private rooms, sitting nervously on leather sofas. Muttered private conversations were held; finally before nightfall several gentlemen also departed hurriedly from London.

All had arrived in Christchurch by Friday morning.

On Saturday morning a second telegram arrived for Mr Frederick Ouvry, marked EXTREMELY PRIVATE. It was signed W. H. ROBERTS.

Soon afterwards a hand-delivered letter, marked EXTREMELY PRIVATE, arrived for the Prime Minister of Great Britain at his home. Mr Gladstone, just leaving for a Saturday-afternoon cabinet meeting, recognised the handwriting of Mr Frederick Ouvry; he opened the letter slightly awkwardly, holding his hat in his hand also.

66 Lincolns Inn Fields
London, W. C.
18 June 1870

My Dear Sir

Lord Arthur Clinton is dead. At an obscure cottage in Hampshire under an assumed name.

He has succumbed to an attack of scarlet fever.

I have seen Lord Edward, and hope to see the Duke tonight on his arrival from Paris.

Believe me,
Your obliged and faithful servant,
Frederick Ouvry

Mr Gladstone read the contents again and then stood, very still, half in and half out of the doorway in Carlton House Terrace, staring at the paper. Mrs Gladstone was away. Mr Gladstone did not see the figure of the departing messenger at the corner of the square; he did not hear the hooves of a passing horse in the terrace. He folded the letter and bowed his bare head in the warm sunshine: perhaps in thought; perhaps in prayer.

The cabinet meeting that Saturday afternoon lasted two and three quarter hours. Greece was discussed, and the colonies, and the Irish Land Bill.

28

Of course news travels.

However, although on the following day, a Sunday, certain vague rumours swirled about the upper echelons of noble society, the rumours did not, in this case, reach the *Reynolds Newspaper* in time for publication, nor 13 Wakefield-street, nor Isabella Stacey (provider of some of the finance involved), who usually knew everything. So Billy did not know the latest developments either, when very early on Monday morning he left home in his best suit and his silk top hat, picked up a copy of *The Times* as usual, and then walked briskly to the Houses of Parliament as if he still worked there.

He had made a decision. He would not leave the building until he had had a conversation with the Prime Minister. All he wanted was his position back; he did not want to share his information with another person, he only wanted the Prime Minister to see that they had both been caught up in a situation not of their making, and that Billy, too, should still be able to work in the place he loved so much. He believed Mr Gladstone would see the honour in this. As he had now been dismissed from the Houses of Parliament he knew he would require the assistance of Elijah Fortune, and was confident it would be given.

However, when he reached the Central Lobby of the Parliament Elijah Fortune was not there; a large man in uniform loomed.

'Yes, sir?'

'Where's Elijah?'

'Mr Fortune no longer works in this place.'

Billy could hardly believe his ears. 'Is he *dead*?'

'He is dismissed.'

Billy looked around the Central Lobby in dismay. He saw two messengers he knew, huddling and laughing together beside carved kings and queens and a few saints: marble folds and upraised eyes. He approached them.

'Where's Elijah?'

'Your sort and his sort aren't welcome here no more!'

'What d'you mean, *my sort*?'

'You finger-twirlers!'

'What?'

'You ponces! You filthy buggers!'

'*Listen, you pigs!*' Billy grabbed the jacketed arms of one of his erstwhile colleagues and lifted him off the marble-tiled floor. '*Where's Elijah?*'

'Oy!' yelled the clerk in alarm.

'Oy!' shouted the new man in uniform.

And Mr William Stacey, who had worked in and loved this illustrious building since he was thirteen, found himself being ejected by three men – not without much protestation – out of the Central Lobby, down past Westminster Hall, and out on to the street, his beautiful silk hat and his copy of *The Times* lost in the mêlée.

Mr John Jenkins, Head Clerk, was to be seen remonstrating with the new uniformed man. He came quickly to the door of the Houses of Parliament, carrying Billy's unopened but somewhat trampled-upon copy of *The Times*, and called out loudly to the disappearing figure. Billy turned and walked slowly back again.

'Where's Elijah?'

Mr Jenkins handed him his newspaper. 'It was decided it was not in the best interests to have him as the public face of the estimable House.' And then the Head Clerk relented. 'It was discovered that he was trying to gather together some money for Lord Arthur. He was straightway dismissed.'

'But he lived here as well! He's been here for a lifetime! And his wife – she can hardly walk! What will happen to them? Have they been evicted from their home?'

'I'm sorry, Mr Stacey.' Spiced pomade wafted out into the morning. 'I am sorry about everything. That same hypocrite bishop was here in a flash when he heard Elijah was involved. The bishops in the House of Lords are a powerful force in this building; there is rather a large number of them, I'm afraid.' Mr Jenkins tapped Billy's unread copy of *The Times*. 'Hounded,' he said.

'What?'

'Read.' Again Mr Jenkins tapped *The Times*. 'Hounded. In my opinion.'

Then the Head Clerk turned back through the big doors and was swallowed.

Billy stared at the entrance he knew so well and then at the newspaper in his hands.

He did not open it at once; some intimation drifted.

He walked round the Houses of Parliament as Big Ben struck eight. Morning activity bustled and jostled past him: carriages, people, carts; there was the usual smell of horses and shit and humans and coal and fish and ale and fresh bread and factories. And, now, his own dread.

He walked away from the Parliament along the Thames, not seeing the coal barges and the small steam boats and the ferries that crowded the river. He was always so careful of his suit that he wore to the Palace of Westminster. Today he finally sat down in that best suit on a grimy, mouldy concrete step leading down to the water. He opened *The Times*. He could not find anything at all at first; it did not occur to him to look at the letters page. At last he saw the two letters. The smell of piss steamed up from the steps as the summer sun rose while he read. By the time he had finished both the letters, he was bathed in perspiration.

He then walked home to Wakefield-street, his precious suit filthy, to read what he had found to his mother and his sister.

Sir,
In confirming the announcement of the death of my unfortunate client Lord Arthur Pelham Clinton, I beg you will allow me space in your journal to enable me to carry out his last wishes in reference to the charges preferred against him, the awful nature of which in no slight degree hastened his end.

'He's dead?' cried Mattie in horror and disbelief.

It was on Friday morning that I was informed by telegram from his medical attendants—

'We only left on Thursday!' said Mattie. 'He didn't have any medical attendants, he means a smuggler!'

—by telegram from his medical attendants of his critical state, when I immediately proceeded to Christchurch, where he had been staying for some time past, and remained there—

'No, he didn't remain there!' said Mattie. 'That's a lie!'

> *—until his death, which occurred on Saturday morning at 1.05 from exhaustion resulting from scarlet fever.*

'Saturday morning!' said Mattie.

'*Scarlet fever!*' Isabella's voice was suddenly shrill with fear as she looked at her two children.

'Maybe,' said Billy. His voice was dry, expressionless.

But Mattie felt her heart beat faster, saw the hot, stuffy room and the moths banging against the lamp. 'He killed himself didn't he Billy.' It was a statement not a question. 'He said he would.'

> *In pursuance of his instructions, I had previously prepared, and he had approved, the letter of which I enclose you a copy, and which I beg you will, in justice to his memory, insert with this. His state however of utter prostration did not permit him to sign the copies which were made, although in full possession of his mental faculties.*

Billy stopped reading for a moment. 'That's convenient for friends and family.'

> *It may be satisfactory to his relatives and friends to know that, in the presence of Dr Wade and myself he, when conscious of his approaching end, in a most earnest manner reiterated his denial of any complicity whatsoever in the wretched case and alleged conspiracy, and his entire innocence of the graver charges imputed to him.*
>
> *I am, sir, yr obedient servant,*
>
> *W. H. Roberts*

'There's that W. H. Roberts person again,' said Mattie. She thought of the hysterical words, only a few days ago: *They don't care about me, it is for the Family, it is only for the Family!* 'And Johnny Hewlettson said he'd get a good doctor called Robbie Thompson and no elegant-refined doctor from Christchurch, that's what he said. Who's Dr Wade?'

'Lord Arthur's own letter – or perhaps his purported own letter – is directly underneath,' said Billy in the same expressionless tone. 'It is even headed MEN IN WOMEN'S ATTIRE so that nobody will miss it.'

To the Editor of The Times

Sir,
In the extraordinary position I find myself placed, and from the peculiar course adopted by the Crown in this matter, I feel justified in asking for the insertion of a letter in your journal.

I am now, as I hitherto have been, anxious to give the most unequivocal denial to the accusations which have been made against me and I most earnestly beg the public to suspend its judgement until the full investigation of a public trial has cleared away and explained the circumstances of suspicion alleged against me.

'Lord Arthur wrote this?' said Mattie, disbelief all over her face.

I pledge myself to surrender to trial at the Central Criminal Court on the day appointed as I am desirous of courting the fullest possible inquiry, being conscious that the greater the light which can be thrown upon this unfortunate case the clearer will be my exculpation.

'Poor sad thing,' said Mattie despite herself, despite what he had said about Freddie; she kept seeing Lord Arthur in her head, in the tiny, airless room, clutching the embroidered handkerchief and their mother's money, shouting and crying. 'It's not what he said to us at all, Billy, he didn't talk about any letter, he doesn't even talk like that.'

'No,' said Billy. 'It's not what he said to us at all, he said he wanted to get to France. I doubt very much that this letter was in the "pursuance of his instructions".'

I am now, and have been for sometime past, prostrate on a bed of sickness, or I would before this have surrendered to the warrant and submitted myself to the authority of the Court.

I have instructed my solicitor to retain services of counsel to represent me in my trial—

'Who's paying for that?' said Mrs Stacey, but the other words kept echoing in her head *scarlet fever scarlet fever* and she looked at them both to see if they were pale, or flushed. She thought her son looked feverish as he read.

—when I shall clearly and honestly show that nothing can be laid to my charge other than the foolish continuance of the impersonation of theatrical characters, which arose from a simple frolic in which I permitted myself to become an actor.

It would ill become me to animadvert upon the course—

Mattie stopped her brother again. 'What does *animadvert* mean?' she said.

'Criticise,' he said.

'How much longer does this go on?' asked Mrs Stacey. 'They said *scarlet fever*! Billy! You're all hot-faced and your eyes are glittery. Are you all right?'

Billy ignored the question and went on reading.

It would ill become me to animadvert upon the course the prosecution has deemed fit to pursue in silencing, by including in the indictment, those who could otherwise throw light upon this case; that I leave to my counsel and advisors on the fitting occasion, and to the common sense of the community, whose calmer judgement cannot possibly exert itself until the mists of prejudice, naturally excited by the enormity of the offence charged against me, shall have been dispelled by the full light of a free and impartial trial.

I am, sir, your obedient servant

——

June 1870

At last Billy put down the newspaper. 'No signature, just a blank.'

'That's just all blooming lies,' said Mattie. 'And he didn't talk anything like that, he was talking about how he loved Ernest and escaping to France with money that was supposed to arrive from your friend Elijah! He killed himself didn't he, Billy? This is done for the family, like he told us, this is them covering everything up.'

'*Never mind all this!*' Fear made Isabella shout at them wildly. 'Could you two have caught scarlet fever from him? You don't look quite right, Billy, and Mattie, you're all hot.' She was literally unable to stop herself feeling their foreheads as if they were children.

'Poor beggar,' said Billy. 'It might have been scarlet fever. Or – it might have been his own choice. And I suppose we'll never know.' He stared down at the letters page. 'My God, they got these two letters out so damn quick, didn't they? We only left on Thursday. It says he died early on Saturday morning. And now it's Monday and here are these masterful letters already published. Very speedy.'

They were in the basement kitchen; he suddenly got up as if he could not stay still any longer. His eyes were certainly glittering and he hadn't yet told them his news.

'Well, well, well. And my position as a clerk in the Houses of Parliament is definitely terminated for good. Elijah's gone as well.'

'*What?*' His mother stared; perhaps she hadn't heard, or perhaps she couldn't believe it, or perhaps she was only thinking of scarlet fever.

At last Billy shouted, 'Elijah's dismissed as well! I can't get back into Parliament to do what I want to do without him to assist me. I went there early this morning to talk to Mr Gladstone – including to give him a message from Lord Arthur – and I've just been thrown out on to the street by a new man in a uniform just like Elijah's!'

And then he caught himself and spoke more quietly.

'Of course they always win, don't they, Ma, one way or another! Lord Arthur could have said in the witness box at the trial all the things he told us at Mudeford, I suppose, and that would have caused an uproar. I wonder what Mr Gladstone is thinking, right now, on this fine June morning.'

Mattie said: 'Surely he's sad. I expect he remembers him when he was a little boy, when his mother ran away.'

'Oh for goodness sake, Mattie!' yelled Mrs Stacey. She stared at her son. 'They actually *threw you out the door*, Billy?'

He nodded.

'Ye gods, ye gods, ye gods! Will this never end!' She ran her hands through her hair. 'Listen to me, both of you! *Listen*! Mr Gladstone probably gave up Lord Arthur long ago as a feckless liability! Mr Gladstone is the Prime Minister of Great Britain and the British Empire, for God's sake, there are wars, there is Ireland, there is the world: how can this matter very much? That business with his old friend the Duke of Newcastle was long ago! Lord Arthur was a sad specimen – Ernest only cared about his title, oh – blooming damn, what a mess these boys have got us into, and now scarlet fever! And what d'you mean, Elijah's dismissed? What about his little home down there you told of? What about his Dodo, you said her arthritis is terrible now! Where would they go? And *do you feel sick*, Billy? Answer me properly. You're all hot.'

'I don't know where Elijah is,' said Billy, slow and calm again. 'All I know is he's fired too because he was trying to raise money for Lord Arthur.' He looked down again for one more moment at *The Times*. 'Do you know what I think, Ma? I think the case might just fade away now in some legally suitable way.'

'Because he's dead?'

'Nobody knew who Ernest and Freddie were before this. They're not important any more. It simply won't be as interesting to many of the interested people – or as dangerous – now that the most noble of all its participants can no longer appear.'

'And it's certainly not bloody interesting to me!' shouted his mother. Then she suddenly pulled herself together. 'Billy, I don't give a thruppeny damn about this case any more! Answer me! *Do you feel all right?*'

'It's hot, Ma, that's all,' said Billy. 'And since you keep asking me, no, I don't feel all right. Not because I'm ill but because I *always* believed I'd get my job back but I've just been thrown out of the Parliament. And for the very first time I don't believe any longer that I'll get back inside.'

He went towards the stairs that led upwards from the basement kitchen but turned back for a moment.

'Maybe of course – just maybe – whoever came from London rammed his own suicide medicine that he told us about down his throat to make bloody sure he wouldn't cause any more trouble.'

They heard his footsteps: up the stairs and out of the house. They heard the front door bang in the hot muggy morning.

❦

Hot, muggy June days indeed that year. In Mudeford, Lord Arthur Clinton's body lay unclaimed with Mr W. H. Roberts leaving so hurriedly again for London. The Newcastle family had not sent any message to Mudeford regarding the body's removal to the family vault, or elsewhere.

Johnny Hewlettson and Mackie shook their heads over the ways of the mighty. On the third day after the death, while Lord Arthur's posthumous epistle so quickly published in *The Times* was being pored over by interested persons in London, in Mudeford there was, nevertheless, still no money sent nor even instructions given for any sort of burial. But Lord Arthur's facial features had changed, stiffened; in the very hot weather he had also begun to smell slightly in the tiny cottage.

Mackie the fisherman helped the local carpenter to build a casket.

Johnny Hewlettson, Esq. sent one more telegram to the lawyer, Mr Frederick Ouvry. One more time Mr Ouvry reached into his own pocket and on the fifth day dispatched the sum of one pound seventeen shillings and sixpence to the Christchurch Cemetery (in the name of the Duke of Newcastle), to secure a plot for the Duke's brother, Lord Arthur Pelham Clinton.

On the sixth day Johnny Hewlettson and Mackie accompanied the body from Mudeford because even busy smugglers and busy fishermen couldn't think that a man should be buried alone. Marigold, the little girl, had laid her own shawl over the coffin before it left, because it looked lonely.

When they got to Christchurch Cemetery the curate was waiting.

Three gentlemen in top hats emerged from a parked cabriolet as the coffin arrived in a cart. One of them was the solicitor who had been to Mudeford, Mr W. H. Roberts; they all smelled strongly of brandy.

The gentlemen stayed for about fifteen minutes as the coffin was lowered into the newly dug – and consecrated – ground and the curate said a few brief words about God. Mr W. H. Roberts had nodded briefly to Johnny Hewlettson and Mackie; the other two gentlemen, who had not spoken nor introduced themselves nor asked questions nor thanked anybody, disappeared back into the waiting cab and were driven towards the railway station.

Before they too disappeared, towards the Old George Inn, Johnny Hewlettson and Mackie stood a moment longer beside the unmarked plot behind the small stone chapel. The curate informed them with a slightly disbelieving look on his face that the two unknown gentlemen had said they were the Duke of Newcastle and his uncle.

'Grieving, loving, noble family, aren't they?' said Johnny Hewlettson, smuggler.

29

The rumours flew about London: that Lord Arthur Clinton had been seen in Paris; that he had been hounded to death and had committed suicide; that he had been got aboard a ship for the Antipodes; that he had been seen, inebriated and dressed in women's clothing, dancing at the Alhambra Music Hall in Leicester Square, laughing.

The *Reynolds Newspaper* pronounced:

A MIS-SPENT LIFE

Lord Arthur Clinton is said to be dead and we most sincerely hope that such is the case. This depraved and dissolute young nobleman seems to have been the presiding genius of the clique to which Boulton and Park belonged.

'If there was any presiding genius,' said Mattie slowly, 'I think it was Ernest.' She thought of Lord Arthur Clinton, crying in the small, hot room.

Isabella Stacey – despite her dislike and suspicion of members of the medical profession (no doctor had been called to Wakefield-street since one had told Mattie to *pull herself together* after Jamey's death) – on seeing her beloved son still sometimes pale, still sometimes feverish, finally sent Mattie, who was obviously not feverish, with a message to fetch one. When he arrived, Mattie, hovering, heard her mother mention the dreaded words *scarlet fever.* The doctor asked Billy if he had a sore throat.

'No,' said Billy. 'Not at all.'

'Do you feel nauseous?'

'No,' said Billy. 'Not at all.'

'Your mother seems to fear scarlet fever. Why would she do that? There isn't any more around London than is usual at this time of the year. Have you been in contact with someone who has had scarlet fever?'

'I don't believe I have,' said Billy.

'Half a guinea,' said the doctor, 'and drink warm liquids.'

'*Half a guinea?*' said Mrs Stacey.

'In case of scarlet fever,' said the doctor.

❦

The workload of Mr William Gladstone was always heavy.

He wrote to, and attended meetings with, many and varied people. He spoke in the House about the teaching of religion with regard to the Education Act; he spoke in the House about the removal of British troops from New Zealand and the loan that country had requested; he debated further intricacies of the Irish Land Act. He sat long hours in the House of Commons as was his custom. He made speeches in all sorts of places. He dealt with the difficult Queen as best as he was able. He continued his Rescue Work (as he called it) in the streets around the Strand. He saw regularly the once-notorious, newly religious lady who was not his mistress (perhaps regarding these emotionally-charged meetings as Rescue Work also). He had dinner with friends. He wrote to his wife who was away on one of her family visits.

But when the letters from Mr W. H. Roberts and Lord Arthur Clinton appeared in those many newspapers including *The Times*, and when the swirling rumours became more and more damaging, he had lain awake long into the hot nights, fearing another bout of illness. Finally he had met with several people early one morning, in Carlton House Gardens.

And then Mr Gladstone wrote a short note to the Editor of *The Times*.

Will you do me the favour to come to my room at the House of Commons this afternoon at 4.30 and to send me word of your arrival? I make the proposal in conformity with your permission, and name the hour, because I hope it may suit your convenience with reference to the House of Lords.

A message was duly delivered to Mr Gladstone as he sat in the House of Commons. He bowed to the Speaker as he left the chamber temporarily. His offices were just along the corridor; his visitor was waiting; the Editor of *The Times* and the Prime Minister of Great Britain shook hands briefly and disappeared alone into the private office.

A further column regarding Lord Arthur Clinton appeared in *The Times* soon thereafter.

Billy Stacey, no work to go to, sat in the hot kitchen, read from *The Times* to his mother and his sister.

We are in a position to give a trustworthy account of Lord Arthur Clinton's fatal illness. He was staying at the King's Arms Hotel in Christchurch when on Monday 13th inst. Mr Wade, in the unavoidable absence of Mr Fitzmorris, was called to see him. He found him suffering from sore throat and other symptoms of scarlet fever, which has been widely prevalent in the area. Lodgings in the village were found for him to which he was safely removed.

'What? He was already dying of scarlet fever before he left Christchurch?' said Mattie scornfully. 'No he wasn't. He wasn't "safely removed", he was jumping into a cab on his way to this village the next day and talking about money he was expecting. We saw him, Billy! And who *is* this Mr Wade? he's the one Mr Roberts said witnessed Lord Arthur's last letter. Billy, I bet he was one of those fellows in the dark behind the King's Arms!'

She looked across the kitchen at her brother. It was so strange to have Billy at home reading to them in the daytime while they worked. Clean sheets, washed yesterday in a huge bucket then wrung out by hand, had been hung to dry over the oven; now the heat of the day had finished drying them in the small backyard and Billy had carried them all back inside. In the kitchen the women stood apart, pulling and stretching the sides of the sheets; they moved towards each other, as in a stately dance, to fold them and refold them, as they listened to Billy.

The disease, though virulent, ran a normal course—

'See! Virulent! While you two were sitting there with him!'

'—and appeared to be gaining ground up to the morning of Thursday 16th – when ischuria supervened.

'That's when we left, Billy! We left Mudeford on Thursday morning – and he was dead by Saturday! He was *frightened*, but that's not the same as scarlet fever! And what's that thing? That *ischuria*?'

'I don't know,' said Billy, frowning over the newspaper.

'It's the flow stopping,' said Mrs Stacey.

'The flow of what?'

'Your water!'

'Oh God, it's hot!' muttered Billy.

'Are you sure you're not sick, Billy? You're still not yourself!'

'Ma,' said Billy. 'Will you please stop asking me that. I am not sick. I have seen a doctor. I have not got any of the symptoms of scarlet fever. And despite what it says in the newspaper about scarlet fever, Lord Arthur told us he was in Mudeford because the King's Arms in Christchurch wouldn't give him more credit. It's very hot but I am not sick, it's just that I'm not used to being at home without work. And where's Elijah? He's lost his home as well as his work and his wife can hardly walk and I've tried all morning but I can't find out where he is.'

He breathed deeply. Then he went on reading in a monotone.

> *Dr R. Thompson was quickly in attendance from Bournemouth—*

'Aha! Well, we know that bit's true,' said Mattie, '*that*'s the name of the doctor Johnny Hewlettson said he'd call – with your money, Ma!'

> *—and by evening renal function was restored. The patient, however, had sunk very low, and, in spite of the free administration of stimulants, failed to rally. Telegrams were immediately dispatched to his friends and on Friday morning Mr W. H. Roberts, his solicitor, arrived.*

'Ask for a friend, receive a solicitor,' he commented mildly as he read.

After a short interview, he declared, in the presence of Mr Wade—

'There's that Mr Wade again,' said Mattie. 'He keeps popping up.'

—he declared in the presence of Mr Wade and Mr Roberts, that the letter drawn up and since published by the latter was in every respect true. He was too exhausted to add his signature, but his mind was quite clear enough to apprehend its full meaning. He was seen again in the evening by Dr Robert Thompson, and at five minutes past one on Saturday morning he died in the presence of his medical attendant, the landlady, and Mr Newlyn Jnr of the King's Arms Hotel.

'A medical attendant and a landlady and Mr Newlyn Junior of the King's Arms, all in that hot little room in Mudeford?' interrupted Mattie again. 'And if he *was* dying where were Mr Roberts and this Mr Wade person? In a cupboard? They should've been with him!'

'This article,' said Billy, 'is published in *The Times*, and signed by *The Lancet*, very official and reliable. Someone has arranged for this article to be printed – to stop all the gossip.' He looked at his mother. 'And Mattie and I know it's a truer version at least, whether there was scarlet fever or not.'

'Billy, stop all this, please,' said Mrs Stacey. 'This is ridiculous.'

'However,' Billy continued, speaking in the same mild manner, 'I notice this Mr Wade was called a doctor in Mr W. H. Roberts's earlier letter – and asked for a medical opinion – but appearing in *The Lancet* report he seems to have lost his title.

The only real doctor we can be sure existed is this Dr Robert Thompson from Bournemouth – the one you paid for, Ma! And as he was a connection of the smugglers he's probably used to discreet consultations. But I bet they wrote the letter that's supposed to be from Lord Arthur *after* he died anyway, however he died. Poor beggar.'

'You read out just now that they sent a telegram to all his friends,' said Mattie. 'If that's true why didn't anybody at all come except a solicitor?' and she pulled fiercely at a sheet. 'And there *wasn't* any landlady, or medical attendant—'

'Yes, there was, Mattie,' said Billy. 'There was that little girl, Marigold, being both. And if the man from the King's Arms was there he was probably looking for his bills to be paid!'

'But surely *someone* would have come from his family to be with him when they heard? Or one friend? Just one! Not just a *solicitor*!'

'Perhaps that Mr Wade was really a friend, Mattie,' said her mother, 'perhaps there was someone else there too, but they don't want to say any names. It's too dangerous to be a friend or relation of Lord Arthur Clinton at the moment, I'm blooming glad nobody knows you two were there!'

The sheets were now stretched and folded. Mattie leaned against the table and said casually, 'Do you think – do you think Freddie and Ernest know he's dead?' A Plan was formulating.

'Course newspapers make their way into Newgate, Mattie,' said her mother. 'They'll know all right.'

Billy stood up and threw *The Times* in a corner. 'I'm going out for a walk,' he said quickly and once again they heard his footsteps going upwards and the front door bang. Since he'd been fired, he often just disappeared. They presumed he was walking the streets.

'Billy must *not* feel we cannot manage.'

'I can make more hats, Ma.'

Isabella Stacey was talking to herself as much as to her daughter. 'We'll manage. We'll find other lodgers somehow. I'll take in sewing. We'll manage.'

'Billy's always just – vanishing,' said Mattie crossly. 'I hope he comes back soon, I wanted to talk to him very important, and he's always rushing about!'

And then she suddenly dived into the pot cupboard; pots of all sizes immediately appeared on the kitchen floor in disarray, as if a burglar was searching the cupboard for treasure. Then she scrubbed the cupboard walls with a brush. Mrs Stacey, thumping the folded sheets with the iron which had been heating on the stove, watched her daughter carefully. Neither of them spoke further.

The basement kitchen got hotter and stuffy even though the door to the small, dark backyard was open. There, three stray cats lay stretched out in the shade.

After a time Billy returned. He looked calmer, cooler, not like someone with scarlet fever, and he was carrying a very battered top hat.

'I've got work.'

'*What?*'

'*Have* you, Billy? Already?'

He handed them an advertisement.

Clerk and hearse-follower required.
Must have excellent handwriting
Grave mien and good manners.

INQUIRE WITHIN.

'It's a funeral parlour along Tottenham Court Road,' he said. 'I saw the advertisement in the window, and I had in my pocket my reference from the Parliament that the Head Clerk gave to me. And I put on my gravest mien and was offered exactly half of the salary I was earning at the Parliament. Will you refine this hat for me, Mattie? Mine was lost when they threw me out. I picked up this old one from the market for you to improve upon because I start on Monday.'

Mattie answered calmly, 'I'll start it tonight if you come to Newgate Prison with me now, this afternoon.'

Her brother and her mother stared at her.

'I think we should tell Freddie and Ernest we saw Lord Arthur in Mudeford before he died. They were his friends once and we're the only people who can tell them we at least went to see him, and talked to him about them, and gave him some money and arranged for a doctor.' The other two remained silent. 'It's not just to see Freddie any more. I know I was lonely, I know I made his friendship bigger than it was. But I will always remember him for his kindness. And I think we should do this.'

Mrs Stacey stirred something on the stove, regarded her children. She knew Mattie so well, but she must be allowed to manage her heart in her own way.

'Perhaps she's right, Billy. It would be respectful of a death and there doesn't seem to have been much respect around.' She suddenly banged at the stove. 'But that's the end of it, do you hear me, both of you? No more talk of murder or suicide or "Mr Wade" or anybody else. And I'm very glad and proud of you, Billy, that you've found work so soon, even if it isn't really what you want – it'll do for just now till this blooming business fades away and I love you, do you hear me? Both of you! You are a brave, true, loyal girl, Mattie. And I'll make a jacket with those long tails for you, Billy, like they wear at funerals. I'll start it while you're gone.'

When Billy laughed he looked like Joe Stacey, stage carpenter and visionary of real stage doors. 'For bribes of a top hat *and* a new jacket,' said Billy, 'I'll go to Newgate Prison.'

30

UGH! WHEN WE got to the corner of Newgate Street – ugh, honestly, it's this ugly horrible ghastly stinking filthy place, the prison is, grim gates and walls and a sewer near by – or probably the sewer's actually inside – I reckon it must be, from the stink there. And all the dirt and all the damp seeping out of the wet walls and something like pain coming right out at you through the bricks and concrete, they've just started to do hangings inside there now instead of out in the street. Billy told me they used to hang sodomites at Tyburn and people threw stones at them and spat. They used to put them in the stocks too – and throw stones and spit at them there too – why do people *spit* at them? I saw those ugly spitting faces outside the Magistrates' Court.

Just as we got to the big horrible entrance a carriage drew up with two fine gentlemen in it, they brushed past us, very important and high-hatted and high-tone with some official-looking papers under their arms. We were all in the entrance at the same time so I heard them with their barking voices: 'Mr Frederick Park,' and they gave their names in confidential tones – I couldn't hear that bit though I tried. The gaoler bowed and went away and then he came back and opened a big iron gate with a big clanging noise and the gentlemen disappeared through an arch and an iron door – and you know what? even those two fine gentlemen had the clanging door locked behind them and the keys turned! We heard footsteps echoing away down a long dark corridor and a loud voice barked back: '*What an odour!*'

'They must be their lawyers,' said Billy. 'Arranging things. Wonder who's paying?'

We told one of the prison officers we would wait till they came back, they took blooming ages, we listened to the noises of the prison, there was shouting coming from all different parts and lots of banging and clanging. We stood outside, occasionally we spoke quiet to each other, leaning against the damp stinking walls – imagine being here, locked up, imagine even working here.

Sometimes I took little looks at Billy, he was pale still but much more himself somehow. I gave him a hug because I felt sort of happy to see him not looking like scarlet fever was eating him, dear old Billy, he smiled. The afternoon had got used up with walking and waiting: the light was going now, I watched strange red sun-lines stretched out across the darkening sky and I wondered if Freddie and Ernest could see them too, down in the cells and it made me shiver to think of them, no sky I expect, either dark or light.

At last the gentlemen came back with their elegant kerchiefs over their elegant noses, they called quickly and loudly for their waiting carriage and ordered it to take them to Piccadilly. 'Thank the Lord it will only take another week or two at the most,' said one to the other as they climbed in. Billy gave our names to the gaoler who stomped away again.

We'd brought cheese and apples and bread and Billy had three half-sovereigns in his pocket.

The gaoler came back. He didn't even unlock the big gate this time, just talked through it. He had a lamp now, it cast strange shadows.

'Not today, youse,' he said.

'What do you mean?' said Billy. 'The others went in. Mr Park and Mr Boulton are not convicted prisoners yet.'

'They dont know you,' said the gaoler bluntly. My heart dropped down to my feet as if it had fallen out of my body.

Billy stepped forward, nearer to the man. 'Course they know us,' he said. 'It must be a mistake. Would you be so kind as to tell them,' he said, 'that Mattie and Billy Stacey have news for them.' He wasn't menacing, but there's something about Billy as I've said before.

'News?' The gaoler didn't budge.

'Tell them – this is important – tell them we have news of Lord Arthur Clinton because we – met with him.'

The old gaoler had lines of tiredness on his face, we could see he wasn't keen to go back yet again along the long, long corridor, but I saw Billy give him a coin and off he went, the footsteps echoing heavy and weary, the lamplight disappearing.

'Surely they'll want to see us?' I said to Billy, confused. 'Perhaps they didn't understand. Freddie always came over and spoke to us at the court, *always*.'

He gave me an odd look but didn't say anything, not then.

Back echoed the tired footsteps, nearer and nearer, we saw the light flickering towards us again. His face shadowed through the iron gate. 'Sorry, lad,' he said to Billy quite kindly. 'They said they dont know you. They said they had no idea who you are and please stop bothering them.'

Stop bothering them? I couldn't believe Freddie would say that. 'But – did you tell them we had been with Lord Arthur Clinton?' My face must've looked distressed because he didn't speak rude.

'They've got big important gentlemen lawyers and suchlike visiting them, miss, not people like you. Off you go now.'

We trudged back home again in silence, still carrying the

apples and the cheese, through the unfriendly streets where people screamed and shadows lurked. Finally Billy did speak.

'Mattie. Try not to mind. We're part of the world they have to distance themselves from now,' he said. 'To get out of prison.'

'How do you mean?' Even in the dark I saw him think how best to say it.

'We're from Wakefield-street, Mattie. We're from all the criminal things – the gowns and the wigs and the perfume and the jewellery. That all has to be cancelled now, so they can – get out of here.'

I didn't say anything for a while as we walked on. I thought of the days when they came and went in 13 Wakefield-street, and the laughter and the song drifting down:

Which is the fairest gem?
Eileen Aroon.

I spoke half to myself, as we walked home in the night.

'Music cant be cancelled,' I said.

31

Lord Thomas Clinton, uncle to Lord Arthur and younger brother of the late lamented fifth Duke of Newcastle, understood that the Prime Minister of England had daily meetings with many people, as part of his routine: some in his private study in his private house; some in his office in the House of Commons. Lord Thomas Clinton did not have an appointment; he came early, on extremely private business, to Carlton House Terrace.

When he arrived the Prime Minister was engaged. One of Mr Gladstone's daughters, whom Lord Thomas might have met when she was a child (was it Agnes? was it Mary? he had forgot), greeted him politely.

'Good morning, Lord Thomas,' she said. She led him to a seat in the wide hallway and reception area and placed his top hat on a table there for the purpose. 'The weather seems at last to be giving us some relief.'

'Indeed, my dear. It was very trying – and particularly so for us, the older generation. Today is fine but fresher, for which we are glad! How is Mrs Gladstone?'

'She is well, thank you, Lord Thomas. Still as busy as she always was.'

'Does she still swim?' Miss Gladstone laughed that he should remember.

'She still swims! She is intrepid and not to be deterred! She was swimming in Kent not long ago.'

Neither of them mentioned the bereavement suffered by the Clinton family not two weeks previously, that is, the death of Lord Thomas's nephew, Arthur Clinton. Their polite conversation would no doubt have continued but the door to the study was opened, another visitor was ushered out and Lord Thomas Clinton was ushered in.

'Good morning, Mr Gladstone. Just a few moments of your valuable time.'

'Good morning, Lord Thomas.'

Always with this family, always, despite the close ties he had had with Lord Thomas's older brother, the fifth Duke of Newcastle, William Gladstone was aware that they were of noble blood. And he himself was not. He indicated a chair on the other side of his small desk.

'Please make yourself comfortable here.' Then the two men sat in silence for some moments.

Finally Lord Thomas sighed. 'This has been a sorry business. And a stain upon the name of Newcastle and its family. I am glad my brother the Duke is dead and knows nothing of this shame. Dear young Susan is prostrated of course. She so loved her brother. She weeps and weeps and will not be consoled.'

Mr Gladstone bowed his head briefly. And then he said: 'What can I do for you, Lord Thomas?'

Lord Thomas shifted slightly in the damnably uncomfortable chair he had been offered and cleared his throat. 'I come to you, sir, in your capacity as a trustee of the Newcastle Estate. Our family has been made aware that there is a sum of money owing to Mr W. H. Roberts, who dealt so – delicately – with my poor nephew's illness and death. Something over two hundred pounds is due to him in monies paid out to others. And indeed there are debts around Christchurch left also by Arthur that, for the honour of the family, should be paid. And Arthur's estate unfortunately does not have the wherewithal.'

'Indeed those debts should be paid, and the family are responsible.'

'Unfortunately – for I have spoken to the young Duke and to Lord Edward – no family member – nor I myself – is in the position to be able to repay those debts. The young Duke suggested that the Newcastle Estate, concerning which you and your fellow trustee Lord de Tabley alone can make decisions, could – in this particular instance – pay.'

Mr Gladstone – his expression stern and deeply disapproving – looked across the desk at his visitor.

'As I understand it, the trust, as I think you know, is not there for "family matters". It is there for the preservation of the Newcastle Estate itself. As I am sure you realise, this is a confidential family matter, Lord Thomas, for you and the family to deal with.'

Lord Thomas Clinton's face flushed, but he added nothing more.

Mr Gladstone stood. 'I shall write to the estate's solicitor, Mr Ouvry, who is more familiar with the particulars of the legal situation than I am. But I would suggest the family should not raise their hopes over this matter. I will contact you, Lord Thomas, when I have an answer from Mr Ouvry.'

Lord Thomas Clinton nevertheless had the last word as he rose from the uncomfortable chair. 'Thank you, Mr Gladstone.'

(Had he perhaps – just slightly – emphasised *Mr* Gladstone?)

'We are a long way indeed from those happy days in our old and noble family home, around our piano with my late brother's wife singing so sweetly – the days that you and I both remember, Mr Gladstone, for you were – well, of course – always made so welcome by our family. I do believe that my late brother – for whom you are speaking – would not want the Newcastle name shamed further. I shall await your answer. Good morning.'

And Lord Thomas Clinton came out into the wide hallway, where he received his hat from the Gladstone daughter whose name he had forgot, and emerged into the brisk, fresh sunshine in Carlton House Terrace.

A brief correspondence ensued after this meeting.

Mr Ouvry, solicitor for the Newcastle Estate, locked himself in his private office to answer the Prime Minister's query.

66 Lincoln's Inn Fields
London W.C.
30 June 1870

To the Prime Minister.

My Dear Sir,
Under the Duke's will no apportionment of Lord Arthur's annuity is payable so that nothing is coming to his estate. In fact I have advanced to Mr Roberts £50 which I have no means of repaying myself.
The trustees have no power to deal with these expenses and therefore members of the family must supply them.

Mr Ouvry put down his pen: there was no one else there of course; these kinds of letters he always wrote privately in a small back office in the building. He put his head in his hands.

Mr Ouvry felt that Mr Roberts had dealt with this extremely

difficult and unfortunately somewhat notorious matter in as private and confidential way as he was able, in all the circumstances. Mr Roberts had acted as he thought best to uphold the honour of the Newcastle family, yet the family refused to reimburse the expenses, and pay his, very reasonable, fee. Mr Ouvry had worked for the old Duke before he died, and had understood that his family had caused him much pain and trouble. Mr Ouvry was certain the fifth Duke of Newcastle would not have stood by idly at this point as the younger members of the family were doing – as was the brother of the late Duke – expecting anyone but themselves to pay the debts and so end this sad story. He picked up his pen again; the nib scratched as he wrote fast because he was angry.

It is impossible that they should allow Mr Roberts, who really has behaved most kindly in this matter, to be out of pocket. The Duke would have paid for getting him abroad and I should have thought would not have hesitated to meet this claim.

Believe me, my dear Sir
Your obliged and faithful servant
Frederick Ouvry

11 Carlton House Terrace
30 June 1870

Dear Lord Thomas Clinton,
I am sorry to say that as I expected Mr Ouvry's reply to my query is unfavourable. He tells me the Trustees have no power to deal with the expenses of your nephew's illness and

funeral, and as regards the Estate it appears that Mr Ouvry himself is out of pocket in acct with it.

Believe me, Sir
Sincerely yours
W. E. Gladstone

The Newcastle family having been thus advised, the debts pertaining to the death of the late Lord Arthur Clinton remained unpaid.

32

It came softly and silently when it came: a small paragraph in the newspapers. Billy had come home with *The Times* after a long and tedious funeral of an alderman; he had walked slowly for miles behind the hearse, and the black horses with their feathers dancing.

'Look what I've found,' he said and he spread out the newspaper on the kitchen table, leaned over it and began reading.

On Wednesday the parties in the case of the Queen v. Boulton and Park appeared by summons before the Lord Chief Justice Cockburn in his private room at the Guildhall. The Crown having withdrawn the charge of Felony the writ of certiorari was granted and the Defendants are to be admitted to bail.

'What's that thing – *certiorari*?' said Mrs Stacey.

'What does that all *mean*?' said Mattie.

Billy looked over the short paragraph quietly for a moment and then to their utter astonishment – still in his funeral clothes, still staring at the words – he started to casually sing.

Half a pound of tuppenny rice
Half a pound of treacle
See the money rolling in
QUASH goes the conviction!

'What it all means is that "somehow" the worst charge, the felony charge – which is the sodomy charge – has been magically withdrawn. *That* must be what Freddie's father knew was coming – and Lord Arthur hadn't even conveniently died then, so this must have been planned all along to keep noble sodomy out of the newspapers. Well, now at least they can resurrect Lord Arthur's good character, in death. Now I wonder, who would those people have been, working so quietly behind the scenes?' And Billy half laughed, pushing *The Times* away. 'And I'm sure it also means that the jurisdiction will be taken elsewhere.'

'Talk in sensible sentences, Billy!'

'I think the case will now go to a civil court, a different kind of court, which is run by a different class of people with a special jury of – I believe they're called "propertied gentlemen". They understand things better – man to man.'

'How *could* that suddenly happen?'

'The world is a mysterious place,' said Billy dryly. 'But I think two useful words would be *money* and *influence*.'

And he sighed. And then he took off his fine black mourning jacket with tails, and the top hat that could have been fashioned by a royal hatter: his new life.

He was stoic, he had not complained about his new position, not once. But his sister and his mother saw that even though he had *sung* to them – a most unusual occurance – his spirits were so low.

On Sunday, *Reynolds News* was absolutely furious. Perhaps it was righteously furious from a moral perspective; on the other hand its profits had recently soared: were they to so suddenly recede?

Billy declined to read the newspaper to them. 'You read, Mattie,' was all he said. So she sat facing their mother so that she wouldn't miss anything, and began.

ANOTHER JUDICIAL FARCE

A writ removing the trial of 'The Men in Petticoats' from the Central Criminal Court to that of the Queen's Bench is nothing more than a loophole afforded to wealthy and influential parties to get out of the fangs of justice. Poor people are tried at the Central Criminal Court – the fact is our judicial system is a scandal to the age and a reproach to the English nation; the custom of removing trials from a criminal to a civil court, by means of money, being perhaps the greatest iniquity in the system. The prosecution by the Treasury has cost an enormous amount of money, and now, forsooth, it completely breaks down! Why has the prosecution of the major offence, the charge of committing unnatural crimes, dropped through?

We feel certain that some sinister influence has been at work to screen people of higher position from being placed in the same predicament as Boulton and Park, and hence their prison doors are thrown open—

She stopped reading. 'Are they free *now*?'

'Keep reading,' said Billy.

—and hence their prison doors are thrown open, bail for ten times the required amount will be forthcoming; the trial if it ever takes place will be postponed for months, no further exposures will be made – and so the farce is ended! It would have been more complete, perhaps, if Lord Chief Justice Cockburn had stood upon his head, or turned a somersault, after granting the writ of 'certiorari' and before the curtain fell on the first act of this comedy.

Billy started to laugh despite himself. But Mrs Stacey stared into her glass of port. 'And that's why Sir Alexander Cockburn, that old party fellow, was sitting at the back of the Old Bailey that day, directing the proceedings, I knew it!'

'And *Reynolds News* will lose hundreds of pounds!' said Billy. 'No wonder they're furious. All the Sunday readers – like us – deprived of the Scandal of the Men in Petticoats!'

Mattie neatly folded the newspaper. 'And Freddie and Ernest will now be freed on bail.'

'So it is reported.'

'And that must be what Freddie's father knew.' Mattie was still folding and refolding the *Reynolds News* into smaller and smaller squares. 'Well. That's it then. I don't suppose they will visit us ever again. Like you said to me, Billy, when we went to Newgate, we're the "criminal element" at 13 Wakefield-street, not to be mixed with. The End.'

'And I suppose I'll work at the funeral parlour at half my erstwhile salary until I am a very old man,' said Billy. 'And all because we rented rooms to Ernest and Freddie.' He looked at his mother. 'They always win in the end.'

Both women saw his somehow resigned face and it hurt their hearts for they had never in all their lives seen Billy *resigned*.

Neither Mattie Stacey nor Mrs Stacey said anything more.

However, that Sunday both women – each quite independently, and without consulting the other – decided, for Billy's sake, to act further.

33

I MADE A Plan.

Our life with Freddie and Ernest was over for ever but I made one of my Plans, for Billy, because it wasn't fair. Everyone else to live happily ever after more or less but Billy without his work that he loved, my brother Billy deserved better than this. It was a bit hard to arrange because I had to wait till Ma and Billy had gone to bed, or be sure Billy was still out with death duties.

I started going down the Strand late at night. I didn't want to wait in the Strand itself exactly, the other girls might have gone after me for walking in their streets but there's a pump at the top of Whitehall just before it joins to the Strand and I waited there, good for leaning on. Night people walked past about their business, carriages still rolling along Whitehall, even a few ladies and gentlemen walking past, but nobody took any notice of me, good.

Billy had always said they often worked late in the Parliament, they were often there in the House of Commons, he said, till midnight or after, and I'd seen him and knew what he looked like, so I used to get there before midnight, walking the busier, bigger streets from Wakefield-street to be safer, didn't take that long, and always making sure I had my sharp rock and some hatpins.

I was lucky the first night, I didn't talk to him but, well at least I knew this was the way he came like Billy said, it was nearly one o'clock and I was thinking of going home, *is this what it's going to be like waiting, boring and tiring*? – but then there he was, walking and talking with another man, they were in serious conversation – loud booming voices too! he didn't seem to think he had to be quieter in the street so I supposed it couldn't have been very private, I could hear them clear, they were talking about Canada, I suppose Canada's not private, anyway I couldn't stop him with the other man there, but I could have a proper look at him, Prime Minister of England, very tall, funny high collar he had and walked very upright, booming along.

Billy had told me he wanted to talk to Mr Gladstone. Well if he couldn't, I would.

The second night he didn't come at all, damn. I waited till half past one in the morning, funny people going past, servants, and gentlemen in top hats and a policeman but he was drunk and oblivious, lucky for me. I felt a bit dejected going home, sneaking in the door and up the creaky stairs, lucky Ma's deaf. Maybe this wasn't going to work.

The third night he was by himself. I'd thought and thought how I would do it, what I might say to introduce myself. I sort of stepped forward and looked at him wondering how to start but all he did was – very courteous – move out of my way and walk on, well that was a lot of bleeding use, I had to be more blooming urgent than that to stop him. It was tiring this pump-waiting, next night I was so weary I didn't go at all, went to bed at eight o'clock!

'You all right, Mattie?' said Ma.

'Course. I was sitting up too late sewing that's all.'

I didn't go back for a couple of nights and then I saw Billy's face one afternoon as he was called out to walk behind the hearse to Highgate. That night I went again.

When he came past I just stepped forward very firm and said,

'Mr Gladstone, sir!' He looked like he didn't like being accosted (maybe he did the accosting) but anyway I couldn't stop now.

'Could I speak to you, Mr Gladstone? I so very much require your assistance.'

His voice in answer wasn't unfriendly but it wasn't friendly either, I saw him looking at me. I remembered Billy saying he only talked to young, pretty girls so I hoped I was pretty enough. I was young anyway.

'What is it?' he said.

I didn't want to walk with him really, he would see my leg. But I s'pose we could hardly discuss Billy's future over a street pump. So I took a deep breath. 'Could I walk with you for a few moments, sir? That's all.'

'Very well.'

He straightway saw me limping, he frowned and I thought, *oh my God limping makes me not pretty enough* but he seemed to be thinking something, or puzzling about something.

'Do I know you?'

'No, sir.'

'Have you damaged your leg?'

'I was born this way, sir. But as you see I do not have to walk slowly, I can walk just as fast as you.' But he slowed a little bit, I thought that was kind. We turned into the Strand and in the darkness the gas lamps caught his face, one by one, his face was bright and then dark as we walked, mine too I suppose.

And then I plunged in. 'My brother has lost his position. We can manage, he has found other work but he is not happy, he so loved the work he used to do and he was so good at it and he misses it so dreadfully. Now he works in a funeral parlour and me and my mother cannot bear to see the spirit knocked from him. It's as if his soul is a little bit dead itself, because of the unfairness that happened to him.'

He looked a bit surprised – that I could speak in sentences I suppose! He seemed to have forgotten the rotten limp anyway. 'How did your brother lose the work he was so fond of?'

Having got to speak to him at last I couldn't stop myself, out came the words. 'It was so *unfair*! He is such a good person, and such a clever worker and no action of his was responsible. I am not asking anything for myself, Mr Gladstone. I am not a street-girl, I have just waited there some nights in the hope that you might hear my story. I knew I would never get near to you if I came to the Parliament.'

Again he looked at me very carefully, then he nodded very slightly, and then he did a gentle thing, he might have been the Prime Minister of England but he gave me his arm in a courteous manner as we walked along the Strand. Night people still passed on their night business, I bet not many saw it was the Prime Minister of England walking with a cripple.

'What is your name, my dear?' he said.

'My name is Martha, sir. People call me Mattie.' (Me, Mattie Stacey along the Strand on the arm of Mr Gladstone.)

'What is the work that you do yourself?'

'I am a milliner, sir. Actually, I make ladies' hats.'

He smiled. 'You are a hard worker I am sure. I see your determination.'

'I *am* a hard worker.' I didn't say yet about us running a boarding house. 'I am sure you are a hard worker also, but, Mr Gladstone – can I ask you something, can a Prime Minister do *anything* he wants in the whole world?' My hand rested lightly on the sleeve of his jacket, I didn't lean on him of course but I felt a deep sigh from somewhere inside him. He was silent for a few moments as we walked.

'Not, alas, my dear, everything. Although I often wish that it was so.' And I tell you what, I heard something in his voice, some

– regret. *Something.* As if his answer held more than he was saying. 'Not everything he wants, alas,' he said again, and it was almost to himself as if I wasn't there. 'The world cannot be like that.'

'No, I s'pose some things none of us can do,' I said, 'even if we are hard workers.' I didn't mean to say the next words, I didn't know I was going to say them in the darkness, I dont know how they got there. 'I was married. My husband was killed by a drunk cart driver who was going too fast. I could not do anything about that.'

For a brief second he put his hand on mine; I could feel the old, dry skin. And I saw a clear half-moon in the sky and thought, like a heart-stab, of Jamey.

For a few moments then we walked in silence.

But I had to say what I came for.

'Could I speak of my brother? I am so grateful for your time, Mr Gladstone, when you are such a busy man, but I must help him if I can.'

'I do not know if I can help him. What was his work?'

The words rushed out at last. 'He was a clerk in the Parliament, he sometimes worked even in your office because he was so clever, his name was William Stacey.' At once, I could tell, Mr Gladstone knew what I was talking about, that Billy was the clerk involved with the Men in Petticoats.

He was so shocked that – he couldn't help himself he just stopped abruptly in the Strand, I could feel he was trying not to be rude, trying to control himself, when he quickly took his arm away from me, but I couldn't help it, I staggered a bit because he moved so quick from me, as if I would poison him. But still I saw how he still controlled himself – he didn't turn away at once. 'I am afraid I do not have anything to do with the employing and dismissing of clerical staff in the Houses of Parliament, Miss Stacey.

And if you approach me again I will inform the constabulary. Good evening to you.'

He didn't even get a chance to turn away properly because my words stopped him. 'My brother and I went to see Lord Arthur Clinton in Mudeford, Mr Gladstone, a few days before he died, now surely you of all people would want to know that?' And of course he couldn't go: he turned back to me completely. 'He was so *alone*, Lord Arthur – no friends or family came, he had no money, my Ma gave him some money, my brother who has now lost his position was one of the last people to talk to him and told him things might get better, and that friends might still help him, and Lord Arthur who you knew when he was a little boy, cried. My brother is not one of those kinds of men, Mr Gladstone, in case that is occurring to you, but he is an honourable person and there is something wrong in this world when an honourable person is kind, and loses his work, while people in high positions shelter each other from scandal.'

It was as if I was possessed, I couldn't stop – and it was as if he was mesmerised, he could not turn away either.

'Are you sure he died of scarlet fever, Mr Gladstone? In that case you better watch out because maybe you have caught it from me breathing beside you, because I wiped Lord Arthur's face when he was crying, and nobody else in Mudeford died of scarlet fever, Mr Gladstone. In Mudeford they wonder how he died too. He sent you a message by the way, that if you didn't help him he would haunt you. All my family ever did to even be part of this story – and my brother had nothing at all to do with it – was rent them a room sometimes, Freddie and Ernest, who told us they used to do acting parts as women sometimes, and they were pleasant tenants and no trouble to us or other tenants. We were not running a bawdy house or a criminal headquarters for sodomites whatever the papers say, we were just a boarding house like hundreds of boarding houses all over London. And this is not some blackmail attempt like in books just because Lord Arthur told us you were once named his guardian though you can call the constabulary if you want to. And I wont be hanging around the pump in the middle of the night and looking for you again so you dont have to be fearful. *But Billy should not have lost his position in the Parliament to save other people's reputations*. You should be grateful that Billy was kind to Lord Arthur before he died, not take his work from him – and Billy is not the only one!'

I stopped at last. I saw his shadowed face – he was completely stunned and shocked, he seemed as if he literally couldn't move or speak. So – I dunno – I was the one who turned away in the end, and I left the Prime Minister of England there, on the Strand.

I was so exhausted on my way home I was careless, didn't notice three drunk men on one corner of a side street near the rougher part of Gray's Inn Road, and they come round me, pushed me against a wall, I could feel the bricks in my back. 'Come on, pretty lady, we'll give you tuppence if you suck us all,' and they started tearing at my clothes and their own clothes and I gave them such a bloody swearing and screaming that they were surprised just for a second and in that second I got the sharp stone from the pocket in my cloak that was now all torn and I scratched it really violent down the face of the nearest man who screamed and stumbled and up above a window opened and another woman screamed as well and poured the contents of a chamber pot on all our heads, turds and all, some of it got on me as well as them but it meant I could get away in all the row and I went home just as fast as I bleeding could to our famous house.

I was shaking and shaking.

No one was awake. I soaked part of my gown that had turds on in one of the big buckets, I washed my face and my hair in a bowl even though the water from the tap outside was so cold. The stove had gone out but there was some warmth still and I slept beside it, till dawn.

34

Billy says they always win in the end. Well to hell with them all, I thought, we'll get on with our lives. And I decided maybe Billy wouldn't feel so low and so lonely for his old life if he could talk to Elijah, who got dismissed as well.

So I found Elijah Fortune and Dodo.

I put on my best hat, made by Mattie of course, and went again to see my friend Louisa Peck, the wife of the Managing Clerk of the Sacred Harmonic Society.

'Isabella Stacey! The Madam of the Bordello!' she said at the door, despite her respectable curls and cap, and she ushered me in and we both laughed but rueful too, and she moved the kettle so that it was right over her big stove fire.

'Didn't you get words written all over your walls, Louisa? Did any of your tenants leave like they've left Wakefield-street?'

'Nah. I let rooms to people of class, that's different! Dead and all now, poor sod. I'm full, are you full?' I shook my head. 'It'll blow over, Isabella,' she said.

She knew I was deaf, talked loudly. She bustled about with cups and biscuits. 'Silly little cow, she is, that Maria

Duffin, only here for a month and puffing up her evidence. And now the trial's called off, eh? I see them gentlemen in charge of England all the time, going to their gentlemen's clubs with their top hats or their clerical collars, so pleased with theirselves and ruling the world and calling off trials.'

Already the kettle hissed and steamed.

'One of my nieces works in the kitchen of one of them gentlemen's clubs and she says it sounds like horses neighing all over the big dining room when they're all laughing and drinking and stuffing their faces.'

Which made me and Louisa laugh too, and I dunno what *we* sounded like, cows laughing maybe, but anyway a visit to Louisa always cheered me up.

'I'm trying to find Elijah and Dodo, Louisa. Did you know my Billy and Elijah both lost their positions at the Parliament over this blessed business?'

'I heard of course. Bastards. Well I tell you what, poor old Freda will know where they are maybe. She's Dodo's cousin, got a couple of rooms at the Elephant, Peacock-street. You know what I heard last night at the Sacred Harmonic Society? They say Lord Arthur Clinton committed suicide, right in the middle of the most respectable hotel in Christchurch, dressed as a woman in stays and corsets, and feathers in his hair! Dancing! And then dying! What do you think of that!'

Somehow I didn't say anything about Billy and Mattie seeing Lord Arthur.

I followed round the streets behind the Elephant till I came to Peacock-street, bloody awful run-down place, I knocked at the number Louisa had given me. All I could hear was children crying and yelling and I thought I must be at the wrong place. I knocked again very loud and at last the door opened and I saw a poor, vexed-looking woman about my own age with a baby in one arm and a small child held firmly by the hand, and yelling coming from somewhere inside.

'Yes?'

'I might be at the wrong place. I'm looking for Freda.'

'I'm Freda.'

'Louisa Peck at the Sacred Harmonic Society gave me your address because I'm looking for Elijah and Dodo Fortune and she thought you might know where they are.'

She opened the door a bit wider. She was neither welcoming or unwelcoming, just harassed and the place stank but I could also smell a cake baking at the same time which made a strange-smelling combination indeed. And then I saw another child, a small boy, tied with a rope to the leg of a big table in the main room, kicking and yelling.

Above that noise the woman called Freda yelled also. 'DODO! VISITOR!' then she disappeared down a dark corridor with the two younger children and I was left with the tied-up one who stopped kicking for a moment to look at me.

'I knew a man who could make the sky move,' I said.

He kept staring but said nothing.

'He could make clouds go fast or slow.'

'Was he God?'

'No, he was a carpenter.'

'Was he Jesus?'

I was taken aback. 'Do you go to a school?' He shook his head. 'How did you know Jesus was a carpenter?'

'I learnt it from the Bible lady.'

'What?'

He shouted, 'I learnt it from the Bible lady, you silly old cow.'

'Can you read?'

'Nah, course not, she reads it to me. But my Uncle Elijah says he's going to teach me to read, he's going to get me a book for me own.'

'Where's your ma and your pa?'

'Dunno, you silly old cow.'

Dodo Fortune rescued both the boy and me from this interesting conversation. She stood in the doorway like a bent crab, holding a plate of little cakes and looking at me. It was still her face. But even though I knew about the arthritis I was shocked beyond belief at how crumpled and crippled she was. Dodo Fortune, once one of the most popular dancers of them all.

'Isabella Stacey!' she said and she still had that smiling voice she had when she was young. She gave the boy a cake, smiling at him. He sat awkward with one leg tied and devoured the cake, pushing it into his mouth fast and getting it all over his face.

There was a chair. I put the chair by her and took the plate of cakes from her. She bent to sit in it, but awkwardly, smiling and smiling, and a sound of pain came out even as she smiled.

'I met your lad,' she said. 'He looked just like Joe.' I nodded. She looked terrible but cheerful.

'Are you and Elijah staying here, Dodo, or are you perhaps just visiting?'

'We haven't had time to properly organise ourselves and Freda has so kindly let us stay here just till we do. I am so useless of course and Elijah must find another position urgently, but they wouldn't give him a reference paper which makes it more difficult, especially a man of his age. I was so sorry that your lad lost his work as well.'

I nodded again. 'Where's all your lovely red cushions and curtains? Billy told me you still had them all in the Parliament. And your clothes and that red table you always had? Where's all your things?' I was still stood there, holding the cakes.

'There wasn't time. A big new doorkeeper fellow – already in a uniform – came down early one morning, I was hardly out of bed, Elijah just about ready to go upstairs. But this man – in a Head Doorkeeper's uniform, only Elijah was the Head Doorkeeper! – was carrying some cases and bags and told us to go, and that he was the new Head Doorkeeper, and was moving into our home. He had some other new men with him and we had about five minutes.'

Her smiling voice told their sad story.

'Elijah rushed about of course, looking for people to stop this nonsense, he knows so many Members, course he does. But the House doesn't sit in the morning and any doorkeepers who were still there, well obviously they was terrified of losing their jobs too, like Elijah and your Billy. He knew at once it was because he'd tried to get some money together for Lord Arthur. Do you know, some of the clerks and porters were calling out "ponce" and such words. "Sodomite." So many years he's been in that place. It's damaged his spirit terribly, Isabella. I've never seen him so sad.' She suddenly looked very distressed, but then she smiled again, Dodo always smiled. 'But Freda has been very kind. We managed to bring some of our blankets with us and we put them on the floor for sleeping.'

I saw the blankets neatly folded in a corner. I tried to imagine Dodo getting down on the filthy, greasy wooden floor.

'That's a lovely hat you're wearing, Isabella.'

'Mattie my daughter made it. Do you remember her when you two used to come back to the theatre to see me and Joe?'

'Course I do. She ran about Drury Lane, that pretty little child, as if there was almost nothing wrong with her leg at all.'

'That's Mattie. She shall make you a lovely new red hat, Dodo, I promise.'

'CAKE!' the boy shouted and I gave him another so that we could go on talking and Dodo said something but I could not hear.

'I'm deaf now, Dodo,' I said. 'We've all grown old. Though I can hear quite a lot all the same,' and it was true, I was sure I could hear that tied-up boy eating, stuffing cake so noisily into his mouth and giving little grunts of pleasure.

'Elijah, he will find another position very soon,' Dodo said, louder. 'He knows lots of people. It is only that this – this petticoat business seems to have put a curse on people.'

'On the wrong people,' I said firmly. 'Of course he'll get another position, Elijah knows everybody! In the meantime, I've got a big room free on the ground floor in my house in Wakefield-street, near Kings Cross. What about you and Elijah come and stay there for a while, Dodo? You know about that house from the newspapers now I'm sure, but you know about it too, from long ago, and how I got that house.'

And Dodo nodded, of course she knew about Mr Rowbottom, but she knew the reason also, because she had known Joe.

'Me and Billy and Mattie will come tomorrow night and carry what you do have. Would that be suitable? See what Elijah says.'

She looked at me. 'We have some money–'

'I dont want money at the moment, Dodo,' I said. 'Billy's found another job, Mattie makes hats, we've got enough in the meantime. You'd be doing me a real favour frankly, Billy is so downhearted just like Elijah and maybe they'll cheer each other up. Till everyone's settled again. We'll come tomorrow evening before it gets dark. And if Elijah is against it because of it being' – I had to say it – '13 Wakefield-street and Mr Rowbottom and you decide not to come, then at least he and Billy can say hello.'

Dodo looked quite shocked. 'Me and Elijah never, ever judged you, Isabella, you should have known that!'

Then Dodo looked at the room and the boy and the blankets and the dirt. 'Thank you for inviting us,' she said. And then she said, 'O Isabella Stacey! Of course we'll come!'

I heard the boy yelling, 'CAKE!' as I left.

Next day me and Mattie got up very early and made red velvet flouncy curtains, and a soft bedcover from material with red and pink flowers I had in my big store cupboard. We got everything as nice as we could in the downstairs room that once held that bad Ronald Duggan, and then Mr Amos Gibbings' glories. And now was hard-pressed to find a cotton salesman, ha. I told Mattie about smiling cheery Dodo remembering her, about her singing and dancing in some of the early music halls when Joe and me and Elijah were working at Drury Lane, and how ever since she was young, Dodo had loved red, she said it made her feel warm and happy.

'I'll make her a red hat,' said Mattie.

We all went back to Peacock-street the next night. I hadn't seen Elijah for years, but I thought he looked terrible, not the way Billy had described him at all. And I suddenly saw him so clearly: standing outside the stage door at Drury Lane, tall and young and whistling. Still, anyone could've seen how pleased Billy and Elijah were to see each other, and Mattie and Dodo were greatly taken with each other at once. In the room the younger children were asleep in a big drawer and Freda in a world of her own didn't seem to mind or notice whether Elijah and Dodo came or went.

But the boy who had been tied up was untied now and sitting close to Elijah when we arrived, listening intently to a story; he took no notice of us coming in but when he realised that Elijah was leaving he screamed and kicked and yelled and wept and finally Freda just grabbed him and grabbed the rope round the big heavy table, and knotted them together. And then she sat down on the chair and fell asleep. Elijah bent down with the book, and gave it to the boy who looked at it for a moment. But it was clear the words meant nothing, only Elijah could tell them, and the boy yelled and wept and kicked again, while we stood about like simpletons. Then, exhausted, he lay down on the floor with his arms round his head and I saw a cockroach scuttle away across the bare floorboards.

'I will come back and see you, Henry,' said Elijah.

But Dodo had gone out of the room and come back again. 'Henry,' she said. 'Look.' She was bent enough to almost reach the floor. He looked up. She had a cake and somehow she had wrote HENRY on it. 'That is your name,' she said.

He looked at the writing on the top of the cake, and looked at Elijah. 'Does that write Henry?'

'It does.'

'Does that mean the whole cake is mine?'

Elijah looked at Freda. But Freda was asleep.

'It does,' he said. 'But if you write your name on that paper I gave you before you eat it, with that pencil I gave you, then you will always be able to write your name.'

The paper and the pencil were on the big table which was covered with newspaper and dirty plates. The boy could not reach it for being tied. He started to stuff the whole cake in his mouth but Elijah stopped him, very firm, and gave him the paper and the pencil.

'Write first, Henry,' he insisted.

And we all stood there, almost holding our breath while Freda snored and Henry looked at the cake and looked at the paper. Finally he copied the word, more or less. H. E. N. R. Y. Mattie in relief clapped her hands.

'That's very good, Henry,' she said.

'You're clever, Henry,' Billy said.

'Did I write me name?' said Henry to Elijah. 'What I writ says HENRY?'

'You wrote your name, lad. You wrote Henry. And I'll come back and teach you more.'

As we left the last thing we saw was Henry not smashing the cake into his mouth but eating round the edges, so that the word HENRY was still there.

All the way home on three omnibuses, with all five of us, even Dodo, holding belongings, cases, a coat, some tins and pots, on our backs or in our arms and trying not to knock ladies' hats off. Billy's face. It looked almost like his old face, so pleased he was. But Elijah's face, I could see it, was thin and pale. He and Billy laughed with each other about unimportant things and I could see that they was bursting to talk about the Parliament but the omnibus was full and they could hardly do that. Nobody even gave up a seat for poor Dodo and we were all carrying so much stuff it was hard to kick people so we stood around her to stop her being too shaken and pressed, but she smiled and the horses trotted and the conductor rang a bell.

Then Dodo saw the red curtains in her new room.

It was the only moment the smile went from her. Her face crumpled up and she looked at me with tears in her eyes and she put her hand that looked like a claw up to her mouth to try to stop herself from making any sound.

35

Ernest Boulton and Frederick Park were quietly released on bail. Very small paragraphs in newspapers.

And then Ernest Boulton and Frederick Park seemed quite to disappear.

Dodo Fortune's favourite newspaper was the *Illustrated Police News*; she delighted in it for days after its weekly publication. She delighted in particular, as Mrs Stacey and Mattie did, in the large violent drawings on the front page: scenes of mayhem and murder; people stabbing each other to death with knives; bold blackmailing ladies; a woman attacked by a rattlesnake; one particularly ferocious murder evinced dead bodies strewn across the whole front page. For some weeks of course the Men in Petticoats had been drawn most dramatically; now it was as if they had not existed.

And the headlines – sometime Dodo longed to turn them into music-hall songs: EXTRAORDINARY ESCAPE BY LADY ATTACKED BY INDIANS (this turned out to be telegraphed from America); EXTRAORDINARY DISCOVERY IN LADY'S CHIGNON (in this case a rat jumped out, followed by a tribe of little rats).

Today however, in her new and wonderful accommodation in Wakefield-street, Dodo gave a little cry of surprise.

THE MEN IN PETTICOATS

CONVICTION OF PARK'S BROTHER

At the Middlesex Sessions on Monday, Edward Henry Park, 26, brother of the Park who has been so notoriously mixed up with Boulton in recent proceedings, was indicted for neglecting to appear at the sitting of this court on 7 April 1862 and plead to an indictment charging him with having indecently assaulted one George White, a police constable, on 1 April 1862. The bench and court were densely crowded by persons anxious to hear the trial.

Dodo thought perhaps there was some mistake. Brother? 1862? *Eight years ago?* Elijah was out looking for work. Laboriously but determinedly, Dodo made her way down to the basement kitchen, holding the *Illustrated Police News* in the best way she could manage.

'Isabella?' she said. 'Mattie?'

But they were reading also.

'It says here, CONVICTION OF A FILTHY FELLOW: EIGHT YEARS LATER,' said Mattie. 'It says here, *Edward Henry Park, a robust man of regular features and a good figure, brother of Park, associate of Boulton, and son of the Master of the Court of Common Pleas.*'

She looked up at her mother and Dodo in disbelief.

'It says here, *This case was remarkable, not merely for the nature of the charge, but for the length of the time between the commission of this offence and the offender being brought to trial.* It says here that Mr Edward Henry Park asked the policeman to go down a mews and then he—' Mattie sighed, then read on quickly. *He exposed his own person, and laid his hands upon the private parts of the constable and kissed him. The prisoner was sentenced to twelve months' imprisonment with hard labour.*

And Mattie thought of the old man she had met with the strained, anxious face in the dingy office where she had waited all day. She knew Mr Park, and she knew his proper title because Freddie had told her: Mr Park, the Senior Master of the Court of Common Pleas.

'We're not the only people to have our lives changed by all this,' she said. 'That Mr Park's face was so – *troubled*. He must have known about this other son too.' And then a memory, like smoke, drifted.

'*I miss my favourite brother Harry who has gone away*,' Freddie had said, as he held her.

❧

The extremely respectable household in Isleworth of Mr Alexander Atherton Park, the Senior Master of the Court of Common Pleas (perhaps not now considered so respectable as it once had been), was cold and silent – and filled with sadness. Anger, disgust, condemnation, censure – Mr Park had long used up such feelings. Now every Victorian nook and cranny and ticking clock and carved table-leg seeped pain.

Mr Park could not understand. He had somehow, among his other, most sensible, children, sired two sons with Tendencies of a Sodomite Nature. Their mother had died, but he had been loving as well as strict. He knew perfectly well his beloved elder son Edward Henry, known to them all as Harry, had gone to Scotland when he had skipped bail. He had lived there for years quietly under an assumed name and his father had sent him an allowance; occasionally he even saw Harry, brother of Freddie, but mostly he had learned to live without him. But the police had found him through the case of the other son (although the court had somehow managed to mostly keep the connection from the newspapers at the time of the trial). For when Ernest Boulton had gone to Scotland to spend time with wealthy admirers, Harry, brother of Freddie, had of course gone to see him. A letter to 'Stella', mentioning filthy photographs and glycerine, signed by 'Harry P.', had been discovered with an address upon it, and the police had quietly put it to one side to be dealt with later.

They had decided that if they were to be thwarted of one brother, they would have the other.

And now they had.

Sometimes now Mr Park could hardly breathe, for the pain.

When the case for absconding had been brought (almost as soon as Freddie was released on bail), the assistant judge who was hearing the trial leaned down to speak privately to Harry Park. 'I have some slight knowledge of your father and your family and it is to me a most difficult task to pass sentence upon you but I can do no other.'

And then he did indeed pass a sentence. Twelve months' imprisonment with hard labour.

As the gaolers were taking him away Harry looked only for his father who he knew was in court. Even the police officers moved away slightly in deference to the distress of the father, whom they of course knew. Harry clasped the old man in his arms.

'You know that I am a sodomite and a fool, dearest, dearest Papa,' Harry had whispered. 'And I cannot help myself. But as I told you so often – those policemen trapped and enticed me in the mews all those years ago – *it is what they do*. Tell Freddie to trust no one.' And for one more moment he held his father tightly and then he stood straight, and was led away.

Who better than Mr Park, Senior Master of the Court of Common Pleas, to know what hard labour meant in England's prisons? It was treadmills and back-breaking work and the birch and punishment.

He still attended the Court of Common Pleas with diligence every day, as he had always done, where of course everybody knew perfectly well his family disgrace. Where once callow and youthful young clerks had nudged each other and winked about the Men in Petticoats as he appeared, they were now somehow silent. For they saw a face that seemed smashed with suffering.

Frederick William Park had always loved his elder, sodomite brother also.

Frederick William Park had now been re-articled to a legal practice near Isleworth run by a cousin of Mr Park's brother-in-law. Frederick worked unseen, in the back offices, never viewed by members of the public. Had he been seen, as time passed, it would have been harder and harder to believe this young man had earlier been arrested as one of the notorious Men in Petticoats, for he was fatter, hairier, broader. And his face was harried in a new way: he had nightmares.

The first weeks were the worst. Every time the door-knocker echoed through the sad house, every delivery, every letter – although reassurances had been quietly given – *everything* contained the possibility of the inevitable call to court or – the worst scenario – a return for Freddie to Newgate Prison. But then various messages did arrive. Frederick Park was to keep his head down, name no names, and the case would not be called again until at least the following year. He was not to have any contact at all with Ernest Boulton. Ernest Boulton and Frederick Park would not be charged with any felonious crime and only the lesser crime of 'misdemeanour'. Higher powers had intervened. If they kept quiet now, it was possible they might escape without any charge at all.

Freddie thought of Ernest. He thought of Wakefield-street. He thought of their nights in the theatres, at the balls. He went to work as an articled law clerk. He came home to his father's house. He saw his father's suffering face. He thought of the weeks in Newgate Prison and dreamed of that place, often.

And now his loved brother Harry had been sentenced to hard labour for the same offence. Freddie had seen a treadmill now. He had heard many stories.

Living now as he was, under such restriction and guilt in mind, body and spirit, Frederick William Park bore the look of a man who had been to hell. And who, inside his head, still resided there.

Things were somewhat different in the Boulton household in Peckham. Mrs Boulton considered Ernest's health to be so delicate that it was inconceivable to her that he might ever go back to the bank where he had worked briefly years ago, or indeed that he should work at all. But the family finances were in dire straits. Mr Boulton, a stockbroker, had decided that he needed to go abroad on certain business.

He did not give a date for his return.

If he had left enough money for their comfort and survival, this would have suited both Mrs Boulton (and her son Ernest) very well; her younger son Gerard had been dispatched to richer relatives; the richer relatives also dispensed largesse to Mrs Boulton when absolutely necessary. But the family finances were, frankly, incoherent.

As soon as her husband had left, Mrs Boulton (who had waved goodbye to him at the railway station, dabbing her eyes with a delicate handkerchief) came home in relief and lay upon her pretty chaise longue. She asked the one maid for Madeira wine and Ernest, both of which appeared.

'Now, my darling. Now that your dear father has gone at last I want you to cheer me up in my *immense* loneliness and sadness. Especially as he is no longer here to forbid it. Oh darling boy, go and put on one of your pretty gowns and play to me.' She indicated the piano.

'My gowns, as you well know, have been – confiscated,' said Ernest sulkily, helping himself to Madeira wine, and he tossed his head so that little curls, which he had worked upon with his mother's curling tongs while she had gone farewelling, bounced and danced.

'But you still have the several gowns that you left here earlier. The pretty primrose with the blue, for instance.'

Ernest quibbled for a few minutes, imbibed a further quantity of the Madeira, but then went away while Mrs Boulton rested from her grief; when he returned about an hour later, he simply looked like a young woman of the household, instead of a young man.

'Oh that's better, my darling. Oh – remember when your grandmother thought you were the maid that time – "too pretty" was what she said – she was very disapproving. "Maids should be plain, not pretty." She never ever knew I put you up to it!'

Ernest was sorting through the music on the piano, but in the end he pushed it all away. 'I am so *bored*,' he complained. 'Worse than bored – buried!'

He felt the skirt swishing as he walked about the room idly, the curls falling now across his forehead, the undergarments soft on his body: all the feelings he liked so much. He wanted to go out and about in the town as he was so used to doing and here he was, caged up with his mother, impecunious once more.

But Ernest was not stupid. He too dreamed terrible dreams of Newgate Prison. Then he also received messages. Ernest Boulton was to keep his head down, name no names, and the case would not be called again until at least the following year. He was not to have any contact at all with Frederick Park. Ernest Boulton and Frederick Park would not be charged with any felonious crime, only the lesser crime of 'misdemeanour'. It was possible he might escape without charge.

He understood that being encased with his mother, with at least also the Madeira wine, and even visits from a friend or two – for his mother was very fond of many of his friends, and liked to be entertained, and encouraged theatricals – was the most he could hope for at the moment. But he began to consider, just a little, that he might, when this was all over, go back and perform in the pottery towns where he had had some success; also, in particular, he thought of Scarborough, where he and Lord Arthur Clinton had once toured and been written about. *I am, after all, famous now. Audiences would queue to see me.*

'A *song*, my darling!'

Ernest sighed theatrically and went back to the piano. He sat and ran his well-manicured fingers over the keys, thinking of how it had been, and how it was now, and Freddie, and Wakefield-street, and assignations, and Porterbury's Hotel and performances, and the excitement, and the *fun* – for 'fun' to Ernest encompassed many things – they had had. He sighed again at his fate and all the things he had been deprived of. And, finally, he began to sing mournfully.

Rose in the garden
Blushing and gay
E'en as we pluck them
Fading away . . .

and the words suddenly struck both him and his mother as so befitting, so apt to his present predicament, that they both wept and then had some more Madeira wine.

36

Summer was long gone.

The days had turned cold and leaves fell from the trees and rattled along Gray's Inn Road. Near Lincoln's Inn Fields beggars huddled by the church, hoping for Christian charity.

Lady Susan Vane-Tempest, sister of Lord Arthur Clinton, had most gladly and relievedly and lovingly resumed her usual relationship with the Prince of Wales when talk of the scandal had drifted away.

But for her brother, she wept alone.

The mistresses of great men survive only if they know the limits of their situation; she understood he could not be publicly involved with her, and that there were certain things she could not share with him. So she never spoke of the pain of losing her brother. She had mothered Arthur the most, even more than his younger brother, Albert; she had teased Artie the most, and comforted him the most, and laughed with him the most. She had loved him the most in that loveless household.

But the Prince of Wales never spoke to her of Arthur and she did not share her pain.

She and the Prince of Wales now met often again, as usual, on arranged afternoons, either at her house in Chapel-street, or, especially if he was pressed for time, at the house of a discreet friend off Whitehall. His Royal Highness could be dropped off there and picked up at a pre-arranged hour without attracting notice, or too much notice, and she would arrive and leave separately, having ordered her own carriage.

But she had had a terrible fright.

So awful had been the temporary parting, so great her fear of losing him, that Lady Susan Vane-Tempest decided – next time the Prince went away somewhere – to go away herself: to France, to discuss matters with her mother.

Lady Susan Opdebeck in Paris (whose own history might perhaps have suggested she was a less than wise counsellor) nevertheless advised her daughter firmly.

'Be guided by me, Susan. You must somehow regularise your position. You are no longer young, you are turned thirty, and more. He will be King. And if Arthur had not died and had instead been brought to court, the Prince would have discarded you for ever and you know it! No doubt the case will now be hushed up in some way – that is how things are *done*, Susan, I assure you – but you must now somehow find an *irreversible* place in his life. There are always official mistresses and they have standing and respect! You understand him; he needs you, he relies on you and of course he can pay for it – but I reiterate: you are not getting any younger; you must keep your hold over him.'

The mother reached for the laudanum.

'Susan, in clear language you need to be bold, and you need to make yourself safe, and I speak these words to you from bitter experience as you know.' She repeated her words. 'You need to make a bold move now: *now*, Susan, before it is too late, for your future.'

At this point her daughter, shaken, reached for the laudanum also.

❦

Mr Gladstone's life continued extremely busy and full. In the Houses of Parliament, the Franco-Prussian War was much discussed, and reparation from France was called for, and education in Scotland was debated, and the un-English behaviour of some of the settlers in the colonies of the Empire commented upon. Mr Gladstone made many speeches, held many cabinet meetings, wrote many letters and discussion papers. He continued to be emotionally but not physically unfaithful to the matrimonial bed. He endured, no change, his uneasy relationship with Her Majesty Queen Victoria. He continued his Rescue Work with street women whom he sometimes brought home to be dealt with by his wife.

The lame girl was not seen near the Strand again but his heart was not easy over this matter: *I knew I'd seen her before. I'd seen her with her brother.* He somehow did not expect her to reappear, or cause trouble, but he told his wife of the disturbing meeting.

'She said that the people in Mudeford do not believe he died of scarlet fever.' He shook his head. 'We may never know. Perhaps he took his own sad life, but it is over. We must leave poor Arthur where he is.'

'Do you believe the girl even saw Arthur before he died?'

'Yes,' he said shortly. 'I do not like the story. But I believe it. I believe she must have talked to him because she said that he had told her to warn me that if I did not assist him he would – haunt me.'

Mrs Gladstone's face showed her shock.

The words Arthur's mother had once used, so long ago.

She pulled herself together. 'Can you help her brother?'

'Of course I cannot do anything so foolish as to interfere in

– housekeeping matters of the building that do not concern me when matters are so – delicate. And they must have known, Catherine, what those fools were doing in their house!'

'She will not follow you again? Or discuss matters with someone else?'

'She said she would not. I cannot say why I believed her exactly, but I did.' But his heart was not easy.

He discussed monarchical – and private – matters with the Prince of Wales. A rather large number of meetings also took place between the Prime Minister (Eton, Oxford), and the Solicitor-General (Eton, Oxford).

❧

In prison, Mr Edward Henry Park, son of the Senior Master of the Court of Common Pleas, brother to the notorious Frederick William Park, did hard labour. Which included many hours strapped to a large treadmill in the centre of the prison, struggling uselessly on a moving wheel, endlessly, strenuously: going nowhere, getting nowhere, and then all over again. At the beginning other prisoners spat at him, a sodomite; now, as they saw his body and his spirit crumble, they felt he was under punishment enough.

❧

In Wakefield-street Dodo made many cakes.

But everyone who had known Elijah Fortune understood what Dodo had understood: that something had happened to his spirit. His work and his home had been conjoined; they were his life. He had been at the heart of the Parliament buildings; what he had not realised was that the Parliament buildings had been at the heart of himself.

Members of Parliament missed him. He had been there

always; so many of them had taken advice and tea in the doorkeeper's cubby: 'Where is Elijah?' they asked. But word very quickly got around that he had been somehow involved in the scandalous business of Lord Arthur Clinton, and that of course made things tricky for his parliamentary acquaintances.

Stage-doorkeepers of London theatres, knowing him from his old days at Drury Lane, heard of his trouble, asked for news of him, didn't give a threepenny damn about Men in Petticoats: they saw men, and women, in petticoats, often. But none had work for him. Old friends asked for him in the Central Lobby; they were told that he was no longer in the red room in the bowels of the building where he and Dodo had lived for so long, and that his whereabouts were unknown. A porter at Billingsgate heard of Elijah's fate, said, 'Them bleeding hypocrites!' and went to find him at the Palace of Westminster with a large basket of fish; he was turned away most rudely from the Central Lobby. (The new Head Doorkeeper tried to keep the fish, but met his match in the Billingsgate man, whose loud and violent swearing was unmatched by mere parliamentary doorkeepers.)

Elijah Fortune, who had known everybody in London, suddenly had no job and no references, and he was the same age as the Prime Minister of England: sixty-one years old.

Finally Billy was able to obtain clerical work for him at the funeral parlour in Tottenham Court Road. Occasionally, when they were short of staff or death was busy, Elijah too had to walk with Billy behind the black horses with their funereal plumes. Sometimes they spoke as they walked, even joked with a grave black humour, but keeping their faces solemn at all times, of the Palace of Westminster. Elijah and Dodo insisted on paying Mrs Stacey something for the room; in vain she told them that there was enough money in the house: there were two salesmen from the North who still took rooms when they came to

London, who were much taken with the cakes that were pressed upon them by the new lodger. Mr Flamp still lived in his small room and received cakes also, and Mattie Stacey continued to make beautiful hats.

Then Elijah, with the help of one of the many people he knew in London, found extra work, unpaid but very interesting, teaching grown men to read and write at a working men's night school near Tavistock Square, which gave him some pleasure; he whistled occasionally. But there was something sad about him; the old Elijah Fortune was missing.

❦

Expenses incurred by Lord Arthur Pelham Clinton remained unpaid and no memorial was placed upon his grave in Christchurch Cemetery.

37

IN WINTER, SCRUBBING our steps, I'd often hear boots walking before I could see them, with the mornings so foggy and cold. So I was scrubbing our steps one morning, God my hands were red and chilled, when I heard feet, then I saw feet – some boots stopped just by where I was scrubbing. I looked up.

'Hello, Miss Mattie,' said the boot owner. And guess what! it was that Mackie, that smuggler, or fisherman – the man from Mudeford who gave me rides on the back of his horse. I was so surprised that I laughed, kneeling there, which might have seemed a bit rude but he looked so out of place in Wakefield-street with his sea-cloak and that beard and wild hair like someone from history, different from most Londoners, and that deep slow rumbling voice with that different way of talking. He laughed too, at my amazed face I suppose.

'However did you know where we lived?' I asked him.

'Can you believe it – even in Mudeford we read the newspapers.'

'Well – well – that was months and months ago, whatever are you doing here?'

'Business,' he said. 'You could say.' (I supposed smuggling went on in London as well only we didn't know about it; or he could fish in the Thames.)

'Well – well – would you like to have a cup of tea with our Ma? We told her you were kind to us.'

'I would,' he said.

There is one thing that is hard having a thing wrong with your foot and that's standing up from kneeling on our front steps. But Mackie knew of course, and helped me and picked up my bucket and my scrubbing brush.

He came down to our kitchen, Ma was making one of her big stews. She and Dodo had taken no time to have an arrangement – Dodo made her cakes really early in the morning, there was something lovely about getting dressed to the smell of cooking cakes wafting up the stairs. Billy had painted the table in their room red, we'd found some cosy red cushions and made her a comfortable chair by the window where even winter sun came in sometimes, if there was any, so when she'd finished her cakes she came back to the red room and read her newspapers and her novels. (I gave her *Agnes Grey* and *The Woman in White*.) And then Ma made stews and things later in the day. And by the way we were all getting fat in our family, because the cakes were so enticing.

So: I took Mackie in and introduced him to Ma – she offered the parlour first but he said no, then he'd feel he should take off his boots and Ma laughed and gave him some bread and jam and put a plate of Dodo's cakes out, we all sat at our kitchen table and the fire in the stove made it cosy and warm.

'Thank you for being kind to my children, Mackie,' said Ma and he said, 'I thought your children were kind too.'

'How's the fishing, Mackie?' I asked (well, I couldn't very well say, 'How's the smuggling?').

He shook his head. 'There was an almighty storm,' he said. 'One of those once in a lifetime storms and I was out at sea. I got back to the coast but my *Annabelle* didn't make it.' He shook his head again as if he still didn't quite believe it. 'I'd had her for years.' (And I immediately imagined smuggling in storms and coastguards and wild adventures.)

'Did you have to *swim*?'

'I held on to part of the hull and one of the other fishermen found me, they'd come looking for me.' We listened, fascinated. 'I've got some work for a while on one of those ferries that ply from Blackfriars to Gravesend, we know one of the owners, he's from Mudeford long ago.' We all spread jam on our bread. 'Where's your lad?'

'He's gone to a funeral,' said Ma.

'Oh. I'm sorry.'

'Nah – he works for a funeral parlour,' I said. 'He got dismissed from his job as a clerk in the Houses of Parliament when our name got in the newspapers. He was so good at writing that he actually worked sometimes with Mr Gladstone – and now he's blooming walking behind hearses.'

'Is that right?' said Mackie.

'Billy might be home soon, it was a very early funeral today because the man was a burglar.'

'Is there some logic in that?' asked Mackie, but as if I had conjured a spirit, the front door banged and Billy in his long-tailed black jacket and with his fine top hat in his hand came down the stairs and into the kitchen. When he saw Mackie sitting at our kitchen table it was as if he had to look twice, to make sure of what he was seeing: there was the Mudeford man eating bread and jam with me and Ma.

'Hello, Mr Stacey,' said Mackie.

'Hello, Mackie,' said Billy, 'call me Billy,' and then he laughed, looking like our Pa. 'Well – welcome to 13 Wakefield-street, but what are you doing here? Fishing in the Thames?'

'Lost my boat in a storm. Looking to buy a new one, I'm working on a ferry till I decide what to do next.'

'Aint they got boats in Christchurch?' said Ma.

'I felt like a visit to London,' he said calmly, 'just to have a look.'

'He's going to work on one of them ferries from Blackfriars,' I said to Billy and I gave him a little look. Those ferries weren't *fishing* boats, we knew that! They took people to Gravesend to get on huge steamers to cross the world but there might be smuggling chances there, for smugglers.

'Well,' said Billy. 'I am sorry about your fishing boat. And glad to see you, excuse my funeral attire but I've got a couple of hours off till the next one so I'll have some bread and jam.' He carefully took off his beautiful jacket Ma had made and hung it behind the door and then he sat at the table and reached for the bread knife.

'Very gentlemanly clothes you have for your new position,' said Mackie dryly.

Billy nodded, spread jam, said nothing more. We were all silent for a moment as if we were shy.

Then Mackie said quietly: 'Those hypocrites,' surprising Ma and Billy and me. 'All the noble gentlemen, saved from scandal and it was you who lost your job I hear, lad. Did you know Lord Arthur Clinton was the brother of the Duke of Newcastle, that young fella that gambles all the time in Paris and his father was in the government?'

'It never exactly mentioned all that in the newspapers,' said Ma. 'How did you know that?'

'We're not stupid down in Mudeford. We even saw that young duke briefly. Or at least, it was said to be him but no one was really sure. Whoever it was couldn't get away from the funeral quick enough, him and that Mr Roberts. I reckon they weren't there above fifteen minutes.' He put down a piece of bread he was in the middle of eating and leaned back in our chair that was almost too small for him. 'What happened in the end to those young fellows Lord Arthur was involved with that lived here? It all went very quiet after he died didn't it?'

'Freddie and Ernest?' Ma's voice was scornful. '*We* dont know. Our lives have been turned upside down and Billy fired but I suppose they wont come near Wakefield-street again. They let them out on bail months ago but we aint seen them, never saw them again. The papers said there would be a trial "one day", ha!'

'Do you know what?' said Mackie. 'Hardly anyone in Mudeford or Christchurch got paid for spending money to look after that sad fellow. Except the King's Arms Hotel – owned by a big businessman in the town and known to a few royals who sometimes stay along the Mudeford coast. You two came to the egg lady's house – do you know where she was? She took a blanket and lived down the back with her hens those days he was there, she didn't have a good year and Johnny Hewlettson thought she could make a bit extra, giving a hiding nobleman in trouble her own house. Eightpence a night was all she asked him, eightpence – not even a shilling! To a Lord – and who'd look for Lord Arthur Clinton in the egg lady's house? Not a penny has she seen. Other debts everywhere, most of them with people who dont have much money and put themselves out for him – and they're still unpaid. And he the brother of the Duke of Newcastle.' He shook his head and then he looked at Ma.

'Mrs Stacey, do you have a room for a few weeks?' All our faces must've looked really surprised. 'I can work on this ferry as long as I like and I have to – decide what to do next.'

'It's a bit of a walk to Blackfriars and back from here,' said Ma.

'We're walkers in Mudeford,' said Mackie. 'Even though we own a horse.'

'We do have a room on the first floor,' said Ma, but I could tell she was a bit reluctant. 'We're not as full as we used to be, thanks to Ernest and Freddie and Lord Arthur. Ten and sixpence per week.'

He took out his purse from his waistcoat and immediately put a guinea on the table.

'Where's your things?'

He looked a bit surprised. From the big pocket inside his cloak he pulled out a toothbrush that was all the rage, and some folded gentleman's undergarments. He placed these next to his purse.

'Those are my things,' he said. 'I'll buy another shirt. If you'll show me the room and give me a key I'd best be off to Blackfriars,' and he stood.

'Wait,' said Billy quickly. He stopped eating, looked at Mackie very carefully. 'Could you stay for a minute?' Mackie waited, but a bit careful also: they were both looking at each other, sort of weighing each other. Then Billy said: 'Would you sit down again?' Mackie sat, didn't speak. Then Billy just plunged in, like diving. 'About what you said. There's another man living here in our house who lost his job also. Elijah Fortune, he was the Head Doorkeeper at the Parliament, been there for years and years. And he was trying to raise some money to help Lord Arthur to get to France, because he knew Lord Arthur's father. So he lost his position too.' Again he looked at Mackie carefully before he spoke further. 'We found out things about Lord Arthur Clinton. Did you find out things, Mackie?'

Mackie's voice was suddenly very quiet, rumbling quietness. 'We had a few suspicions,' he said. 'What did you find out?'

I looked at Billy's face looking at Mackie: he had decided to share what we knew. 'Mr Gladstone was made Lord Arthur's guardian when he was a little boy for one thing. And Mr Gladstone is a trustee of the Newcastle family estate and would know all their affairs.'

If it was possible, Mackie's voice was even quieter. 'Is that so?' he said. He repeated the words, only even softer, like an echo. 'Is that so? Perhaps Mr Gladstone should have guarded him more carefully in Mudeford then.'

'Do you think he killed himself?'

'Do you?'

'He threatened it but – I wonder if—' Billy looked at Ma, he looked at me. 'I cant help wondering if – *someone else* might have been there,' said Billy finally, watching Mackie warily.

I felt a bit blooming hot. This conversation was not going the way I had expected when I invited Mackie in for a cup of tea, and I suddenly thought: what if Mackie and Johnny Hewlettson had killed Lord Arthur for – I dunno – becoming too much of a danger to smugglers? and now he was sitting in our downstairs kitchen and asking to stay in our house? Well – it wasn't that far-fetched – he said he was a fisherman but he *was* probably a smuggler, we didn't even know him, not really. Maybe I've got a face that shows too much of what I think – anyway Mackie suddenly laughed.

'Do you think Mudeford's full of murderers, Miss Mattie?' he said in that strange, different Mudeford voice. 'You saw us, you make up your own mind.' He thought for a while and then he sighed. 'We've had our suspicions too,' he said. 'But we cant prove anything like that – and the people in Mudeford had only taken him in because nobody else would. They are very good people in their way – but – weren't too keen to have policemen swarming all over our quay frankly – especially on account of someone they didn't even know, who was on the run, who they'd taken in, in kindness, and who was only there for four or five days. Johnny Hewlettson said: *he's dead, leave it.* So we left it – it was hard enough anyway to get some instructions from his family about his burial, never mind look into his possible murder!' But Mackie then regarded Billy again. 'I hear you worked with Mr Gladstone himself, and him more involved you say than people know. Well now, would he be able to arrange a murder?'

Billy looked shocked at the question. '*Mr Gladstone?* No, I wasn't thinking like that,' he said. But he stared at Mackie thoughtfully for a few moments. Mackie waited. 'No,' said Billy. 'He's a very religious man.'

'Religious men have been murdering for centuries,' said Mackie dryly and Billy laughed.

'No. I mean something else entirely.' Billy considered how to say it. 'I used to watch Mr Gladstone a lot, course I did, working for such a famous man. He's too – moral, too strict, even with himself. I've seen it somehow. He's sometimes not very – well – he's pompous – he booms and talks very loudly, well he's Prime Minister – among all those Lords too, *Mr* Gladstone, no wonder people in the street like him! But he's – I just think he's a good man. Well. If you think high moral purpose – for others as well as himself – is a good thing then – he is a good person. In my opinion.' Again he looked at Mackie. 'What I *do* think is he may – just possibly – have had something to do with the main charge of sodomy in the case being quietly dropped, course I do. Now that I know what I know. But – no, not that other sort of stuff. I'm certain.'

Again he was quiet, again Mackie simply waited. Me, I wasn't going to say anything at all about Mr Gladstone, I never told anyone what had happened, and I failed anyway.

Billy pulled at a piece of bread but didn't eat it. 'We read in the papers – so it might or might not be true – that there's many other people probably involved in this case in some way—'

'Course that's true,' said Ma scornfully.

'—churchmen and noblemen—'

'But people like that dont murder people, not in modern times!' I said.

'—people with money to arrange things. He told Mattie and me he was going to kill himself if he couldn't get any money to get away. He said he had the means. He said he would never let them take him to prison.'

'Did he indeed?' Mackie stared down for a long time at his big weather-beaten hands. He shook his head. 'People came after Johnny sent the telegram to London. There was a man Roberts came – he said he was his lawyer. And he came to the cemetery also and—'

'That name was his lawyer,' I interrupted. 'We saw him in the court.'

'Well, a few others appeared – from Christchurch, from London, who knows? – a youngish man told Johnny Hewlettson he was Lord Arthur's surgeon, but he looked too young to be a surgeon I thought. I think his name might have been Wade but how would we know about any of them?'

'There was definitely someone there called Wade,' said Billy, 'all the papers agree on that. He witnessed what they call Lord Arthur's last letter.'

'Well, we didn't have polite introductions,' said Mackie dryly, 'course we didn't, it wasn't a tea party, we just left them to it when they arrived. We were bloody relieved, that's all, we didn't listen at the door! Of course we assumed they were his friends, we expected they would take over the situation, however it developed.' Mackie shrugged. 'We didn't consider for a moment they might *help* with the development as it were. And – we all of us in Mudeford know young Mr Newlyn from the King's Arms, who was there just before he died. He would have told the whole of Christchurch in five minutes if they'd done something obvious like put a pillow over his Lordship's face to stop him breathing!'

I couldn't help it, I got carried away with all the possibilities and Billy had suggested all this long ago and I said, 'Maybe – maybe someone else stuffed Lord Arthur's own "means" right down his throat in that little room *just* while Mr Newlyn from the

King's Arms was trying to get a breath of air.' They looked at me as if I was mad. 'Well that tiny room in the egg lady's house was so hot, Mr Newlyn might have gone down the stairs to have a swig of brandy from a flask he probably carried in his cloak. Well I wished I had a brandy in *my* cloak when we got out of that tiny room!' And it came instantly into my head: *Everyone in London knows his arse is as big as the Thames Tunnel, and most of them have been through it!*

'This is not one of your novels, Mattie,' said Ma, sounding as if she was starting to ruffle. 'This is real life. Dont get carried away entirely.' But I saw she looked at Mackie sharply to see what he would say.

'Well let's put it like this,' his voice rumbled. I suddenly wondered if the deep rumbling sound of his voice made it easier for Ma to hear. 'None of the rest of us who were involved in this matter have got scarlet fever. Nor you two, I'm presuming. So I think we can go so far as to say it is possible, but highly unlikely, that Lord Arthur Clinton died last June of scarlet fever. Which is the official story in the newspapers.'

Ma suddenly got up from the kitchen table. Mackie's money still lay there. 'I think we should leave the subject!' she said. 'Talk it over all you want, youse and Elijah, all walking down Tottenham Court Road plotting and gossiping but I dont want *any more trouble* here in Wakefield-street. We could be glad to have you stay, Mackie, most of our regulars have drifted away now, people who have been coming here for years suddenly not coming any more because of all this. But not if you're going to be trouble also. The real court case is over and damage has been done, but nobody in noble society has been harmed except that sad specimen Lord Arthur and the rest will be covered up. But damage *has* been done.'

She looked really angry. Not even ruffling like the turkey but a different anger that made her seem sort of tall.

'Lord Arthur died somehow. Our lives have certainly been damaged, especially Billy's life and Elijah's life, and that sad man Mattie has told us of, Freddie's father – not to mention my daughter being called a whore. The case will have to come back one day, not the same, no noble names – but no doubt *our* address smeared and advertised all over again, and nobody wanting to stay in a bordello and things writ on our walls again, O ye gods!' She pushed at her hair. 'You'd be welcome to a room, Mackie, and we'd be glad of your custom but I dont want any more trouble, and I certainly dont want any blooming amateur detectives talking about blooming murder in my kitchen! I want this whole case to *die*, do you all hear me?' She was unstoppable by now, that way she gets, just sometimes. 'Frankly, Mackie, Mattie and Billy told me they thought you might be a smuggler, well I dont really want smugglers here to be honest.'

He stood at once. 'That's fine then,' he said. 'And understood.' He took his seaman's cloak and when he'd put it on, and looking so completely out of place in our kitchen, he said to Ma: 'I'm a fisherman actually, Mrs Stacey, never quite got the feel for smuggling – I used to go out with Johnny in the old days but – well, I'd rather be a fisherman, I like to go right out into the open sea, free, so that I can see France. Not weaving and diving and running up the channel from customs boats. Me and the fish and the sea. But at the moment I'm not anything because I was out in that open sea when the storm came. And I decided to come to London and work the ferries for a while.'

'Do you have police looking for you for anything?'

'I do not.' Me and Billy watched this exchange in fascinated silence: we waited to see what would happen next. 'And I thank you for the food and I'm glad to meet you. I liked your lad and lass, and always remembered them, they were the only people who came to see Lord Arthur of their own account, and they gave him money – it was their money Johnny Hewlettson used to get the doctor from Bournemouth in the first place and send a telegram to that Mr Ouvry – even smugglers have hearts by the way.'

We watched Ma. We heard the stew bubbling.

'Oh – sit down, Mackie,' said Ma, at last, and she again pushed at her hair. 'You cant be more trouble than sodomites I suppose!'

He stood there looking at her. I thought she had offended him.

'We weren't just being kind, Mackie,' said Billy. 'We did go there to try and find out things. I was trying to find out how to get my job in the Parliament back.'

'Actually it was our Ma's money we gave, Mackie,' I said, but still I thought he was leaving.

Mackie, this unlikely visitor, looked at us all. And then suddenly he laughed and the laugh rumbled out round the kitchen. 'I wont be trouble, Mrs Stacey,' he said firmly. 'To be honest I knew I could easily get a bed with the sailors down by the docks but some of them'd knife you soon as look as you. And – it is true that I was curious whether your Billy and your Mattie had been wondering about Lord Arthur's death also. So I walked to Wakefield-street from the railway. I might not be here for long, depends what happens. But I wont be trouble.'

Ma studied him for a moment longer. And then she shook herself almost: the anger was gone and she laughed too. 'If you're trouble as well, Mackie,' she said, 'I give you my word, never mind the sailors down by the docks, *I'll* bleeding knife you myself!'

38

Nevertheless, Mackie had not, quite, discussed all his London business with the Stacey family.

A fisherman in the offices surrounding Lincoln's Inn Fields is a somewhat unusual visitor; clients, even shady gentlemen, were usually seen in very respectable attire. Mackie was not in the least imperfectly dressed, and his beard and his hair were combed, but he definitely looked out of place as he walked up the steps of the huge formal building that was number 66. He had the address from Johnny Hewlettson, who had got it from Lord Arthur Clinton to telegraph for money and family. Now, with no appointment, Mackie simply presented himself to the stern gentleman in the reception area, asked to speak to Mr Frederick Ouvry, and waited.

Several times other gentlemen appeared, told him that Mr Ouvry was unavailable, asked him firmly to state his name and business. Finally Mackie simply said, 'Please tell Mr Ouvry I have come to see him from Mudeford. It is a small village near Christchurch. He will understand.'

And certainly Mr Ouvry understood, for after that it was not long before Mackie was ushered into a private, dark, mahogany-panelled back office; it looked out not over Lincoln's Inn Fields but over a smaller back street and other buildings, and even this view was partly obscured by blinds.

'I am Frederick Ouvry,' said the man on the other side of the desk. 'This is my private office and we can speak freely. Please sit down, sir.'

Mackie did so, but seemed too large somehow for the fine straight-backed chair that had held many respectable posteriors. 'Everybody calls me Mackie, Mr Ouvry. I'm a fisherman from Mudeford and I have been asked by a number of people in the area to tell you that money spent regarding Lord Arthur Clinton's last weeks, and his death, has not been paid to people who can ill afford to wait any longer.'

'I am not sure that I understand you, sir,' said Mr Ouvry stiffly.

Mackie sighed. 'The builder made a coffin and why? Because it was not possible to leave Lord Arthur's uncollected body unattended any longer, in a house where he was residing on the promise of rent to be paid that wasn't. Incidentally a young girl of ten wrapped his body in her shawl because it seemed to her unkind not to, even though he was a stranger to her, because her parents had taught her charity. The cart-driver came from Christchurch to drive the body to Christchurch Cemetery: why? Because nobody had engaged anybody to do so. As you know, the cemetery *was* paid because the body would not have been buried there else.'

Mr Ouvry did indeed know this last piece of information, having telegraphed the money himself, from his own pocket, under the name of the Duke of Newcastle. However, he spoke firmly.

'The lawyer engaged by the family, Mr Roberts, paid bills. He paid the money owing to the King's Arms Hotel: of that I am certain, I have the receipt.'

'Oh yes of course! The King's Arms is run by an important

businessman of the town, who has many important contacts as you and I both know. The people who have asked me to speak to you are not of that class, but they're not less worthy of payment – in fact more so, for many of them did what they did out of kindness. The King's Arms Hotel, as you possibly also know, refused to extend further credit to this person, which is the reason he came to Mudeford in an unpaid-for cabriolet, not scarlet fever. The Nelson Inn in Mudeford, forewarned, would not take him in. So the egg lady gave him her small cottage as refuge.'

'The – excuse me – egg lady?'

'Not everybody, even in Mudeford, was interested in sheltering Lord Arthur Clinton, Mr Ouvry, once they realised who he was, which wasn't very difficult – Mr Newlyn at the King's Arms told us who he was, course he did. We all know each other round the area, and we all read the newspapers, Mr Ouvry. We guessed the rest. The egg lady – that's her trade, she sells eggs – her name is actually Marguerita but I am sure that's not information of interest – lives very frugal, but she gave him her cottage and moved into the hen shed, hoping to earn eightpence per night while she did so, which would have been a useful sum to her if he'd stayed a while. Johnny Hewlettson and his daughter took it in turn to bring food every day, cooked by his wife. And Johnny Hewlettson telegraphed you about the situation, and called for a doctor from Bournemouth. Those two young people who came down from London to see Lord Arthur gave the money for that.'

'What two young people?' Mr Ouvry was at once alert, but so was Mackie, at once realising his mistake. He shrugged.

'I don't know who they were, sorry. But I'm talking for the people who asked me to come to you because I had to come to London on other business. They deserve to be paid and, if you will excuse me, they were a bloody sight kinder to Lord Arthur, it seems to me, than his friends in London or his family. I tell you what, Mr Ouvry, I'm lodging with a very kind family in London so I know kindness can be found in cities also, but not everywhere. And I miss the real sea so much I can hardly bear to spend another day here. I like to fall asleep to the sound of the sea coming and going, not carriages and carts and cabs and shouting and your filthy river. But I'm here, and because I'm here I've come on behalf of the people I know.'

And then Mackie simply stopped speaking. He had said what he had come to say; he had no more to say to this man about the death of Lord Arthur; that was not his mission; he now sat silent, and waited. He saw Mr Ouvry on the other side of the desk thinking, and he did not interrupt him. He smelled tobacco wafting from somewhere and yearned to light his own pipe but did not; somewhere outside the room there was the sound of men's voices, talking together.

'Are there vouchers or receipts of some kind?'

'Some of the services were not – receiptable, Mr Ouvry. But I made a list.'

Mackie pulled a paper from his pocket, which he passed across the desk and which Mr Ouvry perused.

'Everything can be sent safe to Johnny Hewlettson.'

'Is there money owing to you, Mr Mackie?'

'No, Mr Ouvry.'

'Nothing in it for you?' But it did not sound offensive somehow, merely an enquiry.

'No, Mr Ouvry. Anything in it for you?'

Mr Ouvry actually laughed, and for a moment each man looked in some measure of appreciation at the other and understood they were both doing other people's business in a situation that was, to say the least, somewhat delicate. Then Mr Ouvry shook his head in a kind of exasperation that for a moment he did not even trouble to hide.

'I will do my very best, Mr Mackie, to deal with this matter and I am, myself, very grateful for things that – I know were done in Mudeford.'

He did not, being the most reliable and discreet of lawyers, say that he knew there was a possibility that Lord Arthur had killed himself; he did not say it was like wrestling with sand, trying to persuade the family of the present young Duke of Newcastle to pay for anything other than their own pleasure. Mackie did not say that he now knew the Prime Minister of England was a trustee of the Newcastle Estate and therefore probably had some influence in this financial matter.

'Two young people, you say,' said Mr Ouvry.

'They came briefly and spoke to Lord Arthur. Weren't there long.'

'Not newspaper people?'

'We wouldn't have let newspaper people into Mudeford, Mr Ouvry.'

Silence.

At last Frederick Ouvry, Esquire, lawyer to the nobility, stood up to end the interview. Mackie stood also.

'I myself knew Lord Arthur when he was a sad little boy with no mother,' said Mr Ouvry. 'The late Duke of Newcastle, the father of Lord Arthur, was a man whom I admired, who suffered much misfortune.' Mr Ouvry had put his hand into his own pocket and drawn out half a sovereign.

'Give this to – to the egg lady, Mr Mackie.' He cleared his throat. 'The thought of the egg lady sleeping outside with her hens, while Lord Arthur Clinton died in her bed in Mudeford, disturbs some part of my heart with its – its incongruity and – ah, the pity of it, all of it.'

39

After he had courteously escorted his strange visitor to the door, Mr Frederick Ouvry, a very honourable man, sat alone for a long time back in his private office. He thought of Lord Arthur. He thought of the story he had been told, of the small kindnesses of strangers and an egg lady called Marguerita. It was not his business to judge his clients, but he sometimes wondered how long the Newcastle Estate would remain in existence.

He sighed as he unlocked a drawer and took out all the financial papers relating to Mr W. H. Roberts and the death of Lord Arthur Clinton, and his burial far away from the family home. Some more important bills paid – by Mr Roberts himself; some still remaining. Mr Roberts had written to Mr Ouvry several times, asking if he was able to facilitate the repayment of the money owing to himself and the remaining creditors. Mr Ouvry laid out all the bills carefully, then attached Mackie's list: the almost pitiable sums still owing in the village of Mudeford. He added up everything. Then very slowly he picked up his quill. He knew very well that honourable men come in all guises, and he felt he had been in the presence today of an honourable man from Mudeford.

Finally he began writing to a man who received the adjective *honourable* by virtue of his position but who, Mr Ouvry believed, deserved the word also.

66 Lincoln's Inn Fields
2 November 1870

To the Honourable Mr Gladstone

My Dear Sir,

Mr Roberts' expenses come to £251.14.00. Many payments have been made in cash for which he has no vouchers. The rest he will vouch to me. I do not see that the matter can be carried further and he is much in want of the money.

I send a cheque in his favour in case you decide to pay him.

Believe me, my dear Sir,
Your obliged and faithful servant
Frederick Ouvry

This letter was received and considered by the recipient. There were two trustees dealing with the Newcastle Estate; the other was Lord de Tabley, another old friend of the old Duke of Newcastle.

Finally Mr Gladstone made his decision.

11 Carlton House Terrace
3 November 1870

My Dear De Tabley,

I send you a letter from Mr Ouvry with a cheque in favour of Mr Roberts, which I have signed but it is evident if this act of discretion is to be done it should have the support of our joint judgement. Mr Ouvry has not explicitly advised it though I have always gathered from him that he sees no other course. For my own part it is with a feeling approaching to disgust that I am prepared to accept this charge, which ought undoubtedly to be borne by others, at least out of regard to the memory of the dead. My motive is simply this; I ask myself the question, what would our friend have wished? We are advised that the charge is bona fide, and apparently reasonable; and we find that none of the Duke's family will pay it. Given these circumstances I believe that he for whom we are acting would wish us to do it. Therefore I have signed to express my willingness, if not wholly without doubt, to proceed.

At the same time I suppose it to be certain that, if the act were to be challenged hereafter, a Court would have no option, and would be obliged to make us pay up with interest from our own funds.

Believe me,
Most sincerely yours

W.E.Gladstone

And so it was – although of course the matter was always kept confidential – that, as the grey, cold days of the year drew down and the case of the Men in Petticoats moved very quietly on, the cheque for the expenses incurred by one of the accused, Lord Arthur Clinton, as he had hurried in cabriolets that summer from one place to another, looking over his shoulder; the expenses he ran up at the King's Arms Hotel, Christchurch, until they would give no further credit; the expenses incurred in Mudeford because he died there; and the expenses incurred when he was buried so far from home – so it was that this cheque was finally signed, not by Lord Arthur Clinton's family but by the Prime Minister of Great Britain.

40

ONE COLD FREEZING Sunday everybody was there, in our house in Wakefield-street. Billy had lit the fire in the back parlour, Dodo had made cakes, Ma was simmering a lamb stew with barley. Mackie was still working on the Blackfriars to Gravesend ferry and he came in with a great big magnificent bottle of port which he presented to Ma. 'I smuggled it,' he said and she laughed. Me and Mackie and Elijah settled down to play cards like we often did on Sunday. Newspapers – especially *Reynolds News* – was read from, nothing these days about Men in Petticoats, hadn't heard of them for months. Sometimes there was something about Lord Arthur Clinton, arisen from his coffin, carousing in Amsterdam or Africa. But there were other scandals now.

Just last week Ma had got Mackie and Billy to manoeuvre the little piano down the narrow stairs from Freddie and Ernest's old room. It was a blooming hard job and they banged and swore a bit but they finally got it into the parlour, because Ma wanted Dodo to have a chance to sing again. Elijah played for her when he wasn't walking behind hearses, and I could play, not very good but I could manage a tune. On this day, in our cosy parlour, Ma asked her: 'Sing for us, Dodo. Sing one of the old music hall songs and make us laugh like you always did.'

And dear old Elijah with his sort of sad eyes smiled and put down his hand at the card game and went to the piano. And although Dodo's body was so bent, her voice was still strong and she smiled as she sang.

A jolly shoemaker, John Hobbs, John Hobbs
A jolly shoemaker was he
He married Jane Carter, no damsel looked smarter,
But he'd caught a tartar, yes he'd caught a tartar
John Hobbs did he.

He tied a rope to her, John Hobbs, John Hobbs
He tied a rope to her did he,
To 'scape from hot water, to Smithfield he brought her
But nobody bought her, no nobody bought her
They were all afraid of Jane Hobbs, were they!

Oh who'll buy my wife? says John Hobbs, John Hobbs,
A sweet pretty wife, says he . . .

While she was singing the front door-knocker sounded loudly – Ma was nearest the door, she sighed but went along the hall. There were voices at the door but we were all listening to Dodo and laughing.

When the visitors appeared not everybody knew who they were but of course I had to go and drop my port on the rug. I bent down quick, the glass hadn't broken but there was red port everywhere. 'Sorry, Ma,' I said, and then I said: 'Hello, Freddie. Hello, Ernest,' and then of course Dodo and Elijah and Mackie all understood at once. That these were the two Men in Petticoats.

They weren't dressed in petticoats but in gentlemen's attire; they both held top hats in their hands. Ernest had a small moustache but otherwise looked exactly the same. But Freddie looked so different to me. He was fatter and – I dunno – coarser somehow, older, with a beard.

'Oh,' said Ernest, almost petulantly. 'You've brought the piano downstairs,' and I saw him looking at Mackie in his seaman's clothes with great interest, sort of from under his eyelashes the way he did. 'I am sure I can guess who did the lifting and carrying!'

Mackie regarded Ernest for a moment and then his voice rumbled out. 'Where were you when your friend Lord Arthur Clinton died by himself in my village?' he said without any expression. Ernest's face went a bit red.

'I was detained by Her Majesty,' he said quickly. 'And anyway I'd hardly seen him for months.'

'I see,' was all Mackie answered but you could see Ernest's bravado was gone.

So far Freddie hadn't spoken. He looked round at the fire and the glasses and the cards; they must've heard Dodo singing. 'I believe we are interrupting you—'

'What did you come for, Freddie?' asked Ma suddenly. 'After so many months? A room? We have plenty of rooms free. Our house is known as a bawdy house and the headquarters of criminal activities and we get graffiti on the walls so we dont get the customers we used to.'

'Ma!' Billy said quickly. He is so fair, my brother, even in everything that had happened to him. 'That's not exactly Ernest's and Freddie's fault.'

'Isn't it? Perhaps someone ought to tell them what's been going on in the real world since they dont seem to notice it greatly,' Ma went on calmly. 'You probably dont know that Billy lost his position in the Parliament because it was known you had a room here. And this is Elijah Fortune, and the lady in the red shawl is his wife Dodo who was once a famous singer and dancer in the music halls and was singing when you arrived.'

Freddie and Ernest stared at the bent woman with the claw-like hands.

'Elijah was the Head Doorkeeper in the Parliament and he and Dodo had a home there as well, which they have lost. Because Elijah tried to get some money to help Lord Arthur when he was dying.'

'*Ma!*' said Billy again.

'None of that is exactly your fault, and I know that as well as Billy. In fact maybe some of all this is my fault, I never thought the word "naïve" would apply to me, but perhaps I was naïve to take you in; I believed what you told me, you were pleasant gentlemen.'

I blushed, tried to say something, but somehow there was nothing now that could stop Ma and as she stood tall in the doorway it was like – like the parlour was under a spell.

'I dont blame you or judge you for being different, sodomites, buggers – whatever words are used, we dont judge you on that, and you knew that. I judge you on something else. There is much talk of you being no different from the chirruping gay ladies in some of the theatres and Burlington Arcade – well some of my friends and acquaintances are the gay ladies and the bordello madams of the Strand and the Haymarket, and they are people too, although most of the gay ladies I know carry out their business because they have no choice, no work, not educated and no chances – no food sometimes – no family or loving friends to care for them.' For a moment she stopped herself. 'Though I have never for a moment thought you brought any such business to my house, whatever has been said about you.'

'But.' She pushed her hair back from her forehead, that way she does. 'We were not your friends perhaps, but we were your acquaintances, we made you welcome in our own home where we also live, we have given a good account of you to anybody who asked and will continue to do so. We have now lost most of our regular lodgers. We have lost a deal of our income. Billy hates the job he has now when he loved the work he did once. Like Elijah did. Still I cant really blame you for none of this, the world is full of hypocrisy and powerful hypocrites always get their way in this world we have to live in.

'But Mattie. She cared for you, Freddie, and you knew it.' All I could feel was my face going red. 'She stood up in court and spoke for you and she was called a prostitute and a crippled whore and had stones thrown at her outside the court and our house – our home where we live – got SODOMITE LOVERS writ on it in big letters.'

I thought I would faint from embarrassment. Freddie's face looked shocked, even Ernest looked funny and he said, 'Is that really what happened?' in a small voice.

'Yes,' said Ma. 'That's really what happened. Yet Mattie went to see your father, Freddie, as I am sure you know, and spoke for you in case it would be useful. Most of all she wanted to repay you for your kindness in – in the – sadness that happened to her.'

'*Ma!*' I could hardly even whisper the word, I thought I would die of blushing, I wished the floor would open up and swallow me up and still Ma didn't stop.

'No doubt she'll be forced to give evidence for you all over again one day and be called a whore, and more rude words writ on our house. You cant help that either. But it *is* your fault that when Billy and Mattie came to Newgate, brought you fruit and money and proper news of the death of the friend – so proud you was once to be acquainted with him because he was a Noble Lord – you sent a message to say you didn't know them and for them to stop bothering you – yet they were some of the last people to see him alive. *That's* what I blame you for. You need to accept that other things have happened to other people as well as to you. And because of you. First you knew that that would hurt Mattie who had been so staunch in speaking well of you. And second you didn't want to know of a man you once both called much more than your friend as all the world now knows. You were both keen enough on knowing him once, you might at least – even in your own trouble – have asked how he died, poor sad fellow. By himself, in case you're interested, with not one person by him who cared for him. But decency and loyalty and understanding, and most of all respecting that *other people* have feelings and have had bad things happen to them because of knowing you, does not seem to be part of your exciting world of dressing up and gowns and perfume and larks and balls and loving men. And it is for *that* that I hold hard feelings.'

'Ma!' I think I was crying but I got my voice working at last. '*Stop!* They couldn't see us at Newgate, it was too dangerous.'

'What – you and Billy *dangerous*? And how did our house become "criminal headquarters" and get SODOMITE LOVERS writ on the wall and us scrubbing it off in the night? By anything you and Billy done? It's Ernest and Freddie who are dangerous to anyone who knows them, and even to people like Elijah and Dodo here who have lost their whole lives almost – these two people hardly knew you existed!'

'Ma, they *couldn't* see us I expect – because Billy and I were' – I didn't know how to say it, looked at Billy for words – 'we were from the world forbidden to them by then, all the fun and the dressing-up and – we were, well you know' – I sort of nodded at our little piano – 'the music.'

Ma made an odd gesture of frustration with her hand, and closed her eyes, as if to close out everything and just for a moment nobody spoke in this whole roomful of people whose lives had all changed, and the fire spat.

It was Dodo who finally said something, she said to Ma: 'Should we perhaps have some cake?' and she put out one of the hands that were bent like claws and touched Billy's arm. 'There is a plateful of cakes in the red cupboard in the kitchen.' And as we heard Billy's footsteps going downwards Dodo turned to Ernest: 'I believe you sing, young man. As you no doubt heard, I was once a singer myself but, as you no doubt could hear also, that was long ago. Could we hear you?'

Ernest looked at Freddie.

Freddie looked at Ma. She gave a tiny nod and said, 'Sing Mattie's favourite.'

Ernest looked puzzled but Freddie knew. He put his top hat on the card table, Ernest did the same and touched his own hair fussily, as a woman might. Billy came up the stairs again with the cakes from the red cupboard and Ernest's sweet voice drifted around us.

When, like the early rose
Eileen Aroon . . .

That song I loved.

And as the verse finished Freddie stopped playing suddenly. I saw his rougher hands, which he had once manicured so carefully while he was laughing and preening, lying quite still now on the piano even as the last notes still echoed and he began speaking, but he didn't look at any of us.

'We came to say how sorry we are that everything we did has rebounded on the people who were kindest to us. Not for what we did, but for what happened to you because of it. Mattie is right – it hasn't been safe for us – for the court case that must eventually be heard in whatever form – to see you or to come here or talk of Lord Arthur. I could have written a letter, but now we know how private letters can be used in evidence against us. We are warned that we have to – "lie low" as they put it. Ernest and I who have been each other's constant companions and friends for so many years are not supposed to meet – in case it affects our court case. We are not supposed to meet with any of our friends – in case it affects our court case. We will do *anything* not to go back to Newgate Prison and you should not judge us for that, because you have not been held in there. But we knew we owed some sort of apology nevertheless to the people in this particular house who made us welcome and were good to us and where we were' – the only time his voice showed any sign of any emotion – 'happy.'

'And I say the same,' said Ernest.

No one quite knew what to say next; it was Elijah who finally answered, 'You're not the only people who have behaved badly, lads.'

And Ernest tossed his head, and looked not at kind Elijah, but at Mackie, from under his eyelashes in the way he always did. I've said before, Mackie was wild and arresting somehow and biblical-looking with his long hair and his beard and I suppose Ernest couldn't help but want to impress.

'We have the absolutely very best barristers in England working for us,' he said to Mackie. He repeated it proudly: 'The absolutely very best.'

'Who's paying for them?' said Mackie.

'Oh absolutely everybody. So many people wanting to contribute so they say. Dont they, Freddie?' Freddie was still looking down at his hands on the piano. 'Even the Church, we believe, has put some money towards our case.'

'Is that so,' said Mackie. 'Well that is a surprise,' and I saw him and Billy exchange a look – but Ernest caught it too.

'Well of course, we're not *stupid,*' he said sharply. 'We know perfectly well they're afraid we might be indiscreet if we are convicted. Bring a few more important people along with us! Bishop Julius wouldn't like it to be known he was at Mr Porterbury's ball in the Strand, would he, Freddie!'

'Bishop Julius, eh?' said Elijah. 'Well that would hardly be a revelation in the Houses of Parliament.'

'Ernest, that's enough,' said Freddie quietly. He got up from the piano and I knew he wanted to go but Ernest tossed his head again.

'Tell about Lord Arthur,' Ernest said. And because he could not help it he then added: 'Did he mention me?'

'No,' said Mackie.

And I thought of poor sad Lord Arthur in the little horrible room, tears running down his face and saying, *Stella broke my heart.*

Dodo suddenly bustled – if you could call Dodo's bent walk bustling – about the parlour, offering cake, it was just so mad and bizarre but we all politely accepted cake and ate it, all of us except her, and the fire crackled and crumbs got in Mackie's beard, and Freddie's, and I could hear myself swallowing and nobody said anything.

And while we were eating Dodo sat on the chair where Freddie had been. She put her bent fingers along the piano keys and knocked one or two of them, but she couldn't play.

And soon afterwards Freddie and Ernest left.

They said goodbye to the room, and thanked Dodo who was now making her way slowly to Mr Flamp's room with the remaining cake.

Billy went with them to the door. I watched from the hall, we hadn't yet lit the hall lamps and I stayed there in shadow. Freddie and Ernest said goodbye to Billy and put on their hats and went out into the cold, darkening afternoon, pulling their cloaks tightly about them outside this famous bordello, 13 Wakefield-street.

41

I WAS GLAD they'd come, that strange afternoon. I was glad I'd seen Freddie, I was even glad I'd heard again that lovely old Irish song that Ernest sang. I knew I would never forget kind Freddie that night when I lost the baby. But I didn't have any dreams about him any more. And I saw, that afternoon when she was so angry and so painful, how very hard in the end it had all been on Ma, including my part. The strongest woman I know, and keeping things close to her heart. I wanted to tell her I saw – and that I loved her. So I made her a new hat even though she didn't need one, and I think it was one of the most beautiful hats I ever made and Ma looked at me so special when she saw it. And I knew she understood.

Our house was nice again. Elijah and Mackie and Billy came and went, and sometimes in the evenings the lovely smell of a pipe like our Pa smoked would be drifting about the house. Dodo baked cakes, and Mr Flamp even got a bit fatter! and Dodo still sang, and told us old music hall jokes and read her novels and newspapers. Elijah and Billy and Mackie often worked late. Two of the salesmen still came occasionally, none of the others, but we were all right, and I was sewing more hats than I'd ever done, that lady in Mortimer-street had now passed me on to three of her friends and they kept me really busy and didn't seem to know – or if they did know didn't mind – about Men in Petticoats at all.

And best of all Billy was happier. Elijah had got him to come and help at the night classes for the working men and Billy just loved that and one night when they came home I looked at his face and it was almost like the old Billy had come down to the basement kitchen, with the newspapers under his arm.

Then one day Elijah confided in Ma and me that he thought Billy had a sweetheart.

'*What?*' We both spoke at the same time. Knowing how discreet Elijah was we both thought Billy must have got *married* for Elijah to mention it!

'There's a very nice young woman who teaches at the night school sometimes, called Emily. Mark my words!' We heard him whistling 'Rose of Tralee' as he went upstairs to Dodo.

But there was something sad about Elijah himself, he missed the Parliament buildings so much, no matter how he tried to whistle cheerfully.

Of course, as soon as I got Billy alone in the kitchen I asked him if he had a girl.

'Who said that?'

'Elijah.'

'Well that's very unlike Elijah!' But Billy grinned all the same. 'Elijah's the most diplomatic man I've ever met.'

'Yes, but how was he to know having a girl is a diplomatic matter! Only you would make it a state secret! I'd shout from the blooming rooftops if I had a boy!' This wasn't exactly true but it made Billy laugh. 'Well – well at least tell me her name then.'

'Emily,' said Billy calmly. 'She's a teacher. A real one, not part time and unpaid like me and Elijah.'

'Wont you bring her home,' said Ma – who was not only supposed to be deaf but suddenly blooming appeared out of blooming nowhere!

I've told before about Billy. No one can tell him to do anything till he's ready. But I still said it anyway, echoing Ma: 'Bring her home, Billy, so we can look her over and see if she's good enough for the famous 13 Wakefield-street!' and that made Billy laugh again, and he looked like our pa, and then he went out again, to deal with death.

Mackie went home to Mudeford sometimes, but he always came back. He worked long hours on the Thames – some nights I dont think he even came home and me and Billy used to discuss whether he really was out ferrying, or smuggling, or just gone fishing. Sometimes he brought fish home. In the end he captained one of the Gravesend ferries himself. He told how he felt half sorry half envious of the people in the big ships crossing the seas to other continents, waving goodbye, not knowing when they would see the people they waved to again, or if they ever would, ever again. And whenever he brought us port for our Sundays he always said that it was straight off a smuggler's boat, and for all we knew it might have been but we liked having him there so much, it seemed odd that if we hadn't gone to Mudeford about Lord Arthur Clinton we wouldn't have him living with us.

But it was so clear that in London Mackie missed the sea, not sea like Gravesend and docks and bustle but 'the real sea' he called it, 'the coast and the far horizon' and sometimes as he said it, you could feel it: loss and longing. Once Billy said to him:

The sea is calm tonight
The tide is full, the moon lies fair
Upon the straits; – on the French coast the light
Gleams and is gone; the cliffs of England stand
Glimmering and vast, out in the tranquil bay.

Mackie looked at Billy as if he was a ghost.

'How do you know that?'

Billy grinned. 'I learned it.'

'No, I mean how do you know about the lights?'

'What lights?'

'The lights on the French coast when you get nearer. Like that, coming and going.'

'It's a poem, Mackie. It's written by a poet. Mr Matthew Arnold came to see Mr Gladstone one day so I got his poetry from the lending library. I think he could see the lights from Dover beach on a calm night.'

'Is that right?' said Mackie slowly. 'A poem.' And after a moment he said it again. 'A poem.'

One night I noticed that Mackie called Ma 'Isabella' – that was a bit queer but she didn't say anything. Then I noticed that he often sat and talked late to her, and asked her about her life at the theatre and listened, I mean not polite questions but he just sat back in a chair and listened to her properly and Ma, who didn't talk about the old days much, spoke of Pa, and our room at the top of Drury Lane, and Dodo so clever and popular and Billy calculating the speed of falling plums. I wondered if I was making things up in my head but I finally asked Billy and he nodded and said, yes he'd noticed too. Finally we understood that wild old Mackie was sweet on Ma, well we knew she'd soon put him in his place, plenty of lodgers had been sweet on Ma before of course, like I said, lonely old men from the North and a kind woman like Ma, still beautiful, looking after them, but she'd certainly laughed at anything like that and kindly sent them packing.

And then one night I had left the others talking downstairs and gone to my room, I hadn't quite finished a hat due tomorrow, just some ribbons to be sewed.

'Hello, Hortense,' I said and I took the hat off her head and picked up the ribbons and then instead of taking everything down to the warm kitchen I sat right under the lamp as Ma always said and sewed the ribbons there, it was easier – and I fell asleep over the hat. When I woke up I finished the last bit of ribbon and I went to get a cup of water and warm myself by the stove before I got into bed and just from the top of the stairs as I looked down I saw the strangest, strangest thing in the hallway below.

Mackie had his arms round Ma, his face was in her hair. And her face was hidden in his shoulder. They didn't move. They didn't speak. They didn't see me. I thought, *they'll move in a minute*, but they didn't, just stood there. Enclosed. And suddenly the extraordinary thought – but of course it wasn't extraordinary at all, I just hadn't considered – jumped into my mind: *Ma must've missed being held too.*

It was such a strange realisation: *my Ma.* But Pa had died so long ago, and I never saw that Mr Rowbottom much, and I never ever saw him hold Ma in this strange, still, quiet, long embrace.

It's quite hard for a cripple to move silently, and in our house there's so many boards that creak, but I tried, and when I went back into my room I didn't quite close the door in case Mackie heard the click, and I lay in my bed, amazed.

42

SPRING FRONT-STEP-SCRUBBING, like summer step-scrubbing, they're all right. I do them mornings, and I suppose people come mostly to Wakefield-street in the mornings and because I'm kneeled down I often see their boots first, like when Mackie came.

Mackie. I couldn't forget what I saw that night, they were so, well – well so still and loving together, or relieved, or – I dont know. Something I cant forget. But me and Billy dont quite know what it is that's going on, for they talk normal and somehow you dont ask Ma things like that.

I was thinking about this that spring day when more boots arrived. Nobody spoke, just the boots there. So I stopped thinking and scrubbing.

'Yes?' I said. Looked up, saw a young man in a suit.

'Could I speak to Mrs Stacey, the landlady?'

'What about?'

There was a pause. Then the boots and the legs and the whole person crouched down to my level. 'Sorry, miss. I dont want to shout my business to the street.' He had a nice, open face and he was being kind and I wasn't being very kind.

'Are you looking for a room?' I said, more friendly.

'No I'm looking for Martha Stacey.'

‘I’m Martha Stacey, who are you?’ We were still kneeling down on the steps, he wasn’t to know I found it hard to get up. (I fell down these steps once, long ago. When they brought Jamey from Kings Cross and I was trying to run to get to him.)

‘I’m Tom Dent.’ He spoke quietly. ‘I work for Lewis and Lewis, solicitors.’

I whispered. ‘Is it about Freddie and Ernest?’

‘Yes.’

‘We better go in.’ He helped me up at once, but how would he know it was hard for me? *he must be very well-mannered* I thought. He had a shiny polished face and nice eyes. We took in the bucket and the scrubbing brush and put them in the hall and I closed the front door and dried my hands on my apron.

‘Mrs Stacey. You are a witness for the prosecution at the upcoming trial—’

‘*What?*’

‘Well – you are a prosecution witness.’

‘I’m blooming not! I’m not prosecuting them! Those rude policemen are and if you’re working with them you can just go back again and leave me to my work because I’ve got nothing to say to you thank you! *Dodo!*’ I called into her room.

‘No – Mrs Stacey, wait, please. I should have explained. We are working for the defence of Mr Boulton and Mr Park – of all the accused, and *especially* Mr Boulton and Mr Park for if they are not guilty, then nobody can be found guilty.’

‘Well dont call me a witness for the prosecution.’

‘Yes, dear? Oh – good morning, young man.’ Dodo came walking in her laborious way out of their room. She’s pretty, still, you know, Dodo is. She was holding *Bleak House* in her curled-up hand and even though she was all bent and crumpled she looked pretty, and smiled at Mr Tom Dent. ‘What is it, Mattie dear?’

Mr Tom Dent must've thought he'd come to the Home for the Incurables, me limping in from the steps, Dodo all crooked, I saw he was looking a bit bemused – specially as he probably thought he was coming to a criminal headquarters or a bordello.

'Could we come and sit in your room, Dodo? This man Mr Dent says the trial is upcoming, and he's come about Freddie and Ernest. This is Mrs Dodo Fortune who used to be a music-hall singer and dancer.'

'Come in and have a cake,' said Dodo.

So Mr Tom Dent explained it all to us – that the real trial was starting quite soon, and that because Freddie and Ernest had lived here, and their women's clothes had been found here, I was a prosecution witness, not because of anything that I'd said but because of the evidence that was found, but this Mr Lewis and Lewis he worked for had read my evidence from the Magistrates' Court– 'and Mr Park also advised us that maybe you could be helpfully cross-examined by the defence and help Freddie and Ernest. If you are willing.' He ate Dodo's cake with great enjoyment while he was explaining all this.

I said: 'It feels – peculiar – it all coming up again after so long, it's almost a blooming year since last time! D'you go round all the witnesses?'

'I'm just a solicitor's clerk but I have to find out somehow who might be – sympathetic to Mr Boulton and Mr Park – and who is not.'

Dodo and me were both thinking of their visit, I know, and Ma's outburst.

'Mr Dent,' said Dodo. 'Much damage has been done in this' – and I saw her stop, decide not to make it personal – 'in many people's lives who have been – without understanding almost – caught up in this case.'

Tom Dent said: 'If you are a lawyer—'

'Are you a lawyer?'

'No, I'm just a clerk, like I said. But before too long I'll have my solicitor's credentials. No one in my family has had such an exalted position in the world! Lewis and Lewis work for the nobility and even the monarchy, and usually use only very noble clerks but I'm considered a bit clever so they took me,' and he laughed, sort of like Billy would have laughed if he'd been talking like that, and it made me and Dodo laugh too. 'But if you work in a lawyers' practice, Mrs Fortune, then you often see that people get caught up in things and have their lives changed and it's nothing they did at all, just circumstances.' He bit into the last mouthful of cake. 'And if you work in a lawyers' practice you find out that the world is full of hypocrites. Especially in this case.'

'You're like my brother,' I said.

He swallowed cake rather nervously and then coughed. 'I'm sorry, I think – um – I think I have just now been a little indiscreet,' he said ruefully. 'It was the cake. And the company.'

'You dont have to butter us up,' I said, but I was only teasing because he had been nice. 'I'll say like I said last time, they were very pleasant tenants and we liked having them here and we knew they did some acting and they used our house to put on their women's clothes and we saw them, course we did, it wasn't in the least secret – even old Mr Flamp saw them and he clapped!'

'Who?'

'Mr Flamp. He's our permanent tenant and very old.'

'And he was never shocked?'

'Course not!'

'May I make a note of that?'

'Yes! And you can cross-examine me all you like and try and turn me into knots but I'll say the same.'

'Good Lord, it wont be me! Mr Boulton and Mr Park and the

others are going to be represented by some of the greatest barristers in England!'

'What, Mr Lewis and Lewis?'

'No, no! We're just the organisers at the back, arranging, escorting, taking notes. Really famous barristers. On both sides – the prosecution is using the Attorney-General, the highest lawyer in the land! It's a show-off trial.'

'What does that mean?'

Mr Tom Dent looked a bit embarrassed. 'I didn't mean to say that at all,' he said, like he was taken aback at himself, and he stood up. 'I must go on to the other witnesses. You've filled me with cake, Mrs Fortune, and made me injudicious! But – Mr Park did say I might talk freely here.'

And Tom Dent bowed to Dodo, and thanked her, and I took him to the door. Just before I opened it he said: 'I'll probably have to come back once more before the trial. I think Mr Park's barrister might want to give you a private message about your evidence beforehand, about the cross-examination. Mr Park has the best barrister in England! Mr Serjeant Parry.'

'Serjeant? Is he a soldier or something?

'No, no – it's the way very senior barristers are addressed. Mr Serjeant Parry is my – my mark.'

'Your mark?'

'I – I would like to be as good as him one day. You know what they say about him? They say he speaks like an angel – but cross-examines like a knife.

'And you said he wants to give me a private message? *Really?*'

'Really.'

'I s'pose he thinks I might mess it up because I'm uneducated, but I wont – please tell Mr – Serjeant – Parry that I want to help Freddie and Ernest in any way I can.'

He looked at me. 'Mrs Stacey, I know perfectly well you are not uneducated at all. Can I say something private to you and you keep it to yourself?'

I saw his open, honest face and big eyes, he had blond floppy hair and he kept pushing it away from his eyes impatiently. He didn't *look* like Billy but he reminded me of Billy. 'Course you can.'

'Barristers send private messages to all sorts of people.' He lowered his voice even though there was no one there. 'And when the Prince of Wales was called in the Mordaunt divorce case last year, a particular person – somebody very legally important – went over and over with him what it would be like to be cross-examined if – that is – I mean – if cross-examination couldn't be prevented. I know this because the firm of Lewis and Lewis were involved in that case too.'

'*Really?* Is – is *that* how it all works? Behind the doors?'

'But of course lawyers prepare their witnesses. That's part of their work! That's how it all happens, especially in big important cases.'

'Is this a big important case?'

'In an odd way it has become so, yes.'

'Is it – legal?'

'I think many things are legal to a lawyer, to win his case. And everyone knew that time that they had to keep the Prince of Wales from scandal.'

I thought quickly. 'Does that "everyone" include the Prime Minister?'

'Mrs Stacey, *everybody* had to help the Prince of Wales. It was a very dangerous time for the monarchy. Should one so care.'

'You'll like my brother!' I said. 'I'm not Mrs Stacey.'

'That's your name on the Magistrates' Court reports.'

'I just wanted to give evidence for them, so I said I was the landlady instead of my mother. My name is Mattie.'

'I know. Freddie – Mr Park – told me.'

'Can you say – am I allowed to ask – is Mr Gladstone involved this time?'

His face closed slightly. 'I cant say anything more, Miss Mattie,' he said. 'I've been very indiscreet and said far too much already. And it wont help Mr Park and Mr Boulton – talking about others working behind the scenes – in fact it will do the opposite – they have to seem *not guilty* of what they are accused, dont you see that? It must *not* seem that they are getting assistance from higher places!'

'I can see that,' I said. 'But I know that Freddie and Ernest aren't important people, not really – and I know they would *never* have been able to afford all this – paraphernalia and big lawyers without—'

'Other important people did – become involved, yes.' But I saw he was discomforted at having been so open and I touched his arm.

'You can trust me, Mr Dent,' I said.

He looked at me carefully and I saw him nod very slightly, as if he had decided he could, but he said no more. He didn't know what to do next, he looked around at the flowers and the polished table by the door. 'This is nothing like I first thought 13 Wakefield-street would be,' he said. 'But Mr Park, he said I would like it.'

'Did he? Do you talk to him?'

'Of course. We are preparing the defence case and we talk to them a lot. Mr Park said' – he cleared his throat – 'he said that I would like you too, Miss Mattie, as well as the house. And I do.' I felt myself go a bit red, in surprise, but also in embarrassment because his cheeks were red too. 'And that I was to be sure to give you his very best wishes and' – he was looking slightly puzzled as well as embarrassed but he had obviously been given some particular words – 'to thank you for all the good memories and the sad ones.'

It's strange how tears just – they just get there in your eyes when you're not even expecting them and I had to really bite my lip for a minute, really really hard, as I opened the front door.

43

The sad announcement was made that His Royal Highness the Prince of Wales and Her Royal Highness the Princess of Wales had lost a child, their sixth, born too early to live. It was christened Prince Alexander John Charles Albert, was given a solemn funeral, and the court went into mourning.

The *Reynolds Newspaper* wrote an editorial.

> *We have much satisfaction in announcing that the newly born child of the Prince and Princess of Wales died shortly after its birth, thus relieving the working men of England from having to support hereafter another addition to the long roll of State beggars they at present maintain.*

'That's cruel,' said Mattie Stacey sharply to her brother. 'Don't read any more.' But afterwards, satisfied that nobody was watching her, Mattie picked up the newspaper and read further.

> *The miserable mockery of interring with a Royal Funeral ceremony a shrivelled piece of skin and bone grandiloquently entitled 'Prince' not twenty-four hours old took place at Sandringham on Monday, as described in the Court Circular. And to augment the folly of the entire proceeding,*

the Court goes into mourning for the loss of the wretched abortion, which our readers will observe was carried to the grave by four stalwart men!

Next day when everybody was at work and her mother was with her soup-ladies and Dodo was reading *Bleak House*, Mattie went to the nearby churchyard and pulled up a small honeysuckle, already in flower, as she and Jamey had done so long ago. She took it into the back of 13 Wakefield-street and carefully planted it near the old covered cesspit. While she was digging the earth she came across some strands of Freddie's blue shawl. She suddenly did not dig any further. But she mixed the loose blue strands with the earth, and planted the small honeysuckle carefully. She wished happiness for the Princess of Wales.

Her mother saw, of course, and understood.

❧

Isabella Stacey's theory that Freddie and Ernest were dangerous to know for the people who were around them applied – she had supposed – only to the people who didn't really matter, although the case had obviously reached right up to Freddie's poor father, certainly. But he was not the nobility. The nobility as usual, she believed, apart from that sad and balding Lord Arthur Clinton, would emerge safely from the scandal of the Men in Petticoats unchanged, unscathed: the way they always did.

This was not exactly true.

Because also that year the spring brought not only the death of a baby Prince, but the confirmation for Lady Susan Vane-Tempest, widow, mistress to the Prince of Wales (and sister of Lord Arthur Clinton), that she was also with child.

Her mother had insisted she be bold.

The desperate fear she had experienced when she had realised she might lose the Prince because of her brother's involvement in a huge scandal had finally made her bold.

Lady Susan Vane-Tempest was bold enough to make sure she would not be able to be 'treated' by the discreet and pomade-scented Dr Oscar Clayton, who was always brought forth *at once* by the Prince of Wales, if required.

She told herself it would be cruel to give the Prince the news so soon after the death of his sixth child, which had made him so sad, when he came to her after the sad death, for consolation.

Soon.

She would tell him soon.

On his next visit, as he smoked his cigar and she smoked her long Turkish cigarette, the Prince told her that the final trial of the Men in Petticoats was about to begin, and would take no more than one week.

'That old thing,' said Lady Susan lightly. 'I thought it was all forgot.'

'It has been decided that the matter must be dealt with for once and for all, and quietly die.'

'For Arthur's sake?'

'For the sake of the country. The felony charge has already been removed.' (Of course Lady Susan had in fact been following matters very carefully indeed, and knew this.)

The Prince explained that a few other really very unimportant men, as well as the unimportant Mr Boulton and Mr Park, would now also be tried at the Court of the Queen's Bench at Westminster, a much more refined place than the Old Bailey. And that with the very, very important legal team that had been set up for them, they would all – including her brother – be likely found not guilty, unless of a minor misdemeanour to pacify public opinion, but probably not even that.

Smoke drifted upwards. 'I am so glad, for Arthur's sake.' (She knew she also meant, for her own.) 'For surely, my dearest sir, they will not even mention poor Arthur now!'

'His name is still attached, of course, but only to the minor charge. And it is indeed hoped he will be mentioned solely with the respect and decorum due to those who have passed on, my dear Susan. To that end I believe it has been arranged that the same solicitors will be used who advised me in the Mordaunt case, that is, the Lewis firm.'

She did not ask how he knew it had 'been arranged' but she suddenly stubbed out her cigarette and leaned quickly and lovingly towards him.

'Your Royal Highness is always so kind and generous and thoughtful and I adore Him!' She knew there would always be other mistresses; now it would not matter. 'And I happen to know that, as well as being kind, you have also been *naughty*. It has come to my attention that you have been a very naughty Prince again.'

'I have. Yes. Yes, yes, I have.' And she moved across him in the old familiar way.

'*Yes*.'

It was early days; there might even be some miscalculation on her part. She would mention the matter when the trial was over.

44

A fine May spring day; a smaller, well-behaved and somewhat noble crowd controlled (in a deferential manner) by police constables; an old regal court inside the famous Palace of Westminster.

Mattie Stacey could not attend until she was called as witness; one of Mrs Stacey's soup-ladies was very ill and cried for Isabella to sit with her; Elijah and Billy were walking behind hearses. But Dodo Fortune was determined to attend the trial. 'I shall take an omnibus and return to my old haunts,' she said. 'Where once I fed noble stomachs!'

'My dear, it might be too far,' said Elijah, anxious.

'I'll take you, Dodo,' said Mackie, 'on my way to Blackfriars.'

'But you always walk, dear fellow,' Dodo said, 'I'm not sure that I could . . .'

'I've never even seen the Palace of Westminster! I'll take you on the omnibus.'

'And I'll collect you at the end of the day, Dodo,' said Mrs Stacey. 'If I have to hear Freddie and Ernest's story all over again a whole year after it all began I'd rather hear it from you anyway, who at least can make me laugh, you can tell us it much better than *Reynolds News* and *The Times* rolled into one!' She whispered, 'And don't drink too much tea before you go.'

'Don't worry, dear, I know a place or two. I didn't work in that building for twenty years for nothing!' And they both laughed for although London provided conveniences for gentlemen, women were ill served, as if it were unseemly that they should be inconvenienced anywhere except in their own homes.

Today on the omnibus a young man offered Dodo a seat (not surprisingly after the way Mackie the fisherman loomed over him). They endured a crowded and somewhat rollicking ride because of the antics of one of the horses, which was skittish, or sick, or insane; they were grateful to arrive at all. There were people outside the Houses of Westminster certainly, but not the wild, roistering, unruly mobs of Bow-street, although the usual placarded gentleman stood on a corner:

THOU SHALT NOT LIE WITH MANKIND AS
WITH WOMANKIND: IT IS AN ABOMINATION.
Leviticus 18:26

Mackie got Dodo to a special part inside Westminster Hall where the Court of the Queen's Bench was sitting, away from the public who very often came from far and near to stare at the famous, high-curved wooden roof of the famous building.

'How does it stay up without anything to hold it?' marvelled visitors, fearful even, gazing upwards. 'It might fall on our heads!' And Mackie too had looked upwards carefully as they entered, thinking of how boats were built.

He placed Dodo on the end of a row of chairs. Dodo looked about her; people were mostly very well dressed, with lots of hats. She turned to thank Mackie for his kindness. And was struck suddenly at how he looked: his stillness as he stared across the court area. His cloak was a seaman's cloak, not that of a city gentleman, and somehow it gave him a strange timeless look in this historic building. She watched him for several moments; she thought he looked like an old painting.

'Do you by any chance know that man, Dodo?' Mackie pointed out a particular young gentleman with wavy brown hair on the other side of the court. She looked carefully.

'No, dear. Oh – but I do recognise the gentleman sitting right in front of him, who has turned to speak to the one you pointed out, look.' She indicated a fine, white-haired gentleman in a clerical collar and a cassock, now talking to the young man behind him. 'He's one of the bishops from the House of Lords. He used to like my cakes when I was a housekeeper.'

'Is that right?' said Mackie. 'One of the bishops from the House of Lords.' He looked carefully across the crowd. 'Is that right?' he said again very quietly.

And then, seeing she was comfortable, and that her shawl was about her shoulders, Mackie was gone from her sight. But when he got to the doorway he looked back at the two men he and Dodo had been discussing.

One of whom he recognised.

Of the newly-accused called in this trial, one was dead, two had disappeared, and frankly most people paid little attention to the other two who did appear: Mr Fiske and Mr Hurt. The American Embassy did pay attention because John Fiske was unfortunately their consul in Edinburgh; the higher echelons of the Post Office did pay attention because Mr Louis Hurt was unfortunately one of them – but otherwise everybody else was looking for Mr Frederick Park and – in particular – Mr Ernest Boulton, Star of the Strand.

It was noted by many familiar with the case that Mr Park's appearance was somewhat changed. He had put on much weight and had grown much facial hair; he almost looked like a different person; he certainly did not have an effeminate appearance. Mr Boulton now had a small moustache but it did not change him very much. All the accused wore sober suits – although Mr Park and Mr Boulton each wore a flower in their lapel, but then so did the Prime Minister sometimes. The demeanour of all four gentlemen was solemn. Ernest Boulton (although he may have been sorely tempted) was under strict instructions, and did not wave to the crowd.

The Lord Chief Justice was, of course, under no such orders. With the theatrical aplomb for which he was well known, the Lord Chief Justice, Sir Alexander Cockburn – whom one newspaper had suggested earlier should do a somersault, and whom the Queen had refused a peerage on account of his immoral life – made his stately, bewigged way to his judge's bench in the Queen's Court. He was accompanied by the highest legal minds in the land; the case was to be prosecuted for the government by the Attorney-General himself, accompanied by the Solicitor-General. Four very famous defence barristers walked solemnly in their grandeur. (Who was paying for them all had, all week, been the subject of much debate among some of the more scurrilous newspapers.)

As it was not often that she got out and about any more, Dodo Fortune observed everything with extremely bright eyes. Apart from recognising the Attorney-General and the Solicitor-General, of course, from her time in the bowels of the Parliament, she was interested to see that various other Members of Parliament were attending; she looked carefully at the bishop and the other man that Mackie had pointed out. As they waited, the bishop occasionally exchanged a terse word with the younger man with the wavy hair directly behind him; the younger man fidgeted, looked about the court.

A jury of propertied gentlemen were sworn in, the charge was read, the prisoners one by one pleaded not guilty and the Attorney-General stood.

'The conduct of a prosecution is at all times the most painful duty of my office, but when it is conducted against four gentlemen, and such they are, well educated and well connected – two of whom have borne a high character – it is with pain and sorrow that I feel constrained to accuse them of an odious crime. But I have no alternative.'

He summed up the histories of each of the defendants who were present, in particular stressing that although Ernest Boulton had once worked in a bank, he seemed to have had, since about 1867, no visible means of support.

'A not altogether immaterial point,' said the Attorney-General more than once, looking meaningfully at the judge. He regretted that several of the accused had disappeared; he reminded everybody that the secret and clandestine criminal headquarters of this criminal fraternity had been a boarding house at 13 Wakefield-street, Regent-Square, where they had kept an extensive wardrobe of female attire and female ornaments.

And then he sighed heavily. 'Now, gentlemen. It is with the *utmost* reluctance that I feel myself bound to introduce the name of a defendant who is now dead. I am aware of the *great* pain this will necessarily inflict upon his relatives. I am deeply grieved at the fact that I have positively no choice in the matter. The public interest, which is concerned in the thorough investigation of things of this sort, must be paramount to any commiseration which can be entertained for private individuals and therefore I am compelled to state that I will discuss the relations between Boulton and Park and the late Lord Arthur Clinton.' The Attorney-General sighed heavily once more and brought out a large white handkerchief.

At the back of the court Mackie looked around at the high

ornate building and the high ornate people. He thought of Lord Arthur Clinton in the egg lady's cottage, and the body, left unclaimed to smell before the coffin-maker refused to countenance such disrespect any longer.

And then Mackie left Westminster Hall and walked to Blackfriars, where ferry passengers were waiting to be transported to Gravesend.

Having finished his sighing, the Attorney-General began his evidence.

Over an hour and a half later he was still standing and still talking, and Dodo, who was familiar with so much of it, felt by then how very nice it would be to have a cup of tea. It was all very sonorous and repetitive.

She looked at Ernest and Freddie, quiet and decorous, except for those flowers in their buttonholes; Ernest was pretty, even if he was described as a gentleman and she thought of Freddie with his hands very still on the piano that cold afternoon. She thought of her husband Elijah, working now in a funeral parlour and sometimes walking behind a hearse in the sunshine or the rain or the snow, somehow because of these men and Lord Arthur Clinton. She looked again at the bishop she had pointed out to Mackie. He was staring intently at Ernest, and at the very instant she watched, she saw that Ernest was aware of the bishop, and, delicately, fluttered his eyelashes. The bishop's face turned very red. The younger man behind the bishop stared only at the Attorney-General, listening to his every word.

The Attorney-General was now reading letters found, and many of the letters he read out in his long speech were – 'Mark!' he said to the jury – letters to Lord Arthur Clinton about money, in Ernest Boulton's handwriting: *Send money, Wretch*, signed *Stella Clinton* and *If you have a little coin I could do with it*, signed *your loving Stella*, and one saying, *Dear Arthur, don't tell Papa you have given me money, I don't want him to know.*

Other letters were read. Frederick Park's letters to Lord Arthur Clinton, signed *from your loving sister-in-law, Fanny Winifred Park*. The loving letters from the United States consul in Edinburgh to *My darling Ernie* about those ancients, *Antinous and Lais*, and about marrying thirty thousand pounds a year, signed *with all my love in the world*. The United States consul in Edinburgh stared straight ahead, not looking at Ernest Boulton who had inspired these transports not so very long ago.

Finally, his voice rising, the Attorney-General told the jury that if they were led to the conclusion that the defendants were guilty, they would not hesitate: '*You will not hesitate*,' he declaimed, 'to stay a plague which, if it were to spread without let or hindrance, must prove a serious contamination of our national morals!' At last he sat down heavily, spent, and mopped his brow somewhat theatrically with the large handkerchief. Dodo saw the bishop get up abruptly, mutter something to the young man behind him, and leave the courtroom.

Isabella Stacey came for Dodo as promised; kicked a young man into giving Dodo his seat on the omnibus that took them nearly all the way home. They walked down towards Wakefield-street very slowly, Dodo on Isabella's arm. Dodo did not know that she made small sounds of pain as she walked. She was exhausted. 'It was interesting, but it did go on, and – well – we know the story.' Dodo sighed, holding on to Isabella. 'And odd to be back there in that building that has been so much part of my life. And not to be part of it any more. Poor, dear Elijah.'

Isabella Stacey put her hand over Dodo's bent one for a moment. Dodo never, ever complained.

‘That young man from the solicitor’s office, Mr Tom Dent, he didn’t mean to, but he said it would be a “show-off” trial. And it *was* – that Attorney-General actually “mopped his brow” with a big white handkerchief – it was just like in the novels I read!’

Isabella Stacey half laughed, half sighed, a strange, disquieting sound as they made their very slow journey. ‘Blooming hell, Dodo, you and me know perfectly well sodomy goes on, high and low, course we do, we’ve worked in theatres for years. I bet the Queen knows! I bet a lot of them in the Parliament and the Church were bleeding terrified when Ernest and Freddie was first picked up. Haven’t things turned out nicely?’ They came to the old churchyard at the end of Wakefield-street. Isabella stopped. ‘Rest here for a moment, Dodo. Not far now.’

‘Is it – a cemetery, dear?’

‘It’s an old graveyard full of good spirits, some of whom I know, and – look – honeysuckle and wild roses and daisies. It’s where I often get our flowers from.’

Dodo was so glad to rest among wild flowers; they sat together on a seat that proclaimed GOD LIVES as dusk fell. Further away children were skipping with a piece of rope among old graves: *Half a pound of tuppenny rice, half a pound of treacle.*

‘I don’t think I’ll go again,’ Dodo said. ‘Sir Alexander Cockburn kept saying they must finish in one week. But it was the same old things, I read it all last time around. Oh, and the prosecutors tried to bring the other Mr Park into the story, Freddie’s brother, but Sir Alexander stopped them.’

‘That was kind to Freddie’s father. I expect they all know him. I keep reminding myself that we’re not the only casualties.’ Isabella bent down, pulled at a dandelion. Finally she said: ‘But – ah, Dodo – just what say Lord Arthur *had* been there, and he actually stood up and told that the Prime Minister of Great

Britain had been made his guardian? – and was also in charge of the Newcastle Estate? And just what say he told that his sister was a mistress to the Prince of Wales? He was loose-tongued enough to tell somebody like Ernest, and Ernest was loose-tongued enough to tell people like us. Think of *Reynolds News* then! 13 Wakefield-street would have been quite forgot!' And she laughed, half angrily. 'It was indeed providential for many that Lord Arthur Clinton died.'

'That's what Mackie and your Billy say all the time!'

Children's voices drifted across the shadowy gravestones.

That's the way the money goes
POP goes the weasel!

And Isabella thought of Billy, singing in his funeral clothes: *Quash goes the conviction!*

She saw some early-flowering wild roses nearby; she had a small knife that she always carried in her pocket: she got up now and cut some of the flowers. 'Smell these, Dodo.'

And Dodo Fortune buried her face for a moment in the roses; prickles stuck to her. Isabella carefully unhooked her, pulled Dodo gently to her feet.

'Nearly home, Dodo.'

They started walking again, but at Dodo's slow pace, Isabella carrying her armful of roses. She said: 'But I tell you something, Dodo, after Mattie gives her evidence tomorrow, I'm absolutely *finished* with it, this case, this business, all the bleeding difficulties, *finished, finished finished*! And that means Mackie and Billy and their theorising too! It'll take a long time to recover from being a bawdy house in the newspapers, this just bleeding reminds people all over again. Let them have their big fat show-off trial and prove everybody's not guilty after all and then

Great Britain can live on, happy and glorious, all over the world and not a bugger in sight, magic! And we'll be left alone at last.'

They came to their front door.

'We're only tiny little cogs at the bottom, Dodo, who got caught up.' And Isabella Stacey sighed. 'Welcome home to the criminal headquarters.'

45

MA CAME WITH me to the court when it was my turn; 'I must see Sir Alexander Cockburn performing!' she said in that dry voice.

Mr Tom Dent that nice legal clerk had come back to Wakefield-street and told me to expect it to be long, the questioning, and I said I didn't care. I wasn't nervous this time. 'And Mr Serjeant Parry, Freddie's lawyer as I explained, Miss Mattie, he wants you to be prepared to answer questions about prices for rooms.'

''What for?'

'They have to prove that Ernest and Freddie weren't in need of money, that they weren't – excuse me, Miss Mattie – soliciting money in their ladies' attire from – from other people.' I didn't say anything to that (but I could've said that I knew Ernest had been in need of money all the time we knew him!).

'You tell Mr Serjeant Parry to ask away, Mr Dent!'

'Would you call me Tom?' he had said, quite shyly.

Westminster Hall and its wonderful high curving roof that didn't fall down though there were no pillars holding it up was amazing to look at, even going to give evidence at a sodomite trial, I'd never seen it before and I stared up with my neck falling off nearly.

'Gothic!' people kept saying around us, craning also. 'Gothic!'

And then we were ushered through to the Queen's Bench area. Crowded, but nothing like the Magistrates' Court. Ma sat down, I was taken to a side room, soon I was called, didn't care any more about limping in front of people, once you've been called a crippled whore a few times it dont matter any more – I went and stood in the right place, by a little table. I looked round this new, noble court, all the lawyers all the wigs and gowns and – sleek, you know shiny gentlemen's horses? – like that they looked: sleek. I saw Tom Dent, he gave me a tiny little hidden wave as if he wasn't really.

And then I found Ernest and Freddie. They looked quiet and gentlemanly and each wore a flower in their buttonhole and they were both staring at me. Remembering the last afternoon in our house perhaps, and what was said. And now two other gentlemen next to them, as Dodo had told us. Ernest – he still just looked like himself, I mean how he always looked like, with a little moustache but pretty still. But Freddie was – we had already seen it when they came but that was months ago – so different-looking with his beard and his weight but so – I dunno what's the right word – if I say *suffering* it sounds a bit theatrical. But that's what it felt like to me standing there looking at Freddie's face, with his brave flower in his buttonhole and his brother doing hard labour and his sad father.

Well here I was, crippled whore etc and before everything went wrong with all our lives Freddie was kind. And he had sent me a message with Tom Dent. And I had decided that today I would send Freddie one last message too.

Even though Tom Dent had warned me I could not imagine it would all last *so* blooming long and *so* many people questioning me. It was all very – calm, the whole thing, except when the lawyers got politely rude with each other. What it felt like was – was that there was no *feelings*, no emotion like there had been last time – not the applause and noise like in the Magistrates' Court and not so much laughter, and if there was laughter it was polite. The Attorney-General was polite too, but a bit like a polite vicious guard dog I thought when he stood up and questioned me, all the usual stuff.

'My name is Martha Stacey and I am the landlady at 13 Wakefield-street.'

'You are unmarried and childless?'

'Yes.'

'You are in charge of 13 Wakefield-street?'

'Yes.'

'I believe your mother lives in the house. How old is she?'

'My mother is' – I flicked an apologetic glance at Ma, better add on a year – 'seventy-six.'

Then we got to those same old questions: 'Did they dress as women?' 'Did they bring their friends?' After a while I was so bored I thought: *I'll just say back to them what they say to me.*

'Mrs Stacey, you said in the Magistrates' Court that they asked for two rooms.'

'They asked for two rooms.'

'But you only had one room available?'

'We only had one room available.'

'That meant they had to share one room?'

'That meant they had to share one room.'

I was getting the hang of it, I could answer questions like that for hours and we could bore one another to death. I realised the Attorney-General was repeating a question.

'If they had to share one room that meant they had to share one bed?'

'Listen!' I said. 'I told it at Bow-street. Mr Park and Mr Boulton asked for two rooms and we only had one. And it had one bed in it so I suppose they shared it like I share with my mother when we are very busy. I do not make it my business to go into lodgers' rooms in the middle of the night.'

But he went on and on. Who came to the house to see them? Did Mr Amos Gibbings have gentlemen visiting him? (And I suddenly wondered then why Mr Gibbings wasn't arrested. Because he was a gentleman?)

And finally: 'Did you ever meet Lord Arthur Clinton?'

'I believe I may have met briefly with Lord Arthur Clinton.' And I suddenly thought, *whatever would happen if I said the truth? whatever would happen if I really told about Lord Arthur Clinton, crying in Mudeford and holding Ma's sovereigns and speaking of Mr Gladstone?*

At last the Attorney-General sat down.

Then Ernest's lawyer cross-examined me and asked the questions all over again. Sometimes the Judge chipped in with a question too, and I had to answer him as well. My leg was hurting by now but I'd faint rather than admit it. And yet: all the time I had this feeling that we were just going through the motions, so that they could say there's been a Proper Trial.

Then Freddie's barrister stood up and cross-examined me, he was the fourth blooming man to question me while I stood there. This was the man Tom had told me of, Mr Serjeant Parry, who spoke like an angel and cross-examined like a knife. Well I was on Mr Serjeant Parry's side, I knew he knew it, no need to knife me.

Mr Serjeant Parry changed the subject completely. 'I want to ask you about the prices you charged for rooms.'

I answered everything as if I never knew the questions were coming. And then Sergeant Parry looked up pleasedly at the learned Lord Chief Justice.

'Ten shillings and six per week, my lord! Or four shillings for two people for one night which is all they usually asked for. Not an exorbitant amount of money seems to have been required for the rental of these rooms!' and he and the Attorney-General looked daggers but I suppose that was all part of the performance we were all doing. I looked round the court – and I thought I saw Mackie standing right at the back, funny, he never said he was coming.

'Mrs Stacey.'

'Sorry.'

'Did you have a permanent lodger at this time?' Mr Tom Dent had writ that down in his notebook when he first came to see us.

'Yes we had a permanent lodger at this time.'

'Did he know these gentlemen went out in female attire?'

'Course he knew, Mr Flamp. My Ma had told him. And he saw for himself.'

'How old was he?'

I had no idea so I said, 'Eighty-one.'

'Was he shocked?'

'Course not. They *weren't* shocking.' And I thought of old Mr Flamp, puzzled and yet pleased, at the entertainment.

Mr Serjeant Parry smiled at me, like an angel, and bowed.

And then Ernest's lawyer said to me very courteous and gentle: 'Mrs Stacey, did you ever, in all the time the defendants Boulton and Park were at your house, notice a look, a gesture or a word, on the part of the defendants, that was any way improper?'

'No. No I did not! I can say with certitude that at no time did I notice a look, a gesture, or a word, on the part of the defendants, that was any way improper.' And then I gave Freddie my last message. 'I would also like to state so that every single person in this whole court can hear it clear, I have never known a more polite, or kinder lodger in our establishment – ever – than Mr Frederick Park.' I didn't even look at Freddie. But I thought he would understand.

I thought I was finished, blooming time, my leg was pulsating like a drum but blow me down a *Juror* requested to ask me a question and was given permission – that's the *fifth* man asking me things!

'Can she tell us please, were the dresses high-necked or low-necked?'

'Oh – oh high-necked I should think, almost always high-necked.'

'But never low.'

'I dont say never, but they were certainly mostly high. Very high-necked. Whatever was fashionable.' And I thought of Ernest, powdering his bare shoulders and his neck low low down, and the boxes of 'Bloom of Roses'.

I went to sit by Ma when I was finished, I could have used some 'Bloom of Roses' myself by then, I was blooming exhausted. I looked round for Mackie, but if he had been there he was gone. People whispered that the medical evidence was coming next, and I'd seen doctors outside where I'd had to wait but we didn't want to stay and hear again about their rectums and anuses and syphilis (and new talk about Ernest's 'fistula' apparently, which Ma told me came from a burst boil in a bottom) so Ma and me were just about to leave when there was a policeman suddenly appeared, with two large parcels. He put them down on the floor in front of the Judge and undone them. And when I saw what it was I felt a little gasp inside me and I heard another loud gasp at the same time, all through the courtroom. Afterwards I thought it was the saddest part of the whole trial.

It was Ernest and Freddie's women's clothes.

All their exciting gowns and shawls, their boots and their corsets and their feathers and their jewellery and their chignons and their fashionable hats. But I suppose they'd been packed away in some old police cupboard for a year and they were – well most of them weren't fun any more, or lovely, or pretty, or expensive-looking. It certainly didn't look as if they had spent fortunes on clothes. But I suppose the prosecution wanted them to think they were the clothes of cheap prostitutes. Next to the ladies' boots, the policeman lay everything all around the floor to show the judge and the jury, and daylight shone in bright and you could see quite clearly: most of the skirts weren't very clean, or the bodices, there were marks on them. Stains. The chignons were dank and dull, fallen apart. All the once-beautiful gowns: the velvet and the silk and the moiré and the muslin and the satin. Some, you could see, had been elegant once – that one of Ernest's with the pink and white roses was still lovely but they'd taken old gowns Freddie and Ernest had discarded and stuffed in an old bag as well, and now everything had all been squashed up together and now they mostly looked like things from a second-hand clothesman's cart, they didn't look exciting like they used to when Freddie and Ernest laughed down our stairs in the flattering, soft lamplight. And the shiny jewels that had looked so exotic were dull and broken.

And finally the policeman roughly shook the last package upside down and one last rather grubby gown, Freddie's yellow satin gown, fell out and lay with all the others. It had been folded up, it was torn, but the policeman lay it out like the others – and there was a sharp shock-noise in the court. The yellow gown looked as if it had old blood – well – well it had a lot of blood in – well in a most inappropriate place on the skirt. I could feel a feeling around me at once – people thought that was *unbelievably shocking*.

Because these were men.

It was my blood.

46

An editorial in the *Daily Telegraph* stated that it would not be printing some of the Men in Petticoats Trial medical evidence because it was not suitable for a family newspaper. 'In such a case we do not desire to report more than is really necessary.'

Such information would of course, everybody knew, be found in *Reynolds News* on Sunday if it was required.

Nobody in 13 Wakefield-street required it.

In her home in Chapel-street, Westminster, waiting for a visit from the Prince of Wales, Lady Susan Vane-Tempest, widow, dropped the newspapers and dreamed. She dreamed of Palaces and Kings.

She had followed – she could not attend of course – the present trial in which once again her brother's name – despite his tragic death from scarlet fever – was still being impertinently mentioned. However, friends attending had reported to her that when the defence started their case, one of the defence lawyers had made a powerful speech regarding Arthur.

'Do you mean little Mr Roberts who used to be one of my father's secretaries?'

'No, no, no!' Susan's particular and closest friend, Mrs

Harriet Whatman, who filled her in every day after the court closed, had laughed. 'This is a greatly superior defence team. My dear, Mr Digby Seymour it was who spoke of Arthur – he is defending the pretty boy, he defends only in very important cases. And that Mr Serjeant Parry is there who cross-examines so cleverly and so mercilessly, I swear he made that fat Beadle weep and I would not like to be cross-examined by him on my private life, thank you very much! And dear Sir John Karslake is defending the American consul from Edinburgh, no less – Oh my dear, everyone who is everyone is involved, you know, so they have to have the best barristers, and they all, simply all of them, have to defend the pretty boy if the others – including Arthur – are to be found not guilty. And if there was any disrespect in court, dear Sir Alexander – the Lord Chief Justice, naughty old Sir Alexander whom I have sat next to at Lady Hatton's – you know him of course, Susan dear – got very strict and cross. Oh but Mr Digby Seymour was most moving about Arthur.' She picked up one of the strewn newspapers. 'Look – here it is! Word for word, in *The Times*.'

> *Lord Arthur Clinton is dead – aye dead! But he is included in this indictment, and, Members of the Jury, you are trying the living and the dead! And from his grave Lord Arthur Clinton beseeches you to do justice to his memory and to liberate him from the load of infamy which must rest upon him if this young man is convicted.*

'It was *very* moving, darling,' said all her friends to Lord Arthur's sister.

As she waited now for her royal lover, Lady Susan Vane-Tempest considered her situation, and her options – for of course she would say nothing to him until this wretched trial was over and the matter forgotten.

She knew – so long as dear, lost Arthur's name was buried with the end of this trial – that her mother had been right and she had had to be bold.

For she was nearly thirty-two years old.

She dreamed of this child. A son with special – albeit confidential, of course – privileges – and financial security.

She told herself again; she told herself again: the Prince needed her and relied upon her, and was able to talk to her with a confidence and a confidentiality he could not with others. She was from his background and his youth. She was one of the noble families of England; her own father had accompanied the young Prince to Canada, to the United States. She knew the rules. She would *never* be an embarrassment to him.

And he knew that.

It could all be dealt with satisfactorily, and it was already too late for Dr Oscar Clayton and his pomade of roses.

She heard the maid go to the door to open it for the Prince.

She would tell him after the trial.

Or, to be absolutely safe, just a few weeks later.

47

In his opening speech for the defence, the famous barrister Mr Digby Seymour, Ernest Boulton's defence lawyer, apart from saying, 'Lord Arthur Clinton is dead – aye dead,' also said:

> *Gentlemen. I say that in a case like this I trust your verdict will establish that the moral atmosphere of England is not yet tainted with the impurities of continental cities, and that free as we are, from our island position, we are insulated from the crimes to which you have had allusion made, and you will pronounce by your verdict – in this case at all events with regard to these facts – that London is not cursed with the sins of Sodom, nor Westminster tainted with the vices of Gomorrah.*

This sentiment was printed with approval (and the occasional extra flourish) in many newspapers.

A seventeen-year-old boy in Tooting, who worked as a clerk in an ironmonger's, could not understand the almost uncontrollable feelings he had for another young boy who carried watering cans and coal scuttles and large rods of iron from the ironmongers to be delivered to addresses near by.

This boy in Tooting read Mr Digby Seymour's speech.

And then he walked to Blackfriars.

And then he killed himself.

There was no mention of this in either *The Times* or *Reynolds Newspaper* or indeed in any of the newspapers, for people were always jumping off Blackfriars Bridge.

48

'WAS THAT YOU in the court, Mackie, when I was giving evidence?'

'I look in sometimes,' he said in a dry voice. 'To see how the other half dispense justice. You were impressive!' All of us were in the kitchen. Mackie turned to Dodo. 'Who was that bishop in court the first day, Dodo? From the House of Lords.'

'With the young man?'

'Yes.'

Everyone looked at Mackie and Dodo, curious. Then Dodo seemed to go off at a tangent. 'Elijah, you remember in the old days how in the afternoon a gaggle of bishops used to come to the dining room for afternoon tea?'

He nodded. 'Those prune-cake clericals,' he said, and Dodo smiled, and then explained to us: 'That was my name for them – they asked me to put extra prunes in my delicious fruit cake and I understood them to mean it was for their noble bowels,' and everyone in the kitchen laughed. 'He was one of them.'

'D'you know his name?' said Mackie, quiet.

'Oh Mackie, I'm an old woman with a failing memory! They all looked the same to me – no wait, I know, he had something to do with Shakespeare.'

'Shakespeare?'

I saw that Dodo looked at Elijah for help. 'Dearest, you know, from a Shakespeare play.'

Elijah looked puzzled – and then his face suddenly cleared. 'Well of course, I should have guessed straightaway. Would the play be *Julius Caesar*, Dodo?'

'Yes!' and she laughed at once, remembering. 'At least I didn't say Brutus, dearest! That one, Bishop Julius. Of course!'

And Elijah looked at Mackie. 'Julius. Bishop Julius. She means the old hypocrite who got Billy out of his job. Doesn't surprise me to hear he's sitting in court, waiting for a not guilty verdict to celebrate. I always presumed it was him who gave orders for Dodo and me to be thrown out also.'

'Is that right?' said Mackie.

'Ernest mentioned him,' said Billy, looking at Mackie. 'Present at one of their – entertainments, remember?'

'I remember,' said Mackie.

'He was the one who first came and told Mr Gladstone about the arrests,' said Billy. 'I was in the Prime Minister's office.'

'This subject is going to be bleeding banned in my house!' said Ma, sounding like a warning.

'Ma,' I said. 'It's nearly over, they're only allowed a week for the trial and I don't think any of us are interested in hearing all that old stuff any more. But Mr Tom Dent from Mr Lewis and Lewis, he told me that Ernest's mother and Freddie's father are both going to be witnesses for the defence tomorrow. You always said you'd like to meet Ernest's mother because he was so spoilt. You said she had a lot to answer for.'

'I think I can live without knowing her after all,' said Ma. 'I dont really want to go back there again, Mattie. Let's be *finished* with this whole damn business for God's sake.'

'Ma,' I said. 'I wish you'd come with me. It's Freddie's father, I'd like to hear what he will say. He must feel so – anxious till it's over, with one son already doing hard labour for sodomy, he was so troubled when I saw him, poor thing, though I didn't know everything then and I didn't understand. But at the end of meeting him I thought that he might actually be – a nice man.'

'A what?'

'A nice man,' I said, louder.

'Like Freddie.'

'Ma. When I see Freddie now, when I saw him in court, I just felt so, so sorry for him.'

'Yes,' said Ma. And dear old Ma, she sighed. 'So did I. I was hard on them I expect.'

We went back to Westminster Hall.

'I just might see you in there,' said Mackie, who had walked down with us on his way to Blackfriars. He put his hand very gently on Ma's shoulder as he left, I saw, a tiny loving gesture.

'Gothic!' said a lady in an extremely large hat, looking upwards (precariously it seemed to me as a milliner). 'Nothing less than a masterpiece of Gothic architecture and construction!'

When some people came out we sneaked in at the back, I wriggled down the front a bit so's Ma could hear better. The defence was in charge now and Ernest's barrister was talking about Ernest being called Stella.

'Why, gentlemen, I will be bound to say that there are none of us here who have passed through a public school who have not known at least half a dozen boys who have been always called by female names and laughed at and treated as girls, but in ninety-nine cases out of a hundred, as they grow older they object to that kind of familiarity – or to call it by the only name it deserves "chaff" – but as regards this young man the longer it went on the more he became enamoured of these characters and parts which he was constantly playing.' Ma rolled her eyes.

And then that Mr Serjeant Parry stood up, and the court went really quiet, everyone knowing how clever he is. 'Gentlemen. You must not judge these young men by your own circle. You must try to understand the Acting Life. They were stage performers and great familiarity is bred on stage – they were performing characters offstage that they had performed on stage.

'Now, gentlemen, I am told that when those dresses that have been exhibited – I am so short-sighted that without a glass I cannot discern the features of the jury whom I have the honour of addressing – but I am told by those that have a better and sharper sight than I have that a sort of thrill of horror ran through the jury box when all these dresses appeared on the floor of the court. I confess I did not observe it. I do not believe it is true although I was told so by a very respected person. But, gentlemen, these dresses are a *theatrical wardrobe* – neither more nor less – and a witness will be called to say that one was used in the very respectable performance of *Morning Call* in Scarborough – there is paint, there is powder – all this is theatrical. It is *theatrical* and not – I must use the word – *sodomical* – you must excuse me for such a term. There is the powder and there is the paint and they have played the same part in the street as they did on the stage. There is the lace, there is the silk, there are the fans – all theatrical! And now – a year having passed since they were seized by the constabulary – somewhat the worse for wear, as theatrical costumes often are! I confess I cannot understand how my learned friend,' he bowed to the Attorney-General, 'seeks to make out that these dresses mean that an unnatural crime was committed.'

(And Ma leaned over to me and whispered: '*He's* the greatest performer of the lot of them!')

And then came Ernest's mother. To be examined for the defence very politely by Ernest's barrister. There was a rustle of real interest as she had not been seen before.

She was pretty, with curls, not beautiful like Billy and me (and Mackie) think Ma is, but she was of course very much more high-class than any other woman who had appeared, all us land-ladies and maids. She wore a small hat and lady-like gloves and sometimes she dabbed her eyes with a lace handkerchief, she was a life away from that maid who talked of Ernest in a ladies' negligee and Lord Arthur calling him *darling*.

'My name is Mary Anne Sarah Boulton. I am the mother of Ernest Boulton. We live in Peckham. I have two sons, my husband is a stockbroker but he is away at present. In fact he is in the Cape of Good Hope.' She recounted in most respectable tones that Ernest had always delighted in dressing-up and performance from a very young age, they would have performances at home, she and her husband had enjoyed them thoroughly – 'and my Ernest was always the star, there is no denying it.'

'Were you acquainted with Lord Arthur Clinton?'

'Oh, *very* well indeed. We were very pleased to first meet Lord Arthur Clinton' – and she just slightly emphasised 'Lord' just exactly like Ernest used to do – 'nearly three years ago perhaps at the house of friends. He became a great admirer of my son for they had similar theatrical interests and he would come to our house in Peckham.'

'Did he enter into these – home theatricals?'

'Well,' she said, all coy. 'Perhaps once. No more than that I am certain.'

'Did he dress up in dresses?'

'Oh no,' she said smiling. 'Lord Arthur was always the husband, or the father!'

'Did you ever go to his house?'

'We visited him at his quarters at Southampton-street and there we took refreshment before we went with Lord Arthur – that is my husband, my son and myself – to the theatre.'

'When was this?'

'Ah – I do not have a retentive memory I am afraid. Lord Arthur Clinton was the Member of Parliament for Newark at the time you know.'

'Your son was living with Lord Arthur Clinton at this time?'

'No he was not living with Lord Arthur Clinton at this time. He was on a visit to him.'

'Quite so.'

'He never went anywhere without my permission. I always knew where he was. He had a position in a bank, you know, but he had to leave that employment, he was not strong enough. We have tuberculosis in the family and you have heard of his fistula operation also which was very painful and exhausting for him.'

'And you knew Mr Frederick Park.'

'Very well indeed. Mr Park nursed my son in his illness, for I, you know, am also not very strong. You need to understand my son has poor health – as I say he is possibly consumptive, it runs in my family I am sad to say.'

She said she had always been opposed to his acting but she did not forbid it as he was so keen and he had once laughed and told her of his friends calling him 'Stella' and she had laughed too, at their silliness.

The Lord Chief Justice leaned forward. 'Did you ever hear him called by that name, Mrs Boulton?'

She looked up at the learned Judge, deeply shocked. 'Never, my lord!'

'You say Mr Park came to your house,' continued the kind barrister. 'Did your son visit Mr Park in his father's house?'

'Yes. At Isleworth.'

'So the friendship was known to both families?'

'Yes. Of course.'

'Thank you, Mrs Boulton.'

She smiled sweetly, and made to leave the stand. Ma whispered to me she should have had a notice pinned upon her: 'Very Respectable Mother'.

But for the cross-examination up stood the Attorney-General who had been sitting quietly, I already said I thought he looked like a guard dog, now we found he was ready for the vicious bite – but very politely of course.

'Mrs Boulton,' he said most courteously, 'I am sorry to have to ask you, but,' and the teeth went in, 'I am afraid your husband is not very successful in business is he?'

She looked distinctly put out at once. 'He has had great reverses, certainly.' Then she tossed her curls, a little bit like Ernest. 'But I never allowed any cloud to fall upon my children. I always supplied them with everything they required. Whatever trouble we have had I have always shielded them from everything.'

'Had your son any settled allowance?'

'No – he didn't need one of course. I looked after him.'

'He had nothing from his father I think.'

'If he asked his father for anything he always gave it to him.'

'I must ask you, how long has your husband been away?'

'Oh – only – perhaps a fortnight this time.'

'I thought you said he was gone to the Cape.'

'Oh, oh yes but – but he has only been left *here* about a fortnight. Or – no, I may be mistaken, perhaps a little more.'

'Quite a lot more I think, Mrs Boulton.'

Out came the lace handkerchief, she looked around for support, surely he was being rude and intrusive? But the Attorney-General went on and the questions seemed to get faster and faster.

'Your son has no settled allowance you say. Then how did he live?'

'He lived with me. He always lived with me. Oh – I gave him pocket money – at least a pound per week I should think, my family have always given me a great deal of money and I gave him ten pounds for his birthday when he was in Scotland.'

'Do you know if your son received money from Lord Arthur Clinton?'

'I know nothing about that. I kept my son in clothes you know. He did not go short for anything.'

'Your son generally lived at home?'

'Yes. Always.'

'*Always* at home, Mrs Boulton?'

'Yes, I've told you already, he always lived at home, and he never went anywhere without my permission, I always knew where he was.'

Ma and I looked at each other.

'Were you aware of his living in London, in having lodgings in London?' The handkerchief was clenched.

'I was aware he might stay with Mr Park for a short time. I do not think the lodgings were his. I do not think he had anything to do with them. He merely stayed as a guest of Mr Park I think.'

'Did you know where he was staying?'

'I cannot remember. I do not have a retentive memory. But he has never been anywhere that I did not know where he was.'

The Lord Chief Justice leaned down again. 'You knew of Wakefield-street?'

'No. Oh no, my lord, no! No no no! They never stayed there I believe, never, *never*, they merely dressed there if I recollect rightly, but I do not know anything about that.'

The Attorney-General looked at her. 'You do not know anything about that,' he said, saying each word clearly.

She got more and more upset. She looked around for help: where was the polite man? 'I knew he was with Mr Park but I did not always enquire exactly where they were and I may have forgotten it. I cannot remember everything. I do not have a retentive memory.' (I wished I'd thought of that expression.)

'I need scarcely ask you I suppose whether you were aware of his walking about London, night after night, dressed in women's clothes?'

Mrs Boulton burst into tears, put her lace handkerchief to her face.

'Indeed I did not!'

The Attorney-General bowed and sat and poor Mrs Boulton turned to leave, her hat had gone all awry and she looked pale but Ernest's barrister stood again and asked, so very gently: 'I will ask you just one more question, Mrs Boulton. Has Mr Ernest Boulton proved himself as, and acted towards you and your husband as, a dutiful and affectionate son?'

She looked at him most gratefully and pulled herself up to her respectable mother stance again although the handkerchief was still visible and the hat was at a funny angle. 'He has been a most dutiful and affectionate son.' And then she added – perhaps she had even been instructed like me, or perhaps she was tired after such a long time being questioned – 'and the only fault my son ever had was a love of admiration.' And she looked at the other defendants. 'Which has been fed by the gross flattery of some very foolish people!' and then of her own accord she stepped down and went out of the courtroom. People talked and whispered and Ma said, 'She *might* have believed everything she was saying, Mattie. In which case she is a *very* stupid woman.'

'Call Mr Alexander Atherton Park!'

The Court of the Queen's Bench – nothing like Bow-street, or ragamuffiny people, but barristers in their gowns, and respectable-looking gentlemen mostly, and a few ladies with big hats – went quiet at once but I couldn't help a tiny sound when I saw Freddie's father walk very slowly up to the table.

He'd been angry and, when I understood things more clearly, anxious more than angry, when I met him at his office because he must have known that his other son was finally caught also. But now he looked only like a frail, devastated old man. I looked at Freddie, his face was distressed, he half stood to help his father but Mr Serjeant Parry kept him where he was with a little gesture. Of course everybody in the court knew who the old man was: the Lord Chief Justice, all the barristers, some of them looked down at their papers in embarrassment or pity: here was the Senior Master of the Court of Common Pleas, he was never a person to be in the witness box, and he stood here now, the father of two sodomites.

Mr Serjeant Parry spoke gently.

'You are the father of this young man, sir?'

'Yes.'

'I shall but ask you one or two questions. This young man, your son here, was articled, was he not, to a gentleman at Chelmsford? Now during that time that he was so articled, and down I think to the present time, you have made him an allowance. What allowance have you made him?'

'One hundred and sixty pounds per year.'

'Altogether?'

'Yes. That – that was—' The old man stumbled in his words and then spoke again. 'That was his nominal allowance but he spent a great deal more. I believe he had – eighty pounds to spend and eighty pounds for his board and lodgings.'

And of course I thought of all Freddie's board and lodgings: Bruton-street, Wakefield-street, Chelmsford.

'From what time does this extend – when did he go down to Chelmsford to work?'

'In – 1866 I think.'

'From that time down to now altogether what money have you given him from time to time, and at different times?'

'He has had about two and a half thousand pounds – about five hundred pounds each year. Up to the present time.'

Mr Serjeant Parry shot a triumphant look at the Lord Chief Justice, again about money, his look said, *Freddie and Ernest had plenty of money between them.* The old man held on to the table.

'I believe the young man, Mr Boulton, was once for a short time a visitor to your house?'

'Yes. My son brought him there once.'

'And I believe he stayed there about a week?'

'Yes. About a week.' By now I longed to go and help Mr Park myself and I could feel Ma ruffling, wanting to do the same. This was cruel.

'Do you remember when that was?'

'No, I do not. It made no impression.'

'Where do you live now, Mr Park?'

Almost inaudible now. 'Isleworth.'

The Attorney-General stood quickly and said, 'I have nothing to ask Mr Park.'

With the help of a court clerk the Senior Master of the Court of Common Pleas turned and left the Court of the Queen's Bench.

I looked at Ernest and Freddie. Ernest looked perhaps a bit cross at being told he made no impression. From where I sat, perhaps because of the way the light fell, I saw tears on Freddie's face.

49

The last day of the Trial of the Men in Petticoats.

At the end of all the repeated evidence – much of it either medical (anuses, penises, flaps and fistula, not to mention syphilis); domestic (landladies, negligees and rumpled bedsheets; noble lodgers and cards saying LADY CLINTON); or financial (horrified exclamations from the defence: with so much money provided to these young gentlemen from their loving and generous families, the suggestion that they needed other money, from other men for instance, was outrageous and disgusting) – at the end of the evidence, then, final legal statements were made to the jury.

But the inhabitants of 13 Wakefield street had finally had enough of the trial and did not attend. Except for one.

The Attorney-General for the prosecution, and each of the defence lawyers for their four separate clients, summed up the cases. Hours went by. To be truthful, many people left for refreshment – and if they did so they missed some very fine and telling oratory from Mr Serjeant Parry, defence for Frederick Park. As the press later reported, he spoke movingly about Manhood and Empire.

Mackie stood at the back of the court, waiting.

Mr Serjeant Parry concluded with a final exhortation that was carried in several newspapers.

'I do hope, gentlemen, you will find that not only my client, Mr Park, but all of the defendants have not after all been guilty of the loathsome crime that has been charged against them. Such a verdict in its effect – I do not say could leave a stain upon the national character, God forbid I should think so! But perhaps in the press of Europe and of America – gentlemen, if such a verdict were found, it might be, and no doubt would be, treated with some criticism and reproach! *It might be said to be a part of the manners of the English people in this modern nineteenth century!* Gentlemen! Think on it!

'They have been foolish, and great disapprobation of their behaviour should be pronounced. They never can be relieved from a certain kind of scorn and contempt, but I hope, gentlemen, you will not find them guilty of a greater crime than they have committed.'

And Mr Serjeant Parry bowed to the jury and sat down.

Then it was the moment for the most important speech of all: the summing-up speech of the Lord Chief Justice, Sir Alexander Cockburn, who had no intention of being outdone by a barrister. Many people in the court knew of the Lord Chief Justice: in noble circles his un-respectable private life and Queen Victoria's disapproval were much commented upon and enjoyed. However, he not only held the highest legal position in the country, but was a wonderfully entertaining and indiscreet dinner guest with many outrageous stories, and his presence was sought at many noble dining tables, if not at Her Majesty's (for which he might well have been eternally grateful for they were not diverting evenings on the whole; he very much preferred the company of her more amusing son).

It was known that Sir Alexander Cockburn liked an audience.

Whatever Mr Ernest Boulton, and Mr Frederick Park, and

Mr John Fiske (the consul for America in Edinburgh), and Mr Louis Hurt (from the Scottish Post Office) had been hoping for (with the most serious charge dropped long ago), when the Lord Chief Justice shuffled his papers and cleared his throat importantly, their hearts nevertheless clenched suddenly; they had been forewarned that the special jury could be persuaded of their innocence – or guilt – by this dominant, well-known and extremely powerful person – if he so wished.

Word quickly went round the building: the Lord Chief Justice was now standing.

The court filled up again with people who had refreshed themselves. Also Sir Alexander Cockburn knew that many gentlemen of the legal profession, and of the Palace of Westminster, would have arrived in the court especially for his speech, and that the gentlemen of the press would be reporting his words. So before he began, he bowed to his audience in general and when he declaimed: 'Gentlemen' – nominally addressing the propertied gentlemen of the special jury – the word encompassed other gentlemen in the court as well.

'Gentlemen.'

And then he spoke at very great length. He ran through legal matters; suddenly he severely criticised the police for the way they had obtained much of their evidence: what legal right had they to be bringing evidence from Scotland against Mr Fiske and Mr Hurt at all? For Scotland had its own police. And what right had the police surgeon to make a medical inspection of his own volition without an order from the court?

Then, just as suddenly, he strongly built up the whole case of the Attorney-General for the prosecution – the evidence, the letters, the money, the witnesses.

Then he collated the evidence for the defence with a different view regarding letters, money, witnesses. In particular he emphasised the theatrical side of the three principal defendants; when Ernest Boulton wrote to Lord Arthur Clinton, saying, *Send money, Wretch* – although it was in a somewhat inappropriate tone for persons of such a different class – it may have been money owing for performances; when Freddie signed letters to Lord Arthur Clinton *your loving sister-in-law* he was taking stage parts into the real world.

It was a masterly – and extremely long – performance.

'Gentlemen, there can be no doubt, with regard to two of the defendants, that they *have* been in the habit of presenting themselves in public sometimes in the disguise of women. And at other times in their own proper habiliments in the dress of men – but *still* under circumstances which produced a public scandal, by assuming the gait, and manners, and carriage, and appearance, of women, with painted and powdered faces, so as to produce the general impression that, though in male attire, they were of the opposite sex. Gentlemen. It is *impossible* for me to speak in terms of sufficient reprobation of indecent conduct of this description. Such behaviour is an *outrage* against public decency.'

The Lord Chief Justice took a long drink of water. (Perhaps it was water.) The court waited; various hearts about the courtroom were beating rather fast.

A torrent of words suddenly filled the courtroom. 'Gentlemen, I repeat, such petticoat-wearing behaviour is an *outrage* against public decency that ought to offend any right-minded person of either sex, and ought not to tolerated; and in my opinion when it is done even as a frolic it ought to be the object of *severe and summary punishment*. If the law cannot reach it as it is, it ought to be made the subject of such legislation, and a punishment of two or three months' imprisonment – with the treadmill attached to it – and in the case of a repetition of the offence, a little *wholesome corporal discipline* would, I think, be effective, not only in such cases, but in all outrages against public decency.'

The faces of the defendants were suddenly white. Something seemed to have gone wrong; this was not what they had been led to expect.

Sir Alexander Cockburn looked at them in great disdain for a few moments over his spectacles. Not a sound, not a cough in the court.

'However.' And he turned back to the jury. '*That* outrage is not what we are now trying, gentlemen, and you must carefully bear that in mind, and not allow any indignation you may feel at such unmanly and disorderly proceedings to warp your judgement. I must agree with the manly energy and simple beauty of the speech of Mr Serjeant Parry. Never forget this important point' – and as he took a dramatic pause you might well have heard a pin drop in Westminster Hall – 'never forget that *the first and greatest attribute of a great nation is the Moral Character of its People*.'

Then he spoke briskly. 'Nevertheless the second – I might also say of equal importance – is the sacred cause of truth and justice. If you are satisfied of the guilt of these persons, pronounce it, do not be afraid of the consequences! No popular cry, no operation of prejudice, should be allowed to poison justice at its fountain!'

Then the Lord Chief Justice also mopped his brow with an extremely large handkerchief and sat down.

Now, at 4 p.m., the special jury of propertied gentlemen retired to consider their verdict. At 4.53 p.m. they returned to the court.

'Gentlemen, are you all agreed upon your verdict?'

'We are all agreed.'

Do you find the defendants guilty or not guilty?'

'Not guilty.'

At this point – as reported in every newspaper – Mr Ernest Boulton fainted.

At this point the young man whom Mackie had been watching all day got up and almost ran from the courtroom. He was dodging the crowd in his hurry to get out, his face red with excitement. But as he exited the heavy doors of Westminster Hall, his arm was unexpectedly gripped in what felt like an iron vice.

He was immediately shocked, assuming it was a police officer. The sight of his captor looking like some biblical apparition frightened the gentleman even more; he looked about him for assistance; did not, however, call a nearby constable.

Mackie said very quietly into his ear, 'Mr Wade, I think. I saw you in Mudeford,' and then led him, silently, down towards the River Thames and the Embankment.

The terrified man had become very pale and was perspiring profusely. He tried to loosen his cravat with his free arm. He kept casting small, cowed glances at the tall, strange man in the cloak who still held his elbow in such an intimidating manner. He even actually wondered whether he could be having a religious hallucination.

When they got to the river Mackie wasted no time. 'I am not a policeman,' he said quietly, 'and I don't care if you're a sodomite.'

People hurried past, on their own business; the end of the day. The young gentleman stared at the man in the fisherman's cloak. 'Then why are you making me walk here? Are you from the Church? Did the bishop send you? But I am on my way to him now, I told him I would wait until the jury returned.'

'That would be Bishop Julius of course.'

'Yes. Yes, of course. So you must be from the Church, so why are you holding me like – like a prisoner? Who are you?'

'You don't need to know my name but everybody calls me Mackie. I am not from the Church, I'm from Mudeford. I recognise you, Mr Wade. You came to Mudeford the same day as Mr Roberts. The newspapers said you witnessed Lord Arthur Clinton's last letter.'

If it was possible, the gentleman turned paler still as the smoke-darkened sun moved towards the horizon and more and more people hurried by.

Mackie at last let go of the arm of this person, who stared at his tormentor like a mesmerised rabbit.

'What happened to Lord Arthur Clinton in Mudeford?' said Mackie. 'It was not scarlet fever. But I expect you know that, Mr Wade, as you told Johnny Hewlettson you were a doctor, although I think the title was removed from you in later reports. What about the letter you were supposed to have witnessed?'

'But I didn't stay! I don't know anything!'

'Perhaps you witnessed that letter in London after he died?'

'No! I'm not *that* Mr Wade, there must be some mistake, I think there was another Mr Wade, yes, funny coincidence, there were *two* Mr Wades there, yes, I noted that, wasn't that strange? I wasn't there when he died, no, not at all . . . I was on my way back to London.'

Mackie spoke very slowly and softly. 'Try again,' he said. 'Otherwise I'll either take you straight back and give you to the Lord Chief Justice, or throw you into the river. You can choose. What happened to Lord Arthur Clinton in Mudeford?'

The wild man seemed now to loom over the younger man like Judgement Day. Although he kept his voice low, Mr Wade began to gabble, quite certain his fate was the river below, or worse.

'He had taken the poison before we got there, he was raving about everybody, blaming everybody, he was raving about getting to France – but when we got there he couldn't even get out of bed.'

'What poison?'

'He had it there. And then – and then – and then when – when we weren't looking, that is, he – he must've taken more. To be certain. That's all I know.'

'For *who* to be certain? Lord Arthur? Or for you to be certain, Mr Wade?'

To the young man, the bearded, strange-looking Mackie appeared now to be God on the Thames Embankment as the setting sun disappeared completely behind clouds and smoke. Faster and faster he gabbled.

'Mr Newlyn from the King's Arms in Christchurch, he had been there – he knew Arthur was dying, you could tell he was dying. You can ask Mr Newlyn. Arthur was dying when we came.'

'Did you give him more?'

'He was *desperate*. He was terrified of going to prison and scandal, he kept blaming people, naming names, all sorts of names – none of it true, of course, but he was delirious, you should have seen him in that terrible little room.'

'I did see him in that terrible little room as you call it, with the window closed and the curtain drawn and the little girl downstairs.'

This information caused the younger man to look as if he was actually going to faint. His face had acquired a greenish tinge.

'I'll ask you again. *Are* you a doctor, Mr Wade, as you told Johnny Hewlettson and as one of the newspapers seemed to think? And you happened to be in Christchurch, and then you came to Mudeford?'

'Yes. No, no! I am a gentleman. I do not say that I am *that* Mr Wade. I am not a doctor. You have made a mistake. I keep telling you: there must have been two Mr Wades there at the same time. I am someone else. I am being sent as a missionary in Africa.'

'Is that so?' said Mackie. 'Were you in Mudeford then to save Lord Arthur's soul?'

'I – no – yes. To comfort him, of course. I didn't stay. I wasn't there when he died.'

'So it was just to give a *short* bit of comfort?'

'I am to travel to Africa next week, I have nothing to do with any of this, my work is to be in Africa, taking the word of God.'

'Africa.' Mackie mused for a moment beside the Thames. 'To – get you out of the way perhaps. Are you looking forward to Africa?'

Mr Wade burst out suddenly as if he could not help himself, 'If you lived in London, for God's sake, would *you* go to the damned wilds of Africa?'

'Oh, I see. For God's sake. Is the bishop going with you?'

'Of course not.'

'But no doubt, Mr Wade, you will tell the Africans about that biblical law I saw on a sign outside the court every day this week – that man must lie with woman only, and you'll tell them God says so, even if' – Mackie paused – 'even if you yourself were a colleague of Lord Arthur and of several certain bishops?'

'*Me?* A colleague of Arthur? A colleague of bishops? No, no! Of course not – *of course not!* I never met – any of them! I keep telling you, you have made a mistake.'

Mackie looked at him implacably. Finally the man began to weep.

'Someone had to go to see how Arthur was, that's all. *They made me go!*'

'Who? Bishop Julius, Mr Wade?'

It was at this point that the gentleman turned and vomited loudly into the River Thames.

Mackie felt like vomiting himself; he stared at the dirty, stinking, crowded water, saw smoke rising everywhere, heard ferries hooting and boatmen calling as it got darker. The vomiting, sweating man went on weeping amid his vomit; Mackie thought of the sleek, knowing, clever gentlemen in the historic building behind them, making their sleek, clever speeches; this great city: London. Big Ben sonorously chimed just then almost directly above them, as if to confirm matters.

'Where are you meeting the bishop, Mr Wade?'

The younger man stood miserably beside the river, fumbling for a handkerchief, trying to wipe away the vomit and tears that were mixed on his chin.

'It is – a private establishment . . .'

'Let's walk there then, shall we, Mr Wade?'

'You – you would not be allowed in.'

'Well, I'll send you in, Mr Wade.'

The two men walked back from the river, Mackie's hand now lightly holding Mr Wade's arm; back from the River Thames and into the Parliament Square. They turned towards Victoria Railway Station. Mackie looked up at the big, beautiful, glorious Westminster Abbey, shadowed now against the sky, but that glory was not, apparently, to be the meeting place.

They began to turn again, into smaller streets, and then past the remains of a makeshift, empty street market; children yelled from a broken cart, kicked some mouldy carrots and slipped on rotten tomatoes, and as always, but still noticeable to the man from Mudeford, there was the sour, acrid smell of piss. Down a darkening alley street rats were pulling at something under another cart, the smell now of decaying meat was strong; nearby an unmarked door seemed to be their destination and beside it a small gas lamp shone dimly.

'Bring him out,' said Mackie.

'He won't come out,' said Mr Wade.

'Tell him I'm from Mudeford, that I'm known to Mr Ouvry,

the lawyer for the Newcastle Estate. And that I'd like a moment of his time. If he chooses not to meet me I'll go, now, to Lincoln's Inn Fields, and I'll have the conversation with Mr Ouvry instead. That's all.'

He rapped the knocker briskly and then stepped back into the shadows as a small wooden peephole slid open. The dishevelled Mr Wade was admitted.

It was quite some time before anything happened but Mackie waited patiently as darkness fell. At last the wooden peephole was slowly opened again, then the door, and a large figure appeared – not, however, the bishop. Mackie, who was from Mudeford after all, was not exactly certain whether the person in front of him, carrying a stick and dressed in a bright yellow and over-elaborate uniform, was a footman to the episcopacy, or a clown from a particular kind of entertainment. After all, one of the witnesses in the trial had spoke of wrapping Mr Ernest Boulton in a tablecloth, so Mackie tried not to be surprised by London ways.

The emerging figure saw the other, waiting patiently in the shadows.

'Oy, you!' he called, and Mackie stepped forward so that the yellow-clothed person could see him more clearly.

'As usual the Bishop sends someone else to do his business for him,' said Mackie.

'What d'you want?'

'I want to talk to Bishop Julius.'

'The Bishop Julius won't be talking to the likes of you.'

'Is that right?' said Mackie, and something about his appearance and his implacable manner unnerved the other man.

'You a copper?'

'Do I look like a policeman?'

'You look like a bleeding ancient prophet.'

'And you look like a bleeding clown.'

The clown swung at him with his stick; the ancient prophet caught his arm firmly; inside somebody had obviously been listening and the door was opened again. This time the fine-looking, white-haired gentleman whom Mackie had seen in the court materialised in his cassock and his cloak and wearing his jewelled cross. Mackie let the clown go and turned to the clerical personage who, although *he* was supposed to be the man of God, was startled at the sight of the biblical-looking figure in the half-light of the gas lamp.

'What is it you want?' He spoke abruptly.

'I think perhaps you might prefer this conversation to be held in private. I carry no weapon as you can see.'

'I prefer to have my man with me.'

Mackie nodded. 'Fine.'

The bishop tried to pull himself together. 'How can I help you?'

'It is yourself, Bishop Julius, that you might help.'

Then Mackie was silent for a moment, looking at the cleric carefully. The uniformed person standing slightly behind watched Mackie's every move.

'Bishop Julius, you might have a chat, I suggest, to your God at this point. I think you would help yourself immensely by making that long journey to Africa next week. With Mr Wade.'

Bishop Julius was completely taken aback; this was not what the weeping Mr Wade had led him to expect. His hands automatically went to his jewelled cross.

'Don't be ridiculous! Who are you?'

'I am from a place you may have heard of called Mudeford, Bishop. People call me Mackie. I helped bury Lord Arthur Clinton. Mr Ouvry knows that, you see – you may of course ask him about me if you don't think I look like a man who is telling the truth.'

'All this has nothing to do with me. I am afraid I cannot

imagine why you thought it might. I must bid you good evening.' And the clerical gentleman turned back to the wooden door.

'I've met people who remember you at Mr Porterbury's ball in the Strand, Bishop Julius.'

The cassocked man froze. 'I will manage this, thank you, Claude,' he said and the yellow uniform bowed and disappeared through the wooden door, which remained, however, slightly open. 'I will knock, Claude, if I require entrance.'

The wooden door clicked shut. The bishop slowly turned back. The two men stood together under the gaslight.

'I know, Bishop Julius, as I said, people who remember you at Mr Porterbury's ball. I also happen to know you were delighted with Mrs Dodo Fortune's afternoon fruit cake but that didn't stop you helping to hound her and her husband out of their home, which seems to me to be one of a number of unchristian acts I find you seem to have been personally responsible for.'

In the darkness the bishop, transfixed, became suddenly pale at the turn of the conversation.

'And I understand that you sent Mr Wade to Mudeford.'

'Mr Wade is a hysteric and a liar. I know nothing of Mudeford.'

'He may be those things, Bishop, and you may not know Mudeford but I myself – and many of my neighbours – saw Mr Wade in Mudeford. And I think perhaps you sent him there. I know Mr Gladstone is a trustee for the Newcastle Estate and knew Lord Arthur Clinton much better than is public knowledge – at this point in time. I helped put Lord Arthur Clinton in his coffin, and was present at his burial, which you – of course – were not. No headstone has been erected but I could show Mr Ouvry and Mr Gladstone exactly where he is buried, should there ever be any confusion, or question, about his – scarlet fever.'

In the gaslight Mackie saw that the bishop's polished, urbane face was now dripping with sweat.

'Do you believe in your God, Bishop Julius?'

'How dare you blaspheme in my presence! Of course.'

'Are you sure?'

'Of course I am sure.'

'Aren't you therefore terrified?'

'What do you mean?'

'Aren't you terrified that your God – I'm sure you know your Bible well – is all-seeing, and will therefore find out the things that I found out – let alone *Reynolds News* and *The Times*? I would go to Africa if I was you, Bishop Julius, I'm sure of it. Because once you've seen a lonely dead man stinking for want of a coffin – and then seen all the hypocritical cant that covers up such a story, and heard all the speeches regarding the noble nobility – well, you want to spew, like Mr Wade has been spewing. I know so much that I could ruin you, Bishop, and I am not party to your gentlemen's code, which keeps society's secrets.'

'What do you want?' the churchman whispered in the darkness, staring at the looming bearded stranger. '*Who are you?*'

'I'm just a fisherman, Bishop Julius.'

'*A fisherman?*' And, like Mr Wade before him, Bishop Julius (who indeed knew his Bible well, and was also under great stress of course) thought for a moment that he was having a religious hallucination in the dark, stinking alley.

'I think you should go to Africa, Bishop Julius. Not because you're a sodomite too, because that's your business. And not because you are a bishop, because that's your business also. *But because you are a bloody, lying, cowardly hypocrite.*' In the shocked silence Mackie added: 'Although I fear for the Africans.'

And he turned from the man of the Church and left.

Mackie walked back to the river and along to Blackfriars. The last ferry to Gravesend had left, but Mackie stood on the bridge as the young boy from Tooting had stood, staring at the murky water in the darkness, and he thought of the trial that had ended this day; the pomp and the circumstance and the noble speeches. He thought of Lord Arthur Clinton; he thought of Mr Wade vomiting into this river; he thought of the bishop in his cross and cassock. He thought of the ferries in which he took passengers daily through the channels of the great river to Gravesend, where the big ships were waiting to carry them across the seas to build the Empire of Great Britain: the Great British Empire of Mr Gladstone, of the Prince of Wales, and of Queen Victoria.

50

Mackie got back to Wakefield-street late that evening, but Billy and Elijah had also arrived late from the Working Men's Institute and were still eating the sausage and mash that had been kept warm on the stove. Mattie bent over a stiff hat-brim with a large needle and white cotton; everyone was still in the downstairs kitchen, discussing the trial, knowing what anybody in London who was still interested would have known by now: that the case regarding the Men in Petticoats, that had once been labelled 'the Scandal of the Century', had eventuated to nothing at all, and was over.

The front door banged; Mackie's footsteps descended slowly. He stood in his fisherman's cloak at the bottom of the stairs that turned into the kitchen. Everybody stopped talking and looked up, struck by the odd look on his face.

'What, Mackie?' said Isabella.

He answered abruptly: 'I told you that after Johnny Hewlettson sent a telegram to that Mr Ouvry, several people appeared in Mudeford. Billy, you said that Mr Roberts was definitely a lawyer, right, but he came with a few others. The man we were told was Dr Wade – or later Mr Wade – has been in court all week. I've just had a word with him and Dodo's bishop.'

'*No, Mackie!*' said Mrs Stacey.

She saw her son's face.

'*No, Billy, no, no no! I don't want to know! I don't care!* It's all over at last. We've been through all this, what *good* can it do now? – making wild accusations about Lord Arthur's death, next thing you know, you'll all be doing hard labour at Newgate yourselves, ha! Now listen to me, all of you!'

Isabella stood by the stove, facing them all angrily.

'This is the world we live in, this is how it is. We've had a bad time but the trial is now over and we're all safe, in a way. I've been *unsafe* in my life and I don't want it again, for any of us. You've all got jobs of a kind, hopefully you'll get better ones when this is all over, and we've got our house, so no one can throw any of us into the street. Do you want *another* bleeding trial, Mackie? Why not say Queen Victoria and the Archbishop of Canterbury as well as the Prime Minister of England ordered the death of Lord Arthur to save England? Why not bring down the whole country? Let's have ASYLUM FOR THE INSANE writ on our wall this time, ha! This is the end of the trial and this is the end of our involvement, *now*!'

Mackie straightened up from the wall.

'Isabella,' he said gently in the slow deep rumbling voice that she could hear. 'I know the world we live in, just as you do.' He faced her to be absolutely sure she heard. 'It *is* over, in a way. But it's *not* over in this house. I can't do much. Although I hope I might have given that churchman something to ponder. But I know enough now that I think I might be able to go to see Mr Ouvry again and help get Elijah and Billy their jobs back.'

'I don't want my job back any more, Mackie,' said Billy, surprising everybody in the kitchen. 'I thought the Parliament was a good and powerful place and I liked being part of it but I can't feel the same about it any more – of course I'm not going to walk behind black horses with funeral plumes for the rest of my life, but – no, I don't want to go back there now, from where I was thrown out the door. I really like teaching people to read, ones who didn't have the chance Mattie and I had.' He looked at his mother. 'I'm going to be a proper teacher, Ma.'

There was a stunned silence. Mrs Stacey and Mattie exchanged a tiny glance, remembered that the girl they'd heard of, Emily, was a teacher.

The silence was broken by Dodo.

'Nevertheless. If there *was* any way, then I know Elijah would so very much like to go back to the Parliament' – and she put up a bent, clawed hand almost imperiously when Elijah began to interrupt. 'I *am* going to speak, dearest, I've said not one word all these months but now I'm going to speak. You were part of that building.'

Elijah Fortune was sitting near the long table. He stared at the floor. Dodo turned then to all the others.

'It hurt me to be there this week and know Elijah wasn't there along the hall past all the statues, as he was for so many years. *He was part of the Parliament.* Not that we aren't glad that he is at least working. But he wasn't meant, as Billy was never meant, to walk miles behind coffins and horses in bad weather, or sit in a cramped little office, recording deaths of people he doesn't know, through no fault of his own but his kindness.' And she put her bent hand very gently on Elijah's face. Elijah, who had never once complained, could not, for a moment, speak.

Mackie said quietly to Billy: 'Would you teach me?'

Everybody looked surprised.

'Oh yes, you all think I can read, and I *can* read the newspapers, but I can't read proper books; I never learned anything like that poem you told; we never had one book in our house when I was young, only the Bible. I can sign my name and read the papers and make lists and arrange money and keep my eyes and ears open. But I'd like to read real books, like you all do.'

'I don't read much, Mackie,' said Isabella quickly. 'There's plenty of us who can't read well.'

'I'll teach you, Mackie,' said Billy.

Mackie nodded. He still stood there at the bottom of the stairs, still hadn't taken off his cloak.

'I'd be glad to try to help get your position back, Elijah. Because I tell you what, I *can't* just let things be – because somehow it disgusts me, all the pomp and clever phrases and long speeches that I've heard this week – all to cover everything up and save the face of the nobility – and yet I saw that poor pathetic Lord Arthur dying by himself, nobody rushing to help him while he was alive. And you were trying to help him, Elijah, to get him money. I'll go and see Mr Ouvry once more.'

'Do you think he can really influence the Prime Minister?' Elijah spoke at last, but his expression was rueful as he looked at Mackie. 'I'm grateful, Mackie,' he said. 'Thank you. But Mr Gladstone himself is probably the only person who could get me back into the Parliament after all this.'

(And Mattie looked down at her hands, remembering the night she had met Mr Gladstone. Mr Gladstone knew what had happened to Billy. But it had not got Billy's position back.)

After a brief moment Isabella said quietly, 'Mackie, I'll do it.' And she nodded, acknowledging his words. 'You're right. It's the last thing to be done in our world. You're right – it's not over in this house till that's done. I'll make certain Mr Gladstone knows about Elijah.'

Mattie and Billy exchanged glances. There was only one way their mother ever did things like this.

'How will you do that, Ma?' said Billy innocently.

She looked at her son with love. 'I'm glad you want to be a

teacher, son, and if you don't want to go back to the Parliament after all that's happened, well, who can blame you! And I will be so, so proud of you.' Then she turned to the others. 'And we all bleeding know this trial was arranged by people who have the power – who they know, what they can do. But – funny – we have our power too, we know people – you and me, Elijah, we've always known people in this city, haven't we? Known who to talk to, we've got our own circles and influence. Elijah, remember Tussie Heap?'

He nodded at once. 'At Drury Lane. Years ago. Working in the wardrobe when you were. Cutting, she was good at cutting.'

'That's her. All those years ago. Well, I think she can help us. Listen to this: Tussie Heap now works at 11 Carlton House Terrace, the Prime Minister's house.'

'Oh Ma!' said Mattie and she laughed despite the tension in the kitchen, and Billy added: 'We always said, Ma, that you knew everybody in London.'

'I'll go there.'

'Are you sure, Isabella?' said Mackie.

'I'm sure, Mackie,' said Ma.

'Then – I need to go now.'

Everyone in the kitchen stared at Mackie, stunned.

'I need to – I need to go and breathe the real sea and get some of the stench of everything I've seen and heard this week out of my head. And thanks, Billy. I still want teaching. I'll find you. And the first thing I'm going to learn is that poem about the lights of France and the calm sea.' He turned towards the stairs.

'Mackie,' said Isabella.

Something in her voice. He turned back to look at her, his foot on the stair.

'You know them sailor lodgers down by the docks? You said they'd knife you soon as look at you.'

He nodded.

'Come back into the kitchen, take your blooming fisherman's cloak off and eat some blooming sausages and mash or I'll keep my promise and knife you myself!'

But Mackie didn't move. 'I can't, Isabella. *I have to go back to the sea.*'

She looked at him very carefully. 'Because of what you saw and heard at the trial?'

'It's all right. I'm not going to change the world. I'm going to leave that poor sad Lord Arthur Clinton where he is. But—'

He shook his head as if to free himself from his thoughts. They saw he looked like some sort of caged beast as he stood in his fisherman's cloak beside the stairs that led away from the basement kitchen of the house in Wakefield-street. He looked at Isabella.

'Let me go now, love.'

They heard his footsteps going up the stairs.

They heard the front door close.

51

I WATCHED MY Ma so carefully.

I was frightened she might be sad, but you couldn't talk to Ma about such things.

'Would you like me to make you another hat, Ma?'

She smiled at me, and sort of ruffled my hair, which she didn't usually. Being Ma, she understood what I was really saying. 'He'll come back, Mattie. He just had to – breathe fresh air. But he'll come back.'

'Are you *sure*, Ma?'

'I'm sure, Mattie. I literally couldn't *live* if I was away from London. That's how he sometimes feels about the sea.'

'He's such a – good man, Ma.'

'He is. I am glad you met him in Mudeford.'

That's all. That's all she said. That's all we ever discussed. But for my Ma that was like a whole novel.

52

Mrs Catherine Gladstone had just returned to London.

Mrs Gladstone had many family commitments among her own family, the Glynne family, and in Hawarden Castle in Wales, the Glynne family home – which one day her son William would inherit. If it was not her large family taking up her time, it was the estate workers who needed her. Her husband loved Hawarden Castle also; if it had not been for his astute financial acumen and his sheer hard work, the estate could have been lost. He travelled there, especially in the long summer recess, if his wife was there and his workload allowed.

Mrs Gladstone was absent often, certainly. But if her heart suffered sometimes she never said; despite her husband's rescuing interludes with other women, one in particular, she was nevertheless a loyal and fiercely protective wife to the Prime Minister. She perhaps understood him better than he understood himself, and loved him dearly.

It must be said that the success or otherwise of Mr Gladstone's rescue activities could not be measured exactly. Sometimes there was ignominious failure; one rescued lady, sent away to an institution for Fallen Women actually wrote to say thanks all the same but she had run away; she would have committed suicide if she had stayed there longer.

Occasionally Mrs Gladstone was able to find a better class of girl a position among her large network of friends and acquaintances. Sometimes the women just needed to talk. Sometimes they were perfectly happy with their lives but, having been persuaded by Mr Gladstone that there was a more honourable road under a forgiving God, found themselves, before they knew it, being offered a cup of tea in a set of charitable rooms in a narrow lane off Wardour Street, set up for the purpose of good works by good women.

Mrs Gladstone attended when she was able. Mrs Tussie Heap (long ago a member of the wardrobe staff at the Drury Lane Theatre) always accompanied her mistress, Mrs Gladstone, to these encounters. Tussie would sit outside and perhaps speak to other women waiting; Mrs Gladstone had a bell on a table in the room, which just once or twice she had had to ring and Tussie would immediately enter and help deal with any crisis. On the whole the visiting women were well behaved and quiet; just once one tried to attack Mrs Gladstone with her own umbrella, and once a woman collapsed and later died.

Mrs Tussie Heap, this mid-June day, simply added Mrs Isabella Stacey's name to the list she had been given by one of Mr Gladstone's secretaries, which is how Mrs Stacey of 13 Wakefield-street met Mrs Gladstone of 11 Carlton House Terrace and Hawarden Castle, in a room on the ground floor of the charitable premises, which had enriching pictures on all the walls. The pictures had been chosen carefully by Mrs Gladstone herself and some were beautiful as well as evangelical. The lane outside the building was so narrow that only the smallest of carts could navigate it, but footsteps hurried along continuously, and passers-by called and chattered outside the windows.

'Good morning, Mrs – Stacey, is it?'

'Good morning, Mrs Gladstone.'

Although they were so many worlds away from one another, they were both, in their own way, strong and confident women. Both were dressed well and unfussily although Mrs Stacey was in brighter colours. Their voices, of course, denoted their very different lives.

'Please sit here.'

There were comfortable chairs. But for a moment Isabella Stacey simply stared in amazement. Mrs Gladstone was wearing a plain but elegant gown but from a pocket at her breast an embroidered handkerchief could be clearly seen. And the woman from Wakefield-street recognised it at once – for she herself had sewn it; it was a material sample that one of the salesmen had given her, and in the corner she could see the tiny pink embroidered roses that Mattie had loved.

'What can I do for you, Mrs Stacey? Tell me about yourself. What did my husband suggest for you?'

It was unlike Isabella to be lost for words. She sat down slowly, still looking at the handkerchief. The summer day made the small room warm; Isabella looked for inspiration to the pictures on the wall; even the less sentimental and more artistic ones were mostly of fallen women redeemed, presumably by the Lord, or the Gladstones.

Then she looked back at the woman sitting so confidently across from her; if there was such a thing as an aristocratic mien, Mrs Gladstone possessed it. She was not neat and tidy and removed; she seemed warm and sympathetic and somehow unpatronising. But she was from another world.

Isabella moved her chair slightly so that she was directly opposite the other woman in order to be sure to hear her. And then plunged in.

'I'm sorry to start with a surprise for both of us, Mrs Gladstone, but I made the handkerchief that you wear – the cream silk was given me and you will know it has three pink roses in one corner and one in the middle, which I embroidered myself. My daughter gave it to Lord Arthur Clinton in Mudeford when he was – distressed.'

Composed and confident as she was, Catherine Gladstone could not have been more thrown. Her hand had automatically flown to the handkerchief; confronted with this introduction, and with her hand still at her breast, Mrs Gladstone was momentarily speechless. Finally her eyes turned to the little bell on the table.

'I didn't come here to cause you any trouble, Mrs Gladstone, be sure of that. I didn't know you'd be wearing my handkerchief.'

'What have you come here for? How did you get in?'

'How did you get my handkerchief?'

They stared at one another until Isabella pulled herself together and said: 'Do you know Elijah Fortune?'

'Elijah? Of course I do.' This subject was somehow reassuring to Mrs Gladstone, yet also even more bizarre.

'Have you seen him lately?'

'No, and I was so sorry when he left. He was Head Doorkeeper at the House for so long – I often go of course to hear my husband speak. Elijah had reached retirement age, they told me.'

'He's exactly the same age as your husband, Mrs Gladstone. He didn't retire, he was evicted from his position and his home very early one morning about a year ago by some new doorkeepers who had suddenly been appointed. They almost literally threw Elijah and his wife into the street. It is for Elijah I have come to see you this morning. He's never been allowed back in the building since.'

'I cannot believe that!'

'I think you'll find that that is exactly what happened.'

'But why?'

'Because he was trying to collect money from Members of Parliament to help Lord Arthur Clinton get to France, that's why. Elijah's actions were – disapproved of by some.'

'But – Mr Gladstone does not know this, of course. He would never have allowed such a thing!'

'Elijah believed his dismissal was arranged by some of the bishops in the House of Lords. A year ago, during the first trial, it was dangerous, if you remember, Mrs Gladstone, to be connected with Lord Arthur under any circumstances. I am sure you and the Prime Minister were aware of that also because of your own relationship with him.'

Mrs Gladstone rose majestically. 'Surely, Mrs Stacey, you understand it is deeply impertinent of you to speak of such things to me.'

The other woman did not rise. She bowed her head for a moment before she began speaking again. It may have looked like penitence for impertinence; it was actually Isabella trying to control her anger.

'My clever, beloved – much better educated than me – son, William – like your son, I believe, Mrs Gladstone – was a clerk in the Parliament, and much admired. He loved his work, he had been there ten years, he even worked sometimes in your husband's office when there were extra letters to be written, so highly was he thought of. He was dismissed at the same time as Elijah.'

'Why?'

'Because I am the landlady at 13 Wakefield-street, of which you have probably heard.'

'I see.' Icy now at once.

Still Isabella Stacey did not rise. 'It is a lodging house, Mrs Gladstone. Just like a thousand lodging houses in London. We are by Kings Cross Station and we used to have a lot of cotton cloth salesmen from the North as lodgers – which is why I recognise the handkerchief – they used to bring their samples to show to big businesses in London. One of them gave me that beautiful cream silk square you are wearing.'

She too rose at last.

'They had been coming for years. It's changed now of course – we lost many of them after the first trial, my daughter, who had to give evidence, was called a whore and we had SODOMITE LOVERS writ on our walls, which I do not expect was your own experience. Mr Boulton and Mr Park – let's not pretend you don't know who I'm talking about – told me they were actors and needed somewhere to keep their costumes for private theatricals. I worked at the wardrobes in Drury Lane and the Haymarket for many years, so I know actors often have to provide their own costumes.'

Mrs Stacey moved towards the door, but turned back.

'Now at least you know truthfully why Elijah Fortune and my son lost their positions in the noble Parliament of Great Britain: because of their connection – however indirect and Elijah's through nothing but kindness – to Lord Arthur Clinton, someone you were connected with also.'

Quickly Mrs Gladstone put out a hand to stop her leaving. 'Please, Mrs Stacey.' Mrs Gladstone took a deep breath. 'Let us both sit again.' She gestured graciously. Almost reluctantly the other woman came back; they both sat.

There was something about Isabella Stacey: it was quite clear to Catherine Gladstone that she was speaking completely honestly. Mrs Gladstone, who had experience of listening to women from a different class than her own, got caught up in the story despite herself, and believed it. Besides, she realised now she knew part of this woman's story already, but did not yet say so.

'You – you may have – met Arthur, Lord Arthur, perhaps?'

'We did, yes.'

Mrs Gladstone looked down at her own hands for a moment and then said: 'Would you like it if I ordered tea?'

'Good God above, I'd love that! It would be – easier.'

Tea was brought in by Tussie Heap, who did not of course acknowledge her old friend Isabella Stacey. Mrs Gladstone and Mrs Stacey talked briefly of the pleasant weather. When they were alone they sat in silence for a time.

Mrs Gladstone said at last: 'Arthur was always so. From a boy. His mother – had to leave her children.' She poured tea.

'She came to the theatre once,' said Mrs Stacey. 'His mother. Years and years ago when she was young. To see one of the actresses, and I met her briefly. She was very lovely.'

It would seem that Mrs Gladstone could no longer be surprised by anything in this strange conversation. If Mrs Stacey said she had met her friend of long ago, Lady Susan – Lady Susan Opdebeck as she was now – Mrs Gladstone was sure it was true.

She passed a cup and saucer of immaculate heritage to the other woman, who continued: 'My children went to see Lord Arthur in Mudeford. Lord Arthur told my son and daughter that Mr Gladstone was made his guardian when he was a boy. That is why I came to see you, to ask for help, because I understood you had some involvement in this matter also.'

Very slowly Mrs Gladstone put her cup and saucer back upon the table.

'Has your daughter – forgive me – is your daughter crippled?'

Mrs Stacey was caught between anger and surprise. Every time she heard the word *cripple* used about her beloved daughter she wanted to hit someone. Mattie was not *crippled*. She ran, almost; she could walk for miles.

'She has a limp. Yes.'

'I believe she accosted my husband.'

'*What?*'

Mrs Gladstone had recognised that the other woman was slightly deaf; she raised her voice a little. 'I believe your daughter accosted my husband in the Strand.'

Now it was Mrs Stacey's turn to look stunned. 'Blooming hell! Did she ask for Billy's job back?'

'Yes.'

'So you knew something of this story and you never said? Mattie never told me, the foolish, foolish girl, on her own down the Strand in the middle of the night. I suppose it was late at night?'

'Yes. About one o'clock in the morning, I believe.'

'What was she *thinking* of!' Isabella gulped her tea. 'Well, of course I know what she was thinking of – Mattie loves her brother. She'd do anything for him.'

Now both women were silent again, glad of the tea.

'Why did your children go to Mudeford in the first place?'

'Billy was desperate to get his position back, he loved working in the Parliament so much, especially for your husband who he admired very much. Elijah told him where Lord Arthur was – hiding, waiting for someone to give him financial help, and Billy had already understood there was some connection with you and your husband. He wanted to find out what it was. Lord Arthur told him.'

Silence.

At last Mrs Gladstone said, 'Can you tell me of Arthur's death?'

'I don't suppose you can tell *me* of it?'

'What do you mean?' and Isabella saw at once the genuine surprise. Of course Mrs Gladstone would know nothing. 'Mrs Stacey, he died almost a year ago today. That much I know. Which is why

I am wearing the handkerchief. Just my own thoughts for someone I was fond of when he was a small child, and so miserable.'

'Oh. Oh of course. A year ago. For days I was terrified my children had scarlet fever.' For a moment Isabella was silent. 'But I think Lord Arthur didn't die of scarlet fever, Mrs Gladstone. Mattie and Billy were close with him in the tiny room where he was hiding. None of the people who were looking after him got scarlet fever. He said he had the means to take his own life if he couldn't get to his mother in France.'

Mrs Gladstone's eyes filled with unexpected tears at the mention of people she had known and loved long ago. Automatically she felt for the handkerchief. Girls' voices called from the lane: '*We're late, Effie, we're late!*' Footsteps clattered, and laughter.

'How did you come by the handkerchief, Mrs Gladstone?'

Mrs Gladstone sighed. The handkerchief was in her hand now and she looked down at it: the cream square, the beautifully embroidered pink roses.

'Lord Arthur's solicitor had gone to Mudeford. When Arthur died Mr Roberts brought it back to London and gave it to the solicitor of the Newcastle Estate, thinking it might be' – she shrugged, knowing how it sounded – 'some sort of evidence perhaps to show Arthur's partiality to women. Finally Mr Ouvry gave it to me as a – memento. He knew I had been very fond of that sad little boy long ago.' She looked up at her visitor. 'Are you suggesting that – that it was suicide?'

'My children believed—' But Isabella knew she did not want to say more to the wife of the Prime Minister of England. 'Well, it is possible. They said Lord Arthur was distressed and frightened. Not dying. And then he died.'

'There were rumours he had got away. Perhaps he did.'

'No, Mrs Gladstone,' said Mrs Stacey gently. 'I know one of

the men who put him in the coffin, which was made by the local carpenter.'

Another long, long silence.

Then Mrs Gladstone said, 'I used to take him to the zoo when he was young.' A sigh. 'God will judge, but I will not.'

Silence.

'Is there any proof that Arthur killed himself?'

'There is no proof of – anything.'

Silence.

'Mrs Stacey, I believe many people were made uneasy about Lord Arthur's involvement in the – the scandal of the court case. Possibly others have also been made uneasy by his death. But – as he is dead I myself would leave poor Arthur where he is.'

'As it happens, I couldn't agree with you more, Mrs Gladstone. You asked me about his death, so I told you – something of the things that people say.'

If the wife of the Prime Minister of England noticed the particular choice of words, she did not say. For just a moment they sat there in silence together, then Mrs Gladstone spoke.

'I am certain I can arrange for Elijah Fortune to get his position back. I know my husband will be shocked by his story. I do not know your son, but I will – I will remind my husband again about his fate.'

'Billy does not want to return, Mrs Gladstone. He does not have the – respect – for the place that he once held so dear. They have lost a good man, but he has decided to become a teacher.'

'It seems then that the teaching profession will be fortunate. I will tell my husband that too – you may know of his passion for education.'

Mrs Gladstone rose again now, to close one of the strangest interviews she had ever conducted.

'And, Mrs Stacey, your son may, in his new profession, come

to understand one day that the Houses of Parliament of this great country are run by men who were born and educated to rule and are indeed deserving of his respect.'

Mrs Isabella Stacey rose also. 'Like Lord Arthur Clinton.'

'Like the late Lord Palmerston, like the late Sir Robert Peel, like the late Duke of Newcastle, Lord Arthur's father. Like the late Earl of Clarendon, like Earl Granville, like the Duke of Argyll, like the Earl of Kimberley, like Baron Aberdere, like the Marquess of Hartington, and I name only a few. And, most of all, like my very honourable husband. We do not really know each other, Mrs Stacey, we live in different worlds, and it is mine that rules this country. I do not believe that you will find a dishonourable man among those I have mentioned. I have listened to your story with respect and discretion. You must treat me in the same manner.'

Isabella Stacey saw the honour, if not the truth, in this. Elijah anyway would get his old position back. Now it was she who nodded, and put out her hand graciously. 'Thank you, Mrs Gladstone,' she said. 'This is an encounter I will certainly remember always.'

'I shall remember it also,' said the wife of the Prime Minister of England. 'May I keep the handkerchief?'

It had remained in her hand while they talked.

'I'll be glad to know that you have it,' said Isabella Stacey.

53

Today they were in Whitehall at the home belonging to the discreet friend as his available time was very short.

They never spoke of Arthur. But she believed he had been in some way involved in the way the trial had ended so quietly and so quickly, with her brother spoken of so respectfully, and she had rewarded him for his kindness in this matter in the ways that she knew pleased him.

She had been holding back from telling him her news. She knew he would be out of London for most of August as absolutely everybody would be; this perhaps was the time to advise him of her condition, for it was now indeed advanced; she thought he might even have noticed. She waited till he was relaxed and mellow: a last cigar, his arm lightly resting on her breast before he returned to Marlborough House to prepare for the evening's entertainment. The late-afternoon sun of high summer slanted across the borrowed bed that supported their noble forms.

'Your Royal Highness.' She stroked his royal face. 'I shall miss you while you are gone, and I adore you as I have done since you were ten years old!' He smiled lazily at this woman who had known him always, and moved his hand slightly across her breast.

'Your Royal Highness. I have found that I am – with child.'

His relaxed, gentle, loving demeanour changed in one single, absolute instant. He removed his arm and sat up.

'Go to Dr Clayton now.'

'I will, sir, of course.'

His face was red with immediate anger. 'This is most inconsiderate and inconvenient, Susan. You know that.'

'Of course.'

'How long have you known?' For a moment he looked carefully, but already with distaste, at her body. 'Is it advanced, and you did not tell me?'

'I – I have not been certain.'

He angrily fastened his garments, gesturing to her to assist him. 'Go to Dr Clayton and deal with it at once, this evening. – and do not under any circumstances come to Marlborough House. I do not know this. I have no knowledge of it. It is nothing at all to do with me. Only you and Dr Clayton will be involved – not one other person.'

She dealt with his buttons. 'Of course.'

The cigar was already stamped out on the carpet on the floor of the discreet friend's bedroom, a sign of terrible displeasure indeed.

'I am going away,' he said, averting his eyes from her still partially naked body. 'It is your responsibility. I expect it to be dealt with.'

'But – my dearest sir – just one warm word from you! We are such friends – you are always so kind.'

And it was true that he was kind, many said so, and he had been kind to her a hundred times.

But he was also the Prince of Wales and the heir to Queen Victoria. One day he would be King. Lady Susan could not have chosen a worse time to reveal her condition; she knew many of his secrets but she was not aware, as he was, that his private secretaries were already trying to deal with a dangerous blackmail attempt from his adventures in Europe. And now this. Public scandal was to be avoided at all cost.

The cost of this would, of course, be Susan.

'Susan. The public humiliation of my being called in the Mordaunt divorce case last year cannot *under any circumstances* be repeated. I was booed and shouted at, at the races, damn them! Booed by my own subjects! – my own one-day subjects if my mother ever leaves this earth, which is sometimes doubtful. Your idiotic, stupid, impecunious, sodomite brother is gone but not forgotten – *never, ever* can there be *any hint* of any scandalous connection between Arthur Clinton's sister and myself! You have always known that, always!'

He saw her devastated, disbelieving face.

'But – I am not my brother. I am not Harriet Mordaunt, Your Royal Highness. I am myself.'

He kissed her cheek very briefly. 'I know. And you will deal with it, I know. You are not the daughter of the Duke of Newcastle for nothing. You are one of us.'

And he was gone.

Lady Susan Vane-Tempest emerged alone some time later from the premises in Whitehall. A carriage was waiting for the extremely pale – nay, trembling – lady. She sat back, hidden, as the carriage delivered her through the busy central London traffic, to her home in Chapel-street.

She knew it was now too late for anything to be safely arranged by the pomade-scented Dr Clayton or anybody else.

That is what she had done.

54

SCRUBBING THE STEPS in early autumn was still scrubbing, but the mornings were only crisp not cold, and sometimes a bit of cloudy sun still, and it wasn't so hard for my hands like in dark winter when I had big chilblains and sores under the mittens Ma knitted me. And I always made our steps really really clean and we didn't get no words like SODOMITE LOVERS writ the second time, so 13 Wakefield-street even if it couldn't ever be quite respectable again, could be very, very clean.

And I was singing actually.

A jolly shoemaker, John Hobbs, John Hobbs
A jolly shoemaker was he
He'd married Jane Carter, no damsel looked smarter
But he'd caught a tartar, yes he'd caught a tartar . . .

I was singing because I was happy. Because Mr Tom Dent of Mr Lewis and Lewis obviously didn't find 13 Wakefield-street like a bordello and didn't seem to care that I limped and – he's been *courting* me. And he's so nice and so clever and so dear, and it is the loveliest feeling and we've even been reading *Moby Dick* to each other, what a hard book! But wonderful too and we talk about it as we read along. And Ma likes him and Tom and Billy talk about laws and voting and the Parliament, you should hear them! And Tom holds my hand.

I got a big surprise at the pair of feet that came up to me scrubbing this singing day, it's funny seeing feet and judging who they belong to – these were neat and smallish and Ernest.

'Hello, Mattie.'

Because almost *always* he'd been with Freddie (except that night coming home inebriated from the Holborn Casino) it was almost odd to see him by himself. 'Hello, Ernest. Welcome to the Bordello of Wakefield-street,' but I was smiling and just teasing.

He was still pretty, but was in gentlemen's clothes of course and not even a cutaway jacket. 'Can I talk to you for a minute?' he said politely.

Getting up from scrubbing is that hard thing, because of the steps, I remembered Freddie helping me up once or twice. I remembered Mackie helping me up when he first arrived, and Tom Dent the very first time he came. But Ernest didn't think like that, he waited for me to get up, looking about Wakefield-street, wondering if people were staring at him I suppose.

'Ma's not home.'

'Then she will not rebuke me!' He was only half joking.

'Do you want tea?' I said as we went into the hall.

'No, no we dont need to go down there, let's just sit in your little parlour. Who's here? Where's that man with the beard?'

'He comes and he goes.'

He does too, Mackie, and he insists on paying rent still even though Ma doesn't want him to pay anything at all. But he and Ma have the big front room downstairs now that Dodo and Elijah have gone, Mackie painted it blue like the sea.

Ernest came into the parlour, saw the piano at once, sat at the piano stool, ran his fingers over the keys. 'Where's that old lady who used to be in the music halls?'

'They got their rooms back in the Parliament, Elijah, that was her husband, is the Head Doorkeeper again.'

'Because of our acquittal.'

'Maybe.'

He looked quite pleased and proud. Of course we knew it was because of Ma's visit to Mrs Gladstone but I didn't tell him that. Dodo and Elijah had worried we might not be able to manage if they left but we all laughed, 'We always manage,' we said and we helped them – even kind Billy came with us, came back at last, to his once beloved workplace, the Houses of Parliament – to settle them back into that dear dark little place under the scurrying floors of the government, the red was still on the walls, and we put up the red curtains me and Ma had made and the bedcover on the bed, and we scrubbed and scrubbed till the smell of the other people was gone and Billy and Mackie painted another big table from the market red and Elijah was welcomed back by so many people like a blooming hero! And Dodo told us she missed us, but she felt happy because she had got the real Elijah back.

And you know what? We knew a way to get into the Parliament now, if we sent Elijah a message first, through some dark alleys and a small door left unlocked, and down some corridors and sometimes we went and had cake and gossip and heard the rumbling of the drains in the basement. But we did miss them, although we all got a bit thinner.

'Mattie,' said Ernest now, 'there were a few of our things left here I think. Maybe a gown or two?'

'Oh – well, well I dont think there's much, Ernest, well, you know the policeman took most, even your old ones. A few skirts maybe, and a petticoat and some hairpins and some "Bloom of Roses". And a corset I think. I packed them up in one of your little bags. But that was – ages and ages ago!' (And I had a sudden flash of memory of all the sad packed-up dresses the rude policeman took, laid out in the courtroom months and months later. Freddie's discarded yellow dress covered in my blood.)

Then I realised what he was asking and looked at him in amazement. 'Are you going to dress up again? You're mad!'

Ernest tossed his head, that way he had. 'I'm an actor. An actress. I'm famous – that's what brings in audiences. I'm going on tour. I shall go about the country—'

'With Freddie?'

'No, not with Freddie. He is no longer interested he says. He was always best at character parts, and so now he is wearing his Matron's costume—'

'What are you talking about?'

'He's become all sombre and spends most of his time' – here Ernest almost shuddered – 'in *Isleworth*!'

'With his family?'

'With his unfortunate family certainly. His father is very ill. And his brother – poor dear Harry, who was *such* fun and deeply naughty, is also ill after his incarceration – mind you, a year on that treadmill and I should not have been merely ill, I should have died! Oh – he was simply made to be a nurse, Freddie!' (And I saw him, half-carrying me, not minding the blood, that night.)

Ernest smoothed his hair. 'However, as I say, I have decided to take to the boards again, there are plenty who will be glad to perform with me for I shall draw crowds and we shall make money. A girl has to live, Mattie!' But I saw it was true: what else could Ernest Boulton do? 'I have already advertised for a leading man and I have hopes of great success.'

'Come upstairs,' I said.

The portmanteau was in the back of a cupboard in my room where it had been for months and months.

'Hello, Hortense!' said Ernest and he took the half-finished hat from her head and twirled about my room for a moment, wearing it, looking at himself in the mirror. The portmanteau wasn't locked, I dusted the top, I could feel Ernest was excited and hopeful, and then we opened it up, again a little echo from the sad clothes in the courtroom. We found that white petticoat, a man's waistcoat, a rather dirty blue skirt, two opened boxes of 'Bloom of Roses', a tarnished bangle. A pair of boots. And there was a corset. And a pretty pink shawl.

Ernest held them up one by one, his head on one side. If he was disappointed he didn't let it show.

'I can make use of some of this,' he said finally. 'My mother will help. She is very neat with a needle.'

I wondered if that stupid, pretty little lady *I do not have a retentive memory* (though of course perhaps she was not stupid at all, but clever) thought about Ernest resuming his career. But I thought perhaps that they didn't have any money – for of course I had now realised that many people from different classes than ours had money problems also, just – different kinds of problems.

As if he knew what I was thinking Ernest said, 'What else can I do, Mattie?' in a rather dramatic voice.

I shrugged, understanding that even if, in the most unlikely circumstances, he had wanted to go back to a bank again, no bank would have him now.

'And Freddie becoming a nurse!' His voice had a bitter little tone to it and just for a moment I think I saw that he missed Freddie, but certainly wasn't going to say so. 'I think it is better,' he continued, 'to strike while the iron is still hot and people are interested in seeing me and will – or so I believe – queue to see me.' Then he fluttered his eyelashes just a tiny bit. 'Mattie. Would you make me – just one – really lovely hat? A lovely hat can make all the difference! You know I cant pay you now but when we have made some money I would of course pay the bill then.' He must've saw my somewhat astonished face. He added: 'For Freddie's sake.'

'What do you mean, for Freddie's sake?'

'I suppose I mean for all the – you used to like us staying here, Mattie, in the old days, and you were fond of Freddie.'

'He was very kind to me.'

'He is indeed kind, he's even nursed me! As I said he is no doubt dashing about in a Matron's costume even as we speak, dispensing kindness to the old man and Harry. I meant – for the old days, Mattie.' And then all the optimistic bravado fell away for a moment. 'I *have* to do public performances of some kind, Mattie. I dont have as many – supporters – at the moment, as I used to.'

'What happened to those other two men in court with you who wrote you all those love letters?'

The old Ernest, tossing his head. 'I believe the American consul for Edinburgh left the diplomatic service and went back to his rich family in America. I believe Mr Hurt left the Post Office and went to escort his rich mother round Europe somewhere, France I expect.' He shrugged. 'So much for Lais and Antinous!'

'And where's Mr Amos Gibbings? Where did he disappear to so suddenly after the first trial?'

'Oh Amos Gibbings, he went away with his rich mother too, I believe.' He sighed. 'Very many people went away, Mattie. Although I hear Amos still plays dowagers discreetly when he can!'

'I'll make you a hat, Ernest. I'll take the measurements now and I'll make it as soon as possible.'

We talked about how it might look and he looked again in the glass as he always did, studying his face from different angles.

He wrote his address in Peckham, very neatly in his almost childlike handwriting, on one of my hatboxes and went off to see if he could take the world by storm.

55

Lady Susan Vane-Tempest was unable to stop weeping.

The band of tension around her head felt as if it was crushing her mind. The constriction around her breast felt as if it was crushing her heart. Without the laudanum she took, she believed that both her mind and her heart would explode.

'I was not my brother's keeper! The Prince needed me, always! I shall go to Scotland! I shall go straight to the Royal Household and I shall show my condition! He cannot do this!' Tears falling, Lady Susan threw the very short, cold, royal note she had just received across the room of her house in Westminster, together with a copy of *The Times*.

All mistresses of famous men know how to correspond with their lovers in a discreet and private manner. Lady Susan Vane-Tempest was no exception; since she last saw him, over a month ago, she had written him distraught letters (saying only of course that she must see him urgently).

Nobody who was anybody had stayed in London over August, except, for every day of that particular August, Lady Susan Vane-Tempest. She had stayed, in disarray, and needing her lover to make some contact. For days and nights she had waited there, in her house in Chapel-street – waiting in vain, as the sun rose over London in the morning and set over London in the evening, for just one kind message from her kind and holidaying lover – but no message came.

Nor had he come to see her on his return from his summer travels with his family, although she was humiliated to discover – not from himself, but from the newspapers – that he had indeed returned. And yesterday he had sent the short note, saying he was just leaving again, for autumn shooting in Scotland, and would be away for some time.

Her situation was not mentioned.

He had instructed her; he expected her to carry out his instructions.

He would know that she had not been to Dr Clayton.

The Prince of Wales avoided her, and any scandal.

Her present position was now very much more difficult because her condition had become more obvious. It was much too late for the pregnancy to be terminated safely; it could be terminated now only with great danger to herself. Susan, distraught with anger and unhappiness, turned, at last, to her old and trusted friend, Mrs Harriet Whatman.

She and Harriet talked and talked and talked together.

'He cannot do this!' Lady Susan cried again, still weeping. 'I have my own doctors who have all told me it is far too late! Why should I be poked about by that horrible man and have to breathe in pomade of roses? I should never be able to breathe it out again and I should probably die anyway if I am forced to go anywhere near him! I shall present myself to the Prince in public and tell him so!'

Harriet passed the laudanum. Susan was wild, but not that wild.

Harriet knew that Susan would not embarrass Royalty.

Harriet knew how Susan had grown up: in that mournful house of her childhood with a series of governesses and sad maiden aunts while her brothers had been sent away to school to be educated. Harriet knew that Susan's strict and humourless father (but who would have been humourful in such a situation?) might possibly have been a good Secretary of State for War (though there were some after Crimea who queried that) but he had been an unhappy man, ill fitted to deal with a small girl. Her flight to a mad nobleman had shown the world that she had inherited – just as her father had feared – the same wantonness as her mother; many had said it: almost everybody said it: *just like her mother*. Harriet knew that only a few kind souls had said: ***because of her mother***.

But there were rules to be obeyed nevertheless. Susan had grown up as a young woman of exceptional bravery, or wildness, or stupidity, depending on one's point of view, but Mrs Harriet Whatman knew Susan would not follow the Prince to Scotland.

She would not embarrass Royalty.

'We must make a sensible plan,' said Harriet.

Susan tried to pull herself together. 'He obviously will *never* give me the protection and position I had planned and hoped for.'

'Then he must be induced, Susan, to give you money at least.'

'But he never, ever answers my letters, or visits me – not even one single visit to at least discuss what is to be done! I cannot stay here much longer – my condition is obvious now!'

Finally Harriet said crisply: 'If the Prince is so afraid of scandal, then I'm afraid scandal must be placed in front of his eyes. But not in person,' she added hastily. 'I think, Susan, that the best plan is that *I* write to him. I shall explain your predicament.'

'He knows my predicament!' cried Susan wildly, tears now pouring down her face once more. But once again she tried to control herself. 'Yes,' she said. 'You write, Harriet.'

Finally the two women discussed how this letter from someone else, a concerned and discreet friend, should be written. The biggest scandal in his life had been the Mordaunt divorce case when the pregnant lady in question had run wild and mad. Very well. They decided it would therefore be best to threaten that Lady Susan Vane-Tempest, in her present situation, might run wild and mad also.

Harriet sat at Susan's *escritoire* and dipped the quilled pen into the ink.

'And there is no need to go over the obvious details,' said Susan. 'He knows all that. Just tell him I need assistance in the present circumstances.'

Harriet wrote carefully and dutifully and respectfully to the Prince of Wales but made Lady Susan's Vane-Tempest's present emotional and financial predicament very clear. (She did not mention in words her physical predicament of course.)

'And I might become insane,' said Susan coldly.

Harriet wrote carefully and dutifully and respectfully. 'Shall I say you keep calling your dead brother's name?'

'Perhaps not that,' said Susan. 'Mention members of his family, not members of my family. Make him nervous of scandal.' Mrs Harriet Whatman wrote carefully and dutifully and respectfully. 'Ask for a sum of money. He knows perfectly well that I—' but then Susan's control broke once more. 'If he had only come to see me himself I would have talked all this over with him in strictest privacy,' she said in tears of such distress that Harriet moved to comfort her. 'I cannot believe he is so changed!'

And Harriet, holding her, felt that Susan shook with what might have been rage or fear. But which, in truth, was heartbreak.

Harriet renewed her efforts; wrote that it was now necessary for Lady Susan to leave London urgently or the secret would be out, and that it would cost money. She signed the letter, addressed it, and looked at the time.

'I must go darling,' she said, putting her arms once more around her shaking, weeping friend in real concern . 'Remember!

You are a brave person! You survived Lord Adolphus throwing knives at you!' and they both tried to smile. 'Be strong and brave, darling Susan!'

'I will,' said Susan. 'I will.'

But when Harriet had left and Lady Susan Vane-Tempest was alone again, she held the letter to be posted to Scotland in her hands and stared at the envelope. And her courage, if it was courage, deserted her and she wept again. *This is not my fault! This is the Prince's fault! This my mother's fault! No – this is Arthur's fault – I was not my brother's keeper!* Yet memory rebuked her: *perhaps Arthur's wicked life was her fault? Who had been her dead brother's keeper if not his nine-year-old sister, when they were, so young, forsaken?*

Forsaken.

With tears pouring down her face she slowly picked up the pen, dipped it into the ink, and wrote a love letter. She asked her lover to see her, just one more time.

She gave the two letters to her maid and they were sent to the Prince of Wales in Scotland (through his private secretary) by the same post.

His Royal Highness would not see her.

Arrangements were coldly made, with money.

She was sent to Ramsgate.

There the Prince's private doctor, Dr Oscar Clayton, attended her.

He advised her of her Duty.

There is no record of this child.

While Lady Susan was living alone in Ramsgate, the Prince of Wales was struck down with typhoid and for some time not expected to live.

Bulletins were posted almost hourly by early December, and churches prayed for his life.

On the Prince's recovery, Mr Gladstone conceived the idea of a thanksgiving service at St Paul's Cathedral. He was certain it would bring the monarchy, and indeed the Prince, once more into the hearts and minds of the people. Queen Victoria was violently opposed, but Mr Gladstone won this battle.

And Mr Gladstone was correct.

The Royal Procession to St Paul's Cathedral – including the almost-never-glimpsed Queen Victoria – passing through the crowded, cheering, weeping streets of London was a monarchical triumph. Isabella rolled her eyes at Mackie, and Billy looked for *Reynolds News*. But the incipient republican movement was for the moment, dead, and even the *Reynolds Newspaper* knew when it was beaten.

The Prince of Wales sent a ticket for the thanksgiving service to Lady Susan Vane-Tempest.

Perhaps he thought that, now, the crises over, she would like to be thankful also in St Paul's Cathedral, for his deliverance.

But ill health made it impossible for her to attend.

1882

56

It was early summer when they came.

I was sitting on the steps like Mattie used to, only I had a little chair on the top step, just outside the open front door. It was so pleasantly warm and the sun just going down behind the other houses in Wakefield-street, my quiet time before the others came home wanting their dinner. Dodo was in her room lying on the red sofa we'd found for her; Billy and Tom had carried it home from the second-hand market behind Kings Cross and Mattie and Emily and I had covered it with soft red velvet. It was Dodo's favourite thing in the world and it is where, now, she spends her days. She can no longer walk but she still entertains us all and marvels at human folly from her beloved newspapers and books.

I could hear Mattie and the children and Elijah from downstairs. Mattie was feeding them and Elijah was keeping order and there was a great deal of laughter. Three young children as well as making hats is no joke but you should see Mattie's face; you might say three young children as well as making hats is no joke, but much joy.

When Elijah finally retired recently, past seventy – though Mr Gladstone was Prime Minister again by then and no talk of retirement from him – there was a clock presented, and both the Prime Minister and that Mr Disraeli made speeches in the Members' Lobby. Dodo was carried up by the other doorkeepers and was sat by Elijah in a special chair of honour and her cakes were mentioned! And now they've came back to live with us at 13 Wakefield-street.

We had never heard anything more from, or even about, Freddie or Ernest except we read, only a few months after the trial, of the death of Mr Alexander Atherton Park, the Senior Master of the Court of Common Pleas. Poor sad old man. He was a casualty of the Men in Petticoats I think you might say. The only other thing we ever read about any of them ever again was when Lord Arthur's sister died young, years ago, that pretty lady we saw being introduced to Ernest the night we went to see them acting in Clapham, before any of this happened, who Ernest said was the mistress of the Prince of Wales. There was a tiny half-hearted paragraph somewhere saying that Lady Susan Vane-Tempest, only sister of Lord Arthur Clinton, had died of rheumatic fever and was that Lord Arthur, seen at the funeral? So I suppose some journalist was hoping for scandal. But really the Men in Petticoats had been completely forgot.

So Dodo was on the red sofa, and I was sitting on the steps in the last of the evening sun when two gentlemen approached the house on foot. I would of course know Ernest Bolton anywhere, but the other man wasn't Freddie.

'Good evening, Mrs Stacey,' said Ernest. He looked the same, but – older of course, it must have been more than ten years since we'd seen him I expect – and still like a woman in his features somehow, but – I was going to say 'raddled' but that would not be exactly fair. Worn, I suppose you might say. Still quite pretty, but worn – well we'd all worn in all that passing time.

'Well well. Ernest Boulton,' I said.

'Good evening, Mrs Stacey. This is my brother Gerard.'

'Hello, Gerard.' He was almost nice-looking, in a more manly way; but not as striking as Ernest.

'Good evening, Mrs Stacey. I have heard a great deal of you.'

'I expect you have, Gerard. But it was all a long time ago.'

'Gerard is my leading man these days. I had various leading men but they were all problems, and then Mama said, "Why not Gerard?" We toured with great success in America – did you hear?'

'No. No we didn't hear anything, Ernest. But that's good. I've thought of you and Freddie sometimes, wondered how you were faring.'

Someone's head had by now popped interestedly out of a window in the next-door house.

'Could we – would you allow us to come inside briefly and speak to you?'

I looked at them carefully. 'We dont have a single spare room in the house, Ernest. It's mostly full of our rather large family.'

'Not that,' he said. 'And also – I would like to show Gerard the house where we were – where we had happy times. If you didn't mind.' He didn't look at me coyly from under his eyelashes, but almost.

'All right, Ernest,' I said. And I heard myself give an

involuntary little groan as I stood, my blooming old bones.

Ernest showed Gerard the hallway, and the narrow staircase they used to sweep down in such excitement. I looked in on Dodo, she loved to have visitors, but she was asleep on the red sofa. Her clawed hands held a copy of the *Illustrated London News* to her breast. So I took them along to the back parlour: the old piano and the Joshua tree, both of them polished and shining, the way we always kept them still. Children's voices and laughter echoed up from the downstairs kitchen but Ernest didn't hear perhaps, or think about it. He looked about the parlour.

'We twirled our gowns round here sometimes,' he said to Gerard.

'Where are you, my love?' I'd left the front door open, Mackie would have seen the chair still there on the top step where I waited for him.

'In the back parlour! We have visitors.'

Mackie did get a surprise to see Ernest, and Ernest to see him. He still looked like a fisherman, or a smuggler, Mackie, even though he was now the captain in charge of all the Gravesend ferries; he still had the beard and the long hair. Like Joseph the carpenter, someone once said long ago.

'This is Gerard, Ernest's brother. This is Mackie.'

They nodded to each other.

'I'm glad you're here,' said Ernest to Mackie. But not coy; angry rather for some reason.

'What are you doing these days, lad?'

'We went to America for a while, Gerard and I – Gerard had talent for the stage, and though I say so myself, I took New York by storm!' From his pocket he took some old newspaper clippings. He looked at them carefully, handed one to me. 'It's a poem dedicated to my talents. "Ernest Byne", that's what I called myself.'

ERNEST BYNE

Your airs and graces make us all
Believe you must be feminine;
Your acts, though you're no Harlequin,
Do well deserve a column, Byne.

'Columbine, you see!' said Ernest modestly.

'I do see,' I said. 'I'm glad you've had success, Ernest. And what about Freddie?'

'Nan! Nan! Nan! Nan! Nan!' Children ran in, followed by Mattie and Elijah.

'Blooming heck! Ernest!' Mattie was so surprised she stood stock still in the middle of the room. She automatically put out her hand to seven-year-old Dorothy (after Dodo), and stared at him and the boys stopped their running and calling for a moment and stared too. After a moment she said: 'We've got no rooms left, Ernest!' but she said it with a smile.

'No,' he said, 'we dont need rooms. This is my brother Gerard.'

'Sit down, Ernest,' I said. 'What is it?'

He didn't sit but he carefully took another of the old news clippings. It was to Mackie he spoke. 'Last time I came here you accused me of not caring about old friends.' He tossed his head just a little. 'I didn't mean to remember your words but I did, though I never thought to see you again. Anyway, it was said Lord Arthur escaped to France, or somewhere.'

'He didn't escape, lad. I helped put him in the coffin that the local man made.'

The room was silent. The children still stared, all shy at the visitors, big eyes looking out from the safety of their mother.

'Where's Billy?' said Ernest to me at last. 'Did he get his job in the Parliament back? We were found not guilty of anything!'

'He's a teacher, Ernest. With a wife who's a teacher also. He didn't want his job back in the end.'

'I got mine back,' offered Elijah. 'The second day I was back, Members were coming crying to me with their problems as if I'd never been away! So it was all right, after all.'

And then we heard Billy and Emily talking together as they too came in the open front door.

'In the parlour!' I called.

'Well! Ernest!' said Billy, and he shook his hand and grinned at him, seemed really pleased to see Ernest after all this time. 'This is Emily, my wife.' 'This is Gerard, my brother.' And there was some rather embarrassed handshaking all round.

'Go on, Ernest,' I said. But I think I knew.

He simply handed the newspaper clipping to Mackie. Mackie winked at Billy before he read it, for now Mackie could read to us as well as anyone. I had loved to see them with their heads together evening after evening and books on the table and now Mackie reads to me sometimes.

But then the smile was gone. He read it out.

FREDERICK WILLIAM PARK, an Englishman. Died Newark, NJ, 29 March. Several years ago he entered the dramatic profession under the name of Fred Fenton but he never rose above small business. He was at one time at Fifth-Avenue Theatre. His remains were sent to Rochester, NY, where he had made his residence for some years, and were interred in Mount Hope Cemetery 2 April.

And then the room was quite silent as if some of us could hear kind Freddie laughing and rustling down the stairs in one of his satin gowns. I looked at Mattie's face. I wished Tom was here also. She held Dorothy very tightly to her against her apron.

'How did he die?' said Mattie. 'Were you with him, Ernest? Did he have friends in America? He was only your age, Billy.'

Ernest shrugged. 'He was ill,' was all he said. And then he turned back to Mackie. 'You once accused me,' he said again, 'of not caring for my friends and living a life without caring. You know nothing of our lives, or what we might die of, but I remembered what you said. I've been carrying it around with me for over a year, I kept it for Mattie really, but I'm glad you are here.' And he tossed his head as if he didn't care at all.

'I'm sorry about your friend,' said Mackie. 'I remember what he said to us that day you came.'

And I could see Freddie sitting there with his hands quite still on the piano as the notes died away and saying he was sorry for our trouble and I who *never* cry felt tears in my eyes of all things, for it was me who had been hard on them, not Mackie, not really, and our lives had been so changed.

Into this silence Tom Dent walked, in his solicitor's

suit and with his shiny, open face. 'Ernest Boulton!' he said in amazement.

'Tom Dent!' said Ernest in surprise. 'From Lewis and Lewis! Whatever are you doing here?' but he saw my two grandsons run to their father. Tom looked across at Mattie, his dear shining face and she walked across to him at the doorway with Dorothy, stood close to him.

'We met because of the trial, Ernest,' she said simply.

'Mr Park sent me here,' said Tom. 'He told me to ask for Mattie, and how glad I am that he did.'

'Mr Park is dead in America,' said Elijah.

'Oh – oh I am so sorry,' said Tom, shocked. 'I'm so sorry, Ernest, I liked him very much. Did he get my letter? Telling him I was to marry Mattie. I thought he would be pleased, for he sent me here, to her, he sent me here on purpose, I'm so sure he did. I posted the letter to his father's house in Isleworth.'

'I dont know if he got it,' said Ernest. 'His father died soon after the trial. I – I didn't see Freddie so much after that. He went to America before we did. And I hardly even saw his brother. He was never the same again, Harry – and he had been such *good fun* and' – Ernest shrugged his still elegant shoulders – 'fun! But – even though he was very fit and strong the treadmill in the prison damaged him too much. He died.' Ernest shuddered slightly. 'Freddie was – changed. We tried to work together again in America at first but—' He shrugged again. 'It was no good. He was too changed.'

I was looking at Mattie. She stood surrounded by her family and listened grave and pale to the conversation.

'Freddie didn't, after all, have your resilience, Ernest,' I said and I remembered the day in court when I had thought that. Ernest was the tough one after all. And I saw that it was me had to make the final peace at this strange meeting. 'Ernest, I was very hard on you both that day you came to apologise to us. It wasn't Mackie, not really. I was angry at what had happened to our lives, especially Billy losing his position and Mattie – for her to be called a crippled whore because of you seemed unforgivable. But' – I looked across at all the dear faces in the room – 'other things happened after all.'

'Nan! Nan! Nan!' Young Will was bored now, ran over and pulled at me to play but I held him tight by the hand for a moment more.

'Thank you for coming and letting us know about Freddie,' I said.

'Thank you, Ernest,' said Mattie. 'I have never ever forgot his kindness to me.'

'He was kind,' said Ernest.

But he was looking now for his hat, and Gerard though he had remained very manly throughout was clearly embarrassed by the whole conversation.

'What do you do now, Ernest?' said Mattie.

'Oh we perform still, of course! Round England. We do very well, Gerard and I,' but it sounded like bravado, he was not like a pretty young girl any more, and Ernest tossed his hair from his eyes, anxious to go now. Mackie still held the clipping about Freddie. Now he gave it back to Ernest.

'Thank you, lad,' said Mackie and he put out his hand and Ernest shook it in his limp way.

'Ernest,' Mattie said.

He looked at her, but almost as if he knew.

Her face was pale but she smiled at him. 'I can play,' she said. 'Once more for the good times and – in memory of Freddie in Wakefield-street, shall we, Ernest?'

That Ernest, he couldn't resist it, even now. He immediately put his hat back down on the table and touched his hair fussily, and stood beside the piano as Mattie played the first note. And – yes – he could still sing. I turned away slightly until the song had finished.

Which is the fairest gem?
Eileen Aroon.

As Billy took them to the front door they passed Dodo's room. She waved.

'That was lovely, dear,' she said to Ernest from her red sofa. 'I was so glad to hear you sing again, young man. Thank you.'

When Ernest and Gerard had gone we went down to the basement kitchen where one of my eternal stews was simmering by the fire. Mattie and Tom were putting the children in bed.

'It's all been a very strange tale!' said Elijah to me wryly, and he took two platefuls and went upstairs again to sit with Dodo and tell the story. And Mackie held me for a moment, beside the stove.

Billy's wife, Emily, cut up some parsley she had brought home to scatter on the top of the stew. 'That was such a beautiful song,' she said to me. 'Did he used to sing it here in the old days?'

'He did,' I said, and I thought one more time of Freddie with his hands very still on the piano even as the notes echoed, the final time he came to 13 Wakefield-street.

'Ernest used to sing it here in the old days. It was Mattie's favourite.'

And Emily smiled across at Billy and said: 'I am so glad then, that I have heard it too.'

And Mattie and Tom came down into the kitchen, young Will still awake, his arms clinging round Tom's neck, and we served out the stew to our dear people.

So I suppose you might say – in the most unlikely way from this most unlikely story of the Men in Petticoats which has been quite forgot – that we all lived happily ever after.

Except for Lord Arthur Pelham Clinton who died in whatever way he died, aged twenty-nine in Mudeford, and Frederick William Park who died in whatever way he died, not much older in America. Young men die all the time, including in accidents at Kings Cross long ago.

But they were near Billy's age and I felt sad for them all, all the casualties.

57

With both his hands, Elijah held Dodo's small, bent, swollen one. 'I have been *so* lucky,' she whispered, smiling still.

When Dodo Fortune died in her beloved red room in Wakefield-street, Mattie's daughter, Dorothy, who had been named for Dodo and who had inherited her love of baking, made a beautiful cake decorated with a pretty lady in a red dress, smiling and dancing.

At the death of Mr William Ewart Gladstone – Prime Minister of Great Britain four times, the last time when he was over eighty – there was possibly cake also. And so greatly was he held in the people's affection that his casket lay, in public, in Westminster Hall (that same famous Gothic edifice of the final trial of the Men in Petticoats). Queen Victoria, still going strong, refused to attend his funeral, but the Prince of Wales, still the Prince of Wales, loyally, with his son, actually helped carry the casket into Westminster Abbey, incurring his mother's wrath although he was by now a man in his late fifties.

Concerning also death, and loyalty: Lady Susan Vane-Tempest died, (perhaps of rheumatic fever as obituaries advised), aged thirty-six. Scandal had been averted in that matter, certainly (she had not embarrassed Royalty), and some time later Dr Oscar Clayton was discreetly knighted 'for personal services to the Prince of Wales'. That morning pomade of roses filled the air in royal corridors.

At the time, the newspapers had called the Men in Petticoats story THE SCANDAL OF THE CENTURY. Yet despite all those headlines, miraculously – as if by some sleight of hand, which indeed you might say it was – in the end there was no case at all to answer. Which did not happen later (Isabella and Mattie and Billy noted) when Mr Oscar Wilde was arrested. Possibly the fact that the nobility was on the other side made a difference; Lewis and Lewis, solicitors, popped up again, but not for Mr Wilde, who was sent to prison, with hard labour.

But nobody heard of the Men in Petticoats ever again, nobody even remembered the names, despite Ernest Boulton still trying valiantly to tour the country, still singing (to smaller and smaller audiences) of 'Fading Away' and 'Eileen Aroon', and a bishop who had once been in the House of Lords was praised in many circles for his zealous Christian influence, in Africa.

For in England's partially green, and partially pleasant, land, there are always secrets. And there have always been ways of dealing and concealing (as Billy Stacey had noted all those years ago), when scandal threatens power.

58

I STILL MAKE hats.

I still work in this room, me and Hortense with her red lips I painted and her big eyes, and the hats and the long work-table and the big mirror. The children love Hortense and Dorothy used to stroke her face and say, so serious, 'You are Us too, Hortense.'

Not much time for writing though, and the story about the Men in Petticoats has been over for years. Except . . . life's not exactly a straight line is it? And things are never *over* exactly. I saw Jamey in the moon the night I walked on the arm of Mr Gladstone in the Strand.

That night, after Ernest and his brother had come and told us about Freddie being dead, I came in here in the darkness with a lamp when everyone else was asleep. And in the shadows – just sudden and odd – I found I was remembering that time when they were in the House of Detention and I had crept with my same little lamp into Freddie and Ernest's room and there was that petticoat sticking out of a wardrobe like a ghost and hairpins on the floor, and 'Bloom of Roses'. And in my work-room as I sat there knowing Freddie had died now, it seemed like something drifted, like it brushed the air and the mirror. Drifting, and a bit cold, and I felt a tiny shiver or a memory or – well I dont blooming know what it was but tears came in my eyes.

I wonder if that's what ghosts are? Memories?

And I quickly turned the lamp up high and there was Hortense and a half-made hat with ribbons hanging down and the sounds of – of Us – sleeping all around me and Freddie dead in America.

I loved Freddie. Yes for the hundredth time I *know*, I know I loved him because I was lonely and he was kind whatever else he was as well. I made it up. But I did love Frederick Park all the same – and it was through him that I am so happy now. And I sat with my little lamp that night beside Hortense and thought about him dying in another country far away and I *wished* I knew that he, well – well what I wished for Freddie was that there was somebody holding on to his hand tight, when he died.

I thought I was just writing the story of us in 13 Wakefield-street because I was so wild at it being called a bordello which it wasn't and the big rude writing on our walls and me being called a crippled whore which I wasn't and all the lies and secrets that we found. But all the time that I was writing things were changing: Billy losing one position and finding another, and Emily; and Mackie riding into our lives in the early morning along the Mudeford Road and Dodo and Elijah living with us and Tom Dent working for Lewis and Lewis.

I've read all those novels and – they're about places and people and the sea and thieves and madness and murder, but – really – I think most of them are about love and maybe I've been writing about love too, all different kinds of love, and it was like I said all those years ago, you cant always tell your heart what to do.

This Men in Petticoats was about certain people in charge wanting everyone to love the same. Someone should tell them that everyone is not the same and love is not the same but, whoever we are, we have to fill up that big waiting space inside our hearts.

ACKNOWLEDGEMENTS

This historical novel started off being about something else, with the 1870 trial of Ernest Boulton and Frederick Park as background. But as I began to research this slightly mysterious trial, I by chance found some surprising new information; I finally realised the novel had to be about the trial itself. I have woven three primary sources into my story and quoted from them freely: the extraordinary trial records, the huge newspaper coverage of the scandal at the time, and some unpublished letters. All letters in the novel are genuine.

The trial records used can be found in the National Archives at Kew, where patient staff made big boxes of these original papers available. The newspaper reports quoted can be found in the British Library Newspaper Collection, where again I was assisted by helpful staff: at Colindale, and in the newly-opened premises at the British Library in St Pancras. And I am grateful to Mr C. A. Gladstone for permission to use the genuine 1870 letters, all but one unpublished, which I found in the Gladstone collection in the Additional Manuscripts Room at the British Library and in the Glynne/Gladstone collection at the Flintshire Record Office. I was not able to receive permission from the Royal Archives to use the 1871 letters of Lady Susan Vane-Tempest (nee Clinton) to the Prince of Wales, but these can be found in both the biographies of Edward VII listed below.

I have received an enormous amount of help and support while writing this novel. My thanks for their advice to Sarah Baxter at the Society of Authors; Caroline Kelly from the Department of

Manuscripts and Special Collections at Nottingham University; and Claire Harrington and Sue Copp at the Flintshire Record Office. I was given invaluable legal information by Nicholas Bamforth, Fellow in Law at The Queen's College, Oxford University and have received much support from Professor Richard Parkinson at The Queen's College, Oxford University, author of the British Museum's *A Little Gay History*. Gratitude also to Ben Campbell and Dick Drinkrow for emergency technical advice, and to Kitty Williston for research in America.

My ongoing journey took me to all sorts of places: I was taken through Burlington Arcade by the present Head Beadle, Mr Mark Lord – including down to where a real underground tunnel did once run. I was shown all around the House of Commons – including the basement – by Austin Mitchell MP and had many questions patiently answered by his Parliamentary Assistant, Matthew Kay. I was taken through the corridors and offices of the House of Lords by Lord Alan Hawath. In Christchurch I was given invaluable information about funereal history by Mr Stuart Major of the funeral directors Miller & Butler, and by Christine Mockett of the Christchurch Borough Council; and shown historical records and graves in Christchurch Cemetery by the caretaker, Steve Ryan.

To all these people my grateful thanks.

I would also like to thank my editor at Head of Zeus, Laura Palmer, whose brain seemed to attach itself to mine during the editing of the manuscript.

And, finally, to my beloved British Library, where I have just about taken up permanent residence, and the patient staff there, my gratitude for providing me with most of the books listed below, to the authors of which I am indebted.

Victorian London: the life of a city 1840–1870 by Liza Picard (Weidenfeld & Nicolson, London 2003)

Lost London 1870–1945 by Philip Davies (Trans Atlantic, Amersham 2009)

Gladstone: 1809–1898 by H.C.G. Matthew (Clarendon Press, Oxford 1997)

Gladstone's Diaries: with cabinet minutes and prime ministerial correspondence (1869–1871) edited by H.C.G. Matthew (Clarendon Press, Oxford 1982)

Gladstone and Women by Anne Isba (Hambledon Continuum, London 2006)

A Beckford Inheritance: the Lady Lincoln scandal by Virginia Surtees (Michael Russell Publishing Ltd, Salisbury 1977)

Edward VII: Prince and King by Giles St Aubyn (Collins, London 1979)

Bertie: a life of Edward VII by Jane Ridley (Chatto & Windus, London 2012)

Masculinity and Male Homosexuality in Britain 1861–1913 by Sean Brady (Palgrave Macmillan, Basingstoke 2005)

The Changing Room: sex, drag & theatre by Laurence Senelick (Routledge, London 2000)

Men in Petticoats: The Lives of Boulton & Park, Extraordinary Revelations (pamphlet: George Clarke, London 1870)

Sodom on the Thames by Morris B. Kaplan (Cornell University Press, Ithaca NY 2005)

Nameless Offences by H.G. Cocks (I.B. Tauris, London 2010)

Crossing the Stage: controversies on cross-dressing edited by Lesley Ferris (Routledge, London 1993)

Reclaiming Sodom edited by Jonathan Goldberg (Routledge, London 1994)

London and the Culture of Homosexuality 1885–1914 by Matt Cook (Cambridge University Press, Cambridge 2003)

The Sins of the Cities of the Plain by "Jack Saul" (Privately printed, London 1881)

Bad Companions by William Roughead (W. Green & Son, Edinburgh 1930)
Who Was that Man?: a present for Mr Oscar Wilde by Neil Bartlett (Serpent's Tail, London 1988)
Lewis & Lewis by John Juxon (Collins, London 1983)
A Little Gay History by R.B. Parkinson (The British Museum, London, 2013)

The trial records can be consulted at Kew under the numbers KB 6/3 and DPP 4/6.